KNIFE EDGE

WHEN DUTY CALLS

HARVEY CLEGGETT

Published in Australia by Sid Harta Books & Print Pty Ltd,
ABN: 34632585293
23 Stirling Crescent, Glen Waverley, Victoria 3150 Australia
Telephone: +61 3 9560 9920, Facsimile: +61 3 9545 1742
E-mail: author@sidharta.com.au

First published in Australia 2023
This edition published 2023
Copyright © Harvey Cleggett 2023

Cover design, typesetting: WorkingType (www.workingtype.com.au)

ISBN: 978-1-922958-29-7

To my wife Leanne,
whom I love and cherish as my companion for life.

To my son Steven and daughter Lauren,
may your hard work and dedication remain
the bedrock of your lives.

PROLOGUE

The blades of the Eurocopter 135 were already spinning as Superintendent Peter Donaldson braked hard outside the enormous Essendon hangar. The name FERGUSON AVIATION, bold and imposing in huge block letters was centred above the gaping entrance; Malcolm Ferguson's less-than-subtle declaration as to who was boss. One of his staff waved for Peter to park the police car inside, which he did, the tyres protesting on the polished concrete. Leaping out, he, along with his Homicide colleagues, Michael Ballard and John Henderson, slammed their doors in unison, the sound echoing inside the cavernous hangar. Sprinting over to the helicopter they scrambled aboard.

Malcolm leaned across from the controls and shook their hands. "Perfect timing gentlemen. Now buckle up and put on your headsets." He eyed their shoulder holsters, but their grave expressions had him facing forward without comment.

The detectives did as instructed, each testing that the billionaire property developer could hear them. With everyone settled, Malcolm radioed the Essendon Control Tower, repeating the flight plan he had submitted earlier. Granted permission to lift off, he announced to his eager passengers, "We'll be cruising at a hundred and thirty knots, just over two hundred and thirty kilometres an hour. At that speed we only have a six-hundred-kilometre flight range, so for safety reasons I'll refuel at the Horsham Airport. I have a man on standby there for a top-up of avgas. We'll then fly due north towards Ouyen and onto the nuclear waste facility. If you give me the coordinates I'll get you onsite in less than two hours. By my reckoning ..." his eyes narrowed as he inspected the digital clock on the instrument panel, "that'll make it 0100 hours." It was obvious from his crisp and concise instructions he wasn't an ex-Vietnam chopper pilot for nothing.

Ballard leaned forward. "Will do Malcolm, but I need to make a call first. Our SOG commander, Tim Robbins is at the ambush site with his team—they flew up on PolAir."

The billionaire flashed a brief smile. "Well then, let's get this show underway."

John uttered an extended moan as the twin Pratt & Whitney jet engines increased in intensity. His balled fists whitened as the chopper lifted effortlessly into the night sky, the rapid ascent akin to an express lift. Ballard winked at Peter, sensing Malcolm was giving the motors greater stick than usual to stir John's already jangled nerves.

Peter shifted to face Ballard who was behind him, forgetting he didn't need to. "I can't get over how bloody quiet this thing is."

Ballard grunted in agreement, seizing the opportunity to further annoy John by ambushing him with an avalanche of mindless technical jargon, an ongoing prank he often played on his long-suffering partner. "Oh, that'll be due to its sophisticated cabin insulation properties ... along with the special design of the fenestron tail rotor ... and let's not forget the intelligent piezoelectric actuators on the trailing edges of the main blades which helps reduce vector slap." He pointed a forefinger skyward while uttering his tongue-in-cheek monologue.

Malcolm emitted a barking laugh, enjoying the torment being inflicted.

Dropping his chin and blowing out his cheeks in disgust, John bleated, "You know something detective inspector? You can be a right smart-arse at times … no, come to think of it, make that most of the time."

With a grin, Ballard removed his headset to call Tim. "I know this is a stupid question to ask at a time like this, but what's happening up there?"

The SOG officer sounded tense, and for good reason. "Surprisingly not much. I'm assuming Pete's already told you the locomotive hauling the nuclear waste cannisters was derailed, a result of the track spikes being ripped out. From that point on it was open season on the security detail guarding the train. Presumably the attack was carried out by The Board's death squad. All up, fourteen have been slaughtered. Getting enough ambulances out here to transport the bodies when you and forensic have finished processing the crime scene will be a challenge in itself due to the remoteness of the bloody place. My guys have already taken God knows how many photos in situ. Delwyn and her team, along with the forensic crew, will be at least another two hours before they lob—" He broke off to utter a series of orders, his words muffled by the sound of rustling fabric.

There was a pause. "Sorry about that. On a more personal note, I'm guessing this was a bitch of an ending for your Italian getaway, and John's—even more so for Natalie and Sonia. Pete mentioned earlier he was collecting you both from Tullamarine prior to heading on up here. I gather you're on the way … how far off are you?"

Ballard gazed out the window at the ground below, the almost full moon creating a kaleidoscope of mysterious shadows; lights from outer suburban homes appeared as a twinkling carpet stretching to the horizon. Having difficulty comprehending that the train transporting Australia's first shipment of nuclear waste to the new storage site in outback Victoria had been attacked, he brought himself back to the moment.

"Nat and Sonia were picked up by Dave, my travel agent—and you're right, they weren't the least bit happy about the way the holiday ended, but they accepted we had no choice. As to your question, we're enroute at a fair rate of knots aboard Malcolm's Eurocopter."

The billionaire glanced behind him, having heard his name being mentioned.

"With the second PolAir restricted to the metropolitan area, I rang Malcolm and he kindly agreed to save us the five-hour road trip. We should be wheels down in under two hours."

John dropped his head a second time as he growled an aside to Peter, "Wheels down? Christ, now he's pretending to be a damn chopper pilot."

Tim was impressed. "Not bad going. It pays to have wealthy contacts, and considering how you and John saved Malcolm's wife a while back, well, I'm guessing you both have your share of brownie points tucked away in the bank." He grew serious. "Apart from the tragedy of the massacre, the big issue biting us in the backside right now is how we go about recovering the two cannisters containing the U-235 that have been knocked off—"

"*You're kidding me!*"

"At a time like this?"

Ballard could only blink as he digested the information. "Bloody hell Tim. Bernard's CIA contact in Venice told us the uranium from Italy was in cannisters that weigh less than five tonnes."

Tim responded, "If that's true then a decent forklift would have had *no* trouble moving them off the flatbeds."

"Are there any tyre tracks leading from the train which can be followed?" Ballard wasn't hopeful.

"Yeah, you'd think there would be, but a massive downpour half an hour before we got here put paid to that. All this red dirt has turned into five centimetres of sodden mush. They chose the ambush site near one of the all-weather metal roads in the area, so they were smart enough to consider there might be unforeseen circumstances. Saying that, whoever did this got lucky and pulled off the raid *before* the rain set in. But from what you've just told me, the cannisters are most likely in containers on tray-trucks heading into the wide blue yonder." He uttered several choice expletives. "By the time *we* got here the damn things would have been hundreds of kilometres away. As for the forklift, it'll be tucked inside one of the containers along with the cannister."

Ballard sympathised, noting the frustration in Tim's voice. "Hang in there, buddy. The rest of your guys should get there in the next hour or so. Oh ... before I forget, I need your coordinates. Flick me a text when you can."

"Roger that."

Ballard slipped his headset back on and after adjusting the mike, repeated Tim's startling news about the two missing cannisters. His announcement had everyone on edge, including Malcolm.

Peter, forever practical, nailed the gravity of the situation. "Every terrorist group in the world would give their eyeteeth to get their hands on that stuff—including the lunatic fat boy in North Korea."

John attempted to flatten his wayward hair, but failed as usual. "At least now we know what The Board's plans were, but I have to admit, I thought they'd have been more interested with the storage site itself…" he shook his head. "Apparently not."

Ballard considered his partner beside him, not entirely convinced, and eyeing Peter who had twisted around in his seat, it was obvious the new developments were troubling him equally. "OK, Pete, spit it out."

"I'm thinking back to what Bernard told me after he spoke with his CIA contact in Venice, Vincenzo Ricardo, raising the possibility the Ndrangheta mafia is poking its nose into the storage facility here in Australia. They desperately want it to fail so Italy can build their own. Any turf war between them and The Board would be a nightmare for our agencies. Never mind the truckloads of corrupt money that would be sloshing around from such a deal, putting us on a collision course with The Board … *and* the mafia."

Hearing the discussion, Malcolm chose discretion, opting to say nothing. Glancing around he saw the detectives staring at him, resulting in a shrug. "Don't worry about me, fellas, chat away amongst yourselves. None of this is my business, and it certainly won't pass my lips, I'm just the pilot."

Ballard scoffed, reflecting on the billionaire and his wife Teresa, their lives unwittingly linked to the current investigation against The Board. "Hardly. Considering your, and Teresa's, disastrous history with Vladimir and Sergey, you've got more than your fair share of skin in the game. Rest assured, you're *definitely* one of us."

Malcolm didn't bother to hide his appreciation of the accolade.

All sank into deep contemplation, Ballard retracing the multiple avenues of inquiry the department was forced to pursue regarding The Board's criminal activities. On a positive note, he was relieved he had convinced the Crime Department's Assistant Commissioner, Kevin Thompson, to take on the services of Bernard Winters, a retired CIA operative, along with his son's private investigation agency, claiming both would be invaluable intelligence assets in the fight against The Board's clandestine pursuits.

Glancing across at Malcolm, who was systematically checking his instruments, Ballard was reminded how consummate a pilot the billionaire was. Equally comforting was the solid character of the man, in the vein of Bernard Winters, each in their own way able to be relied upon in a crisis.

Ably assisted by John, Ballard reflected back to when they saved Teresa from Sergey's clutches. The ex-Spetsnaz soldier and Vladimir were in the throes of extorting money from Bernard in the couple's Eureka Tower penthouse, with Teresa kidnapped by Sergey to apply additional leverage on the billionaire. The resultant bond that the detectives now enjoyed with the high-profile couple was unbreakable, forged through perilous times.

Ballard refocussed on Vladimir and his connection with The Board, the Russian operating as a commercial property developer similar to Malcolm, but choosing to walk on the dark side, his financing of the siege on Parliament House affording him a shot at his ultimate goal of becoming the group's next cell leader in Australia. Despite being recently arrested, it was still unclear whether he had any role in financing the ambush and removal of the two nuclear cannisters; and if not, was it indeed the Ndrangheta who committed the crime? Those questions and more swirled unanswered in Ballard's head like bees in a bottle as they progressed towards their refuelling stop.

The avgas top-up at Horsham was executed with Formula One efficiency, the three policemen impressed by the speed of the operation. Back in the air, Malcolm set a course due north after punching the coordinates provided by Tim into the autopilot. "By my calculation we'll still be landing at 0100 hours, give or take a few minutes." He was pleased they were on schedule.

Ballard craned his neck to observe the almost full moon high to his left, for once Mother Nature onside, affording what would prove to be much-needed visibility on the ground. While the drone of the jet motors was hypnotic, the circumstances were such that none of the detectives were in fear of dozing off, anticipating the horror they would witness at the attack site. The distress of seeing human flesh torn apart by the brutality of modern weaponry was a fact of life in their profession, but something they never got used to, and prayed they never would.

The first indication they were approaching their destination was a bright light in the distance, diverging into a cluster as they neared. All presumed the local police had organised the installation of a generator and floodlights to assist Tim and his crew. Circling low before setting down, Malcolm chose a flat stretch of ground behind PolAir, ensuring there was ample separation between the two sets of rotors. The earlier rain meant no dust cloud was created as they landed on the sparsely grassed patch.

Malcolm cut the motors then swung around to face the detectives. "I'll keep out of your hair, gentlemen. To fill in time I might nip over and have a chinwag with the PolAir pilot. The last thing you need is for me to get in the way of your crime scene." The three men echoed their appreciation, thanking him for the faultless flight.

Exiting the chopper, careful to navigate the areas of deep mud and puddles, they were staggered at the enormity of the ambush. Harshly illuminated, the locomotive leaned off the tracks at an alarming angle. Despite this, it remained coupled to seven flatbed rolling stock as well as the damaged rear carriage which would have housed the security detail. Five enormous nuclear waste cannisters were strapped in place on the flatbeds, with two rolling stock conspicuously bare.

Strategically positioned floodlights provided limited lighting, powered by a generator whose monotonous drone could be heard from across the far side of one of the flatbeds. Several local police stood nearby as members of the specialist teams crisscrossed the area casting competing shadows.

Tim approached, evading large areas of mud. He appeared tired but left no one in any doubt he was very much in control. He shook the detectives' hands, noting wryly, "Arriving in style I see." He waved at the chaotic scene behind him. "As I said, fourteen dead, a veritable bloodbath ... never seen anything like it. I assume you know about the support chopper being blown out of the sky?"

Ballard and John indicated they did, Peter confirming he had phoned them before their landing at Tullamarine, passing on the distressing news.

"Whoever did this had one objective in mind, secure the two cannisters and take out any witnesses."

They began assessing everything around them, noting the bodies lying beside the track, all covered with blankets. It was apparent that those in the security contingent who were not injured or killed in the rocket attack on the rear carriage had attempted to take offensive action, but had been caught in the crossfire, cut down by a hail of bullets.

John was thunderstruck. "You're right, Tim, the miserable bastards weren't taking any prisoners. Have you heard when Delwyn and her team will get here to start making sense of all this?"

"She rang a few minutes ago." Tim consulted his watch. "They'll be at least another hour, Forensics the same."

"Any clues as to whether The Board was responsible?" Peter understood the question was a difficult one with so much material evidence still to be collated.

Tim deliberated for several seconds. "We've sighted a ton of empty shells and I'm pretty certain they were using HK416s. Now whose fingers were on the triggers is anyone's guess, but undoubtably the death squad are front runners—the sheer viciousness of the attack is their MO through and through."

"What about the storage site, what's happening there?" Ballard's gnawing apprehension continued to mount.

"I spoke with one of the security guards on duty there when we first landed, and again thirty minutes ago. He claims it's all quiet on the western front."

"How many guards do they have?"

"Not sure John, I get the impression only three or four." Tim pointed towards the covered bodies. "They were to be supplemented by these poor buggers had they got the shipment through."

John's face reddened. "*Three or four*? How bloody stupid can the government be? Don't they know this stuff is gold for major crooks?"

Peter was thoughtful as he pointed to the nearest cannister. "My guess is they assumed the sheer size of these damn things would have required serious lifting capacity, along with suitable transportation. What everyone failed to consider was how compact the Italian cannisters were ... well by comparison. Christ Michael, your motor cruiser is *way* heavier, and you say a forklift gets it out of the water without any trouble?"

Ballard agreed. "Yep, all eight tonnes of it, so any cannister coming in at around five would be easy pickings." He hesitated, then came to a decision. "Tim, there's nothing we can do here until Forensics arrive, so in the meantime I want to drop in on the storage facility and check it out. Malcolm can fly us there."

Peter was keen to get underway, with John already heading towards the Eurocopter.

Agreeing, Tim declared, "Can't do any harm. Like I said, there's not much going on here other than us having to guard these cannisters. I'll wager though, whoever did this isn't coming back now they've got what they wanted." He made to move back to his team; over his shoulder he directed, "Give me a sitrep when you get there."

CHAPTER 1

Malcolm didn't need convincing. "I've always wanted to see inside a nuclear bunker."

He fired the jet engines, the four blades on the Eurocopter commencing their rhythmic rotation. John braced himself, the rapid ascents the one aspect of the chopper flight his stomach still hadn't come to terms with.

"I'm assuming all I need to do is follow the rail line to the end and that's where the site will be?" Having stated the obvious, Malcolm switched on the chopper's powerful floodlight, directing it so the train line remained in view as they flew at low speed. "How far away is the bunker?"

His eyes glued to the tracks below, Peter responded, "According to Tim, about twenty kilometres."

Malcolm performed a rapid calculation. "Ok, ten minutes will have us there at this rate."

Everyone sat in silence, pondering their own dark thoughts, the scale of the massacre they had just witnessed a shocking reality; the carnage becoming an all-too-familiar occurrence in The Board's relentless pursuit of money, greed their ever-present mantra. The Note Printing Australia robbery, and the siege on Parliament House were perfect examples of their technical capabilities, amassing them well over a billion dollars of government money. Now their insatiable appetite for more was firmly directed towards wrecking Australia's chance of becoming the world's solution for nuclear waste storage. Escalating the stakes with each tragic event, Sergey emerged as the common factor, his elite Spetsnaz training amply equipping him with the necessary skills to achieve The Board's objectives.

True to his word, Malcolm had them landing to the minute, on this occasion in a cloud of dust, the rain at the attack site not as widespread as first thought. A high chain-wire fence topped with razor wire, and sporting multiple signs warning the public to stay out, stretched into the distance in either direction. Ballard recalled the earlier briefing by Robert Mayne, the department's ballistic expert, his presentation expounding on all things nuclear, indicating the enclosed area was just shy of fifty hectares.

All four men approached the perimeter fence which was illuminated by floodlights evenly spaced atop metal poles. The rail line continued inside the compound, ending in two black rubber bumper blocks. Illuminated by more floodlights, a long, grey, menacing concrete bunker was the only sign of any physical structure above ground, other than a guard hut off to one side; the detectives were conscious that the real action was focussed hundreds of metres below.

An immense gantry crane equipped with canvas slings towered beside the rail line to lift the nuclear cannisters from the flatbeds. At right angles to the line, horizontal steel girders extended to the building's concrete wall, each supporting rows of heavy-duty rubber rollers.

Assessing what was before them, Peter summarised the operation. "Ok, so the crane lifts the cannister off the flatbed and lowers it onto the rollers. The cannister is then drawn sideways into the building. Christ, that means a bloody great section of the concrete wall must slide hydraulically to one side, allowing the cannister to be loaded onto whatever the hell it is they use to transport the damn thing down into the guts of the place. The train then repositions further along the track for the next, and the next, cannister. *Simple as she goes!*"

Ballard filled in the gaps. "A movable section of wall would have been simpler had the building been made of steel, but I'm guessing the Regulatory Commission demanded the bunker be nuclear bomb proof, fireproof, floodproof, and for good measure, earthquake proof."

They studied the compound, searching for an entrance, and it was at this point that Ballard's suspicions became a nightmare reality. Having approached the brick guard post, he peered through the slide window which was partly ajar. Summoning the others with a hand gesture, everyone's senses became hyperalert as each viewed the uniformed body slumped in a chair. Mouth gaping, arms dangling, rivulets of drying blood appearing black under the stark fluorescent light, the source a small but obvious bullet hole in the centre of the guard's forehead.

Turning their attention, an examination of the lock on the reinforced steel entry gate, normally released from inside the security post, revealed it was torn from its anchor point—the tell-tale signs of explosives indicated by the darkened metal. John glanced at Ballard, both men echoing, "*Sergey!*"

Ballard turned to Malcolm. "I'm sorry, but you need to get back to the chopper and be ready to lift off at a moment's notice." Embarrassed, he added, "Unfortunately we can't loan you a weapon."

Malcolm's gaze was almost fatherlike. "Michael, I'm a Vietnam vet who flies multi-million dollar choppers ... more often than not alone. Do you *really* think I'd be doing that unarmed?"

Ballard grinned knowingly, with John chipping in, "Mate, whatever you've got, just be sure to pop it on your lap until we get back."

Understanding the seriousness of the situation, Malcolm did as requested, jogging back to the chopper, light on his feet despite his bulk. Each detective took their Smith & Wesson's and pumped a round into the chamber. One-handed, Ballard dialled Tim, impatient at the SOG officer's slow response. Pressing the mobile hard against his ear he explained, "Tim, we're at the storage site. Not sure by whom or when, but a security guard has been shot—"

"Dead?"

"Very much so ... inside his guard post. No sign of anyone about, but there's no doubting—"

"*Michael, get the hell out of there!* You're not equipped to take on this mob." Tim was emphatic, anxiety stressing his voice. Ballard heard him bark a series of orders to his team, including several directions for the PolAir pilot.

Ballard resumed his update. "Malcolm's firing up the chopper as we speak—"

"*Just make sure you get on it.* We'll be there within minutes. Promise me you'll leave this one alone." Tim made no attempt to hide that he was troubled.

Taking the path of least resistance, Ballard blurted, "Will do," then disconnected.

John crowded closer. "What did he say?"

"That we should make tracks out of here."

"*Like hell we will.*" John scrutinised his colleagues, searching for any sign they might be contemplating the prudent course of action prior to Tim arriving. To his relief his fears were unfounded as he further insisted, "At the very least we should conduct a quick recce, that way Tim and his team will know what they're up against."

Ballard agreed, but countered with, "John, if this *is* Sergey's doing, or even Igor's, now we know he's a Board member out here overseeing proceedings, these bastards play for keeps, so let's not go into this hairy-chested ... *OK?*"

The last word demanded an answer, which John jumped at. "Got it. A quick peep 'round the corner then we're gone ... scout's honour." On closer scrutiny it was clear his attempts at sincerity were futile, but Ballard knew there wasn't time for a debate.

In a crouched run they approached the building, avoiding the lit path, thankful they could merge into the shadows. Flattening himself against the concrete wall, Peter hissed, "How the hell did the attackers get into this place, or more to the point, how do *we*?"

The path continued around the far side. Edging up to the corner, each stole a brief look, Peter's question answered with shocking clarity. The entry door was a solid piece of steel, and ominously not fully shut. Its wedge-shaped sides ensured that in the advent of an external explosion the shockwave would further seal the door into the metal frame which had corresponding angled side jams. Above the door a series of cameras and floodlights provided internal guards with a comprehensive view of anyone at the entrance, day or night, now highlighting a harrowing scene. Lying on the path to one side was a second security guard, very much dead, and the probable means by which the attacker's gained entry to the building.

The detectives speculated what would have been demanded of those inside. 'Open up or we'll blow his brains out!' Reasoning that an empty storage site wasn't worth one of their own being executed in cold blood, the bunker guards, despite being wracked with indecision would have allowed the attackers in.

John hissed, "*Now* I'm convinced this is Sergey's doing. Once he got access, he'd have put this poor bastard down without a second thought."

He began approaching the door but Ballard shot out his hand, gripping his jacket and motioning that a call had to be made. Speaking quietly into his mobile, Ballard gave Malcolm brief instructions. "We're about to enter the building. We should be back out before Tim and his crew arrive, but if not, let them know where we are."

Crouching low they peered inside, observing a small reception area. Verifying there was no sign of movement, all three entered and were confronted by more dead security guards; this time two were slumped behind the counter, and as before, blood was congealing from single head wounds.

Peter snarled, "Jesus, is there no end to this prick's murderous rampage?"

John respectfully relieved one of the slain men of his holstered Glock. After checking the magazine he wedged the weapon in his waistband.

A grey door on the far side of the office, ironically plastered with health and safety brochures, led them into a gargantuan loading bay where the cannisters from the train's flatbeds would have been rolled into position. Bolted onto the concrete wall were massive hydraulic arms to operate the movable section. Parked nearby, three purpose-built low-loaders sat idle, the drivers' cabins empty; two of the units had their doors wide open.

Twitchy in the extreme, John searched around him, asking more of himself, "Where in Christ's name are the workers who'd be operating all this gear?"

Staring along the wide roadway sloping down into the bowels of the complex, Peter suggested, "Without knowing why, I'd say they've been herded onto one of those electric buggies and driven down to the storage area." He indicated several multi-seated electric cars parked to one side, the vehicles like overgrown golf carts. "I'd imagine if any of the staff had been witness to the carnage outside, or in the office for that matter, they wouldn't have put up too much resistance." Peter's ominous tone didn't augur well for what he believed was the fate of the workers.

John's expression begged that they had no choice but to investigate whether the missing personnel were still alive. He added as further incentive, "We have to at least take a look and *try* to save them from being slaughtered, if it's not too late already."

Weighing up the risks with their limited weaponry, Ballard faced Peter. "John's right. Who knows how long Tim will be?" He inclined his head towards the nearest buggy. "Ok John, you drive while Pete and I stand in the back riding shotgun." As one they switched their mobiles to vibrate.

Easing into gear, John was grateful the buggy was electric,

the only sound being minimal tyre noise on the relatively smooth road surface. Overhead lights were fixed in the tunnel's concrete ceiling every fifteen metres, and while they were adequate, they were not as illuminating as the detectives would have liked. Approaching each set, their shadows lagged behind them, resembling weary travellers, then as they passed beneath their image leapt ahead like hyperactive children; the process was hypnotic as it repeated over and over. A flat, grey conduit tray at least 600 millimetres wide and fixed high on the concrete panelled wall appeared to house the tunnel's essential services. It stretched endlessly ahead as did the red waterpipe anchored to the ceiling, sporting evenly spaced sprinkler heads in case of a fire.

John steered one-handed, the other clutching the Glock, his own Smith & Wesson remaining holstered, Ballard aware of his partner's preference for the Austrian manufactured, polymer-framed semi-automatic. Weapons drawn, Ballard and Peter grasped the thick metal roll bar which spanned the width of the buggy, their eyes straining ahead, ever vigilant.

Every hundred metres John brought the vehicle to a silent halt, all three straining to hear any sounds in front of them. Under normal circumstances their combined firepower would have been reassuring, a total of sixty rounds before having to reload. This, however, was Sergey they were tracking, his elite Spetsnaz skills and ability to adapt no matter what the odds ensured each detective remained on high alert.

A kilometre from their starting point they maintained their steady progress, the angle of the descent gentle as they snaked back and forth in giant serpentine S's, the temperature dropping as they proceeded. On three occasions they passed exit doors marked by green glowing signage; nearby, instructional symbols were painted in red paint on the walls, the escape routes reassuring. Sections of the concrete panelled walls bore trickles of water that had seeped through hairline cracks, the rivulets reflecting under the overhead lights, the resultant stains now a dirty tan colour, reminding all that nature was active and ever present.

Regular stops and measured bouts of intense listening without hearing anything had them questioning whether anyone was indeed below them. Progressing on, the first faint cries of terrified men echoed up to them. John hit the brakes, causing Ballard and Peter to lurch against the chest-high barrier. They remained motionless, holding their breath, their senses on edge. Satisfied they hadn't drawn attention, John looked up and whispered, "How do we tackle this?"

Ballard and Peter hopped down, indicating for John to turn the buggy around and face it in the direction they had come.

"How fast does this thing go?" Ballard peered over John's shoulder at the speedo, surprised at what he saw. "Ok, more than enough. Pocket the key."

Hugging the wall they proceeded on foot for another fifty metres, the cries of the men now continuous and appreciably louder. Edging up to a bend they were confronted with a substantial widening of the tunnel and a doubling in its height. Just short of where the passageway broadened, two enormous steel doors at least a half-metre thick and suspended on giant hinges were swung to the fully open position—clearly the site's last bastion of defence. On either side wall individual cavities had been carved into the bare rock, large enough to house the cannisters two high, the series of recesses stretching into the distance as far as the eye could see. A massive forklift and various items of machinery were staged near the entrance, along with overhead signage indicating exit, hazard and first-aid points.

Thirty metres in, a buggy identical to their own was parked next to a wire-mesh equipment cage recessed into the rock. Inside at least six men were imprisoned, shouting, pleading, all clutching at the mesh.

Signing their intentions to each other while minimising the risk of being spotted, the detectives crept closer, attempting to see what the men were fixated on. An unmistakable figure outfitted in army fatigues moved into view, working just short of the first set of cavities on the left side of the cavern wall. Following a knowing glance at one another it took a mere instant for the detectives to grasp what Sergey was undertaking before they backed away, all the while keeping him in view.

Unaware he had company, the Russian continued setting explosive charges which he drew from a black satchel slung over his shoulder. The strategically placed packs of C4 were the subject of the workers' mounting horror, and the cause for their desperate pleas for freedom.

Barely audible, Peter hissed, "So that's the plan, blow the shit out of this place and the government kisses goodbye any chance of nuclear storage in Australia ... *forever.*"

John leaned closer to Ballard, whispering. "Do you think the bastard's alone?"

Ballard hesitated. "Hard to tell. If there *is* someone else, he must be further inside the tunnel, perhaps setting more charges."

Assessing the distance between Sergey and themselves, Ballard estimated it to be too great to approach without being spotted, the Russian's combat prowess far superior to their own. Complicating the situation was the risk of friendly fire striking the caged workers.

Frustration and anger coursed through Ballard as it had when trapped in the chopper with Sergey after the Parliament House siege. In the space of seconds each of the murders the Russian had committed flashed before him: the two politicians on the government building's front steps; Sergey's own men inside the parliamentary chamber; the chopper pilot beaten to death with a rock at the Grampians, along with the tragic slaying of the local country policeman; the two New South Wales police officers shot at point-blank range in Sydney Harbour, and now the four security guards slain at the storage site. Fighting an overwhelming urge to leap out and put the ex-soldier down like the mad dog he was, Ballard regained his composure, gesturing for Peter and John to follow him.

"You saw the trigger device hanging from his waist?" They confirmed they had. "Once he's set the charges he'll be hightailing out of here, blowing the site and the workers with it. My guess is it won't be long before he's heading our way."

Looking up, Ballard assessed the height of the ceiling to be just over three metres, the minimum clearance required to accommodate the transportation of the larger cannisters. He whispered, "We need to take at least three of those lights out to darken a section of the tunnel." Shading his eyes, he inspected the one above him. "Thank Christ the cover over the globe is secured by a swivel arm, not screws. This makes for faster bulb replacements."

Peter glanced at Ballard, then John. "We could dink Johno on our shoulders, but the light would still be out of reach."

Not waiting for further discussion, John sprinted back to the buggy, reversing it to beneath the light where they were standing, breathing hard from his exertion. Ballard and Peter checked that Sergey was still occupied with the charges, relieved the frantic shouting from the workers had drowned out the tyre noise from the buggy.

As John scrambled onto the bonnet, bracing one foot on top of the windscreen for stability, Ballard took out a handkerchief and folding it, handed it to his partner. "The bulb will be red hot, use this so you don't drop it."

"Thanks for the vote of confidence … no pressure mind you."

While Peter remained on Sergey watch, Ballard gripped John's legs to stabilise him as he swung open the light cover. Grasping the halogen globe, John pushed up while twisting anticlockwise to unscrew it. The area around them was thrown into partial darkness, and while not total, it was enough for them to appreciate the plan had merit.

Handing the wrapped globe to Ballard who deposited it in the glovebox, John slid into the driver's seat, repositioning the buggy under the next light. An action replay saw the second globe removed and darkness in the tunnel expand.

"One more?"

Ballard waved him on. Under the third light, John reached up, and in his haste he fumbled the bulb. Both men were desperate, Ballard saving the day by clutching the wayward globe to his chest, the glass burning his palms and through his shirt. Wiping sweat from his brow, John took the globe and placed it with the other two, only then muttering, "Nice catch," his expression failing to match his pithy utterance.

Looking back they were impressed how dark the forty-metre stretch of tunnel had become. Peter could be seen in the distance, crouched down as he maintained his vigil. Realising that in a firefight the buggy may offer a degree of protection,

John reversed it level to where Peter was squatting, parking it on the opposite side of the tunnel, reasoning that Sergey would be driving in the middle of the roadway when he exited.

Pleased with their efforts, they crept forward to find the Russian standing impassively in front of the cage, assessing what he was about to do, devoid of any emotion. To him the men were collateral damage, the charges a blatant message to the authorities that The Board wasn't to be messed with. The workers, sensing their time was up, were beyond panicked, their combined voices a desperate primal cry for help.

Their urgency was contagious as Peter glanced about him. "We need to split up so we don't present a group target." He pointed to the opposite side of the tunnel. "I'll wait over there in the shadows while you two take cover behind the buggy. I'm guessing he won't see me because it's unlikely he'll have his headlights on, not knowing he's driving into darkness until he comes around the corner."

Ballard expanded on the required actions. "John and I will take out the tyres to stop him. It's critical he doesn't get past us so he can set off the charges. I'll go for the rear tyre John, you concentrate on the front. Ricochets may be a factor but they can't be helped. We'll challenge him, and if he goes for a weapon or the trigger device, we'll put him down. He's most likely wearing a vest, so John, aim below where the vest ends. Pete, you go for headshots as you'll be closest, I'll aim for high chest and neck area. *And don't spare the rounds.*" The bitterness in his voice had Peter and John second glancing their colleague.

They rechecked their automatics, more to settle their nerves than as a precaution. Peter stepped to the far side of the tunnel and crouching down, braced one knee on the concrete floor just inside the shadow line.

John and Ballard took up position behind the buggy, selecting a stance that gave each a clear field of vision. Nudging Ballard with an elbow, John hissed, "We're doing the right thing Mike. This bastard deserves to be taken out. Hopefully he'll realise he's outnumbered and outgunned and come quietly, but this is Sergey we're dealing with …"

Nodding, Ballard broke away, creeping closer to the corner, a result of hearing the workers' cries grow even more frantic. Flattening against the wall he spotted Sergey hop behind the wheel of the electric car; after one final inspection of his handiwork, the Russian swung the buggy around and drove towards the waiting detectives.

Within seconds he came into view, fifteen metres short of where Peter was crouching. Ballard and John rose up, and employing a two-handed stance, squeezed off three rounds each. The muzzle flashes were vivid in the darkness, the roar of the shots deafening—the acrid stench of metallic sulphur stinging their nostrils. The buggy lurched to the left as the nearside tyres deflated, the vehicle grinding to a halt, still within the orb of the last operating light. Ballard and John leapt forward, shouting for the Russian to put his hands up, John supplementing the command with, "Blink shithead and I'll blow your goddamn brains out!"

Peter remained steadfastly mute, the backup surprise factor, Ballard and John's trump card should the situation turn nasty. Sergey's military training cut in, aware he needed to assess the capability and scope of his enemy before reacting. Raising his hands above his head he watched his attackers approaching from two angles, arms locked, their weapons unwavering.

The sight of the detectives didn't faze him, having overcome greater odds many times before.

Peter chose to ramp up the degree of difficulty. "Don't even think about it. Not even *you* are that fast."

Demonstrating incredible self-control, the Russian didn't bother to look in Peter's direction, Ballard convinced both angle and distance based on Peter's voice had already been calculated. A growing sense of the inevitable pervaded Ballard's thinking, remembering back to when he and John had interviewed Vladimir, the billionaire insisting Sergey would never be taken alive were he to be confronted with certain arrest.

Recognising the detectives, a sardonic, almost fatalistic smile came over the Russian's face, possibly reliving the physical injuries Ballard inflicted upon him in the helicopter. "Well, here we are again ... comrades in arms." Fixing Ballard with an unblinking stare he added, his voice a mere whisper, "It's been a pleasure."

Sensing this was to be his parting utterance, Ballard's finger tightened on his Smith & Wesson a split-second before the Russian's hands dove down from behind his head to activate the trigger mechanism. Bullets from all three directions, each striking with the impact of over five hundred Newton metres of force hurled Sergey from the buggy onto the concrete floor—flesh and bone pulverised, the once-dreaded Spetsnaz soldier reduced to a lifeless form, never to terrorise and murder innocent victims again.

John approached warily, his weapon still levelled, his face contorted with rage, the Russian's death failing to appease his sense of justice. "The shithead had it coming. We should have taken him out months ago when we first had the chance."

Still assessing the body, he claimed, "All that training and experience and here he is put down like a mad dog, lying in his own blood."

Ballard and Peter stood beside their partner, each dropping a heavy hand on his shoulders as they stared at the torn body, blood pooling around it. In an inexplicable way each felt cheated that such a challenging adversary had succumbed so unremarkably; no clever military tactics to foil the standoff he was caught in, no spectacular athleticism to evade his captors for which he was renowned—just a transformation in the blink of an eye from an elite, professional soldier to a lifeless form on the ground.

His eyes blazing, Ballard snapped, "We may have won *this* battle, but with The Board and the Ndrangheta having the makings of a nuclear bomb in their clutches, it's inevitable we'll be engaged in a protracted war with these bastards."

To Peter and John's shocked amazement, Ballard squared up, aggressive, as though about to deliver a savage kick to the inert body as a means of venting his barely contained fury. He held back, wiping his mouth with the back of his hand. In a voice choking with emotion he declared, "And it'll be a war costing God knows how many more lives, and may well involve our loved ones."

CHAPTER
2

Everyone holstered their weapons, with John beginning the task of recording the crime scene as best he could by photographing the body and its surrounds with his mobile. On completion, the detectives turned towards their buggy, checking it over to ensure it hadn't been hit by stray rounds. As they prepared to make the short journey to release the workers who would have heard the gunfire but were unaware their prayers had been answered, they exchanged questioning glances, perplexed why the men's desperate cries had inexplicably risen to a new level.

Without warning a buggy hurtled up the ramp from the direction of the imprisoned men, driven by a thickset man dressed in full camouflage fatigues. The instant he spotted the detectives he released a volley of shots which ricocheted off the walls and whined into the distance. Adjusting his course, he steered straight for all three, who dropped to a crouch to minimise the target area they were offering. The driver squeezed off additional rounds.

Grunting in pain, Peter slumped forward, clutching his left shoulder, blood oozing between his fingers. Ballard and

John crowded closer, protecting their partner as more shots reverberated in the confined space. Levelling his automatic, John discharged four rounds at the shooter as he accelerated past into the darkened section of the tunnel. Realising further attempts to halt the fleeing figure were futile, he lowered his weapon in disgust. Taking in Ballard, he cursed that their earlier efforts to remove the globes had now worked against them, the shooter escaping and well on his way to the exit.

Both men inspected the wound which had stained Peter's suit sleeve a deep burgundy.

The superintendent grimaced in pain. "*Christ* this hurts. I've never been shot before—"

Ballard examined the bullet's exit point. "Stop your moaning, it's a through and through, so you can thank your lucky stars. At least the round didn't hit an artery, and by the position of the wound it appears to have missed any bone." Bunching his handkerchief on the injury under Peter's shirt, Ballard attempted to mask his growing fear as to what may unfold at any moment.

Struggling upright, one hand maintaining pressure to stem the blood flow, Peter gritted his teeth, doing his best to ignore the searing pain. Having seen Ballard's expression he confessed, "You're right, this isn't our biggest problem right now. *But that is.*" He thrust his chin towards the trigger device lying beside Sergey's body.

Ballard sized up the situation, aware there was nothing to be gained by downplaying their extreme predicament. "The question is, does the shooter have the same device as our dead Russian? He went past too fast to see. And once he's clear of the blast zone is he going to light this place up?"

He glanced back to where the workers could still be heard

shouting, then grim-faced he made an abrupt decision. "John ... take Pete in the buggy and get him to the surface for medical treatment. Hopefully Tim's arrived by now and is in the process of taking out our shooter—"

John stiffened, wide-eyed, shocked at what the request implied. "And what the hell are YOU going to be doing?"

Ballard's lips drew back in frustrated anger. *"Don't argue!* We haven't time. Get Pete out of here and bring back the cavalry while I free the men in the cage. Believe me, we won't be far behind you, and a bit of light exercise will do us the world of good."

John and Peter rose up in united defiance, with John bellowing, *"Bullshit we will.* We're not leaving without you. Get in the buggy and we'll *all* go and set them free."

Ballard made to reply but was halted by the ominous rumble of an explosion emanating from the direction in which the shooter had fled. An instant later a blast of scorched, dust-laden air knocked the detectives off their feet. The tunnel lights dipped then came back on, although much dimmer, assumedly on battery backup. A returning rush of air from the opposite direction rocked them again, but it was minimal compared to the initial onslaught. Dust continued to billow in a heavy, rolling cloud, hampering their breathing, their eyes flooding with tears.

Hauling himself upright and retching, Ballard squinted through the haze to where John and Peter lay sprawled on the tunnel floor, also gasping for air, their hair and clothes covered in a fine, grey powder. Relieved, he saw them slowly stagger to their feet, Peter reapplying pressure to his shoulder. Approaching them, equally wobbly, Ballard queried, "No broken bones?"

Peter shook his head, dazed, while John spat out a mouthful of dust. "I'm just pissed I didn't blow the prick's head off." He waved about him. "It would have saved all this."

Feelings of relief grew that the shooter may not have a duplicate of Sergey's trigger device—each assuming that if he had he would have detonated the full series of charges by now. Ballard battled to think of something droll to utter, determined to calm everyone's nerves. "I may be stating the bleeding obvious guys, but we could be down here a damn sight longer than we first planned." They reached out, bunting clenched fists, their cautious grins flashing white in their dust-caked faces, belying the still-dire situation they and the workers were confronting.

Turning towards the buggy, Ballard halted, catching his breath, his newfound euphoria in tatters.

Picking up on his sudden mood change, John blurted, "What is it?"

Hesitating, not wanting to create undue panic, Ballard realised he had no option but to reveal the dread now overwhelming him. "We can assume the explosion was from charges he had with him when he shot past us. But what if the trigger mechanism … which he doesn't appear to have … was only a backup?"

"Go on." John was stone-faced, along with Peter, each sensing the worst.

Ballard attempted to clear his throat, the choking dust reducing his voice to a scratchy whisper. "How do we know the explosives aren't hooked up to a bloody timer set to go off at any second?"

Shocked into action, the three men raced to their buggy.

Snatching out his mobile, Ballard glared at the screen. "No signal goddamn it."

The detectives scrambled aboard, John accelerating towards the cage where the workers were now silent, cowering in fear, uncertain whether those approaching were friend or foe. Leaping out, Ballard fronted them, extending both hands palms outward in a display of friendship. "We're the police. We need to get you out of here as quickly as possible." He glanced across at the packs of C4, willing his worst fears to be unfounded, acutely aware he didn't possess the necessary expertise to diffuse the explosives.

His action and words had an immediate effect. The dust-covered men rose as one and crowded forward, their fingers clawing through the steel mesh, eager to be released.

"Who's in charge?" Ballard prayed there was a foreman among them who could coordinate the men.

A tall man in faded jeans and a blue T-shirt stepped forward, his clothes, hair and handlebar moustache coated with dust. "That'd be me."

"Name?"

"Jack. Jack Wilson."

Ballard inspected the heavy-duty lock on the cage door. "Any thoughts how we spring this thing Jack?"

"You could shoot it off."

John nudged alongside Ballard, snapping in frustration, "Doesn't work, only in the movies. Believe me, I've tried."

Peter peered into the cage, spotting a small jemmy bar lying beside an assortment of tools. "Pass it through." He too eyeballed the explosives, but kept silent for fear of spooking the workers any more than they already were.

Jack did as instructed. "We tried using it before, but we

couldn't reach the padlock through the mesh—and the jemmy isn't long enough to get the leverage we need to force the cage door hinges."

John wrested it from the foreman's hand. Inserting the curved end into the U-shaped shackle of the padlock he began applying pressure, willed on by the desperate men. Straining, John's face turned purple, and just when it appeared his efforts would be in vain there was a sharp metallic crack. The padlock itself remained intact but the surrounding metal bracket hung free, generating a rapturous cheer.

With a series of hefty kicks from within to fully release the door, the men streamed from the cage and bolted for the buggy, their expectations unmistakeable.

Ballard forcibly grabbed Jack by the arm. "Not so fast. We're *hoping* that when the shooter set off the charge, he was on the entrance side of what will be a heap of collapsed rubble, but we can't be certain. He may have seen our rescue team coming down the tunnel in front of him and detonated the explosives to stop them. For all we know he's on his way back here to take hostages so he can bargain his way out." He pointed to Peter and John. "I know this appears selfish, but *we* need to take the buggy and check that he's not hiding out somewhere to pick us off one by one when we all eventually drive out."

Jack took a deep breath, immediately regretting it, coughing fitfully before hawking up a glob of mucus and fine dust. Nodding, he loped over to his team who were already seated and anxious to depart; reluctantly he explained the situation. Cursing and disappointed, the men slowly disembarked, their eyes boring into the detectives as they stood in a dejected huddle.

John swung into the driver's seat as Ballard and Peter climbed into the rear, their automatics drawn, Peter's free hand pressed against his wound. He called to the men, indicating they should begin making a cautious, and above all, silent approach towards the entrance. He added that once the coast was clear, John would return to ferry them the rest of the way. Ballard followed this with strict instructions for the group to keep to the side wall as they passed Sergey's body, ensuring they didn't contaminate the crime scene.

Switching on the headlights, John began the ascent, steering well clear of the slain Russian. The vehicle's lights pierced the darkened section of the tunnel, the suspended dust particles resembling a heavy fog, adding an eeriness to the already tense situation. Emerging into the lit area, John flicked off the headlights so as not to forewarn the shooter of their approach should he still be in the tunnel, again the tyre noise their only giveaway. Glancing back, Ballard observed the twin tracks left by the vehicle, a consequence of the thick layer of settled dust.

They progressed on for several minutes in silence, the suspended particles so dense that vision was reduced to a few metres. Ballard, together with Peter who was bearing his pain through gritted teeth, were forced to balance against the rollbar with their bodies so they could use their free hand to hold their jackets against their nose and mouth.

Driving singlehanded, John did likewise, his complaint muffled in the fabric. "This stuff is like pea soup. The bastard could be off to one side and we'd drive straight past and not even see him—*Jesus!*" He stabbed his foot on the brake, forgetting the impact his action had on the passengers standing in the rear.

Peering through the haze of dust, they saw a stream of

muddy water flowing towards them over the floor of the tunnel, and while it wasn't a torrent, it was constant; within seconds it coursed beneath the buggy. In unison, Ballard and Peter hissed, "The sprinklers." Ballard added, "I'd say the explosion has ruptured not only the fire system, but also the water pipes servicing the workers' amenities area."

Still coughing they progressed on, and after navigating yet another wide sweeping bend, flashes of light ahead caused John to panic, stabbing the brakes once more. Ducking low in his seat he shouted, *"Get down!"*

Ballard and Peter chose to play safe. Seconds later John sheepishly admitted, "Sorry guys. My nerves must be shredded. For a second there I thought the bastard was shooting at us."

Ballard placed a hand on his shoulder. "Don't apologise Johno. Better safe than sorry."

Less than twenty metres in front of them massive slabs of concrete, fallen rocks, reinforcing steel and mounds of earth completely blocked the tunnel, the aftermath of the explosion. The conduit tray was twisted and torn, hanging forlornly from the ceiling. Sparks from the electrical cables shorting out continued to splutter, the source of John's embarrassment.

Coughing, the detectives got out and cautiously approached the impenetrable barrier, checking above to determine whether the remaining sections of roof were stable. Several slabs on the side walls leaned in at an alarming angle, with one piece appearing to be on the verge of collapse.

John turned to Ballard. "Well now we know, the bloody shooter must be on the other side ... unless of course we missed him on the way up here."

Failing to appreciate his partner's black humour, Ballard queried, "How close to the surface do you think we are?"

John inclined his head in deep contemplation. "On the way down, the distance from the loading bay to the cage was just over two kilometres. On the way back we've come a kilometre and a half." Grinning, he tapped a forefinger against his temple. "I checked the speedo before we took off."

Peter held his mobile under the nearest light, exclaiming, "*Two bars*!"

Ballard checked his, relieved it showed the same signal strength. "We must be nearer the surface than we first thought." He dialled Tim's number.

A series of rings were followed by a breathless, "Mike ... are you guys alright? I rang you before but there was no answer." The anguish in the SOG commander's voice was extreme.

Swallowing, Ballard blurted, "Never felt better ... and you?" He switched to speaker mode.

"Considering we had to put down a bloody madman blazing away at us near the tunnel entrance, yeah, everything's tickety-boo." The caustic reply was laced with undisguised relief. "Where in God's name are you?"

"We're facing a bloody great pile of concrete and rock. Where are *you*?"

"Oh, about twenty metres away ... on the other side of that bloody great pile."

Both men laughed, overwhelming relief causing them to feel mildly giddy.

"Is this Sergey's doing?" Tim already knew the answer.

"*Was* his doing."

"What do you mean *was*?"

"He's dead."

"How?"

"We shot him."

There was an extended silence. "You … you *shot* him?"

"Tim, I'll explain later. Right now, I have seven workers hightailing it up the tunnel on foot, and they're pretty keen to put as much distance between themselves and Christ knows how much C4 which may go off any second. Hang five while I speak to John."

Addressing his partner he asked, "Are you ok to go back and pick the guys up and drop them off at the exit door nearest to here?"

John had already hopped into the buggy. Reversing, he called out, "Is the Pope a bloody Catholic?" Accelerating back down the tunnel, this time with headlights blazing, it was obvious he was determined to test the vehicle's top speed.

"Are you there Tim?" Ballard turned back towards the pile of rubble with Peter close by, grimacing as he maintained pressure on his shoulder.

"Yes Mike, I'm not going anywhere until we get you out of there." Tim sounded exasperated.

Ballard felt a rising sense of urgency for Peter. "Tim, we have a slight problem here, Pete's been shot—"

"*What*! I thought you said everyone was ok?" Alarm sharpened Tim's voice.

Peter seized the mobile. "Tim, I copped one in the shoulder. It hurts like a bugger but the bullet passed through and didn't hit anything vital. Even so, we're hoping to get out of here via the closest exit to where we are."

Tim switched to resolution mode. "So there *are* exits in the tunnel?"

Ballard and Peter chorused, "Three of them."

Tim took up the commentary again. "All this happening in the middle of the night isn't making life easy. I've requested a shitload of reinforcing poles to prop up the roof and they're being trucked in as we speak. Once they're in place a front-end loader will begin moving some of the fallen slabs—but all that will take too long for you guys, so yes, the exit is your best bet."

Peter grunted. "Yeah, avoiding a shitload of stairs *would* have been preferable, but dodging a heap of C4 going off is also near the top of my to do list. Somehow, I'll make it. We're just waiting for John to get back with the workers, then we'll get stuck into the climb." To move the focus away from himself he asked, "What's happening at the ambush site?"

Peter handed the mobile back to Ballard so he could take up applying pressure to his wound.

"Delwyn's arrived with Ken, Bobby and Susan, and they're doing what they can to make sense of everything. Forensic is flat out salvaging evidence before there's any more rain, and believe me, there's plenty of it ... evidence that is. The AC ordered the Communications van to be on site when this thing first kicked off—it should be here any time now. I've also included the bomb squad. The other urgent issue will be getting heavy lift equipment to pop the locomotive back on the tracks once the rail line is repaired. This explosion has put paid to moving the cannisters to their final resting place for the time being, but at the very least we'll get them into the loading bay, away from temptation." He hesitated, and in a lowered voice added, "To give you an idea how political all this has become, I've been informed ... no, make that *ordered*, that the bodies are to be removed from the ambush site as soon as possible, and when the press start sniffing around, the official line is the train derailed, killing the security contingent and the driver."

Ballard's eyes almost popped out of his head as he stared at

Peter who was performing a slow head shake. "*Bloody madness. Something as horrendous as this can't be kept under wraps … far too many people know about it.* How are the bodies to be removed without someone leaking the news?"

"Body bags, and would you believe *both* PolAir's will be used to ferry them back to Melbourne."

"What does the AC make of all this?"

"Who do you think gave the order?"

"*Really?*"

"Really."

Ballard's eyebrows arched upwards, copying Peter's who appeared to be struggling to fathom the ever-increasing obstacles surrounding the tragedy. Just as he was about to pump Tim for more information, John returned alone in the buggy, performing a well-executed U-turn in front of them.

Eyes wide, he announced, "Hop aboard folks and I'll take you to the exit. It's not as far down as I first thought." It was obvious he was enjoying himself.

Ballard informed Tim that he would call him back. The moment he and Peter were aboard, John drove along the tunnel for less than two hundred metres, pulling up beside Jack who was standing with his back to the exit door, the illuminated sign above him a feeble, flickering excuse of a light.

John acknowledged the foreman before shuffling around in his seat to face Ballard. "Jack gave me a bunch of figures you may find interesting." His wicked grin widened. "The slope of the tunnel is a one-in-twenty-five gradient and we're about half a kilometre from the entrance, so that puts us at around forty metres below the surface. At six steps a metre, this means we'll be climbing a mere two hundred and forty steps to get us out of this hellhole." Chuckling at Ballard, who was normally the narrator of endless statistics, John spotted the show of alarm on Peter's face.

Mortified, John apologised. "I'm sorry Pete, I shouldn't have been so flippant. Do you think you can make it?"

Climbing out of the buggy with considerable effort, Peter shrugged before replying, "There's only one way to find out." He waved deferentially at Jack. "After you my good man."

With Jack leading the way, the detectives entered the stairwell, which was also lit by ceiling lights now on battery backup. While the illumination was constantly flickering, it was adequate. The metal stairs allowed two abreast, enabling Ballard and John to remain close behind Peter, ever ready to support their colleague should the climb become too arduous. Their combined footsteps, along with those of the workers above, echoed in the confines like a stampeding herd, everyone grateful the air was much cleaner than inside the tunnel.

Grumbling more to himself than to anyone in particular, John snarled, "Considering what the government must have spent on this place, you'd have thought a lift would have been in order."

Even though the foreman was two landings above, he responded, his voice deep and gravelly. "Yeah, that's what we thought, but lifts aren't practical here because for security reasons the exit point has to be *inside* the loading bay, so we're actually climbing at an angle."

John resumed his relentless ascent.

Ballard reached up and tapped Peter on the back. "How're you feeling?"

The superintendent came to an abrupt halt, both hands gripping the rail, blowing heavily. "Ask me in another two hundred steps. If I'm still able to talk I'll let you know." He resumed his climb, and despite concerted efforts not to, regular groans of pain escaped his lips.

Minutes later joyous cries could be heard filtering down to their level. The three detectives assumed the workers had reached the top of the stairs and were now enjoying their hard-won freedom inside the loading bay.

The involuntary grunts of pain from Peter became more frequent, causing Ballard to plead with his partner, "We don't need to do this in one go. Take a break and catch your breath."

Peter's response was a ragged growl, refusing to slow down, and while his stoicism was applauded by John, Ballard feared that should his colleague push his endurance to the limit he may well collapse and have to be carried out.

Fifty steps from the finish line Ballard's prediction proved correct. Peter's foot clipped the front edge of a step and he came down heavily on one knee. Struggling in the narrow staircase, Ballard and John hauled him to his feet. Slinging an arm each around his waist, and careful not to aggravate his shoulder, they continued at a much slower pace, guided him up the remaining steps, his head lolling from side to side.

Propping the exit door open, Jack encouraged the trio on. Exhausted, Peter no longer offered any pretence of independence, accepting that he needed to be carried the final stage. Emerging into the loading bay the detectives spotted the workers in a huddle, many hugging, all exchanging handshakes and high-fives. Realising the air quality in the cavernous surrounds was as bad or worse than in the stairwell, everyone elected to move outside, the moon providing sufficient light for the joyous celebrations to continue.

Tim and two of his team approached at a brisk trot, the SOG commander as emotional as Ballard had ever seen him. "*Bugger me*, I had my doubts I'd ever see you lot in one piece ever again. When the explosion went off, we had no idea whether or not the whole tunnel had been destroyed, with you guys inside. *Damn it*, you buggers have given me more than my fair share of heart attacks over the past few months." He did his best to maintain the rage. "*All this shit has to stop!*" Swallowing several times, he focussed on Peter. "An ambulance should be here any minute to take you to the Ouyen hospital."

Propped on a folding chair taken from the loading bay, Peter managed a weak grin. "Not a problem. I *was* going to suggest a couple of band-aids to cover the bullet holes ... but if you insist."

Tim grimaced as he inspected the wound. Spinning back, the SOG commander unleashed on Ballard and John. "You two couldn't wait, could you?"

Overhearing the volatile exchanges, Jack stepped closer. "If they had then we'd have all been blown to smithereens by that Russian ..." He appeared perplexed. "What was he anyway, some kind of soldier?"

John helped out. "Sergey Alistratov, and yes he *was* a Russian soldier, *once*, before he decided there was more money in it for him becoming a professional criminal."

Jack contemplated what might have been for himself and his men just forty minutes prior, physically shivering. The detectives thanked him for rallying his workers when it was needed, shaking his hand in farewell. The foreman asked them to wait as he called his team over, and together they raised a hearty cheer. The policemen returned an embarrassed wave before walking around the corner of the bunker, Peter having recovered sufficiently to move unaided, but still in considerable pain.

Continuing on, they waited outside the guard post for the ambulance to arrive, watching with interest as forensic officers went about their work, some with cameras, others carrying plastic evidence bags. In the distance Malcolm was seen exiting the chopper, making a beeline towards them. At the same time the ambulance pulled up, shrouded in a cloud of dust, reminding them of the conditions in the tunnel. Piling out, the paramedics checked Peter over before requesting he lie on a stretcher in the rear. After handing the keys of the police car to John, he chose the side bench seat, allowing himself to be buckled up. As the rear doors closed, he managed a weak grin and a wave, then, with the lights flashing the ambulance drove off.

Having stood to one side out of respect while Peter's departure took place, Malcolm approached, his face revealing his relief. "Thank God you're all in one piece." In an attempt at levity he laughed, "I can't *imagine* what Teresa would have said were I to tell her I'd flown you all up here to your deaths."

Tim's mobile rang. Snatching it to his ear he moved away.

Malcolm chose to throw in a rhetorical question. "I take it the cannisters when they get here won't be concreted into their ultimate resting place any time soon?"

John scoffed, "Dead right, and the political fallout from all this is going to be government changing if I'm not mistaken." He knew not to elaborate on how the politicians were choosing to handle the situation in the short term. As a compromise he revealed, "Malcolm, I'm going to let you in on something which you can pass on to Teresa, however, *only* to her, ok? ... Sergey's dead."

The billionaire froze. Digesting the revelation, his face remained impassive, but his eyes gave away his incredible relief. The detectives looking on couldn't blame him considering the grief Sergey had unleashed on him and his wife, but they were mindful they still had to maintain a lid on the information getting out.

Ballard chose to reconfirm John's declaration. "Malcolm, this whole situation is becoming incredibly complicated. Obviously what John told you isn't for public consumption as you can well imagine, so for security reasons we'll be doing everything possible to keep things on a need-to-know basis."

Just as the billionaire was about to affirm his understanding, Tim returned, his brow furrowed. "That was the AC. He's arrived on PolAir 2 and is now ensconced in the mobile communications van at the attack site. Needless to say, he's not a happy camper. He wants to see us ASAP." Turning, he addressed Malcolm. "I feel I should deputise you considering all the assistance you've given us so far, but I need one more favour ... can you fly us back to the derailment site?"

Malcolm's eyes lit up. "I thought you'd never ask."

"OK, while you're firing up the chopper I'll nip over and update my 2IC." Tim left at a brisk jog.

Ballard sidled closer to John. "What's the bet the boss wants to hear firsthand what went down, then we'll be given our marching orders as to what we can and can't pass on to other members and the press?" He turned. "OK, Malcolm, let's do this."

The three men loped over to the Eurocopter and clambered aboard, Malcolm going through his pre-flight checklist as they waited for Tim. In deep thought, Ballard and John relived the preceding chaotic hour and a half, each grateful they had survived to fight another day. Less than five minutes later they were in the air, once more the powerful spotlight highlighting the train line below them. Tim sat opposite Ballard and John, the conversations subdued.

Voicing everyone's thoughts, Ballard commented as he massaged both temples, "Whichever way you cut it, this whole situation has turned out to be as god-awful for those poor security guys as anybody could have possibly feared."

Tim proposed a more optimistic viewpoint. "Maybe so, and as tragic as it clearly is, had the rest of the workers been killed and the storage facility blown sky-high, *that* would have significantly complicated matters. At least those men are alive, and while repairing the tunnel will be a job and a half, it's doable. Once the rubble's cleared the bomb squad will go in and do their thing, and let's pray there are no accidents during that seat-of-your-pants phase."

They lapsed into silence, Malcolm focussing on his instruments, wisely affording them time to reflect, the drone of the jet engines in the background a comforting distraction.

There was a hint of the approaching dawn as they neared the attack site, the floodlights now less distinct. Malcolm set the Eurocopter down on the same spot as before. Just as the policemen were about to climb down, he repeated his previous assurance he would keep out of their way. With mutual thanks they made a beeline for the battleship-grey communications van which was the size of a semi-trailer. They each felt a degree of trepidation; the AC's brutally aggressive manner in getting to the truth of a situation at the forefront of their minds.

Mounting the steps, Ballard knocked on the door. He led the way into the brightly lit van where they found AC Kevin Thompson at the head of the conference table scrawling furiously in his daybook. A female police sergeant and a male senior constable sat at laptops secured on wall-mounted benches. Above them on the perimeter walls were a series of monitors. All were switched off except one, which displayed a live feed of the derailed train thirty metres away. A mass of radio communication equipment was located on a table at the far end of the room. Both junior officers greeted the visitors with a cautious smile and a brief nod; by contrast the AC took in their presence with a penetrating gaze.

"Good morning, sir." Ballard sat to the AC's right, with John and Tim also acknowledging their assistant commissioner as they slipped into chairs opposite. The senior officer's formidable reputation was enhanced by a uniformed, bearlike physique that underscored he was in top shape. His grey hair was slicked back from a broad but lined forehead, and his intelligent, piercing blue eyes completed the picture of a man who was a natural leader. This was an officer who was fair and measured, yet one who had no qualms striking fear into anyone not up to speed on a particular subject he or she should be well versed in.

On this occasion, while his demeanour was that of a troubled man, his eyes were compassionate. "I owe you gentlemen a considerable debt of gratitude, as does Victoria. And seeing you here in one piece is an enormous personal relief. As traumatic as this situation is, it could have been a damn sight worse were it not for your combined, brave efforts. Saving the workers' lives along with the storage site was incredibly important from an individual and political perspective, which I'll go into in a minute."

He drew the attention of the two staff. "My apologies, I need to discuss a number of issues with these members in private."

Rising together, the officers left the van, having expected the request.

Turning to Tim the AC asked, "You mentioned when I rang that Peter's being patched up at the Ouyen hospital?"

Tim shuffled into a more upright position. "That's correct sir. Nothing life threatening it would appear, but that type of wound *can* be tricky. The shoulder contains the subclavian artery which feeds the main artery of the arm, as well as the brachial plexus, the large nerve bundle controlling arm function. In Pete's case the bullet passed through the fleshy part of the deltoid, missing both bone and artery. In short, while he was unlucky, he was actually *very* lucky if you know what I mean."

The AC blinked several times, reminded that in the SOG commander's line of work it was essential he be cognisant as to how gunshot wounds impacted the human body.

John grinned at Ballard, mildly amused that for once it wasn't his partner expounding on a complex issue.

Catching the exchange, the AC changed tack. "Now, this is what I *do* know about this god-awful catastrophe. The train carrying the nuclear cannisters was derailed sometime between 7 and 8 p.m. last night, prior to being attacked. An accompanying support chopper was shot out of the sky, and along with the train's complement of security personnel, a total of fourteen men were murdered in cold blood. Those fourteen consisted of international security officers, the train driver and the engineer. Two cannisters of U-235 were stolen and I'm led to believe all this was the work of The Board. Am I correct so far?"

Ballard felt obliged to divulge disconcerting news. "Either The Board or another group made up of the Italian mafia." He turned to John. "Help me out here Johno. What name do they go under?"

Realising the question was a setup, with Ballard aware his partner had difficulty pronouncing the group's name, John spluttered, directing a death stare towards his colleague.

Relenting, Ballard came to the rescue. "Ah yes, I remember now ... the Ndrangheta."

Despite the seriousness of the situation the AC smiled, fully aware of the pranks his detectives played on one another, an essential element in maintaining their sanity during demanding times. "Could this mob be in partnership with The Board?" The AC was dubious but determined to tick all the boxes.

"Unlikely. From the intelligence we have from Bernard and his CIA contact in Venice, both groups are bitter rivals, but their objective is one and the same. They're hellbent on destroying any chance Australia has of ever becoming a world player in nuclear waste storage."

The AC stroked his chin, his eyes thoughtful. "So, the attack on the train and the theft of the two cannisters could be the doing of either group? But would I be correct in assuming the attack on the bunker was most likely The Board's undertaking?"

"Very much so sir, unless Sergey and his sidekick jumped ship and were working for the mafia." John's expression considered the possibility questionable.

"Christ, as if The Board wasn't enough of a headache, now we have to contend with the bloody mafia." The AC was incensed. Leaning forward he asked, "Which brings me to the incident you two …" he waved a meaty hand at the detectives, "along with Peter found yourselves involved in. Mike, would you care to run me through what went down?"

Clearing his throat, Ballard presented the facts, with the AC raising the occasional question, all the while taking copious notes, occasionally stopping and staring at both detectives as the hairier aspects of the incident were expounded upon.

With the pertinent details revealed, the AC left no one in doubt as to what was needed. "Michael, John … it goes without saying Professional Standards will be interviewing you over the shooting, and I'll also be keeping an eye out should IBAC put their oar in the water. Tim, the same applies to you regarding the shooter in the buggy. I want to emphasise though, this is purely standard procedure, and I'll insist you all be given time to catch your breath from this ordeal before they call you in."

John shot upright in his chair, about to blurt out there was no need to delay the interviews, but the AC square-jawed him to remain silent.

Continuing, the senior officer added, "What's more, you two will require a couple of sessions with Marjorie to get the department off my back." He smirked at the thought. "Considering what she and Delwyn went through at the hands of Sergey, I have no doubt *that* little chat will be very enlightening."

Both detectives agreed, aware none of what the AC was demanding was up for debate. A debriefing with the department's chief psychologist wasn't their first, and wouldn't be their last.

The AC appeared thoughtful. "So the tunnel is currently blocked off near the entrance, with Christ knows how much C4 set in amongst the storage cavities?" His eyes widened as he contemplated the extreme difficulty the bomb squad would experience locating the explosives.

Ballard inclined his head. "Yes, that's it in a nutshell."

Tim reiterated that bracing poles were being installed, and once a path through the debris was made safe, the bomb squad would move in. In a surprise reveal, the AC shared a rare moment of personal reflection. "You know I'm in awe of what those teams do, I wouldn't have the ticker to do it myself. One slip and 'boom', blown to smithereens." He shook his head in admiration. His introspective mood was short lived, his face hardening. "Now, I need to work through the political ramifications of all this. The coroner accompanied me in PolAir. She's literally up to her knees in mud out there doing her level best to make sense of the bloodbath."

All eyes focussed on the monitor, but they couldn't make out the medical examiner amongst the forensic officers roving the area. The AC pushed on. "Her full support team should arrive within the next hour or so, and she commented that her investigation would normally take days. Nonetheless, the Chief has briefed the Premier and between them they've given her a directive that she has hours, not days, to have the bodies removed. The Premier then instructed the Chief ..." his gesture encompassed everyone present, "which as you all know is code for *us* ... to do whatever it takes to find those two cannisters within forty-eight hours."

"Forty-eight hours! That's just bullshit." John was incensed at such an impossible deadline.

"Yes, forty-eight hours is the maximum time the Chief and the Premier will be able to stall the press."

The AC repeated himself, exasperated, "*Forty-eight hours. It's not like we're dealing with bumbling con-artists here. I stressed that our chances are basically zero in recovering the cannisters in such a short timeframe.* That wasn't what the Chief wanted to hear, and he made it patently obvious he expected something, *anything,* to be unearthed to ensure the inevitable mauling by the media wouldn't be a complete bloodbath, ending any chance Australia has of becoming the nuclear storage mecca for the world."

John raked his fingers through his hair, the resultant dust cloud settling on the polished wooden table. He did his best to remove the offending film of grit with his sleeve and several concerted puffs. Hoping no one had noticed, he claimed, "But there are so many groups who know about this already, there's no way this can be kept a secret."

Ballard wasn't convinced. "Communications operators at headquarters know *something* has happened to the train, but not the totality of the massacre. The workers at the storage site aren't aware what's happened at this end, and Tim, you can warn them not to talk to the press about *their* adventures. The local coppers here know and can be ordered to keep this under wraps. The heavy lift machinery operators won't be on site until after the bodies have been removed. Finally, Delwyn and your guys John, along with the forensic team will need to be cautioned." Ballard drew Tim into his deliberations. "Who have I missed?"

"My chaps of course, but I'll sort them out. As for anyone else …" he inspected the ceiling in deep thought, "Malcolm, but he's old-school military, so he knows to keep quiet about this."

Another pause. "I'm assuming sir you'll deal with the coroner, her staff and the two officers that were here in the van?"

"Without a doubt." The AC's growl left no one in any doubt that the threat of instant dismissal would result should anyone break ranks. His scowl lifted. "The sheer remoteness of this place means news won't get out for a while, so that's in our favour." He directed his next order to Tim. "Arrange for all the weapons to be taken back with Michael and John in Malcolm's chopper." He rocked his head from side to side at the detectives' questioning expressions. "Yes, I know, we're breaking protocol, but I don't want that stuff seen by the machinery operators when they arrive, and Michael … see to it the weapons are logged into property as soon as you get back to the office. Now Tim, one more thing, make sure all the cartridge cases have been collected by forensic before the crews arrive. Spent shells lying around would be a dead giveaway." He pursed his lips. "The fire in the chopper they shot down has been out for some time, so tarps can cover the wreckage while the train tracks are being repaired and the locomotive lifted back into position." A significant sigh escaped his lips. "Let's not kid ourselves, details of what happened here *will* get out, there's nothing surer. All we can hope for is that in the forty-eight-hour window we're given we can conjure a miracle. So, get to work and I'll see you all back at the office at 1100 hours." He singled out Michael and John, giving them a wry smile. "I take it you two have a change of clothes at work? Despite your premature grey hair affording you a distinguished persona, I suggest you take a shower and grab a bite to eat first." He leaned forward in his seat. "And before I forget, I really do apologise for ending your holiday on such an abrupt note. When you speak with Natalie and Sonia, please pass on my apologies."

Ballard and John's eyes narrowed as they took in his words, not fully convinced he was as sympathetic as he professed to be. Muttering their thanks, they rose from their chairs.

CHAPTER
4

As they stepped from the communications van, Tim excused himself to visit his team, mentioning he would arrange for the weapons to be loaded into Malcolm's chopper while 'moving heaven and earth' to be back in time for the briefing. In the distance the detectives spotted Delwyn, along with John's team of detectives. Each were writing in their daybooks as they moved throughout the scene of devastation, all wearing mud-covered gumboots.

Looking at John, Ballard queried, "How do you think your guys will be handling this?"

John shrugged, fiercely loyal to his charges, but never one to show his emotions. "It's what they signed up for Mike, and with The Board and the mafia now at each other's throats, it won't be the last bloodbath they'll be witnessing." He motioned with his hand. "Not that they don't know it already, but this kicks home yet again what human beings are capable of when there's a toxic mix of greed, opportunity, power and large sums of money at stake."

Ballard wide eyed his partner. "Hmm, very true."

Their superintendent spotted them and headed over, the

fringe of her steel-grey, short back and sides fluttering in the gentle breeze. The three detectives trailed behind her.

Treading the same empathy path as the AC, the difference being Delwyn appeared genuinely concerned, she apologised for their shortened holiday. "Not the best way to end what must have been a magical time over there."

Bobby, a proud Macedonian, shook their hands. "Welcome back." He included Ken and Susan in his next comment. "We only wish it was on better terms."

Susan's eye-catching cerise ringlets danced as she shook her head. "It's ... it's just *inconceivable* that anyone could do this to so many, and for what?"

"Money, and lots of it." Ken was blunt and to the point, for once his cheeky but melancholy features matching the situation. He gave Susan a tight smile of support.

Getting down to business, Ballard informed them that Sergey was dead.

Bobby's eyes widened, with Delwyn beating him to the obvious question. "*How*?"

"The three of us were in the tunnel at the storage bunker just as Sergey was about to light the place up with God knows how much C4—we had no choice."

All four sets of eyes bulged at the revelation, and remained so as the senior detectives expounded on the events—from when they first landed in Malcolm's chopper, to finally surfacing in the loading bay via the emergency stairs.

Delwyn showed her concern for Peter's well-being. "You're sure Peter will be ok?"

John scoffed. "Pete's not fussed in the least. In fact, he led us to believe all he needed was a couple of band-aids."

Pretending to be reassured, Delwyn quipped, "So it'd be fair to say John, your quads won't need a workout for the next couple of days?" Her eyes narrowed as she assessed how her two senior detectives were coping after their life-and-death ordeal.

"Er, forget the couple of days caper. Try never again!" John was emphatic, with Ballard giving his partner a less than gentle shove in the ribs.

A half smile of relief played out on the superintendent's face, thankful both men appeared to be their chipper selves, at least on the surface, and this despite their dishevelled appearance.

Ballard hooked a thumb over his shoulder. "I won't go into the full particulars of what the AC just told us, but what you're seeing here isn't to be passed on to *anyone* else at the office, and certainly not to family or friends."

All dutifully agreed, aware this entire incident was about to be shrouded in relentless political oversight.

Despite Ballard and John's jocular persona, Delwyn still had misgivings regarding their mental state. "I'm glad to hear Pete's receiving proper medical care, but what about you two? You've backed up a dose of jetlag with a horrendous seven or eight hours being shot at and nearly blown up. You do know you have to recuperate?"

Without looking, Ballard backhanded his partner before he could utter that what they had experienced was all in a day's work. Choosing the wise option, Ballard agreed with her summation. "Pete will be in hospital for at least a couple of days. John and I are about to head back to Melbourne in Malcolm's chopper. The AC has asked us to take the security contingent's weapons with us so John here can ogle the latest in military hardware on the way back. Tim's arranging that now." He chose not to mention that the AC was expecting them to front up to a briefing at 1100 hours.

Although intrigued that the weapons would be transported in a civilian helicopter, Delwyn relaxed. "Good. Go home after that and put your feet up, we have this in hand. We'll stay onsite as long as the forensic teams are here. I'm assuming someone's going to repair the line and get these cannisters to the storage site?"

John reattempted to flatten his hair while offering, "As soon as the bodies are loaded onto the PolAir's, the heavy lift equipment will be allowed in to get this train on its way. The workers we rescued will do their thing at the site, securing the cannisters inside the bunker's staging area."

For the next five minutes discussions centred on the criminal charges to be laid should any of the offenders be arrested. Finishing on a lighter note, Ballard indicated he and John were looking forward to a freshen up and a warm meal. Wishing Delwyn and the team every luck with their investigations, they made their way over to Malcolm's chopper.

As the Eurocopter rose into the morning sky, the sun became visible, peeping over the horizon. Sitting beside Ballard, John salivated at the assortment of military hardware near his feet. The cache of assault rifles ranged from HK416s, Howa 89s, HKG36s to American M16s. There were even two short barrelled Uzis. Unable to hide that he was in seventh heaven, he grinned foolishly at Ballard.

With the course set to Horsham for a refuel before the final leg to Melbourne, Malcolm twisted in his seat to face his passengers. "It may not be my place to make this suggestion, but the trucks moving the cannisters in the middle of the night would have had to travel with their lights on. Being seen wouldn't be a major issue were they closer to civilisation, but out here, literally hundreds of kilometres from nowhere, they'd have stuck out like sore thumbs."

Ballard and John fixed him with mounting interest, aware his Vietnam exploits, along with a proven ability to amass a property fortune were the consequence of him being incredibly capable, as well as mentally astute. Curious, they encouraged him to continue with his line of thought.

"What I'm suggesting is that with the amount of forward planning they undertook, they had to know police choppers and a cavalcade of police vehicles would be travelling up here as soon as the assault took place. Large vehicles with containers onboard in the dead of the night in such a remote location would have drawn more than their fair share of attention. The vehicles moving the cannisters would have been limited to sealed roads, and there aren't too many of those out here. The last thing they'd want is to become bogged on a dirt track."

John was intrigued. "This is all making sense so far, Malcolm."

"Cutting a long story short, in all probability the vehicles would have remained hidden until first light. By that time most of the police movement along the highways would be over, everyone having reached the attack site. What I'm proposing is we fly a grid pattern on the way back, and with luck and a prayer we just *might* stumble on one or both of the trucks heading towards Melbourne, or wherever it is they're off to. I know there's a lot of ifs in that bundle, but I'm happy to give it a shot if you have no objections, and you're not in too much of a hurry."

Neither detective hesitated, remembering the AC's forty-eight-hour deadline, with Ballard adding, "What have we got to lose?"

Malcolm extracted a set of binoculars from the door pocket. Passing them behind him, John snatched them away from Ballard's outstretched hand. "Not so fast, Sonny Jim!"

Grinning, Ballard announced. "Over to you Malcolm. I'll keep an eye out on the starboard side, and John can do the same from the port window."

John rolled his eyes as he muttered under his breath, "Port, starboard ... what's wrong with good old-fashioned left and right?"

Bringing up a map of the area on the navigation screen, Malcolm began a series of wide sweeps, incorporating lesser roads just in case. Both detectives sat glued to their windows, willing a miracle to occur. Ten minutes passed with no result, the one empty tray truck of interest much too small to accommodate a container large enough to house the cannister and possibly the forklift.

For a further ten minutes they patrolled in ever-increasing arcs, with John growling under his breath as his hopes plummeted. Looking to Ballard, he lamented, "I guess it was worth a shot, but Christ there's so much damn *nothing* down there."

Malcolm checked his gauges. "We've enough fuel for another twenty-five minutes before we need to head to Horsham. Do you want me to—"

Ballard's mobile interrupted the billionaire. Waving an apology, Ballard removed his headset as he checked the screen, noting the call was from Tim. The moment he went to respond, Tim barked, "Where are you?" There was tension in the SOG commander's voice.

"Not that far away, perhaps fifty clicks as the crow flies, we've been checking out the surrounding area in case—"

Tim broke in. "Communications in town received a call fifteen minutes ago from a very distressed farmer outside Ouyen who says he heard a shitload of gunfire on his property earlier on. He went to check it out, and on the road running alongside his farm he saw a parked tray truck—"

Ballard couldn't wait. "Did it have a container onboard?"

"No damnit, but nearby was a black Hummer, which considering the remoteness of this place was unusual in itself. The farmer said he was a fair way off, on the opposite side of one of his paddocks, checking what was happening through the scope of his rifle. And just as well he wasn't any closer because the next thing he saw was a couple of guys grab a can each and chuck what he thinks was petrol inside the truck cabin, setting it alight."

"*Jesus*, where's the farmer now?"

"While he was watching all this unfold, he rang 000 to spill the beans. He said the Hummer waited around for a couple of minutes then took off. He's pretty shaken up because he drove across to the truck after ringing the fire brigade and discovered the driver inside, very much toast. Not a pretty sight for the cocky to contend with for the rest of his life."

After swearing in frustration, Tim continued, "PolAir is firing up now. I'm onboard with five of my team to head off and see if we can locate the Hummer. With you guys already in the air, I thought depending on where you are, you might be able to spot the smoke and perhaps the Hummer."

"What's the truck's exact location?" Ballard waved for John to take out his notebook.

Tim rattled off the details, with Ballard repeating them for John.

Showing them to Malcolm, Ballard requested, "We need

to head to this location." Returning to Tim, he asked him to standby while they changed course.

Malcolm got to work, and after punching in the coordinates in the navigation system, he banked the chopper hard to starboard, the jet engines howling enthusiastically, with John moaning that his stomach was coming out through his ears.

Checking his instruments, Malcolm declared, "Fifteen kilometres, dead ahead. Around four minutes."

Training his binoculars through the windscreen, John scanned the horizon, tense, straining forward. "Er ... nothing ... *no wait*! Well bugger me, just as the farmer said, a bloody great column of black smoke, and getting bigger."

Ballard raised his mobile. "*Tim*, we have the smoke in sight, so we're heading in the right direction. Did the farmer indicate which way the Hummer went?"

Tim's voice remained tense. "Apparently Stone Road runs alongside the guy's farm, that's about five kilometres north of the intersection with the Mallee Highway, the B12. He said the Hummer turned *towards* the intersection when it took off. It's unlikely when it got to the T-intersection it would have headed into Ouyen, so it's more than an even bet it'll be going west along the highway."

Tim's voice became more authoritative. "Now all I'm asking you guys to do is *spot* the vehicle—I repeat—*spot* the vehicle if you can, then report back to me. Tell Malcolm to hang behind and we'll catch up and take it from there. Remember, *spot* the vehicle ... do I make myself clear?"

Ballard threw a mock salute inside the cabin to no one in particular. "Perfectly. I'll be in touch."

Hanging up, he replaced his headset and was immediately quizzed by John. "*Well*?"

Ballard thought hard for several seconds, a lopsided grin forming. "The reception wasn't great, but I *think* Tim said we're to *stop* the vehicle if at all possible."

CHAPTER
5

Malcolm maintained an altitude of two thousand metres, with the airspeed set at 220 kilometres per hour. The sun appeared as a vibrant orange ball low in the sky, but visibility was excellent, the morning fog having burnt off. At the three-minute mark they crossed onto the Mallee Highway and began tracking it. As predicted, the intersection with Stone Road flashed past on their right, the smoke from the truck fire in the distance a vertical column marking the location where yet another horrifying murder had taken place, the body count mounting.

All aboard the aircraft were grim-faced, with Ballard questioning, "A black Hummer? Doesn't that strike you as odd John? Every time The Board's death squad have been involved, they've driven Mercs. Me thinks this could be the doings of the Ndrangheta."

"God help us." John reached down and began checking the magazines of the assault rifles. "Malcolm, if it comes to a shootout, can these side doors be partially opened then locked into position?"

The billionaire nodded. "At the bottom you'll find a

securing mechanism. Make sure when you *do* open the door that it's less than your body width … just in case I need to engage in some evasive action. As an additional precaution, reach under your seats, you'll find safety tethers. Put them on and fasten the snap hooks to the bulkhead rings. That way I won't have to catch you two mid-air if you fall out."

Both detectives checked Malcolm's expression, the slight upturn at the corner of his mouth the only indication he was joking. As instructed, they donned the harnesses, clipping the tethers onto the ceiling rings. John slid three assault rifles across the floor so they were within easy reach of Ballard, then positioned three for himself. Feeling confident they had sufficient firepower at hand, they resumed their vigil of the highway below.

In a bid to determine where the Hummer may be, Ballard began a series of calculations. "We're presupposing the guys are avoiding the direct route back to Melbourne, *if* that's where they're ultimately going." Straining forward he studied the console map. "By my reckoning they've been on this highway for thirty minutes. That puts them around fifty to sixty kilometres from Stone Road."

Malcolm placed a forefinger on the potential position on the screen as Ballard added, "If I'm correct, and they haven't stopped off anywhere, or deviated, they'll be somewhere between the towns of Boinka and Cowangie." He tapped into his mobile, snorting before announcing, "Get this … Boinka has a population of thirteen at last count." More tapping followed. "Whereas Cowangie comes in at a crowded thirty-six."

Responding to John's incredulous grunt, he continued. "Populations of that size know what everyone's doing, quite often before the individuals doing it know themselves. It's *very* unlikely the Hummer will be calling in for a cup of tea and a biscuit somewhere ... besides, in those towns there probably isn't anywhere public to have one. Again Malcolm, trusting that all my waffling is on the money, I'll bet my shirt the Hummer's still this side of Cowangie, or if not, just a blink past it. What's our ETA?"

Malcolm inspected his instruments. "We've passed Boinka, so the mighty metropolis of Cowangie you speak of will be coming up in less than five minutes."

Ballard turned to John. "All we have to do now is formulate a plan to stop the Hummer which won't result in us having our privates shot off. Any thoughts?"

"We shoot the bloody tyres out like we did with Sergey's buggy ... really simple."

Ballard permitted himself a fleeting smile. "If only it were. Malcolm, are you comfortable doing a relatively slow fly past of the Hummer to see the crooks' reaction, mindful they'll be armed to the eyeballs?"

The billionaire shrugged, completely at ease with the request. "This being a civilian helicopter with no markings, hopefully they won't be *too* trigger happy and draw unnecessary attention to themselves." His gaze took in the empty highway and even emptier surrounds. "On second thoughts, I take back any concern they may have regarding 'drawing attention'. Nevertheless, we do need to satisfy ourselves that they're the bad guys before we take any action. What do you have in mind?"

Ballard's features hardened. "As Johno said, first we do a fly past, then we double back at speed and shoot the crap out of their tyres. After that, let's put sufficient altitude under us so they can't hit us. Hopefully by then Tim and his cavalry will have arrived to clean up the mess."

Malcolm inclined his head, the beginning of a grin forming. "Sounds like a plan."

Both detectives rechecked the assault rifles while mentally preparing themselves for what lay ahead, knowing they were dealing with professional killers who wouldn't hesitate to shoot them out of the sky. Minutes passed and to their dismay Cowangie appeared before them with no sign of the Hummer. Powering back and initiating a much steeper decent than John would have liked, Malcolm swung to port to position their flightpath directly over the town, which amounted to a mere handful of houses. Three pairs of eyes scanned the streets for the few seconds it took to pass over the township, the Hummer nowhere to be seen.

Breathing hard after realising he had been holding his breath, Ballard remained upbeat. "They're ahead of us on the highway, I'm sure of it."

Malcolm flicked him a brief glance as he increased power, returning the Eurocopter to its previous speed. John backed his partner. "I agree, I mean where else would they be going in this miserable excuse for a countryside?" Seconds after John's words had left his lips, Malcolm thrust out his arm, pointing below. "There they are!"

Ballard and John almost collided heads in their haste to spot the speeding vehicle several kilometres in front of them. Throttling back to 150 kilometres per hour, Malcolm was brutal in his descent, punishing the collective lever much to John's audible protest. Choosing to pass the Hummer on the driver's side meant Ballard had to leave his seat to crowd alongside John, his tether strap just long enough to accommodate his repositioning. Both men's faces pressed against the window.

"I'll be concentrating on flying, so I'll need you to tell me if I have to hightail it out of here." Malcolm's voice was calm, his demeanour now in combat mode; his Vietnam experiences having conditioned him to show little or no emotion during high-pressure situations.

"Will do." By contrast, John's voice was tense, but his expression demonstrated his delight at being able to take decisive action.

Displaying impressive skill, Malcolm manoeuvred the Eurocopter down to a height that would have afforded them a clear view inside the Hummer had the vehicle's side windows not been so heavily tinted. The flightpath resulted in minimal clearance over the trees and power lines. Throttling back even further, he established a parallel course fifty metres to the right of the speeding vehicle.

Seconds passed with no reaction from the occupants of the Hummer, causing Ballard and John to doubt whether they had the correct vehicle. Suddenly the rear driver's side window lowered and the barrel of an assault rifle was thrust through the opening.

"*CLIMB MALCOLM!*" The urgency in Ballard's voice left the billionaire in no doubt as he applied full power, forcing the Eurocopter into a near-vertical ascent, testing the maximum climb rate of thirty metres a second to the limit. Levelling off, Malcolm increased the forward speed to surge ahead of the Hummer which was continuing along the highway, the occupants presumably believing they had frightened off their interloper.

In his element, Malcolm took command. "Open the starboard sliding door part way and engage the locking mechanism. When you're both ready and armed, I'll double back, putting this baby into a dive, passing the Hummer on the *driver's* side. That'll give me half the roadway to play with, allowing me to pass them as low as—"

"How low?" The whites of John's eyes were on display, his fear of heights and flying competing with the adrenaline rush he was now experiencing.

"Oh, around ten metres. I'll be travelling at 150 clicks, so the combined approach speed will be 250 to 260. That means we'll be directly opposite the vehicle for less than a tenth of a second. You'll need to commence your burst of fire prior to us reaching the Hummer, maintaining it as we pass. All this is subject to no other vehicles being on the road. If there are we'll abort and regroup. In case you're wondering, I'm in favour of Michael's head-on approach as we'll be passing the Hummer much faster than were we to travel in the same direction. The downside of going front on is it gives the bad guy's time to see us coming. Attacking from the rear, while the obvious choice, means they'd have a much slower target to have a crack at."

John swallowed hard. "I'm with you Malcolm, head on it is." He slid over to Ballard, both men hauling on the starboard door, opening it part way as instructed, with Ballard securing the locking mechanism. To be certain, John yanked on the doorframe to check it wouldn't budge—it remained firm. The wind howled past the opening, immediately chilling the interior of the chopper, the jet motors painfully loud.

Guiding the Eurocopter into a sweeping arc, Malcolm turned to his partners in crime, his eyes, while not maniacal, were wide and staring. "Are we ready?"

Ballard responded. "As we'll ever be."

The billionaire gave a dry laugh, growling, "I'll be taking

this baby down hard, so John, try not to throw up until *after* all this is over."

An unintelligible mumble was all John could manage while he and Ballard selected an assault rifle each, jacking a round into the chamber then flicking off the safety. Ballard stood braced at the door, his barrel pointing outward while John dropped to one knee beside him, his weapon also at the ready.

Malcolm wasn't exaggerating when he advised the dive would be brutal, both detectives stunned at the rate of descent, blood rushing to their head. The Hummer sped towards them, the occupants registering what was about to unfold only in the final seconds. Malcolm's voice came through the headsets. "Aim low and begin firing when I say so. *Wait ... wait ... wait ... NOW!*"

Ballard and John squeezed off a continuous burst. The Hummer flashed past, in full view for a split-second as Malcolm had predicted; at the time of passing the vehicle was veering off the highway, the driver losing his nerve at the last instant. Even above the noise of the motors and the howling wind, the return gunfire was audible, thankfully the rounds missing their mark.

The rapid climb was as breathtaking as the descent, with Malcolm levelling off at 2,500 metres. Staring below they saw the Hummer was now completely off the road. Their objective of crippling the vehicle a success, whether as a consequence of the rounds into the radiator, the punctured tyres, or both. The occupants were seen piling out and John began a running commentary, his fingers white knuckling the binoculars. "I see three ... *no four* outside the Hummer. *Jesus*, two of them are firing at us—"

Malcolm broke in. "At this height assault rifles are unlikely to hit us. Just pray they don't have *bolt* action rifles ... very unlikely, but keep an eye out for—"

John shouted, "What about shoulder-mounted missile launchers!"

Malcolm stiffened. "*What*?"

John adjusted the focus on his binoculars, with Ballard pressing behind him. "That's what I said! They pulled the bloody thing out from the back of the Hummer."

Unleashing a stream of expletives, Ballard snatched a second assault rifle before thrusting John aside, aiming the barrel out the open doorway. "They may not be able to shoot *up* this far, but we sure as hell can shoot *down* at the bastards. This should keep them honest." He emptied the magazine as he spoke, then throwing down the rifle, took another which John thrust at him, squeezing off a second full magazine.

The two bursts had the desired effect, the men on the ground scrambling to the far side of the Hummer. Malcolm maintained the Eurocopter in a rock steady position. "No point trying to outrun a missile, just give me notice the instant you see them fire the bloody thing ... you'll know when, believe me. Then hang onto anything you can because I'm going to be doing some pretty drastic manoeuvring. Luckily for us, evasion from a missile attack is far more effective in a chopper than in a plane."

John winced as he handed Ballard another rifle. "Yeah, thanks Malcolm, that's reassured me no end ... Mike, perhaps another burst or two might be in order so they don't poke their bloody heads out again."

Ballard obliged just as Malcolm let out a whoop of joy. "My, my, talk about in the nick of time."

"Come again?" John's nerves were fraying, and it was evident by his high-pitched tone.

Malcolm chuckled. "I do believe the cavalry has just arrived." He pointed through the windscreen. The detectives swung around and to their relief they spotted PolAir speeding towards them. Thrusting the rifle into John's hands, who resumed firing, Ballard snatched up his mobile and called Tim. The moment the SOG commander answered, Ballard shouted, "Directly below us, four bandits, automatic weapons … we believe they have at least one missile launcher."

Tim was emphatic. "Ask Malcolm to climb higher and hold his position."

Ballard passed on the order and Malcolm complied, the ascent rapid and gut churning.

Although PolAir was at least 500 metres out, John reported via his one-handed grip on the binoculars that the SOG team had begun laying down heavy fire in an effort to prevent a missile being launched.

Fearful the SOG personnel would have to traverse too great an expanse of bare terrain once they landed, Ballard declared, "Tim, you and your guys will be sitting ducks as you approach on foot. We'll drop down and continue firing until you're in position." Despite Tim's shouted protest, Ballard motioned for Malcolm to descend, which he did in earnest. The detectives armed themselves and began spraying further rounds near the Hummer, ensuring the four men remained hunkered down.

The instant PolAir landed, the SOG personnel leapt out. Spreading wide they began approaching the Hummer, adopting the rapid, short step shuffle unique to security forces, their weapons levelled, firing multiple bursts. One of the offenders leapt up, foolishly aiming his rifle—he was immediately shot, falling in a heap at the rear of the Hummer. Seconds later John reported that raised hands could be seen, the remaining three men emerging from behind their vehicle. SOG officers surged forward and within seconds the offenders were face down on the ground, their hands cuffed behind them.

Ballard placed his weapon on the seat beside him. "Malcolm, I do believe our little adventure is over. John and I can't tell you how much we appreciate you sticking your neck out for us the way you have—"

"*Guys, guys* ... I haven't seen this much action since my last mission in 'Nam." Malcolm appeared ecstatic as he searched for a clearing to land the Eurocopter. A solitary vehicle approached on the highway, slowing, then accelerating hard past the Hummer, the driver wisely deciding the chaotic scene he was witnessing wasn't something he should be part of.

Exiting the chopper, Ballard and John waited for Malcolm to emerge then drew him in for a bear hug and hearty back slaps. Tim finished issuing orders, and turning, jogged in their direction, still carrying his rifle. Even before he got to them, he barked, "Yet again you couldn't wait! *Jesus bloody Christ you two.*" While his words were forceful, the twinkle in his eyes gave away his true feelings.

Malcolm laughed. "I confess Tim, most of the blame must rest with me, the temptation of one last *real* adventure was just too great. For that I owe you all a huge thanks." He paused. "One small favour though, I'd rather none of this, er ... *escapade* be passed onto Teresa."

With Ballard and John beaming at one another, Tim shook his head. "This has turned out to be a bloody excellent catch. Without doubt these are the bastards who shot down the support chopper. Forensics, along with the help of Robert Mayne will confirm the missile launcher was the type used at the ambush site."

Ballard stared back along the highway, reflective. "The missing piece of the puzzle is the tray-truck this lot set on fire after killing the driver. It's almost certainly one of the two that transported the cannisters away from the train. Not having the cannister onboard now means one of two things ..." he considered deliberately delaying his thoughts to annoy John, but catching his partner's tired expression, he chose to press on. "The cannister has either been offloaded onto yet *another* truck, or it's still somewhere in the area. A bit like the Great Bookie Robbery in '76 where the crooks stole the money, then hid the cash upstairs in the same building in an office they'd leased months earlier. Weeks later, when everything had cooled down, they came back and calmly walked the loot out under everyone's noses." He inclined his head. "Could these buggers be doing the same thing, hiding the cannisters in plain sight?"

John scoffed, "Cannisters are a wee bit bigger than a sack full of cash Mike ... but methinks you may be onto something."

Tim agreed. "Yes, it's a distinct possibility, and one we'll need to explore. On the matter at hand, a couple of divisional vans are on the way to pick up these three—"

Ballard cut him short. "Tim, take their photos, as well as the dead guy when you can and forward them to me. I'll send them on to Vincenzo to see if he can ID them as Ndrangheta mafia."

"Will do, and in the meantime, I'll get the AC to organise for Surveillance to send a team up here pronto to start looking in the area for the cannisters ... who knows, we *may* get lucky." Frustration bubbled to the surface, chasing away his short lived positive mood. "Ok, two shipping containers ... assuming the cannisters are still inside, where would you hide them? Under a camouflage net perhaps—?"

Ballard hesitated. "How about alongside a haystack? They have a forklift, so those large rectangular bales could be lifted on top and pushed against the sides. The cannisters could stay hidden for weeks. Unless of course the farmer wants hay for his livestock ..." His voice trailed away, trepidation shadowing his features. "We all know what that scenario will lead to."

John responded, equally worried. "I do indeed. If these shitheads *did* hide the containers at a nearby farm, then you can bet your pension there's a husband and a wife team lying dead in their bed, and out here it'll be days or even weeks before someone drops by and discovers them. By that time the containers will have been reloaded and hauled off to their *intended* destination with no one the wiser."

Tim's angst ramped up a notch. "The sheer remoteness of this damn place, while it may be fantastic for storing nuclear waste, it's a bitch for conducting law and order." He kicked angrily at the red dirt with the tip of his boot. "Ok, onto immediate issues. The murdered security contingent and the dead guards at the storage bunker have been zipped into body bags. Most are already loaded onto PolAir2, and not in the most dignified manner I have to say. Those earmarked for our chopper are under a tarpaulin and will be put aboard when we get back to the site. As for extracting Sergey, he's going to have to wait until the tunnel's been cleared." There was a distinct lack of concern in his voice regarding the Russian's fate.

"Workmen and heavy lift equipment have already arrived, and the locomotive should be back on the tracks within the hour. Once everything is sorted out here, and the Hummer has been popped onto a tray, I'll go back and escort the remaining cannisters to the bunker. As soon as they're secured inside the holding bay, I'll head back to Melbourne with the AC and the remainder of the bodies."

Tim waved at the Eurocopter as he addressed Malcolm. "I take it you'll be flying these two reprobates back to Essendon so they can be out of your hair once they've transferred the weapons into the police car?" He didn't wait for an answer, adding, "Before I forget, the AC has asked to meet with you and your wife at some point when things calm down. He wants to thank you for everything you've done. It's incalculable how you've helped us, and to boot you've kept these two alive ... for that I'm eternally grateful." Tim concluded his borderline formal speech with a heartfelt handshake, Malcolm embarrassed by the accolades heaped upon him.

John returned the billionaire to earth with a thud. "Steady on Tim, after all, Malcolm mentioned at the outset he was only doing this because he needed to give the chopper a weekly burst to clean out the pipes."

Tim flashed John a brief smile before heading back to his men, calling over his shoulder, "I'll see you guys at the briefing."

CHAPTER
6

The flight to Horsham proved low key. Conversation was almost non-existent as Ballard and John sat dozing, the long-haul flight from Italy, followed by the harrowing events of the past ten hours taking their toll. Having rung their respective partners to reassure them they were safe, overwhelming tiredness befell them. Malcolm smiled as he observed their heads dropping forward as they struggled to stay awake, finally succumbing to the laws of nature, John's whistling snore echoing through Malcom's headset.

The refuelling at Horsham saw both partially stir, then once they were in the air, with the jet motors a monotonous background drone, sleep overwhelmed them. Touching down at Essendon Airport, the Eurocopter was towed inside the giant hangar before Ballard and John fully woke, disoriented, attempting to rub the weariness from their eyes.

John glanced about him, spluttering, "You probably thought I was asleep Malcolm. Not true, I think much better when my eyes are closed."

Malcolm laughed. "And I'm guessing heavy snoring helps your concentration also."

The senior sergeant grinned sheepishly. "Ok, you caught me, but don't let on to Teresa or she'll think I'm getting old."

Malcolm scoffed. "Hardly, considering what you both did to save her life."

Reversing the police car alongside the Eurocopter, the assault rifles were loaded into the boot, and after one last round of handshakes, Ballard and John drove out of the hangar. Minutes later they were on the freeway, heading towards the CBD and the Crime building.

After pulling into the second-floor car park, they arranged for the assault weapons to be catalogued and stored in the Property Office, much to the wide-eyed amazement of the public servants handling the collating. Opting for the showers, thirty minutes later John emerged sporting a slightly wrinkled navy-blue suit, a paler blue shirt and bright canary-yellow tie. All the while he eyed Ballard's white business shirt, grey wool Armani suit and highly polished, black Berluti leather brogues. Under his breath, but loud enough for his partner to hear, he grumbled, "Isn't it bloody amazing what money can buy?"

Ballard clapped him on the shoulder. "Johno, considering what we've been through, I suggest it's time for a decent breakfast ... my shout."

Even before he had finished speaking, John was ahead of him, stabbing the lift button. "I thought you'd never offer."

Entering the canteen, now almost empty of breakfast patrons, the wall clock showed 10.15 a.m. John moved to the bain-marie, intent on a gastronomic onslaught of bacon and eggs. Ballard grabbed his arm. "Pace yourself Johno, remember how long it's been since our last meal. Perhaps a bowl of cereal and fruit first up to minimise the shock to our system might be in order."

John's face screwed up. "Not the tucker I would have chosen, but yeah, I guess you're right."

In no time they were sitting together, spooning down a mix of cereals and fresh fruit. A dribble of milk headed south on John's chin, caught with a hastily positioned serviette. A thoughtful expression came over his face as he rhythmically chewed. "Where do you think the AC will kick off?"

"At the briefing?"

"Yeah."

Ballard pushed his bowl away. "I figure the immediate hurdle is for the tunnel to be cleared so the bomb squad can go in and locate the packs of C4 and disarm them. Let's pray no one gets hurt — I take the AC's point though about not wanting to hold up a hand for *that* thankless task."

John scowled at his spoon. "All those bloody catacombs or whatever you call the cavities ... Christ, they went on forever ... can the bomb squad *ever* guarantee all the explosives have been found?"

Ballard thought through his partner's query. "Only one way to find out."

"How so?"

"Disarm all they can find, then clear everyone out before shutting those bloody great steel doors and pressing the button on one of the trigger devices. If nothing blows up, they've got it covered."

"*Jesus!*" John spooned his last mouthful before mumbling, "Talk about all or nothing."

"Then there's the pressing matter of finding two cannisters containing the most radioactive material on the planet—and in the hands of bloody lunatics to boot."

"Mike, I'd hate to be the AC right now, imagine the political pressure he must be under to come up with the goods ... but forty-eight hours ... *it's just bloody ridiculous.*" John almost choked on his partially masticated strawberry as he drew breath. "I mean there's no *way* the cannisters can be found that soon—"

"Unless some country haystack reveals them." Ballard's tone indicated that prospect was a million to one shot.

John reflected aloud. "I know the surveillance teams have been sent up there, but in reality, where the hell do they start?" Wiping his chin again he added with a grin, "It really is a cannister in a haystack proposition ... get it, cannister ... haystack ...?" He gave up in disgust at Ballard's poker face.

Alerted by an incoming text, Ballard studied the screen. Four separate photos of the men from the Hummer appeared, one being of the dead man propped against the vehicle in a sitting position, his eyes closed, multiple blood stains on his shirt. Tim's accompanying text was blunt: 'As requested. Tim'.

John reached out for the mobile, his forefinger flicking the screen sideways through the photos. "Can you believe our rotten luck? First The Board and now this murderous bunch in the mix to make our lives even more shitty."

Ballard agreed as he checked the time. "I'll forward these onto Vincenzo to get his thoughts. By my calculation it's just after 3.30 a.m. over there. He won't be up, but I don't think he'll mind ... considering what we're sending him." Checking the CIA agent's mobile number, Ballard transmitted the photos with a message for Vincenzo to call him when he had an answer.

Both men reflected on their adventure in Venice where they

had tagged along with the agent and his special forces team to arrest Maxim Dabylov, a Board member living in a mansion on the island of Giudecca.

John chuckled, "I wonder if Vincenzo's recovered from the grenade going off in Maxim's swimming pool? All I know is I'd sure hate to be Dabylov with Vincenzo conducting the interrogation—he's a hardnosed bastard ... even I'm impressed by his ruthlessness."

Ballard scratched his head as he thought back to the near fatal incident. "Can you believe all that happened just two days ago?"

They stared at each other, amazed at how much had transpired since the event, with John confessing, "When Nat and Sonia found out *most* of what we got up to while they were at the Murano glass factory ... gee, I don't think I've *ever* seen them so angry—and worried for us." He looked as guilty as he felt.

Ballard sprang to his feet. "I think our bodies have survived the first onslaught of carbs, so how about chancing our luck with some greasy bacon and eggs?"

John needed no encouragement. "And about time."

Minutes later John replaced the previous trickle of milk on his chin with a run of egg yolk which Ballard alerted him to while chewing on a piece of bacon. "I'm assuming Pete's been patched up by now. Like Tim said, that could have been really nasty, a centimetre either way and he'd have bled out, or had bone fragments in his shoulder. No one, and especially Pete, deserves to die in that godforsaken tunnel, it would have been a tragic, unforgivable end to his life."

John stabbed his last piece of bacon with such force it was clear it was the deceased Russian he was impaling. "The deaths that bastard has caused in the months *we've* dealt with him is incredible —but at the end of the day he was just flesh and bone like the rest of us, and as I said, he deserved to be put down."

Ballard took in his partner. "You know Professional Standards are going to drag us through the ringer on this one, even more so over our shootout at the Hummer?"

John's fork remained poised close to his mouth, the morsel of egg that was perched on the speared piece of bacon falling off and landing on the edge of his plate. His mouth opened to voice his indignation at Ballard's claim.

"I know ... I know John, but rushing into the tunnel as we did, not to mention shooting up half the Ouyen countryside from Malcolm's chopper, you don't have to be Einstein to figure out they'll want to kick the crap out of us, perhaps even park us behind a desk from now on." Ballard was serious. "I'm only bringing this up because I don't want you losing it during the interview and getting us busted back to constable."

Having retrieved his fallen piece of egg and delivered it, along with the bacon and some toast to its original destination, John chewed methodically, his eyes narrowing. "I *could* say we saved a heap of lives doing what we did, but fair point Mike. Trust me, I'll be putty in their hands."

Ballard studied his colleague of more than twenty years, aware he was being unconvincingly amenable. "Hmm, that's what I'm afraid of." As he pushed his plate away his mobile rang. Mouthing 'Vincenzo' to John, he answered while his partner crowded closer. "Aha, an early riser I see."

Vincenzo laughed. "When my beloved Aussie compatriots text me with important information I drop everything, and with good reason. It looks as if you've hit the jackpot with those four. I passed the photos on to a colleague who's working nightshift. He ran them through our database ... and it didn't take very long. Yes, our worst fears have been realised, they're bad men through and through."

For the next five minutes Ballard explained what had happened at the ambush and storage sites, describing the events in terms that should their conversation be monitored, it wouldn't make sense, knowing Vincenzo would be more than capable of deciphering what was being relayed. The account complete, Ballard suggested, "Not the most auspicious start to our government's new business venture one would think?"

Vincenzo was unfazed. "Nothing a degree of skilful manipulation by your politicians at a media conference won't overcome. I'm sorry to hear about the collateral damage though. It's always heartbreaking for everyone concerned." He cleared his throat noisily, confirmation it hadn't been long since waking, with breakfast most likely a distant promise. "Now for some news I can pass on. The friend of the family you met in his mansion over here has finally admitted to being a key member of the club we both know so well. He's also confessed that the shipload of canned fruit you were going to store was indeed planned to be stolen by you know who, thus cutting off future supplies."

John smiled at the elaborate doublespeak Vincenzo was engaging in, the CIA agent adding, "In fact, so informative has his story been I'm planning to come down under very soon to discuss the issues with you personally and perhaps ..." he hesitated for dramatic effect, "you can 'throw a shrimp on the barbie' for me. Is that how you Aussies describe it?"

Ballard laughed. "Close enough Vincenzo, and you can be sure John and I will oblige. That's great news, and something your colleague over here will be delighted to hear." Ballard imagined Bernard's reaction on learning one of his closest work partners was about to visit.

Vincenzo's cheeky tone changed. "The only downside is it's moving into summer over here, and I'm told your winters aren't anything to boast about."

John drew even closer. "We'll buy you an extra thick jumper, you'll be fine."

A jovial, "I'll be in touch," ended the conversation.

CHAPTER
7

Over the years the Critical Incident conference room in the St Kilda Road complex was the setting for countless high-profile briefings. Now, in the modern Spencer Street Crime building, the equivalent meeting room was located in the centre of the fifth floor, the absence of any windows a deliberate feature so participants wouldn't be distracted. As Ballard and John entered, they assessed the attendees already seated, realising today's briefing would be yet another highly charged event.

The AC's seat at the head of the table was empty, but sitting to its right was Gerhard Müller, the Counter Terrorist Unit's assistant commissioner, a hard man with an even harder job. To the left of the AC's chair, Bernard Winters was contemplating life, his bearlike Texan frame relaxed as he observed those around him, his years in the CIA equipping him emotionally for any situation that may be thrown his way.

Gerhard and Bernard nodded briefly at the two detectives as they settled between Robert Mayne, the ballistics expert, and Lieutenant Colonel Jordan Hensley attached to the army's Special Operations Command. John smirked at Robert's cobalt blue bow tie while Ballard took in Jordan's immaculate military uniform, both men brilliant in their fields but worlds apart in personality.

John leaned across and whispered in Robert's ear, "Married yet?"

"Wash your mouth out." The reply was instant, accompanied by a look of genuine horror.

Ballard smothered a laugh as he questioned Jordan. "So, you thought the Parliament House caper would be your last involvement with us?"

The army officer scoffed, "Hardly, the boffins at DSTG are still heads down cracking the encrypted files on the iPad."

Ballard nodded, aware the military Defence Science and Technology Group was vital in their efforts to decode the files on the iPad that Igor Greshnev, a senior Board member, had accidentally dropped after diving off the side of a container ship at Swanson Dock. Thankfully he had sealed the computer in a waterproof satchel. Eventually retrieved by the water police from the murky, sludge-filled depths, the information gleaned from each decrypted file had been critical in determining what illegal activities The Board was planning; this, as well as pre-warning the department that the group was displaying an unhealthy interest in the recent consignment of nuclear waste.

The conference room door burst open and AC Kevin Thompson entered, heading straight to his seat. Slumping down with dishevelled hair, he growled, "Well that was an experience and a half. Try sitting in PolAir while it lands on the roof helipad in a force-ten gale. At one point I was wishing I hadn't taken the flight, but it saved a shit load of time getting here."

Ballard pictured the adjoining thirty-nine-storey headquarters building with its purpose-built rooftop helipad, appreciating the skill required by the pilot, who would have been especially anxious, aware that the senior officer onboard was not someone to mess with. John stared at Ballard, clearly curious what was being done to ferry the bodies from the chopper to the mortuary. He knew not to ask, instead, waited for the AC to set the tone and direction of the briefing which he did in no uncertain terms.

"Gentlemen, we have a situation on our hands that if it isn't dealt with appropriately will grab us by the vitals and stuff all our careers." He sat back in his chair, allowing the significance of his declaration to sink in. "*Nothing* discussed here today is to leave this room without my authority. If I find that any one of you has divulged *anything*, even by accident, you'll lose your job … period." Another weighty pause. "We have a total of eighteen good men dead, executed by the Ndrangheta mafia, and by The Board's chief assassin, Sergey Alistratov, who by the way is now deceased, along with, we believe, another member of The Board."

The AC chose not to include Ballard and John in his visual sweep of the table. "At the risk of going over old territory, a train hauling cannisters of nuclear waste was deliberately derailed, then in the ensuing mayhem, the security contingent, along with the train driver and the engineer were massacred. A support chopper containing additional security personnel was blown out of the sky by a missile, with all onboard perishing. We have two cannisters of highly dangerous nuclear waste stolen, their whereabouts unknown. A section of tunnel in the storage site which is located in the godforsaken Victorian outback near Ouyen has been blown up, and there's more unexploded C4 hidden further inside the facility. Overlaying this chaos is an unrealistic request by the government, passed down to me by the chief commissioner, demanding that the two cannisters be located ..." his left arm did a theatrical arc through the air as he inspected his watch, "*before* 7 p.m. the day after tomorrow."

His startling blue eyes bored into every attendee. "Does anybody here have any misgivings that what I've just described to you will be nothing less than a bloody nightmare to resolve?"

The frustration in his barb wasn't lost on his audience as he continued. "Ok, first things first. While I was at the attack site, the rail line was repaired and the locomotive lifted back onto the tracks. Twenty minutes after I left Tim, who by the way can't make it to the briefing ... he rang me to confirm the remaining cannisters had been delivered to the storage site. They're temporarily housed in the loading bay which has been thoroughly searched for explosives by the bomb squad." He added, "Not that any explosion would impact the cannisters."

He paused, taking a mouthful of tea from the steaming mug he had brought in with him. "I guess we have to be grateful for small mercies, at least the remaining cannisters have been secured." A second sip followed. "Tim and his team will stay on site until the tunnel has been cleared of rubble, the roof temporarily repaired, and the bomb squad has moved in and deactivated all the C4 charges."

John perched on the edge of his chair as he made an announcement. "Sir, to be certain they've located all the explosives, it's been suggested the bomb squad move out after they've searched the area and the trigger devices be activated to make sure no additional packs were missed." He winked at Ballard while developing a mischievous grin. "I have to confess I didn't come up with that suggestion sir, Mike did."

The AC's cobalt blues locked onto the two detectives while he did his best to maintain a severe exterior. "Thank you for those words of wisdom, John. Rest assured I'll pass them onto the bomb squad ... just in case their combined years of experience and comprehensive training had them overlooking the bloody obvious."

John's grin stretched wider, satisfied he and Ballard had played their part in protecting their colleagues, pretending not to have registered the AC's overt sarcasm.

Turning to Jordan, it was clear that the AC viewed the army officer with the highest regard. He underscored his respect for the officer with his next comment. "Appropriate approval will need to be sought Jordan, but I'm prepared to go out on a limb here and ask you to pre-empt that sanction by setting in place a military ring of steel around the storage site. Our SOG contingent can't be deployed up there forever. Assuming the necessary consent will be forthcoming, what would you recommend as adequate protection against a beefed-up attack from The Board or Ndrangheta, or both groups simultaneously for that matter?"

As though having anticipated the question, the lieutenant colonel began rattling off facts and figures in a bewildering array, proving yet again he was up to formulating complex operational strategies on the run. "I'm mindful that the total fenced-off area of the site is fifty hectares. That's too large a patch to patrol and secure without utilising an inordinate number of military personnel. Far more effective will be the securing of the ..." he searched for an appropriate description, "the immediate storage bunker itself." Warming to his subject matter, he rolled his chair back from the table, allowing his next comments time to mature. "As a minimum there would need to be a platoon on the ground twenty-four-seven, made up of forty-five soldiers. They would consist of three rifle squads and one weapons group. The rifle squads would be armed with M4A1 carbines with semi- and fully automatic capability. The carbines would be fitted with night vision, laser pointers and grenade launchers. The range of these weapons is 500 metres, with a rate of fire between 700 and 950 rounds per minute."

The silence in the room meant a pin dropping would have seemed a thunderclap.

Maintaining a straight face at the concentrated looks, Jordan continued, "The fourth squad, in addition to being armed with carbines, would have RBS-70 new-generation air-defence tripod-mounted missiles to tackle what most likely would be an initial helicopter attack. The range of this weapon is 250 metres all the way up to eight kilometres. It has night vision capability, and at 580 metres a second flight speed, nothing's going to outrun it." Jordan paused, his face grimacing. "The only downside is the unit's cost—not a heap of change out of two million a pop, so—"

The AC scoffed. "Bearing in mind the revenue the site will generate annually, that degree of expenditure isn't out of the question. I did some maths on the way over here as a result of Robert's earlier briefing." The ballistic expert shot to attention despite not being asked to contribute. "Once the storage site is at capacity, a cool five hundred *billion* will be amassed over a seventy-year period." The AC assessed the group. "I accept seventy years is a very long time, but five hundred billion is a bloody lot of money. Ok, carry on Jordan."

The military officer reflected for several seconds. "I also recommend there be two Boxer CRVs on standby within the perimeter."

John mouthed CRV to Ballard, his eyebrows forming a question mark. Jordan spotted the query. "That's a Combat Reconnaissance Vehicle. Its armament consists of a 7.62-millimetre light machinegun, a 30-millimetre cannon in the turret, and sufficient armour protection to make it basically indestructible. The Boxer's fitted with a 40-millimetre automatic grenade launcher and the vehicle is an all-terrain unit capable of a top speed of 110 kms per hour, notwithstanding its thirty-five-tonne curb weight." He took a breath. "Early detection of a potential attack is vital, and the AN/TPQ-50 counterfire radar is the perfect means of achieving this. It's lightweight at 227 kilograms, can be tripod mounted, and has a fifteen-kilometre detection range. It's an essential piece of equipment to ensure the troops have adequate warning so they can prepare for whatever assault is coming over the horizon.

"Finally, if we're to take the security of this site seriously, keeping at the forefront its potential revenue-generating capability, an EC665 Tiger multirole attack helicopter"—he flashed a boyish grin—"or perhaps two for that matter, need to be on standby. The armament on these units is not something even The Board or Ndrangheta would dare to take on. We have twenty-two of these gunships in Australia, so surely the army can spare two until the storage site is fully utilised and sealed off."

Jordan noted the doubting glances around the table, questioning why such significant capital expenditure should be outlaid. "Perhaps it would help if I put what I've just described in context, and how it's the *minimum* security benchmark that should be established." He cleared his throat. "The AC has mentioned how much revenue will be generated over a seventy-year period as a consequence of the site. I too was at the briefing given by Robert where he detailed that in the first year alone, eight billion would be accrued for the state. To put that into a more relatable context, Fort Knox holds half of America's gold reserves. At the latest count, the stockpile amounts to seven trillion—now while that's a bloody sight more than our gross earnings of five hundred billion, nobody can claim we're not up there with the big boys."

Jordan paused, his eyes assessing his audience over the rim of his mug. "The Fort Knox complex is surrounded by a steel, electrified security fence." He pursed his lips. "Run-of-the-mill situation so far. What *is* incredible though are the 40,000 soldiers on standby who live and work nearby—with over a thousand of them guarding the fort at any one time. The grounds have laser security coverage connected to a battery of machine guns. In addition, anti-personnel mines as a further disincentive are positioned throughout should anyone plan on storming the complex. The concrete and granite walls of the structure itself are steel reinforced, and the door on the vault weighs upwards of twenty tonnes. No one individual has the complete set of codes to open it, and the building has its own power and water supply." Jordan grimaced, clearly in anticipation of his next comment. "Compare that sort of protection against the criminally inadequate handful of guards armed with sidearms that were in place at the storage site here last night and this morning. Forget that the bunkers were empty ... it's *potential* worth is the true value of the complex, full *or* empty. In short, the government was caught with its pants down and are now playing catchup."

Ballard nudged John, impressed that Jordan had the moral fortitude to call out the political shortcomings of the nuclear waste venture, along with the tragic consequences that resulted.

Far from finished, Jordan added, "All the equipment and personnel I'm listing are currently available here in Australia. Putting it bluntly, the Yanks have demanded we spend two percent of our GDP on defence to qualify for their protection in the advent one of the big countries take us on. We already have the military personnel and equipment while we wait for the next war, and that array of shiny toys are sitting idle all over the country. I say we should utilise those resources a hell of a lot more during natural disasters and high security situations.

"Protection of this nuclear waste site *has* to be a sufficient reason to deploy these assets until such time it's filled. One more thing, the escorting of future nuclear waste cannisters should continue to be by train, but with significantly beefed-up protection. The military personnel on the train must be in a carriage which can withstand missile attacks. Two crewed Boxers should be positioned so that one is at the front and one at the rear of the cannisters, each on their own flatbed. The indestructibility and firepower of these units would discourage the two organisations we are currently under siege from, or anyone else for that matter. So Kevin, there's my answer regarding what security should be applied to movement and storage of these cannisters." Leaning back in his chair he checked out the senior officer.

Blinking rapidly, and more than impressed with the detail of the security outlined, the AC asked of the group, "Any questions?"

Ballard was troubled as to how long such a complex task would take. "How soon could you arrange for the soldiers and equipment to be on the ground at the site?"

Jordan was upbeat. "Once I'm given the nod from the chief of army, I could have boots and most of the equipment on the ground within seventy-two hours. A further seventy-two would make everything permanent."

"Jesus, so soon?"

"Like I said, the army prides itself on rapid deployment, and after all, this is merely another exercise in logistics, and one that will be damn good practice for each of the areas involved. Obviously it'll take longer to set up onsite accommodation, canteens, Q stores and other ancillary support for the troops within the fifty hectares. That also includes the ongoing maintenance of the equipment, and specifically the specialised support for the Boxers and the Tigers." He shrugged. "For the airships it's a fifty-fifty ratio of maintenance hours against flying time. So yes, it's a complex operation, but it'll serve as a valuable training exercise while providing vital experience for all concerned. I can promise you, once everything is in place, that fifty-hectare stretch of land will be the most protected real estate in Australia."

The AC expressed his thanks, then ordered, "Start the planning Jordan, I'll get you the approval you need."

Ballard and John eyed one another, comprehending the lengths the department was prepared to go to in their pursuit of adequate security for the site, something that would have to be put to the Premier, perhaps even the federal Attorney-General. The AC cleared his throat noisily, as much to gain attention as to open his airways. "Now you may be wondering why the security outlined by Jordan should focus on anything other than the train trip to get the cannisters to the storage facility—that once the cannisters are inside the building the complex itself is secure enough—impregnable in fact, and as such it shouldn't need guarding." His features became bleak. "We now know all too well how The Board and Ndrangheta operate. They'd think nothing of kidnapping a number of women and children, marching them up to the front door of the bunker after killing the guards, then proceed to execute the hostages one by one until whoever was inside relented and opened the door. It's that simple, and effectively it's what they did this morning for Christ's sake. Were that to happen again, we can kiss goodbye five hundred billion in revenue for the state, not to mention the tragic loss of life."

He waved an apologetic hand towards Jordan. "This is why it's vital the military have carriage of the complete security package to prevent this form of threat ever happening. I need to stress that so-called civilian guards for this role won't cut it. I'm not implying in any way that the military are a heartless bunch of automatons. Far from it, they're pragmatic, they have to be. God, I shudder when I contemplate the decisions they make during wars—*that* type of hardnosed, uncompromising decision-making needs to be in place because I feel in my bones The Board and Ndrangheta haven't finished with the site by a long shot."

The mood in the room, already tense, grew darker, with the AC allowing it to mature to underscore the point he was making. "I can assure you that were the children of the president of the United States kidnapped and hauled off to Fort Knox, the safe door wouldn't be opened no matter what was done to them. To do otherwise would expose every bank and vital facility in the world to the same threat. No gentlemen, the nuclear waste complex here in Victoria *must* be guarded by the military, with my task being to convince the Premier of the appropriate measures that have to be implemented immediately. We cannot tolerate any delays resulting from bureaucratic bungling."

After a studied gaze around the table, and a defiant thrust of his chin, it was clear the AC wasn't in any doubt what his next actions would be after the briefing. "While it may appear churlish mentioning I should have been allowed to implement this form of security *prior* to the cannisters arriving here, had I been given the nod there wouldn't be eighteen innocent lives lost and two high-risk cannisters floating around somewhere in the state. Cannisters that should have been buried beneath a metre of concrete in an impregnable storage site by now. The Premier needs to face up to this reality." The AC bristled, guaranteeing no one challenge his course of action. "Now, changing pace, the emergence of this Ndrangheta group is an unwanted complication to our investigations. It adds a heightened level of brutality to what is already unspeakable cruelty, something we've witnessed many times from The Board."

Turning to Assistant Commissioner Müller, the AC's jaw muscles rippled. "Gerhard, would you provide us with background history of this mob, as well as an update as to how far they've infiltrated into our way of life here in Australia?" He turned to Ballard and John. "Some of this will be old news for you two as I believe your CIA contact gave you a rundown on the group when you were galivanting around in Venice with your wives."

Ballard wasn't troubled by the light-hearted dig. "A refresher course won't do us any harm sir."

Gerhard wiped his mouth with a serviette, his German ancestry coming to the fore to the extent it was feared he was about to spring to attention and click his heels. Instead, he remained seated. "I'll begin with the Australian origins of the Ndrangheta. The 1965 ASIO report spelt out how the society kicked off with the arrival of the ship *Re D'Italia* in

1922. Three members of the group established separate cells in Melbourne, Perth and Sydney. Around 1930 the dominant cell was located here in Melbourne." Gerhard referred to a sheet of paper. "ASIO agent Colin Brown wrote a report titled 'The Italian Criminal Society in Australia', which found that secrecy and allegiance to the organisation was increasingly ensured by the intermarriage of families within it. It'll come as no surprise that Brown's document was never made public."

Everyone sat upright, intrigued.

"Fairly early in the piece the group began controlling the Victoria Market. In fact, one of the store holders was the Melbourne Godfather."

Several whistles broke out.

"From that point on the group's influence increased and diversified. While it'll never be admitted by the Government, or even by our own Command for that matter, this lot have had their claws into the following for umpteen years." He ticked the points off on his fingers. "Labour racketeering, building and road construction, wholesale distribution of alcohol and soft drinks, the importation of olive oil, tomato paste and cheese, the baking and distribution of Italian goods, the vending machine business, the monopolistic ownership of night clubs and taverns, music recording and record distribution companies, even model and theatrical booking agencies ... the list is endless."

John declared to Ballard in a staged whisper for all to hear, "When we were at the Colosseum, didn't I mention the murderous bastards back then only preceded this current bunch by a mere sixty generations or so? Nowhere near long enough for the genetic defect to be bred out of their fairly dubious DNA."

Gerhard permitted himself a tight smile, but it was fleeting. "An accurate summation John. Undoubtedly there are traits in this current mob that match the proclivity of the ancient Romans in getting their way ... ruthless murders and intimidation the primary means to achieving their goal."

The resultant series of nods around the table were a ripple of movement, much like a mini-Mexican wave. Gerhard pressed on. "The deceit, guile, manipulation, threats and intimidation—in summary, the essence of today's mafia criminals, those attributes match in every way the tactics of its founders. What *has* changed dramatically are the financial opportunities and technological advances available to them. Another aspect is the internationalisation of the group. No question they're now the wealthiest, most influential group in the drug trade, with their sticky fingers in most countries, specifically in North America, Canada, Germany, and of course here in Australia. Let's not forget the world's largest ecstasy bust of 4.4 tonnes of MDMA occurred just kilometres from where we are now, at Port Melbourne. That was back in 2008."

The head nodding became monotonous.

Gerhard shot a glance towards the AC, the exchange indicating he was almost done. "To think the Ndrangheta are now in competition with The Board, or even worse, that they may form an alliance with them is something we need to stop at any cost." He drank from his cup of tea, wincing at what now had become a cold brew. "Also, modern technology has made everything the criminals do that much harder to investigate." He lifted a hand towards John. "I'm fully aware of your aversion to technical jargon, so I won't go down that route other than to say, while the internet is a tool for good, it's also a vehicle for evil. The dark web hides a multitude of criminal activities, and it's almost untraceable. Crypto currencies enable criminals to transfer money outside of conventional banking practices, bitcoin being a favourite, and while it's not impossible to trace the origins, it adds a significant layer of complexity that these two groups are taking advantage of. All this makes traditional policing—namely knocking down doors and storming through premises to arrest people—it makes good old fashioned policing a thing of the past."

His almost reflex sigh was clear resignation that those times were long gone. Shutting his folder, he handed back to the AC, his job done. "Thank you Gerhard. Now for a change of pace, we *need* to locate these missing cannisters. I know Surveillance are on the hunt and scouring the local area, but at best this is a hit-and-miss strategy considering the remoteness of the place." He waved a hand towards Robert who snapped his daybook shut and sprang to his feet, powering up the overhead projector as he did so.

"Thank you, sir. I'm certain the Surveillance boys on the ground are doing their best, and of course if they *do* locate one of the cannisters, or better still, both of them, they'll direct Tim's teams to the location as a priority. But what they can't do is provide imagery of the actual massacre and subsequent loading and transportation of the two containers, along with the tracking of the vehicles." A smirk crossed his face as he noted the instant curiosity generated amongst his audience. "Some time back the Federal Government, and specifically the Defence Department went into partnership with a Western Australia hi-tech company, LatConnect 60. The aim was to launch a number of small-scale satellites—each weighing less than a hundred kilograms."

The image of one of the satellites, a rather unspectacular shaped cube, appeared on the screen, undoubtedly packed with mind-numbing technical wizardry.

"The purpose of this constellation of eyes in the sky is to provide, and I quote, 'a sovereign space-based imagery capability for Australia'. In other words, it affords us the opportunity to monitor and photograph any part of Australia without having to pick up the phone and call in favours from the Yanks. I accept that's an oversimplification, but effectively that's what the situation has been for decades. The number of satellites will increase over time, with the degree of coverage expanded so more and more detail is available for Defence, law enforcement and authorised commercial companies such as mining, oil, gas, and agriculture."

He nipped back to the table and briefly inspected his notes. "These satellites are stationary above Australia at an altitude between five and six hundred kilometres. They're fitted with two cameras, a digital single-lens reflex DSLR with a catadioptric optical system, and a compact camera for wide-angle image capture. The cameras will produce high resolution panchromatic and multispectral optical images."

John leaned forward and banged his forehead twice on the tabletop before sitting back upright.

Robert ignored his colleague's open display of intolerance for high-tech verbiage—the display having zero impact on his continued delivery. "The DSLR camera has a viewing frame of three by five kilometres, and can clearly identify objects less than a metre across, day and night. This makes the identification of small objects, including vehicles and the like, invaluable, especially for our line of work. The second camera has a wide-angle frame of five hundred and sixty by seven hundred and forty kilometres. This means a mere handful of satellites can cover the entire state of Victoria."

The AC wasted no time asking the question on everyone's lips. "So, what you're telling us Robert ... and shout me down if I'm wrong ... from what you're saying, we should be able to obtain footage of the attack on the train and the loading and transportation of the two cannisters."

Robert's beaming face said it all. "Indeed it does, but the catch is the request must be made through Signals Directorate, and that may take twenty-four hours. You, as the AC, will have to make the request via Covert Support."

The senior officer's frown spelt out his displeasure. "Hundreds, perhaps a thousand kilometres could be travelled in twenty-four hours. Can the satellite coverage *track* the movement of where the trucks took the cannisters?"

Robert's eyebrows shot north. "Indeed it can, but it'll take additional time, and there's always the possibility the vehicles become lost in traffic, or if they enter a warehouse and the containers are swapped onto different trucks—"

The AC's fist crashed onto the table with such force that cups, saucers and glasses of water jumped and shimmied, along with a number of attendees rising off their seats in shock. "*Then damn it man*, hightail it up to Covert Support as my representative and start the ball rolling. They can obtain final authorisation from me once you've given them all the details. If they ask what's this about, tell them we have high profile offenders in the area who need to be tracked. Not a lie, but it's essential we keep the real purpose under wraps."

Robert took one last look at the AC, realising to his disappointment that his briefing had been terminated. Scooping up his belongings he mumbled his goodbyes to no one in particular as he headed for the door. In his rush to leave, the projector remained on with the photo of the mini satellite still displayed on the screen.

About to resume control of the briefing, the AC's mobile interrupted him. Reaching forward he scooped it off the table, his brow knitted in mild annoyance until he viewed the contents of the screen. His features transformed to acquiescence as he answered. "Good morning, sir."

For the next minute and a half, he scribbled hard and fast in his daybook as the person on the other end spoke. Everyone assumed it had to be the Chief Commissioner for the AC to remain so fixated on the conversation. "Thank you, sir. Yes, I'll be there in thirty minutes."

He replaced the mobile on the table, his action slow and deliberate, emphasised by the manner in which he perfectly aligned the phone to his position, his expression contemplative. Staring into middle distance, he claimed, "As you'll have speculated, that was the Chief. He's at Parliament House with the Premier and the police minister. You can also assume as to what they want to discuss. The good news is that this gives me the perfect opportunity to hammer home the security requirements we need established at the storage site. Make your planning a priority, Jordan. Get back to me as soon as you have a firmer estimate of the implementation date." The glint in his eyes hardened. "As I stressed at the outset, none of what we've just discussed is to leave this room. On that note, thank you all for your input." He pocketed his mobile. "I'll advise you when we'll need to reconvene."

Everyone made to exit the room, but not before the AC halted Ballard and John. "Not so fast you two. While I'm aware you haven't had much sleep in the past couple of days, I'm also cognisant you're the only members who have firsthand knowledge of what transpired up at Ouyen. I want you to accompany me to a meeting you won't forget for a long time to come ... if ever." While his tone was suggestive, his eyes were otherwise. It was obvious to Ballard and John their attendance was mandatory.

CHAPTER
8

The extended metallic shriek of metal on metal, a sound ingrained in the DNA of all Melburnians, was loud as the No. 86 tram performed the tight right turn from Latrobe Street into Spencer. The sleek lines of the E-Class resembled a green-and-yellow mechanical caterpillar as it negotiated its thirty-two-metre bulk around the acute bend. The electric motors propelled the sixty-tonne monster effortlessly along Spencer Street, then powered left into Bourke Street, the familiar columns and expansive front steps of Parliament House coming into view eight city blocks away.

After deciding the quickest means of getting to Parliament House was to catch public transport, all three detectives were thankful they had elected to avoid the midday bumper-to-bumper congestion which was at a standstill in all directions. Minutes prior, the AC had leapt aboard the tram with startling agility, pointing towards the rear which was devoid of passengers, Ballard and John following closely behind.

Having plonked down on a seat, with the detectives sitting opposite, the AC ensured he couldn't be heard before growling, "Again I'm sorry for dragging you two along, but pretty outlandish claims are going to be tossed about today. I'll be looking to you to provide a factual account of what *really* went down at the site so certain deskbound bureaucrats can fully comprehend some home truths associated with our current crop of criminals."

John raised an eyebrow at Ballard, unsure whether the Premier's well-publicised penchant for shooting from the hip could ever be curbed, the politician famous for challenging anyone who disagreed with him.

The AC noted John's scepticism, shrugging in resignation. "We'll just have to do our best and pray the Chief doesn't get carried away with all this—agreeing to an impossible course of action or timetable just to impress the Premier. That can only lead to one thing ... *certain disaster.* Adding to that will be my near-impossible task of convincing the Premier that Jordan's account of what security is necessary at the site is a genuine minimum claim, and not an ambit one. You guys will have to present the attack in all its blood and guts to impress on him we're dealing with organisations who will stop at nothing to get their way."

The detectives realised no response was necessary, their task ahead crucial in the overall scheme of things.

The AC hitched his trouser legs, leaning closer, elbows on knees. "Changing subjects, as I mentioned in the communication van, I'll put in a word to Professional Standards not to get too carried away at your interview, despite them wanting their pound of flesh. Standards will kick up a stink, but too bad—that's the deal, take it or leave it." The AC's focus was on John who wilted under the intense, blue-eyed scrutiny, fully aware the senior officer was hell-bent on minimising the possibility of him losing his cool—Tim and Ballard delegated to custodial duties.

A contrite, "Thank you, sir," passed John's lips as he dragged his eyes back level with the AC's.

Taking a deep breath, the senior officer's brow knitted even further. "When the public get wind of this fiasco, the Government's going to do everything in its power to deflect blame … that'll put the department in the firing line, and by default that means *all* of us will be under the microscope."

John began to protest but the AC cut him short. "None of this is fair John, it's just the way things are. You've both been around the traps long enough to know it's par for the course. There's no doubt our heads will be on the block if we put a foot wrong." He licked his lips. "The game changer will be finding the missing cannisters. Robert's briefing on the satellite coverage is at least *something* we can toss the Premier's way as a positive avenue of inquiry."

Ballard pressed the button to alert the tram driver they wished to get off, this despite being aware that Spring Street was a scheduled stop. "I guess we'll find out soon enough."

Alighting, they crossed at the traffic lights and climbed the Parliament House steps. As on previous visits they acknowledged the Protective Security officers on duty as they progressed upwards, entering through the front door.

After surviving the security screening, with John fumbling as he put his belt back on, having set off the alarm, the AC informed reception that the Premier and the police minister were expecting them. Minutes later they were ushered into the Premier's office on the first floor, the senior politician sitting at the head of a small, polished conference table in the room's annex. To his right the police minister sat glum-faced, on his left the Chief Commissioner was finalising a phone call while appearing equally dejected. All three men wore sombre business suits matching their expressions and had open folders on the table within easy reach. Introductions ensued and were concluded with a minimum of fuss.

The AC took his seat opposite, flanked either side by Ballard and John. Composed, the AC studied the Premier through narrowed eyes, correctly assessing that the career politician wished to open proceedings.

"Thank you all for coming." The Premier ran aggressive fingers through his steel-grey hair, then dived in, circumventing any polite preamble. "It's a nasty pickle we find ourselves in, and one we need to plan a way out of, and fast." Checking himself for what could have been construed as insensitivity, he hurriedly added in his deep baritone, "Of course the loss of so many innocent lives is tragic, and an unforgivable act of barbarity on the part of the criminals." Having voiced his obligatory concern for human life, it was clear there were more pressing matters to be considered, as confirmed by his next statement. "Politically and economically, this state is on a knife edge, balanced to go either way."

He directed a gun-barrel stare at the AC who returned it with equal steadfastness. "So Kevin, we've called you here to brief us on the latest developments, and to detail what options you consider appropriate to resolve this issue."

Picking up their pens, the Premier, Police Minister and Chief Commissioner adopted expectant expressions, each anticipating the AC was about to reveal a miracle. Their hopes were sorely dashed.

"Premier, we have a situation where an elite group of Russian criminals are at war with one of the most dangerous Italian mafia organisations on Earth. Both groups are hellbent on destroying Victoria's ... no, make that *Australia's* ... chance of storing the world's repository of nuclear waste. Further complicating matters, one of these groups, which we believe is the mafia, have stolen two cannisters of the most radioactive substance known to man."

The AC went to continue but the Premier stopped him. "So what you're telling us from the get-go is there are no simple solutions to solving this crisis?"

"Not only are there no *simple* solutions, Premier, realistically there are very few *complex* measures available to us to resolve this emergency." The AC witnessed the looks of gloom on the three faces. "Even so, things could be much worse. For example, seven workers would have been killed, and the storage site totally destroyed were it not for the efforts of these two fine detectives, and another of my team, Peter Donaldson, who was wounded in the ensuing gun battle." He motioned towards Ballard and John, Ballard praying John wouldn't adopt his usual comic routine of glancing over his shoulder in search of the aforementioned fine detectives. The Premier and Police Minister took in the men, expressing their gratitude while the Chief Commissioner studied them with appreciative eyes but no words. The AC continued throwing a lifeline. "Another bonus is the remaining five cannisters are now safely inside the storage area, and the military are assessing what's required to take over external security of the site—something that should have been in place originally. In a moment I'll detail what we believe are the *minimum* security requirements necessary to secure the complex."

An audible sigh of relief escaped the police minister's lips, interposed by a pained expression and an embarrassed shrug, the minister silently conceding there had been a monumental security miscalculation by the Government. The AC pressed on. "The two perpetrators intent on destroying the site have been killed, the main offender being Sergey Alistratov—"

The Premier spluttered, almost choking on a mouthful of water. "That ... that's the bastard who attacked Parliament House!"

"Correct. And I'm here to tell you he'll never kill another human being again, or for that matter demand a ransom of any government."

The AC's declaration caused both politicians to shift uncomfortably, the mention of a ransom invoking painful memories. Proving his previous copious notetaking wasn't for show, the AC cleared his throat before launching into a mini version of Robert's briefing of the satellite coverage of the attack site. He explained what that may reveal. The transformation on the politicians' faces was akin to drowning men being thrown a lifeline. The Premier was the first to respond, addressing his question as much to the Chief Commissioner as to the AC. "So, you're telling us there's a possibility you can track down the location of the cannisters? That's fantastic—"

Again, the AC stepped in with a reality check. "Premier, the vision will only point us in the general direction that they initially took. Identifying their current location is very unlikely. Also, it must be stressed that any request for the necessary footage has to pass through Signals Directorate."

"If there's *any* delay Glen, call me 24/7." The Premier's fierce look was a clear directive to the Chief Commissioner, and it was accompanied by what appeared to be a desire to hammer the table with his fist, but he refrained. The Chief Commissioner dropped into assurance mode. "It won't be a problem. I've a contact in the Directorate who can speed things up." His positive tone underscored his promise that for once bureaucracy wouldn't slow the required actions.

Satisfied at least some positive actions were underway, the Premier looked to the AC. "Without divulging the full details of the conversation, I've already had a lengthy discussion with my Attorney-General about arranging adequate ongoing protection for the site at Ouyen. He's very conscious of the urgency of the situation." The thinly veiled threat to the Attorney-General's future career prospects was duly noted.

"So Kevin, tell us what's required from a hands-on perspective to repel another attack." The Premier's expression was such that he knew what he was about to hear would be confronting and expensive, but his pen remained poised.

Again, the AC didn't disappoint, astounding Ballard and John who looked on as the senior officer rattled off facts and figures associated with the squads of soldiers needed on the ground; the surface-to-air missile defence strategy; the two Boxer Combat Reconnaissance Vehicles and the firepower they were capable of unleashing; the radar early-warning systems; along with the need for at least one Tiger gunship and the deterrent that would represent.

The minister for police spoke first. "Kevin, I'm mindful you believe you should have been involved in determining security for the site from the beginning, and your belief quite tragically has proven to be correct. But with all this equipment and personnel, aren't you now overcompensating?"

John stole a brief glance at Ballard, his eyes wide, both men fearful the barb might set the AC off. To their relief their apprehension was unfounded. Taking a leaf out of Jordan's presentation, the AC coolly detailed the security associated with the Fort Knox Bullion Depository, along with the revenue comparisons. Then, without warning, and in a stunning aside directed at the Premier and the police minister, the AC's frustration unleashed. Continuing his monologue in a business-like tone, he fired both a question and an answer in one, his eyes as cold as granite, locking on the politicians as he delivered the left-field bombshell.

"Premier, minister, if your wives and children were kidnapped by The Board, or possibly by Ndrangheta, and they were marched up to the bunker's front door with the threat of torture, rape or death if access wasn't granted, which type of security would *you* rather have had in place to emphasise the futility of such an action? Standard, run-of-the-mill guards, or a military presence that had earlier broadcast to the world, and to these groups specifically, that kidnapping *anyone* was a futile exercise in the first place? Of course you'd want your families to be spared, but deep down you'd know in your heart that if the site were breached they'd be murdered anyway, the resultant political fallout of the site being destroyed most likely ending both your careers."

Ballard and John held their breath, spellbound. The police minister appeared too shocked to respond, while the Premier's mouth continued to goldfish. The detectives were in two minds which scenario the politicians found more distressing, the harm to their family's wellbeing, or the demise of their political careers. It was at this point that the necessity for heavily weaponised security sank home.

Agreeing, albeit with a degree of angst, the Premier conceded, "Ok Kevin, I take your point. Let's not forget, I've ... *we've* experienced what these bastards are capable of at Parliament House. Clearly, you've brought home in no uncertain terms a scenario that isn't impossible, God forbid. For that I appreciate your candour."

Turning to Ballard, the AC asked, "As you've been personally exposed to how The Board and Ndrangheta operate, in your opinion Michael, what's the likelihood of them having another crack at the disposal site to destroy it once and for all?"

Like the AC, Ballard chose to be blunt. "One hundred percent certainty should the security be anything less than maximum visibility and capability. Our CIA contact in Venice made it abundantly clear to John and myself that criminal elements in Italy and Russia will stop at nothing to destroy the site if they believe they have *any* chance of success. Billions of dollars are at stake for whoever effectively manages waste uranium storage in the future. These organisations have almost limitless resources to take on what has and would have been *sub-standard* security. We need to do something about that … *and now.*"

Listening, the Premier's eyebrows rose, in fact they couldn't have gone any higher, but he didn't say anything. Heartened, Ballard pushed on. "Only those precautions proposed by Lieutenant Hensley, the special operations commander who contributed to the successful end of the Parliament House siege … *only* his recommendations will come anywhere near being a deterrent. And Premier, we don't have *any* time to waste. Our SOG commander, who is currently at the site guarding the cannisters, is exposed and grossly under-manned and under-equipped should The Board or Ndrangheta decide today to have another serious crack at blowing the place up."

A number of seconds passed in which it was clear the Premier was coming to terms with the take-it-or-leave-it briefing, and where polite utterances were not the order of the day. Turning his attention to the police minister and the Chief Commissioner, he stated in a subdued voice, "We've been caught coming up short once. We can't risk a repeat of the tragedy that unfolded out there. We have no alternative but to adopt the recommendations."

To Ballard he asked, "How long will these measures need to be in place?"

Ballard's expression didn't brook any disagreement. "Until the site is at full capacity and the vault doors which are already in place are locked good and tight."

"But it'll be years, perhaps a decade before *all* the world's waste uranium is housed there!" The Premier was seen performing mental arithmetic as he calculated the exorbitant cost of security for such a protracted period.

Ballard laid an irrefutable incentive on the table to which no politician who wished to remain in power could ignore. "Something approaching five hundred billion is at stake."

The silence in the room lasted long enough for John to feel uncomfortable, uncertain from the Premier's demeanour which direction the politician was about to head, conscious this was a grave decision that may cost lives.

A wry smile formed, followed by a long sigh from the politician, occasioning a surprisingly succinct directive. "You're pushing against an already open door Kevin, proceed with what you believe must be done."

Ballard and John winked at one another, prompting John to blurt out before his brain could catchup, "And about bloody time."

The Premier shifted his gaze to the detective, who after being kicked under the table by Ballard, reddened in the face, unsure if his outburst would bring about a rebuke.

"My sentiments exactly John."

Mumbling an unintelligible apology, John broke eye contact, doing his best to hide the upturned corners of his mouth.

Scribbling a note in his folder, the Premier asserted, "I'll have my Attorney-General contact his federal counterpart to seek authorisation from the chief of army." He addressed the commissioner and the AC with a single sweep of his hand. "You'll have authorisation to proceed by close of business today."

Both uttered their thanks, the AC commenting, "Actually, preparations are already underway as I assumed the necessary approvals would be granted."

The Premier rewarded the revelation with another lopsided grin. "I'd have expected nothing less from you Kevin." It was clear he was satisfied this crucial facet of the crisis was now a work in progress. "Moving on, while the political aspects of this incident aren't *your* concern," he focussed on the three policemen, "unfortunately it's *my* immediate challenge, and one that has to be addressed forthwith." He paused, embarrassed by what he was about to ask. "How long have I got before I'm forced to hold a press conference?"

Glances abounded among the group, with the Chief Commissioner requesting from the AC in the bluntest of terms, "Kevin, what's your estimate as to who has knowledge of this debacle?"

The AC began counting on his fingers, the twinkle in his eyes obvious only to those in the know. "There's Michael and John here of course, and Peter Donaldson who was with them in the tunnel. Then the SOG personnel who attended at the attack site. The deceased bodies were moved prior to the heavy lift equipment operators arriving to pop the locomotive back on the tracks, so hopefully they'll believe this was a simple derailment. Now who else is there? Oh yes, the forensic teams and the local police on duty at Ouyen ... but they've all been sworn to secrecy, and I'm certain they got the message. The seven workers at the site are aware of the damage caused to the tunnel, but little else. Then there are the communications radio operators here at headquarters who were in direct contact with the security contingent on the train—"

The Premier held up his hands in surrender. "Ok, enough Kevin, I get it. The probability of this catastrophe being kept a secret even for a number of hours is zero."

The AC presented a poker face with the merest undertone of disparagement, which again only Ballard and John picked up on. "*Damn social media* ... in my day there was no such thing as mobiles, we took photos with a bloody camera, then we sent the film to the chemist for development. From there it was snail mail if we wanted to show the pictures to friends who didn't live close by."

An amused snort escaped John's lips which he attempted to cover by a series of coughs into a clenched fist.

The Premier grimaced before addressing the Chief Commissioner. "Well Glen, once more unto the breach .... Let's schedule a briefing later this afternoon. In the meantime, we'll lay low from reporters."

The commissioner's growl proved amusing for Ballard and John, which they did their best to hide. "I'll make the necessary arrangements. Not that we haven't had our share of practice lately. But this is going to be a tough one."

Ballard's cautioning hand was a warning to John, fearful his partner was about to blurt out that the repercussions were of their own making. The senior sergeant remained silent.

The Premier addressed the AC. "Ok Kevin, let's pretend for a moment you're the media baying for my blood ... what questions are going to be thrown my way? I'll give an answer then you tear it to shreds."

Not one to shy away from a challenge, the AC decided on an initial body blow. "No doubt the first salvo will be something along the line of why the public were kept in the dark about the shipment of nuclear waste being moved through populated suburbs prior to it heading up to Ouyen."

The Premier did his best not to appear evasive, but failed. Squaring his shoulders, he opened with, "The cannisters containing the waste met world's best practice in terms of any possible leakage, and due to their size, we believed they were virtually impossible to steal. It was also in the national interest that this aspect of the operation be kept low key."

The AC remained on the front foot. "The national interest line sounds like a coverup. Further to that, are you saying you didn't know about the two smaller cannisters from Italy?"

"We knew they were in the mix, but we didn't find out about the actual size of their cannisters until after the heist."

Observing the Premier on the defensive was a novel event for Ballard and John.

The AC was relentless. "The press will climb all over that admission when they learn that the two cannisters are missing. This whole episode smacks of poor project management, the planning was substandard whichever way you cut it. You have two choices—tough it out and hope over time something else comes along to occupy the media's attention, or accept responsibility that you got it horribly wrong and cop a short-term belting. I don't have to tell you, Premier, Australians hate being lied to, but once they have the facts they're remarkably forgiving." Somehow the AC managed to turn his statements into questions.

The Premier attempted to drag the situation back onto his terms. "So Kevin, you're obviously beginning with the easy stuff."

His attempt at levity was slapped down hard. "Indeed I am. The more difficult questions will be what amount of responsibility do you take personally, and your government collectively, concerning the eighteen men who died as a result of the inadequate security protocols you put in place. And as a consequence, taking into consideration the Westminster system we operate under, will you and your ministers contemplate resigning?"

The only sound in the room was a combined drawing of breaths, the loudest being John's as it appeared he was about to faint. The Premier drew himself upright in his chair, taking a moment to regroup, his self-survival instincts kicking in. As though he were actually in the media briefing per se, his answer was hard-nosed and defiant. "Mistakes have been made, I can't escape that reality. The loss of life is an abomination, and for that I'm truly sorry, but these criminals can't be seen to have won. As such, my government will move heaven and earth to bring them to justice, and for myself and my ministers to cut and run now would be admitting defeat. We will not be doing that." He sat back, his eyes penetrating.

The AC considered his response while Ballard watched on with interest, intuitively sensing his superior was about to go for the Premier's throat. In a low voice the AC uttered a stark home truth. "If that's all you can offer, Premier, the media will rip you apart because it's a stock-standard political answer. I suggest while it might be an opening gambit, you *must* back it up with details. Tell them what you've done to strengthen security by employing military resources. Spell out all the steps that have and will be taken, and I'd suggest a verbatim account along the lines I've just given wouldn't go amiss—it'll serve multiple purposes. Firstly, it'll reassure the public something concrete is being done to minimise a repeat attack. Secondly, it'll send a clear message to The Board and Ndrangheta that your guns are bigger than theirs, and hopefully that'll be a game-changing deterrent."

The Premier visibly relaxed, the mental image painted by the AC was one that pleased him.

The commissioner stirred in his chair. "If it helps, Premier, I can give an account of the security measures we're going to undertake."

A delayed response had Ballard convinced the Premier was weighing up the repercussions should the Commissioner make the announcement, perhaps stealing the limelight at the briefing. The corollary was if the Premier attempted to detail such a complex scenario, and was then peppered with detailed questions he wasn't technically equipped to answer, he would be found wanting and have to defer to the commissioner anyway. Ballard could almost hear the politician's mind ticking over as he assessed his options.

Drawing a deep breath, the Premier concluded, "Ok Glen. Let's do that, it'll save me memorising a heap of technical jargon."

The AC raised a further consideration. "Another tough one will be whether your government is still committed to using the site as a storage facility, or given the circumstances, you're cutting your losses and shutting the project down." It was obvious the question was rhetorical, the AC mindful such a money-generating proposition was far too enticing for the premier to let slip through his fingers.

The politician tilted his head, almost as though he had misheard, or more to the point, believed the AC had lost his marbles. "The revenue this venture will accrue for Victorians over decades to come will deliver them new infrastructure and services that will immeasurably advance the quality of their lives and those of their children. Most assuredly the site *will* be utilised for the initial purpose for which it was built, that being the secure storage of the world's nuclear waste."

The AC pursed his lips. "Excellent ... grabbing the question by the scruff of the neck is always the best course of action."

"I agree Kevin, and the fact you've approved one out of three answers is better than none."

The sarcasm wasn't meant to be biting, and wasn't taken so by the AC. "I'm only doing your bidding, sir."

Both men respected the role the other had to play considering the situation, conscious tough times lay ahead and setbacks were certain to be regular occurrences in the fight against an enemy who didn't know the meaning of surrender.

Snapping his folder shut, the Premier glanced about him. "Wayne, anything you care to ask these fine gentlemen before they leave?"

Ballard gave John a precautionary kick under the table as the police minister shook his head, having been uncharacteristically subdued throughout the proceedings. "No, Premier, I'll liaise with Glen and Kevin regarding the approvals we're seeking from the chief of army. The sooner we shore up the site at Ouyen the happier I'll be."

"Won't we all." The Premier's reply was aimed at no one in particular. "Kevin, Michael, John ... I appreciate your excellent efforts to this point, as well as what you'll be doing to extricate us out of this mess. I know the public believe we politicians are cold-hearted bastards who view deaths as mere statistics, but this massacre has hit home just how important the role law and order plays in our society—it's the very *backbone* of our existence. We must do everything in our power to preserve it. Christ almighty, I refuse to stand by while Victoria is compared to Afghanistan or damn Iraq in terms of lawlessness … that's not going to happen on my watch."

As they made to leave, the three detectives were convinced of the Premier's unshakable resolve.

CHAPTER
9

John's eyes were appreciative as he settled back in his seat in the tram, the AC opposite, their knees almost touching. "Jesus, boss, now I know why they pay you the big bucks to keep this sort of crap out of our hair."

The senior officer flashed a boyish grin, momentarily wiping years off his age. "I did warn you it'd be an experience you wouldn't forget."

The tram braked hard, causing a group of raucous students along the aisle to stumble against one another, all bursting into peals of laughter. Taking the group in with a hooded brow, the AC turned back, declaring, "Again I need to stress how important it was to have you there. It's bloody imperative we demonstrate to these pollies that their decisions have real-life consequences, and operational police like yourselves are placed in harm's way having to *execute* their directives, at times with fatal results." He nodded emphatically while stabbing a forefinger at an imaginary premier. "Now, the moment we get back to the office I'll arrange to have you both driven home. I *don't* want to see either of you until the day after tomorrow."

As the statement was an order and not a request, the

detectives shrugged their grudging acceptance.

The AC wasn't finished, "In the meantime I'll contact Professional Standards and wise them up on the facts of life as to what it's like being in the field and having crims point guns at you." His fixed stare at John didn't need illumination. Satisfied everything was in order, the AC rested his head against the window of the tram, shutting his eyes against the glare of the sun.

Not speaking for fear of interrupting his catnap, Ballard and John were conscious their boss was juggling multiple balls; should any one of them fall it would spell disaster for both his and a host of other careers.

Alighting from the tram, the senior officer made a beeline across the road to the new headquarters building, having claimed he was scheduled to brief his deputy commissioner.

Ballard and John craned their necks as they took in the glistening glass and steel behemoth before them, John shaking his head in disgust. "Utter bloody stupidity Mike ... seven thousand staff in this monstrosity, and another two thousand-odd in our Crime building, side by side no less—if that isn't putting all your eggs in one basket then I don't know what is."

They continued their disapproving looks before mounting the steps on their way to their office. After chatting with a number of detectives on the floor, Ballard sat back at his desk and called Natalie. Nearby, John was in deep conversation with Sonia.

"Michael, are you *sure* you're Ok? And what about John and Peter ... I know you rang before but I never hear the *real* story up front, and then when the truth comes out—"

"Sweetheart, you'll be happy to know all our fingers and

toes are intact … we're fine." Ballard felt uncomfortable at his omission of Peter's circumstances.

"Thank God, I was so worried."

"Hmm. You're just pleased because you know what I can *do* with my fingers and toes."

Natalie's spontaneous giggle came across loud and clear, her concern dissolving. "Where are you now? I miss you."

"Not as much as I miss you, my darling." Grinning, Ballard scrutinised his partner who was sitting with one leg propped over the corner of his desk, his mobile pressed against his ear. "John and I are in the office and the AC's about to arrange for us to be driven to our respective partners' loving arms."

"Michael, I know you and John are close, but really …" Another giggle. "Don't bother getting a lift. I'll come and get you."

"No need. In the time it'll take you to drive in from the town house I'd already be there at our love nest."

"*Very funny.* No, I'm actually in town at the office. My boss called me in this morning on a work matter, but I'm all done now, so I could be outside your building in fifteen minutes." Natalie's tone implied this was a clear directive. Ballard stood up from his chair, throwing a roundhouse salute that caused John to frown at him, convinced his colleague had gone quite mad. "Well Nat, your command is my wish … or is it, your wish is my desire—"

"Good God Michael, by the sounds of it your sugar levels have dropped. As soon I get you home I'll make sure you tuck into a decent meal then bed."

A cheeky retort was on the tip of Ballard's tongue, but he controlled himself. "Fifteen minutes it is. I'll be around the corner in Latrobe Street … you'll see a one-eighty-six-centimetre guy with brown hair and an athletic build wearing a grey wool Armani suit, a white business shirt and a silk tie. It's been said he looks a lot like a taller version of Sting—"

Natalie chose to ignore his droll rantings and ended the call. Ballard pocketed his phone as John queried, "Is Nat ok?"

"She's at work and wants to pick me up."

John pushed shut the drawer in his desk. "Yeah, Sonia's doing the same, said she'd be half an hour."

Ballard rolled his chair closer, furtively checking around the office to ensure there were no prying ears. "Taking aboard the AC's directive, we'll have to leave our better halves in the dark regarding the attack. Even so, with the Premier and the Commissioner holding a news conference pretty soon, Natalie and Sonia are sure to put two and two together. I guess all we can do is plead we were mere spectators."

"What about Sergey? He's impacted Natalie's life pretty badly with her having to quarantine her two youngsters at her parent's place for so long. Doesn't she deserve to know he's no longer a threat?"

Ballard contemplated his partner for several seconds, his lips compressing. "You're right Johno. Even though Igor's still in the mix, him being a risk to Nat's family isn't as immediate. Yep, as good as done, and the same goes for Sonia. After being held hostage at Parliament House by the bastard means she's entitled to know he's no longer a danger, but nothing more, ok?"

"Roger that." John was delighted he could pass on the news to his pregnant fiancée, knowing it would be an enormous relief to her.

Ballard snatched up the plastic bag containing his soiled shirt, underclothes and socks, holding it aloft with a dubious grin. "Hopefully I can get these soaking before Nat spots them and grills me as to why they're covered in dust. Thank Christ our dry-cleaning service here in the building takes care of our suits."

John's lopsided grin matched Ballard's. "Best of luck smuggling that lot in. I distinctly remember you telling me how fussy Nat is when it comes to washing clothes."

Ballard waved a dismissive hand at him, already halfway to the lift.

Standing in the one patch of direct sunlight near the intersection of Latrobe and Spencer Streets, a chilly breeze lifted his jacket lapels as Ballard checked his watch; it was just after 4 p.m., not yet twenty-four hours since he, along with Natalie, John and Sonia jetted into Tullamarine from their whirlwind Italian holiday. It seemed inconceivable that so much had taken place in such a limited time, registering belatedly that his adrenalin levels had plummeted and fatigue was overwhelming him.

He reflected back to Jordan's comments and what military defences were needed to secure the storage site, and how it would be required for years to come. He prayed the fortifications could be established in time to prevent another bloodbath, the images of the torn bodies of the security teams resurfacing like a terrible dream.

A cobalt-blue BMW pulled up alongside him. Natalie leaned across, gazing up at him, her Gucci sunglasses perched jauntily on her nose. The sight of her broad smile dissolved the exhaustion he had been battling to keep in check. He grinned to the world before opening the passenger door and leaning down. "My mother always warned me against getting into cars driven by beautiful women … but aw, shucks, I guess I can make an exception *just* this once."

"You'd better." Reaching across to draw his head closer, Natalie's kiss was warm and sweet, her lips tasting of peppermint. Eyeing the plastic bag he had tossed in the back, she guessed they contained the clothes he wore on the flight back from Venice. Her brow creased, suspecting for him to have changed meant he had been in the thick of something dangerous. Giving him a reassuring pat to convince herself he was still in one piece, she flicked a glance over her shoulder before pulling out confidently from the kerb, exploiting the red traffic light behind her. Performing a tight U-turn, she travelled up Latrobe Street towards Victoria Parade.

Negotiating the traffic with practised ease, she gave Ballard a scrutinising look through the dark lenses. "Would I be correct in assuming any questions I ask regarding what you and the boys have been up to aren't going to be answered with anything resembling the truth?"

Swallowing hard, Ballard placed a hand on her deliciously exposed thigh. "Actually, I've got some news for you that you'll find *very* comforting, but I think it best I wait until you've stopped at a set of lights before I pass it on."

A head spin was followed by, "Michael, I *can* walk and chew gum at the same time … *as you well know*. So tell me." Her excitement was palpable, almost childlike in its intensity.

"Sergey's dead."

Ballard's belief that he should have waited for a set of lights proved prophetic as Natalie swerved in her lane, correcting instantly. "What! *Really*? My god, what happened? So Josh and Kayla —"

Ballard interrupted her, conceding he had missed his daily interaction with Natalie's two youngest. "Yes, at long last they can leave that dingy, cramped house your parents have been locking them up in for the past few months." Ballard smiled at his own joke, visualising the enormous Box Hill clinker brick mansion Robert and Barbara rattled around in, the ex-Vietnam colonel the king of the castle, with Barbara more than his equal queen.

Happy tears tracked down Natalie's cheek which she didn't attempt to wipe away. "Oh Michael, I've been wanting to get them back home for so long. And this means Emma and Tricia can drop by too whenever they have a free moment." Natalie's voice radiated excitement at the prospect of her two older daughters catching up with their mother after such a long absence. For months she had feared for their safety, requesting they not visit her South Yarra townhouse on the distinct possibility Sergey might find out and harm them.

Ballard chuckled, his fingers stroking the back of her arm. "I can see this has made your day—"

"*Made my day*! Darling, this'll make my entire *life*."

Ballard's lip pouted in indignation. "Steady on. I thought *I* might have figured *somewhere* in your new sense of euphoria."

Natalie drew her glasses down low on the bridge of her nose, her eyes crinkling, content. "Ha ha! Not everything is about you Michael, but of course having you here with me makes it *all* worthwhile."

Settling deep in his seat, Ballard closed his eyes, satisfied Natalie's day-to-day life was returning to normal after months of anxiety. While aware an equally ruthless monster in the form of Igor was stalking the streets, a troubling issue in itself, it was one he didn't need to concern her with right now.

That said, the Russian was an immediate challenge for the department, and one that had to be addressed with urgency.

Responding to the green right-turn arrow, Natalie accelerated into Punt Road and despite the bumper- to-bumper congestion, managed to pull up outside her garage thirty minutes later. Glancing at Ballard, and seemingly reading his thoughts, she declared in a breathless voice, "Can you believe it's just over two days since all four of us were walking the streets of Venice on our after-dark tour? You've no idea how much Sonia enjoyed the trip ... just as I did, and I think John had a ball as well, even though he'd never admit it."

"Oh, he enjoyed it alright, don't you worry about that." Ballard was careful not to let slip that the highlight of the holiday for his partner was the trip to the Island of Giudecca with Vincenzo, accompanied by his heavily armed special forces team to arrest Maxim Dabylov.

Activating the garage door, Natalie pulled in alongside the V12 Bentley Continental GT, its sleek silver bodywork enough to make any high-performance car enthusiast drool. Ballard couldn't help ogling at the engineering masterpiece.

Natalie laughed. "Darling, I know it's been over ten days since you last saw it, but it's been perfectly comfy here in the garage, and Dad's already promised you can keep driving it until his leg heals."

Ballard checked himself. "Sorry Nat, how *is* your father coming along after his tumble off the ladder?" The mental image of the half-trimmed ivy on the front wall of the Box Hill mansion flashed to mind.

Natalie's reply was tongue-in-cheek. "Yes, thank you for asking. He's doing just fine, but as with anyone in their late seventies, it's taking a bit longer to heal. The doctors think he'll be back to his old self in about six weeks." She focussed on Ballard. "Now, I'm fully aware that the longer it takes Dad to mend the more time you'll have to drive this rocket ship. My worry is that when you finally have to hand it over and go back to the Chrysler, you'll be a grumpy hubby for quite some time."

Ballard contemplated the day he would need to return to his Chrysler 300 SRT, a brilliant vehicle in its own right, but sadly not in the GT's class. He braced himself. "Never fear, cars like your father's are for the chosen few, and God knows he deserves it. It may be another decade or two and possibly a robbed bank before we can lash out on one for ourselves."

Natalie gave Ballard a gentle push to get out. "Go on, touch it to settle your nerves, then come inside. You'll be pleased to know I crumbed salmon fillets with polenta and parmesan this morning before shooting into work. That, along with potato wedges and a Greek salad should *really* calm you down."

Ballard's mouth began watering at the prospect. "Sounds fantastic. Any chance you and I can have a quick shower before dinner ... er, what I *meant* to say was, have *I* got time for a freshen up before tucking in?"

Natalie eyed him as he extracted his bundle of clothes. "I know *exactly* what you meant. And yes, providing you don't take longer than your usual twenty minutes, be my guest. Then afterwards you can tell me everything you're allowed to about what happened from the moment you and John abandoned Sonia and I at Tullamarine."

Ballard thought about protesting, but chose discretion. "It's a date." He headed upstairs. Just short of halfway he stopped, an ear cocked, then sneaking back down he established that Natalie was occupied in the kitchen before slipping into the laundry. Shaking his clothes from the plastic bag into the machine, he added washing powder then programmed a heavy-wash cycle, all the while wincing at the noise of the filling water. Spinning around to creep back upstairs he jumped, spotting Natalie in the doorway glaring at him, hands on hips. He inclined his head towards the machine, sheepish. "I thought I'd save you the bother."

Natalie did her best not to show her fear as to what she was about to learn. "Like I said, let's chat after we've eaten." Eyes serious, she returned to the kitchen.

Minutes later Ballard felt the tension flow from his body as the piping hot needles of water cascaded over him. So relaxed was his state of mind that he didn't hear the shower door open, and only when Natalie's deliciously soft hands began washing his back, did he register she had decided to take him up on his offer. Turning, he hugged her long and tenderly, feeling tears of relief stinging his eyes as he relived how close he and his colleagues had come to losing their lives. Intuitively sensing the fragility of his emotions, Natalie hugged him until he regained his composure, not believing for one second that he had rubbed soap into his eyes.

Standing on tiptoes, her breasts firmly against his chest, she kissed both his cheeks before cupping his face in her hands. "So, you thought I'd turned down your suggestion to conserve water? Hardly ... everyone should do their bit for the environment."

His arms encircling her waist, he pulled her closer. "Oh, I intend to do my bit, darling. Don't you worry about that." A spontaneous laugh morphed into deeper, throatier mutterings of appreciation. "Hmm, take your time Michael ... we're in no hurry."

Draining the last of his orange juice, Ballard placed the glass on his empty plate before wiping his mouth with a serviette. "That was a meal fit for a king."

Natalie wasn't convinced. "Perhaps a tad exaggerated, but I'll grant you it was honest tucker." Clearing the dishes from the table, she began washing up. "Wait for me in the lounge, darling, I'll be there in a minute."

Ignoring her, Ballard stole the tea towel draped over her shoulder. "I may have turned fifty a few weeks back, but I'm not ready for the old folks home *just* yet!"

Natalie fluttered her eyelashes. "Yes, I can vouch for *that*." She attacked the dishes, eager to ask what he and his colleagues had been involved in, but aware he could only reveal their actions in general terms. The after-dinner chores complete, they relaxed in the lounge, Natalie's slim legs hooked over his thighs. "Ok buster, let me have it."

Ballard pretended to be confused. "I thought we sorted that out upstairs?"

"*Stop avoiding the issue.*" Natalie punched him in the ribs.

Ballard switched on the twenty-four-hour news channel. "The premier and the commissioner held a news conference this afternoon—" He broke off as the image of the two men appeared on the screen, the repeat of what had been the earlier briefing already underway. Muting the sound, Ballard added, "Sweetheart, depending on what they say will determine what I can tell you."

Natalie nodded, aware of the limitations his work placed on him.

The Premier, wearing the same sombre grey business suit as earlier, was in full flight, standing behind a bouquet of microphones, the setting one of the Government's press rooms in Spring Street. The Chief Commissioner in full dress uniform stood alongside him, the Australian flag and the Victorian Coat of Arms in the background.

Natalie drew a sharp breath. "I can't believe it. This is an action replay when those two got up just weeks ago to explain the attack on the Melbourne Assessment Prison. The public must be wondering whether law and order in this state has totally collapsed."

Ballard remained tight lipped, conscious she and millions of Victorians like her were asking the same question.

"And I'm assuming you three were mixed up in whatever it is the Premier's discussing?" Natalie knew the chance of a direct answer was slim, with Ballard's caught-in-the-car-lights stare confirming her worst fears.

Ballard unmuted the sound on the TV as he shuffled into a more upright position, Natalie following suit. As always, the Premier was confident, his greying hair slicked back from a broad forehead, the familiar deep baritone voice firm and controlled. "The point I'm making is nuclear waste storage at the purpose-built site will be a massive revenue generator for decades to come. The financial rewards we'll be able to funnel into cutting-edge, state-wide infrastructure projects, along with the social advances for all Victorians will span generations, similar to those benefits enjoyed by citizens in oil-rich countries, but without all the nasty pollutants."

Intrigued, Ballard sensed the Premier was positioning himself to hammer home how the project was an undeniable necessity for Victoria's financial prosperity. Conversely, the Commissioner's expression was complex, the senior officer doing his best to hide his pained awareness that the Premier was spelling out the benefits of the venture while leaving the brutal questions about to be posed by the assembled media for him to counter. And he wasn't wrong.

"Chief Commissioner, from a security perspective, how comfortable were you allowing nuclear waste to be transported past people's homes and children's playgrounds?" The TV coverage swapped from the two men to a painfully thin reporter who appeared to be little more than a teenager, yet was experienced enough to ask emotive questions that were certain to generate frontpage headlines.

Normally one who revelled in media attention, the Premier was more than happy to allow the senior officer to respond. By taking a sip of water the Chief Commissioner afforded himself additional thinking time. "The Government and my department have been meticulous in ensuring the nuclear waste is enclosed in specialised cannisters that meet, and in most cases exceed, US Nuclear Regulatory Commission safety guidelines—"

"And did they?" Although young, the reporter wasn't lacking in spunk.

The Commissioner glanced at the Premier who gave the merest hand gesture for him to continue.

"Before the shipments arrived, each country provided in writing their confirmation that the USNRC standards had been met. This gave us the confidence we could safely transport the material."

The reporter wasn't satisfied with the answer but surprisingly didn't attempt a follow-up question.

A reporter wearing a Burberry trench coat, which gave her an aura of a wealthy, cold-war spy, held up her hand. "How many countries were involved in the first shipment?"

The commissioner leaned into the microphones. "Five."

"Which countries?"

"Sorry, that's commercial in confidence."

"Why would that be?"

Multiple eyebrows headed north, with the Premier joining the fray, flashing his well-known 'I'm going to shut this line of inquiry down' smile. "As I mentioned before, these countries are paying vast sums of money for the privilege of storing their nuclear waste at our facility. That permits them anonymity, and that's the last comment I'll be making on the subject." He thrust his chin towards a group of journalists on the opposite side of the room, inviting them to raise more questions.

A veteran reporter took up the offer. "Premier, there are strong rumours that the train transporting the nuclear cannisters was ambushed last night, is this true?"

The Premier didn't flinch, unlike the Commissioner whose jaw muscles flexed several times. "Yes, it is. Four offenders have been arrested and the cannisters are now safely stored inside the complex." The Premier peered over the rim of his glasses, his gaze firm and confident.

Ballard held his breath, waiting to see if the politician's omission of the total truth would be challenged. The momentary delay from the reporters had Ballard astounded that as impossible as it would seem, they were not yet alert to the deaths of the security contingent, or of the two missing cannisters. He put that down to the security perimeter established around the attack site, and the remoteness of the storage bunker.

The moment he assumed a miracle had been achieved, the veteran reporter stepped in again, far from done, dashing Ballard's hopes.

"Premier, how many security personnel died as a result of

the assault on the train?"

There it was, the elephant in the room. Ballard was curious as to her source, but realised that was a moot point. The Premier's worst fears were now realised, the genie was out of the bottle and there was nowhere to hide.

Realising attack was the best policy, the Premier launched into his answer. "Yes, regrettably innocent lives *have* been lost, and every one of them is a tragedy, necessitating the full force of the law to be brought to bear. I won't say how many have perished at this juncture as this is an ongoing investigation, and it will be some time before we know the full details. As I said, the four perpetrators have been arrested, one fatally shot in the process, the remaining three are facing multiple charges, including murder—"

The Premier was interrupted mid-sentence by a reporter who called out, "If there were only four attackers, then surely the security detail had to be grossly inadequate?"

Without drawing breath, the Premier shot back, "Modern weaponry now ensures a small number can achieve what in the past required many boots on the ground." Then in a master stroke of deflection he turned to the commissioner and directed, "Glen, would you detail the security procedures we're applying to the storage site to guarantee ongoing protection of the existing cannisters and future shipments?"

Realising this was his opportunity to prevent, or at least delay additional probing questions regarding the security contingent deaths, the Commissioner launched into an almost word-perfect version of the AC's account of the actions the army had taken, and were still in the process of undertaking, to protect the site.   Natalie leaned across, her lips brushing Ballard's ear. "How long will the site need to be protected by all these soldiers and equipment?"

Without taking his eyes from the screen, Ballard quipped, "Oh, a shade over seven hundred million years, give or take a few million."

Her mouth and eyes wide, Natalie gave him a shove, exclaiming, "Really? Surely not."

Ballard relented. "Once the site is at capacity, and that'll be a number of years at best, it can be sealed off and yes, the soldiers can go home." He paused, reflective. "The complication will be if the nuclear waste is ever reused, which is a distinct possibility as new technology comes online. Then, when access to the site is established again, security will have to resume."

Natalie was pensive, now aware that the storing of the waste wasn't a simple dump-and-forget exercise, yet the enticement of incredible sums of money made it obvious governments of every persuasion would be loath to turn their backs on such a venture—even regrettable deaths failing to be a deterrent.

A host of questions from the media followed, but none refocused on the venture's Achille's heel, namely the transportation of the cannisters from the docks to the site, and that the public had been uninformed regarding the conveyance of the nuclear waste through their suburbs. Ballard was certain the senior reporter would pursue the issue, or worse, raise the question that two cannisters had been stolen. It didn't eventuate and the omission left Ballard dumbfounded.

Alert to his mannerisms, Natalie picked up on his bewilderment. "There's something the reporters aren't asking isn't there?"

Ballard hugged her, impressed by her insightfulness, but by no means surprised at her astute observation. "Very true my love, but by the look on the Commissioner's face he won't be volunteering any more details tonight if he can avoid it."

"Just as you won't be."

"Correctamundo."

Natalie was wise enough to let the matter rest.

Aware they were going to survive the briefing, the Premier concluded by promising to provide further updates when appropriate. He thanked everyone before turning with the Chief Commissioner, both men striding from the room.

"I know I can't ask for specifics Michael, but tell me you weren't in any *real* danger." Her look of hope was fragile at best, pricking Ballard's conscience.

Holding up both hands he began counting his fingers, proving yet again he was in one piece.

Natalie was having none of it. "Ok, smarty, but you can't blame me for being worried."

A prolonged hug was his way of demonstrating to her everything was under control—although deep down he knew that to be far from the truth, including his omission that Peter had been shot. Covering her hands which were cupped to his face, he asked, "Any chance of taking tomorrow off? John and I have been given a leave pass by the AC."

"Wild horses Michael."

"Great, perhaps in the morning we can pop over to your parents to catch up on how your father's coping with his leg in plaster. Afterwards, let's head down to the Botanical Gardens for a stroll around and a bite to eat."

Natalie's face lit up. "This just gets better and better. While we're at Mum and Dad's we can load up some of Kayla's and Josh's things to bring back ... they'll be home tomorrow after school."

Ballard was pleased. "As it should be."

CHAPTER
10

If ever a car can be described as sensual, Ballard was convinced the Bentley Continental was it as he ran his hands over the walnut burl steering wheel. The pitch of the 626 bhp twin-turbo V12 motor was music to his ears as he drove along Whitehorse Road, Natalie beside him, her window partly down, the wind caressing her honey-blonde hair.

She looked his way. "I spoke with Dad this morning and he's still cranky about falling off the ladder. He said it makes him feel decrepit."

"What, that old war horse?" Ballard could only imagine the torrent of choice language the Vietnam veteran would have voiced while lying on the ground, his tibia fractured and his pride dented. "Can you believe it, all that time in the war without suffering a scratch, then he falls victim to a ladder and a set of garden sheers?" With a roguish grin, he added, "There's an upside, darling, like we said last night. We get to tool around in this beast while he's mending. I'm just glad it's his right leg he injured and not his left, otherwise he'd still be driving—"

"It's so good to see you have your priorities in order." Despite an admonishing look, Natalie was aware of the deep affection and respect Ballard had for her father. "I'm concerned about Mum though, having to ferry him everywhere until he mends, with him more often than not nagging her about her driving."

Ballard laughed. "I wouldn't worry, Barbara doesn't do *anything* she doesn't want to, and she's more than a match for Robert ... besides, I've been in the car with her and there's nothing wrong with her driving." In a skillful manoeuvre that produced a barking snarl from the GT, he shot past a very grubby VW beetle driven by a young man who believed weaving in his lane while on his mobile was par for the course.

"Settle down darling. I told Mum we wouldn't be there before eleven."

"I'm only obeying Robert's instructions that I give this beast a caning every now and then so the electronics don't revert to granny mode."

Natalie arched back in the seat, her hands clasped behind her head. "Yes officer, I wasn't *really* speeding, my father-in-law instructed me to do it."

Sitting in the lounge opposite Robert, who was propped in his favourite armchair, his right leg encased in plaster and elevated on a footstool, Ballard asked, "Any idea how long before you're up and about?"

A bear-like growl preceded his answer, "At least another two months, so don't panic, you'll have the Bentley for a while longer. Oh, and I've been kicking over the Chrysler each week so the motor doesn't rust."

"Thanks, and I can't tell you what a blast the GT has been. It's a fantastic machine, and John's green with envy whenever he sees me in it." Ballard chose discretion, deciding not to mention the hair-raising incident at the Geelong docks where John drove the Continental while Ballard rode shotgun, hot on Igor's tail through the streets, only to finish up with the Russian laying down a burst of automatic gunfire either side of Robert's pride and joy as an unsubtle warning to back off. "I just hope going back to the Chrysler won't be too big a shock to my system."

Robert laughed. "Hardly, your SRT may be a hundred and fifty horsepower shy of the GT, but it's still a mighty fine piece of machinery." He shuffled in his seat, his gaze penetrating. "Ok, now that we've aired our love of fast cars, I suspect you've got something to tell me. Well, whatever it is you're *allowed* to tell me." He glanced at the closed loungeroom door, hoping Natalie and Barbara would remain ensconced in the kitchen catching up on family news.

Ballard hesitated, not sure where to begin. "The fact Kayla and Josh can move back into the townhouse is a giveaway that Sergey's no longer a threat."

"So, he's either been arrested or killed. Which is it?" Robert wasn't beating about the bush.

"Killed."

Robert's eyes narrowed as he studied Ballard's face, analysing the tone of his voice. "Tell me if I'm stepping over the line Michael. Would I be correct in assuming you had a hand in the bastard's demise?"

Ballard assessed the trauma the Russian had caused Natalie and her children with his ongoing threats, her two youngest living with their grandparents for months at a time, and by default severely displacing all their lives. Knowing Robert's contribution to his country in Vietnam, and the senior position he held in the army at the end of his career, Ballard believed the retired colonel deserved the truth. "While I can't provide you with specifics, yes, Sergey drew on myself, John and Peter ... we had no choice—"

"So it was you or him?"

"In a nutshell, yes."

"First time you've had to kill someone?"

Coming from anyone else Ballard would have been affronted, but this was Robert, a no-nonsense self-made man who had experienced more in his life than most could ever imagine, thankfully a more compassionate and wiser person for it. "Yes it is, and I've no self-doubts about the justification because his actions had they succeeded would have meant the deaths of many innocent men, as well as John and Peter. But I have to admit, putting the Russian down has shaken me up, and it's something I won't be raising with Natalie any time soon."

Robert checked the lounge room door once more. "Very understandable Michael, and quite normal. Now, what I'm going to tell you won't make you feel any less troubled, but flying helicopter gunships in Vietnam meant I was responsible for the deaths of dozens of young Vietcong soldiers, and tragically, the inevitable collateral deaths of civilians caught in the crossfire."

Ballard blinked hard. "How did you ... *do* you deal with it?"

Robert's face transformed as he relived the horror of what he was ordered to do in the name of war. "I talked things over with my closest army buddies ... and some of the chats went long into the night, let me tell you. Conversations of that nature back then were extremely rare—the majority of the aircrew bottled their feelings, toughing it out, more often than not to their detriment. Expressing my thoughts released *some* of my guilt, however at the end of the day the only thing that blunted the pain was time. Also, I was pragmatic, able to convince myself that what I did *had* to be done—as it was for the Vietcong, told by *their* government *they* had no option but to fight an invading army." It was clear he was recalling memories he had long since suppressed. "The hardest part for me was the futility of it all, I've lost count of the times I've asked myself what in God's name did all that bloodshed achieve? I guess first and second World War soldiers, and those who fought in Korea must have felt the same about the tragic waste of humanity. Now of course we add Afghanistan, Iraq and Ukraine into the disastrous mix, with Taiwan most likely the next cab off the rank."

Directing a determined stare at Ballard, he claimed, "Your situation is clear-cut Michael—the protection of innocent lives, not to mention your own and your colleagues. I'm not saying this because I believe your circumstances are any less traumatic to come to terms with than mine, all I'm stressing is that your actions saved lives. Mine cost them."

"Nightmares?" Ballard felt guilty raising the issue, yet having come this far he wanted to know everything.

"Yes, for the first few years after I got back home … but a wonderful wife and a fulfilling career helped, and now the flashbacks are rare. I just deal with them whenever they surface." He leaned closer. "Like I said, Barbara helped me immensely, so don't think for an instant Natalie won't be able to do the same for you."

Ballard was thoughtful. "I'm sure you're right Robert, and I'm confident down the track I'll be calling on her to keep me from dwelling on this too much." He rubbed his chin, reflective. "Speaking of mental trauma and how it can haunt you, I'm reminded of having bumped into a colleague of mine several years back. We were often rostered together in the van down at St Kilda … in a way he was my mentor, having been in the job a lot longer than me. I'll call him Eric, not his real name by the way. He told me that when he first transferred to the station guys used to sneak a smoke in the divvy van while on shift. Apparently this one time his partner finished his cigarette and had him pull alongside an industrial waste bin, flicking the butt inside."

Robert's eyes narrowed, aware the story was about to take a darker turn.

"Eric said twenty minutes after they returned to the station, they were called back out again to a fire which happened to be the damn bin his partner had chucked his cigarette into. A firetruck was already there hosing out the flames. Then, while Eric and his mate sat watching, the firemen dragged out a burnt body—"

"*Jesus*! What did they do?"

"Eric said they froze. His partner was *convinced* his cigarette was out when he tossed it in. As a consequence they said nothing, and that's when the nightmares began. Eric confessed that had they owned up then and there they'd have got a kick in the pants and that would have been the end of it. The dead guy was a known metho drinker, and a lighter was found alongside him as well as a packet of cigarettes. Eric thinks the poor bugger must have crawled inside to get out of the cold, took a couple of swigs of metho then lit up a ciggy—*poof*, up he went."

Ballard winced as he recalled the conversation. "Despite logic shouting from the tree tops it wasn't their fault, Eric said the image of the dead guy is the last thing he thinks of at night, and the first thing that floods his head in the morning. What's more, the images are getting stronger not weaker as the years go by. I felt so sorry for him. I guess in light of that horror story I haven't got much to complain about."

Shaking himself as though offloading a bad dream, he offered, "Forgive me Robert, talking about all this is indulgent of me, but you've no idea the clarity your revelations have given to *my* situation, and I'll pass on your words of wisdom to John and Peter. Hopefully it'll help them as well. Also, I'll take your advice and confide in Natalie—at the right time."

Robert reached across to shake his hand. "Glad to be of service."

"My, my, this all looks terribly formal." Barbara caught the tail end of the two men's physical exchange as she and Natalie entered the loungeroom.

Without missing a beat, Robert joked, "No mystery at all my dear. I've just sold Michael the GT. He said he's more than happy to take it off my hands—"

Barbara laughed. "*Nonsense Robert*. The chance of that happening is the same as me becoming the Queen of England. Even on your death bed you wouldn't part with it. I'm on to your subterfuge." She gave her husband a look that hinted of a later interrogation. "Hmm, clearly this is secret men's business and we *mere* women folk are going to have to cop it on the chin." The twinkle in her eyes took the heat out of the assertion.

"Yep, that about sums it up." Robert's tone was light-hearted, but Ballard caught the steel in his father-in-law's words. It was obvious the matter wasn't one to be pursued and Barbara was wise enough to recognize that. Deciding to ease the tension in the air, Natalie plonked down alongside Ballard. "I've been catching Mum up on our holiday in Italy. She was *most* impressed that you invited Sonia and John along."

Ballard grinned. "I'm not sure who had the best time, them or us."

Barbara drew his attention while pouring tea. "I'm jealous. Robert and I have never been to that part of the world." Her gaze hinted that their next overseas venture should consider the possibility. "Now on another matter, I hear our grandchildren are to be whisked away from us."

Robert snorted, then did his best to disguise it with a loud clearing of his throat.

Ballard had a twinkle in his eyes as he explained. "It's a complicated story Barbara, but the long and short of it is they told Natalie they're feeling guilty about not being able to do their share of chores around the townhouse—"

"*Ha.* What's with you two never giving straight answers? But perhaps the chores thing has some truth to it because they always made their beds and helped out in the kitchen without being prompted. You did a wonderful job there Natalie."

Ballard concurred. "Speaking of helping around the house Robert, I brought some old clothes with me so I can finish pruning the ivy." He dismissed his father-in-law's protestations that he would do it when he got better. "No. Think of this as part-payment for allowing me to continue driving the Bentley."

An hour later all four stood in the afternoon sunshine admiring the neatly trimmed ivy. Ballard's forehead glistened with sweat, and with shears tucked under his arm he accepted the glass of iced tea from Barbara. With a satisfied lick of his lips he asked, "Mind if I take a quick shower—?"

"Go right ahead. Natalie tells me you're off to the Botanic Gardens, so I've packed a picnic basket to save you having to go back home first."

"That's really kind of you—"

Robert wasn't having any of it. "No, thank *you* Michael. I'll admit I wasn't looking forward to a repeat performance on the ladder. In fact, Barbara has banned me from doing this sort of work from now on ..." He feigned glumness and was very successful at it. "I feel the beginning of the end is nigh."

Barbara produced an unladylike snort. "*What rot.* There's still plenty of life left in you yet ... I can vouch for *that.*"

Ballard was amused as he sensed Natalie's embarrassment at her mother letting slip what should have remained private between two septuagenarians.

Reclining alongside Natalie on their rug under the shade of one of the Botanic Garden's established trees, Ballard couldn't resist a degree of mischief. "Ah yes, if I'm not mistaken this magnificent specimen above us is an English elm. Its botanical name is *Ulmus minor Atinia.*" He propped on his elbows, gazing upwards. "And I suspect the arborists have just completed another round of pollarding."

Natalie knew she was being set up, but chose to participate anyway. "Unlike John who lives in fear of your technical rants, I'll play your game Michael—what on earth is pollarding?"

"I'm glad you asked. It's the periodic lopping of the upper branches to secure the good health and longevity of the tree ... a bit like pruning a hedge to stop it becoming too rangy."

"How do you know all this?"

Ballard shrugged. "Well, regarding the name of the tree, I checked out the plaque at its base while you were unpacking the picnic basket."

"My god, no wonder John pulls his hair out, having to endure your ... revelations."

"Johno? Oh, don't fret over him, he secretly loves it."

Natalie wasn't having any of it. "I very much doubt that." She began repacking the wicker basket. "Now that we've gorged ourselves on everything Mum prepared, let's walk some of it off."

"Good idea." Ballard shook the grass off the travel rug then folded and looped it in the handle of the basket.

Arm in arm they strolled the grounds, marvelling at the stunning array of plants and trees, many of them on the endangered list. In a philosophical mood, Ballard proposed, "You have to hand it to our forefathers ... and foremothers for that matter. They had incredible foresight establishing these grounds for the public's enjoyment. Think about it, everything back then would have been just seedlings."

"I guess so. When *were* these trees planted?" Natalie stood admiring the intricate, gnarled root system of a giant oak towering above them.

Ballard dug deep. "If my memory serves me correctly around 1846—that's eleven years after Melbourne was founded."

They meandered along, enjoying the warmth of the sun and the lushness of their surrounds. Halting, Natalie checked her watch. "Gosh, we need to make tracks Michael. I want to be home to start dinner before Kayla and Josh get back from school."

Ballard smiled at the excitement in her voice, at the same time feeling guilty his work had deprived her of everyday contact with her children for so long. They headed for the exit gate to Alexandra Avenue where the Bentley was parked, the GT still within the shade of one of the magnificent plane trees lining the boulevard. A short fifteen-minute drive had the sports car tucked away in Natalie's garage and Ballard unpacking the picnic basket prior to changing into clothes more suitable for dinner.

As he was about to head downstairs, he heard the front door open and seconds later bang shut. This was followed by a cry of joy from Natalie. Guessing Kayla and Josh had arrived, he hesitated on the upper landing, not wishing to impose on their joyous reunion. Waiting for an appropriate time, he made his way downstairs to be greeted by two very excited teenagers.

Smiling at their youthful exuberance, he enquired what subjects they were studying and when their next holidays would be. Excusing herself, Kayla asked her mother if she could help prepare the evening meal while Ballard sat with Josh at the kitchen table. "Still thinking of joining the police force?"

An ear-to-ear grin from the teenager was followed by an enthusiastic, "You bet."

"How are your grades?"

Josh dipped his head. "Not great, but I'm putting in more hours like you said." He frowned, concerned he may not be living up to Ballard's expectations.

Showing his approval of the additional effort being made, Ballard followed with, "I know this sounds old-fashioned, but the hard yakka you put in now will make your life a *whole* lot easier at the academy. For a start you'll be well-organised, having established a solid study pattern, and believe me, there'll be heaps of that to ensure you get a decent pass mark. It's a fact that trainees who finish in the top ten in their squad are generally those who progress the most through the ranks."

Josh turned wistful, daydreaming when he would stand to attention on the Glen Waverley parade ground, his back straight, head held high. Warming to the subject, he unleashed a barrage of questions which Ballard did his best to answer without embellishing or downplaying the reality of what a police officer's life would entail; describing the rewards, along with the misfortunes and hardships that come with such a demanding profession.

Natalie moved about the kitchen, listening in as she and Kayla organised the meal. She appreciated that Ballard was being careful to answer Josh's questions as honestly as he could, but as a mother and a wife she looked ahead to the day when Josh's partner may well have to endure the anguish of a criminal making threats against her family as she had just suffered herself.

His questions satisfied for now, Josh changed focus, his stomach growling. "What's for dinner, Mum?"

Natalie eyed her son in the unique way mother's do, telepathically instructing him to set the table as she placed cutlery in front of him. "Considering the evening meals your grandparents would have dished up, no doubt each one a full-on formal affair, I thought we might slum it and have egg and bacon salad rolls with fresh fruit and ice cream for dessert."

Josh's eyes lit up as he began setting the placemats. "Thanks Mum, you're the best."

Kayla's look of nausea was followed by her eyeing Ballard as she poked a finger down her throat in a gagging motion.

Not wanting her to be left out of the general conversation, Ballard asked, "So what about *your* career prospects Kayla, what's on the horizon now you're in your last year of high school?"

The teenager was effusive. "I *really* want to be an engineer. I've checked it out and have to decide on a university. I can't wait to build roads and bridges."

Approving, Ballard claimed, "Your mother kept me posted with your marks. I'd say there's every chance the world's about to be your oyster, with a pearl in the middle as a bonus."

A serene expression flooded her face. "Gosh … I really hope so."

Ballard winked at Natalie, excusing himself after explaining he needed to make a quick call to Peter. Entering the lounge, he slumped into an armchair while speed dialing his partner. After six long rings the superintendent came on the line. "Hmm … so you're checking up to see whether being waited on twenty-four-seven has me losing my edge?"

"Yeah, that's about the size of it. How's the shoulder?"

"*Bloody sore*. But the doc said I won't lose any movement or strength, so I can't complain—let's face it, if anyone had to take a bullet for you two it may as well have been me. Last man off the ship and all that."

Ballard's grin widened, relieved Peter's sense of humour was still intact. "When are you back at work? I'm sure Diane will be more than happy to take over your recuperation." He visualised the emergency department's triage nurse with whom Peter had formed a relationship after meeting her at the Williamstown Hospital, a consequence of Delwyn and Marjorie being admitted for observation after being kidnapped by Sergey.

Peter grunted. "I'm told in a couple of days." Swapping subjects, he asked, "So when do you guys front Professional Standards?"

Ballard checked over his shoulder as he answered. "At this

point I'm guessing tomorrow. The boss gave us today off to recuperate."

"How the hell are you going to keep John under control?" There were genuine misgivings in Peter's voice as he added, "Don't be surprised if the buggers go for your throats. Tim gave me an update of your shenanigans in Malcom's chopper. Gutsy stuff, but Standards will have a field day over that one. I guess my turn will come when I get back to the office."

"Actually, the AC wanted all of us in the room at the same time to do just that, keep John in check, but Standards won't want to wait another day."

Peter added, "Oh, before I forget, Tim also mentioned the army's moving heaven and earth to bolster the defences at the storage site. Apparently Jordan's taking no chances, and truth be known he's itching to kick the death squad in the vitals if they're silly enough to have another crack at blowing the site to kingdom come."

Ballard shrugged. "More's the pity all that wasn't in place *prior to* the cannisters arriving."

The lounge door opened and Kayla poked her head around. "Dinner's ready."

Waving an acknowledging hand, Ballard quipped, "Got to go Pete, the boss lady is dishing up another gastronomic chef-d'oeuvre. We'll catch up when you get back."

Peter disconnected, but not before uttering a questioning, "*Chef-d'oeuvre*? Try that one on Johno and see what he says!"

CHAPTER
11

The AC studied the attendees in the Critical Incident conference room, satisfied the appropriate specialists were on hand to advise him. "Jordan, let's kick things off with you. I'm told the deployment of your defences at the storage site are almost complete."

"Indeed, they are. The rifle squads are on the ground and the weapons team have installed four RBS-70 air defence missile launchers. I convinced my boss to provide two Boxer CRVs and they should be arriving today." He paused. "I *didn't* have any luck securing the Tiger attack helicopters, more's the pity. I was informed in very blunt terms it would be a gross underutilisation of a major strategic military asset. So as I said, they remain locked up in their hangars ... doing bugger all."

The AC responded. "That was always going to be icing on the cake, Jordan. Christ almighty, to have established what I consider to be armour-plated defences at the bunker, and in such a limited timeframe, well, it's nothing short of a miracle. What this tells me is the government's *finally* taking this nuclear waste situation seriously. It's just bloody criminal so many lives had to be sacrificed before they got their act together."

James Patterson, the ASIO senior intelligence officer who had been instrumental in helping resolve the Parliament House siege, leaned forward with a question for Jordan. "When will you be fully operational should another major attack occur?"

The Lieutenant Colonel's reply was confident, without being arrogant. "We're ready now. It would require a massive assault for them to get anywhere *near* the site. Our counterfire radars are in place for early warning of an aerial approach. We've also erected five 360-degree lookout posts and installed night-vision cameras throughout. Everything is monitored twenty-four-seven from our command centre."

James was reassured. "For your information, our agents are flat out analysing current online chatter. Nothing's been picked up suggesting there's *going* to be an attack, but as we all know, The Board utilises Cold War communication techniques to get their orders out, which pretty much stymies our efforts to determine what's going down at any point in time."

Ballard stared at John, their mutual understanding almost telepathic, a result of working together for decades. Shuffling upright, John posed a question for Jordan, which Ballard knew was at the forefront of John's mind. "Where are all these soldiers going to be billeted while they're seconded to the site? I'm not convinced the greater metropolis of Ouyen with a population of eleven hundred or so good country folk are geared for such an influx of military personnel."

Jordan began nodding even as the question was being asked. "Robert, you mentioned in a previous briefing that the total area of the site is around fifty hectares." The ballistics expert held up a concurring hand. "Thankfully that affords us sufficient flat ground to begin installing all the portable huts we need, and the mains power lines being so close makes life a hell of a lot easier. RAEME have been working their butts off setting everything up. I'll admit there's still a heap to be done, but should an attack take place, in terms of battle readiness, we're good to go."

The AC was pleased. "Much appreciated Jordan. At least that's one crisis off the table. Now for the current dilemma which will have our backsides in a sling if it's not resolved—the missing cannisters." His piercing blue eyes locked onto Robert's. "No surprise you're up next."

The forensic expert shot from his chair as though fired from a cannon. Flicking on the overhead projector, the image of a Nammo M72 shoulder-mounted rocket launcher appeared on the screen. The AC was perplexed why Robert wasn't focussing on the missing cannisters, but the ballistics expert foreshadowed the question.

"If I may digress for just one moment, sir. I can advise that the rocket launchers found in the Hummer when the Ndrangheta operatives were arrested were the ones used to shoot the support chopper out of the sky and take out the train's security personnel carriage. I ran the comparisons myself and there's no doubt they're the culprits. I also need to point out that launchers like these aren't sitting around on shelves in army disposal stores, so the reach of this group in acquiring top-of-the-line weaponry is every bit as effective as The Board's. Adding to that, this model of launcher has the advantage it can be used in a confined space such as a room, the muzzle flash equivalent to a nine-millimetre pistol fired at night—in other words, bugger-all flare." He addressed everyone present with a sweep of his hand. "This is the scope of firepower this mob has access to, and can employ anywhere, any time. It's vital to keep this in mind when you're making future arrests."

The AC pinched his nose in frustration. "Thanks for clearing that up Robert. Up 'til now I was wondering what could be more challenging than taking on this damn Ruskie mob." He allowed his rhetorical statement to hang for several heartbeats. "That was prior to a bunch of Italian thugs coming along and proving they're just as ruthless and equally determined to make our lives a living hell."

Robert studied his audience. "I thought for safety's sake I should put this information on the record. Now on to the missing cannisters." The image of the rocket launcher was replaced by an aerial shot, clearly taken from a satellite. "Sir, your push up the line to access the Defence Department's LatConnect 60 imagery has paid off. Because we knew to the minute when the attack on the train occurred, we had a definitive starting point. The lead-up to, along with the entire shootout has been captured, as well as the seizing of the two cannisters in a series of static images."

Robert's laser pointer worked overtime as he presented each image, the series displaying the firefight, along with the forklift moving the cannisters off the train's flatbeds into containers on two large tray trucks.

The AC's complexion turned a mottled shade of purple as his blood pressure soared, viewing the savagery of the attack with wide-eyed despair. In an action replay of the earlier meeting, his clenched fist struck the tabletop causing teacups, saucers and glasses of water to wobble and jump. "*The bastards. As God's my witness I'll nail the brains behind this mob before I retire. That's a promise to myself if not to the department.*"

John gave Ballard a quick glance, both men aware that

much blood would be spilt before the warring factional issues were resolved, if ever. Sensing the tension in the room, Robert presented another aerial shot, this time circling the laser pointer around what on closer inspection proved to be a large haystack. Beside it were the two tray trucks still carrying the containers. "Michael, you mentioned that Malcolm had suggested Ndrangheta would choose a hiding place until morning rather than drive the trucks in the middle of the night and stand out like sore thumbs." The laser pointer pierced the centre of the haystack. "That's *exactly* what they did, surrounding the trucks with large bales of hay so passing traffic ... not that there's much of it out there ... wouldn't see them."

Robert checked the AC's demeanour, fearful of setting the senior officer off on another tirade. "Unfortunately, the farmer, his wife and one of their workers met a horrible fate as a consequence."

The AC's eyes hardened but he remained silent, having earlier been informed of the tragic news by Surveillance. Robert turned back to his audience. "This is where things get interesting ... at first light the trucks took off, splitting up. We tracked one of them heading away from the farm and then being stopped in Stone Road by the black Hummer." A number of glances did the rounds of the table. "The container on the original truck was swapped onto another empty tray truck, with the forklift driven back into the container. The truck then headed off towards Melbourne, preceding the Hummer by what appears to be fifteen minutes."

Ballard took in John, then the AC, all realising that by sheer bad luck, and even worse timing, one of the cannisters wasn't able to be recovered there and then. Aware of the painful realisation, Robert pressed on. "As we all know, prior to the Hummer departing Stone Road, the driver of the original truck was shot and the rig torched." Clearing his throat, he revealed, "We've managed to track the replacement truck via the imagery right up until it got to a trucking yard in Braybrook, then it disappeared—"

"What do you mean it disappeared?" The AC, who had been expectant up to this point, was furious.

Nervous, as though he were at fault, Robert confessed, "It was driven through a covered area where it merged with dozens of similar trucks with containers all going in different directions. There was no way of knowing which truck was which."

Just as the AC opened his mouth, Robert continued. "I had a couple from Peter's team grill the manager of the company with no luck. He said he didn't have *any* knowledge of a truck coming from Ouyen with a container onboard. The guys pushed hard, but they believe he was genuine. We think the truck circled through the yard with the express purpose of throwing off any aerial surveillance that there might have been. Long story short, we have no idea where that unit is now."

His blood pressure high, the AC queried through gritted teeth, "And the other truck?"

Robert bravely stepped up to the plate. "The satellite shots tracked it through Bendigo, Seymour, then Yea and onto Healesville. It finally took backroads into the Yarra Ranges National Park and ..." He fell silent, embarrassed yet again.

"*And?*" The AC knew the answer but was committed to hearing it anyway.

"We lost it." The ballistics expert valiantly maintained eye contact. "Surveillance have sent a team out there to search the area, but ..." His voice trailed away, clearly not confident anything would come of it.

"Christ! Ok then, any thoughts why the trucks split up?" The question was directed at Robert and hung in the air, but the AC's tone made it clear that anyone was free to offer their suggestions.

Ballard contemplated out loud. "By splitting up they reduced the chance of being caught and losing *both* cannisters. What doesn't make any sense is why they've moved the second cannister to such an isolated location as the national park." He scratched his head. "The first location holds true if they plan to smuggle it out of the country, or threaten a highly populated area such as the Melbourne CBD."

A wall of glum faces peered back at him. "Look, I don't want to make things appear worse than they already are, but Ndrangheta are certain to know how successful The Board was during the Parliament House siege. After all, we saw that a mere 40,000 litres of ammonium nitrate and diesel fuel brought the State Government to its knees. Imagine what the bastards could demand with a cannister chock full of nuclear waste."

The glum faces turned even more morose as James added, "They're not stupid, and know the longer they wait the greater is their chance of being caught ... they'll act sooner rather than later on their ransom demand." He did his best not to appear worried. "So now we find ourselves fighting on two fronts. Firstly, against The Board who are hell-bent on blowing up our storage site in order to convince the Italian Government to build two of their own outside of Naples. This will impact the International Atomic Energy Agency big time. Those buggers will be caught napping on the job, now having to secure additional storage sites around the world because they've been waiting to see how successful we were going to be at managing things. In the meantime, SOGIN, an engineering and site operation company owned by the Italian Government and controlled by the Ministry of Economy and Finance … this mob is responsible for the decommissioning of *all* their nuclear reactors. Again, The Board is up to its eyeballs in the upper echelons of this group for reasons none other than to make money."

James cleared his throat. "So, onto the second front … the Ndrangheta, who we assume are about to demand some form of outrageous ransom. This'll put our federal Attorney-General under the microscope just as he was for the Parliament House siege. My take is, having already been burnt to the tune of a billion dollars the first time with no result, there's zero chance in hell he'll fork out any more money. As a consequence, this forces the onus back onto us to sort this mess out."

The AC anchored both elbows on the polished woodwork, his forefingers pointing towards Ballard and John. "While you guys were gadding about in Italy, you teamed up with Vincenzo Ricardo, the CIA operative stationed in Venice. As a consequence you were privy to him arresting Maxim Dabylov, a senior Board member." He refocussed on James. "Has anything come of the subsequent interrogation?"

The ASIO agent's face lit up. "After speaking with Bernard yesterday, I put in a call to Vincenzo who was *very* upbeat, claiming Dabylov was singing like a canary."

John grunted. "Yeah, that's what Vincenzo told us, and it's a turnaround from when Dabylov was first arrested. Perhaps Vincenzo's threat of a waterboarding session worked after all."

James' grin was more of a grimace. "Perhaps so John.

Vincenzo went on to say there's to be a major meeting of The Board in Moscow in a week's time, supposedly to discuss a raft of issues. One of them being what Plan B should look like if they're unsuccessful in blowing up our disposal site. Another hot topic is their progress regarding infiltrating our ports, and not least, what to do about the rise and rise of the Ndrangheta and the impact this group's having on The Board's bottom line."

Ballard nudged John. "What I wouldn't give to be a fly on the wall at *that* little get-together."

Overhearing the comment, James quipped, "Be careful what you wish for Michael. Vincenzo was extremely impressed with you two during Dabylov's arrest. Right now he's negotiating with his contacts in Moscow to form a team from key likeminded countries, including America, Britain, France, Italy and Australia to be on standby when they raid the meeting—that's so the spoils can be carved up so to speak." He grimaced. "What could possibly go wrong with *so* many agencies sticking their fingers in the pie? The good news is Vincenzo's arriving in Melbourne in the next few days to thrash out the details." James drew the AC's attention. "I can't tell you how much Bernard's looking forward to catching up with his old work buddy."

The AC pushed his cup away, having drained it. "Ok, we've got work to do. Jordan, I take it your Defence Science and Technology boffins are continuing to break more of the encrypted files on the iPad?"

Jordan concurred. "Indeed they are, and there's still hope we'll turn up something, *anything* that might give us a clue as to what their future plans are."

The senior officer looked up, having completed writing

in his daybook. "Excellent, and again, tremendous work in securing the site." His attention swung to Robert. "I don't care how you do it, but find those damn cannisters ... whatever resources you need you'll get."

The ballistics expert flicked off the projector, smarting at having failed to work a miracle to this point, but determined to succeed or die trying. The AC continued wrapping up the meeting. "Ok James, ensure your electronic ears are peeled for any intel that may point us in the right direction, but I accept your reasoning that these bastards aren't stupid, and most likely won't be passing on anything of importance which may be monitored online." He thought for a second. "And find out what this Vincenzo character is planning, and what's in it for us if they do manage to gatecrash The Board's party."

That brought the AC to stare long and hard at Ballard and John, the latter checking behind him as to whether he was in fact in the firing line of the senior officer's cobalt-blue gaze.

"Very funny, Detective Senior Sergeant. Now I've had a long chat with Professional Standards, setting up parameters with them as best I can, without actually *telling* them how to conduct their inquiry. Nevertheless, a shooting death is a shooting death, and must be handled independently. So John, suck it up and get it over with. As for you Michael, keep a steady hand on the wheel. Unfortunately Peter hasn't been released from hospital as yet so he'll have his turn later on, along with Tim who's currently tied up with a domestic siege in Fitzroy."

Ballard asked, "When do we front up, sir?"

The AC glanced at the wall clock. "You've got ten minutes to get next-door, the twenty-fourth floor. They're expecting you."

The two detectives rolled back their chairs, climbing to their feet.

"Oh, and you'll be pleased to know Marjorie's pencilled in a counselling session with you both immediately after your interview."

A groan escaped John's lips which he attempted to disguise as he pushed his chair into the table, feigning a sore back. "Looking forward to it, sir."

The AC's fierce gaze was unwavering. "Remember Henderson, your actions in the next hour may well determine the rest of your career."

With that warning echoing in their ears, Ballard and John left the room.

CHAPTER
12

Two Professional Standards detectives entered the interview room which Ballard and John had been ushered into five minutes earlier by a diminutive policewoman in uniform. John's nod of thanks to her had been returned with a hesitant smile, the officer unsure as to why the senior detectives were there.

Ballard did a double take when he recognised both men as those who had interviewed him after he had fought for his life at his country property in Gisborne; his attacker, Eric Parnell, subsequently tumbling to his death onto rocks at the bottom of Jackson's Gorge. All four men formally shook hands, with Ballard assessing the two detectives to glean the direction the interview may take. While unable to determine their mood one way or the other, with John just as cautious, both men appreciated the gravity of the situation despite being unimpressed by the youthfulness of their inquisitors.

Settling, the taller of the two detectives addressed Ballard first. "I'm not sure whether you remember me—"

Ballard chuckled. "How could I forget … Detective Sergeant Walter Jamieson, and," he addressed the stockier of the two, "Detective Senior Constable Thomas Sadler."

Walter smirked. "Proof positive you have an excellent memory. Now, as with all police shootings there has to be a thorough investigation of the circumstances, after which we'll write up our reports with recommendations as to what your immediate duties should be."

Not daring to look at his partner, Ballard felt John stiffen beside him, praying his colleague's expression wasn't one of open hostility. "Standard practice Walter. John and I have nothing to hide. Please fire away." He winced at his poor choice of words.

Thomas pointed the remote towards the video recorder above him, activating the ceiling mounted unit.

In the blink of an eye Walter's demeanour changed to that of a take-no-prisoner investigator. Armed with a pen, his hand hovered over a blank page in his daybook. "Interview commenced at 11.30 a.m. on Thursday the 24th of May." He rattled off the names of everyone present.

"I'll begin with a question for both of you. Would it be an accurate assessment that in the last eight months you've been involved in a series of police incidents where your lives and those of your fellow officers have been put at extreme risk?"

This time Ballard did include John, an imperceptible hand gesture passing between them. Turning back, Ballard recognised the path the interview was about to take, deciding not to accept it lying down. "If you're referring to operational circumstances requiring us to react in a decisive and at all times legal manner, then yes, we *have* been confronted with incidents necessitating a strong resolve."

Walter blinked rapidly, a mannerism evident during Ballard's previous interview, brought on when confronted by an officer who was forthright, who never backed down, and was old-school to his bootlaces. Not wanting to be caught off guard, the detective pressed on. "Neither of you need reminding, but these are just a *few* of the incidents in question." He addressed John initially. "You were involved in a near-death experience in the underground loop when in pursuit of an offender who had kidnapped a child, resulting in you being almost flattened by an oncoming suburban train, the offender losing a foot in the process." His pen remained static over the page.

John assessed both detectives, choosing not to respond, the AC's words of caution still fresh in his mind. Realising a reply wasn't to be forthcoming, Walter continued. "While not necessarily in chronological order, you both find yourselves dangling from a cleaning platform on the side of the Eureka Tower complex, climbing container cranes at the docks, imprisoned in a helicopter which subsequently crashed, almost blown up *twice* in Port Phillip Bay during high-speed boat skirmishes, and let me see ... ahh ... yes, facing a Note Printing Australia robber charging at you on a motorbike spraying Uzi rounds in your direction." He lifted his eyes to assess Ballard's and John's reaction to his summary of their escapades. "Finally, and what is the focus of this interview, you enter a restricted area in a nuclear waste facility against the express advice of a special operations commander, and end up shooting dead a fleeing offender, not to mention firing military automatic weapons out of a civilian helicopter in the Victorian outback. Is this correct?" Walter's tone was now confrontational, and it had the desired effect.

John bristled, unable to control himself any longer. "And the point you're making?"

Expecting the outburst, Walter sat back in his chair, arms

folded, observing the focus of his diatribe for several seconds. "The point I'm making, Senior Sergeant, is that all these incidents were high risk and should rightly have been left to specialist officers … *it's what they're trained for.* It's that simple."

"*Bullshit.* And for your education, it's *detective* senior sergeant. Now, had we waited, a billionaire's wife would be dead and God knows what would have happened to that child in the city loop. Let me ask *you* something … were we supposed to stand idly by and allow offenders to escape who had robbed the note printing works of millions of dollars, killing security personnel in the process? Or sit on our hands and do nothing when politicians were held hostage—two of which I point out were murdered in cold blood during the Parliament House siege?" On a roll, John's lips drew back in a ferocious sneer. "Oh, and let's not forget, just standby and allow seven storage site workers to die in a tunnel explosion had we not intervened." He goaded Walter, drawling, "Or is that what *you* would do?"

Mimicking Walter's previous actions, John sat back in his chair, arms folded, chin thrust forward aggressively. Incredibly, his outburst had no effect on either detective, with Thomas offering, "While this all sounds very heroic, there are protocols that *must* be followed, otherwise we'd have police members running riot out there—"

Not done, John challenged, "How long have you been in the job, son?"

Also blinking hard at being referred to as 'son', Thomas debated whether he should answer. "Six years, but—"

John was relentless. "How many years as a detective?"

Like the proverbial deer caught in car lights, the young man blurted, "A bit over a year."

"Jesus Christ Michael! Can you believe it? This little bugger still has soap behind his ears."

Walter lurched forward, fearful the interview was degenerating into a slanging match. "*Detective Senior Sergeant*! This is a formal interview regarding the shooting of an offender and I'll remind you to refrain—"

John's smile was hard and his eyes flint-like, no longer wanting to play ball as he leaned forward, his forefinger stabbing within inches of Walter's face. "*No* ... you listen to *me*. The correct way to go about this interview is to raise questions that allow us to explain the circumstances surrounding our actions, and the limited timeframe within which we had to make decisions, along with the split-second reaction times we had in which to operate. Once you've assessed all *that* information, *then,* and only then can you form an opinion. The moment you stepped into this room buddy boy, you had us painted as gun-toting Clint Eastwoods. I'm here to tell you that couldn't be further from the truth."

Ballard sat with a half grin on his face and a sense of release, relishing his partner's home truths, realising nothing was going to stop John from venting his fury. Addressing Walter, he declared, "I totally concur with my colleague, and in case you're wondering, I'll be backing everything he says."

A look bordering on panic filled the detectives' eyes, each glancing up at the camera, mindful their interview was in total shambles, every second recorded, the footage available for analysis at a later date by their superiors.

In what proved to be a fatal announcement, Walter attempted to wrestle back some form of control. "Bluff and bluster don't diminish the fact you've both placed yourselves in dangerous situations that should have been left to specialist officers."

His declaration pushed John to breaking point, all thoughts of future promotion or even ongoing employment within Victoria Police now irrelevant. He reached forward and snatched up the remote, switching off the camera.

Both Professional Standards' detectives were visibly stunned, Walter blurting, "Turn that back on, *immediately*!"

Hunching forward conspiratorially, John whispered something unintelligible.

Walter squinted and bent closer, confused. "What did you say?"

John curled a forefinger, inviting him to come closer, then in a deliberate action he punched him square on the forehead with a clenched fist. The detective rocked back in his chair, clutching his face, howling in pain and disbelief. Throwing the remote back onto the table, John barked, "Interview concluded at 11.50 a.m. Guys, don't bother getting up, we'll see ourselves out."

Ballard hauled himself to his feet, eyeing Thomas who's mouth was opening and shutting like a goldfish. "I suggest you get an icepack on your mate's forehead before it turns into a nasty bruise." He nodded at John. "I don't think there's anything of substance we can add to further assist these fine officers, so let's bid them good day." Backs straight they strode to the door.

The AC did his best to display genuine anger, and almost succeeded. "So John, it appears my advice to you somehow got misconstrued in the five minutes it took you to walk next-door?"

John shrugged. "It being a new building and all sir, your instruction must have somehow slipped my mind."

The AC's brow darkened. "You'll be pleased to know I've pulled some serious strings, so luckily for you nothing further will come of your ... your shenanigans this morning, *but no more outbursts, ok?* You'll both be reinterviewed at a later date by detectives more akin to your age and experience, if *that's* any consolation." His cobalt blues locked onto John's, the directive unambiguous.

Cooling down, and wise enough to at least appear remorseful, John ate humble pie. "Thank you, sir. I appreciate your intervention."

"Ok, now for something a little less taxing. Your chat with our resident police psychologist, Marjorie. She's downstairs in your office as we speak, and already up to speed regarding this morning's ..." He waved his arms, at a loss for an appropriate word.

Ballard came to his rescue. "*Interview.* Thank you again, sir. We'll be off now." He unceremoniously hauled John from his chair, grabbing the collar of his jacket for leverage. As the two men made to leave, John looked over his shoulder, worried the AC may call him back for another reprimand.

Taking the stairs to their floor, Ballard reasoned drily, "That *could* have been a whole lot worse Johno." His voice echoed in the confined space as they traversed the steps. "I did note however, that you chose to punch the guy on the forehead instead of—"

"A lot less incriminating evidence than a blood spattered shirt. There's always method to my madness."

"Hmm, I guess a degree of logic is lurking in there somewhere."

Entering their floor, they made their way over to their desks where they found Marjorie sitting at Ballard's work pod. She appeared the epitome of cool, wearing a high-collared, white silk blouse, navy slacks and delicate black stilettos. Her hair was piled high and secured with a gold clasp, accentuating her fine features.

On seeing them she sprang to her feet in one lithe movement. "Well, well. If it isn't my two favourite detectives. Up to mischief yet again I hear." Indicating the conference room with a directing inclination of her head, she led the way, settling at the end of the table.

"Michael, John, as you know I've been tasked to provide the department with a report detailing your suitability to continue operational duties." She appeared almost sheepish. "After asking you both down to the Beech Forest safe house to help Delwyn and myself recover from our ordeal with Sergey, this all feels a bit ... *weird!*"

Oozing with charm, John stated, "Marjorie, nothing you do could ever be described as *weird*."

Smiling, she flipped open her folder, scribbling the date on a blank page. She looked at both men and sighed. "Nonetheless, this is serious because what I submit will have a direct bearing on your careers. The AC was categorical that the report be factual and ..." she hesitated, "*professional*."

Ballard scoffed. "I'd have thought that wasn't something he'd need to have asked. You've *always* been upfront in your concerns that we take undue risks, and now on top of everything we have Professional Standards breathing down our necks." He turned to John, shrugging. "Me thinks the walls are closing in on us."

Marjorie was uncertain what approach she should adopt. "I have to admit this is the first time I've interviewed you both where I believe I might not be doing either of you justice. I feel like an imposter considering the tremendous advice you gave Delwyn and myself, but the department still wants me to report whether you're fit for duty. No doubt about it, this is going to be a tough gig all round ... in fact it feels like I'm analysing my father."

John nearly fell off his chair. "I say, steady on with the 'father' analogy, ok? I know we're getting a *bit* long in the tooth, but *father* figure?"

Marjorie laughed. "John, any self-respecting lady would be delighted to have either of you as a father. She'd certainly feel protected and secure."

Taken aback by the unintentional ageism, John turned to Ballard for moral support, but to no avail.

Despite her doubts, Marjorie had no difficulty getting down to business, her professionalism oozing from every pore. "There's no avoiding the reality that shooting and killing an offender, even a monster like Sergey is a traumatic event, and it will have an emotional impact on each of you—whether you care to admit it or not."

Ballard's fierce glance at John prevented him from protesting to the contrary.

Marjorie gave an almost imperceptible shake of her head. "Generally there are three types of reaction we see resulting from a police shooting, and they vary widely as a consequence of the officer's age, length of service, work experience and mental capacity to ... to self-heal—"

Unable to contain himself, John pointed a meaningful forefinger at himself then Ballard, alternating the digit between the two while grinning broadly.

Ignoring his unsubtle gesture of self-survival, Marjorie continued. "In the mildest form of psychological distress there's a transitory period which generally lasts one to three weeks. This involves the officer talking about the incident as many times as is necessary with family and friends, quite often with colleagues, or even a professional counsellor."

This time Ballard pointed a concurring forefinger at Marjorie, followed by a positive thumbs-up, his gesture appreciated by the psychologist. "In most of these instances the officer is capable of functioning normally in both his private and work life.

"The second level of psychological distress is more intense, with post-traumatic symptoms evident and known by everyone as PTSD. These indicators persist for weeks or even months, the officer's everyday functioning is undoubtably impaired. In this instance more formal counselling and support from multiple levels, namely a skilled psychologist, family, work colleagues and friends are required for extended periods before the officer can hopefully recover sufficiently to resume full duties. In some instances, medication prescribed by a doctor may be necessary.

"Now, the third type of psychological reaction becomes a train wreck for the officer, and over time, for everyone around him or her. Effectively, the officer has a mental breakdown. He recalls … I'll say *he* because in the majority it is a he … he recalls over and over in his mind every aspect of the incident. Each time the horror of what he did becomes more and more intense. Help in its multiple forms fails to reduce the mental suffering, and eventually partners, friends and colleagues distance themselves. This is because they feel helpless and hurt, often upset and offended that their efforts haven't been useful or appreciated. This is a critical phase in the officer's life because invariably he turns on everyone, lashing out and alienating those around him. Is this game over for him? For many it is, no longer able to be employed by the department, or not wanting to have anything to do with the hierarchy, blaming them for not providing adequate support, this despite the police force *in the majority* coming to his aid. On the plus side however, time is the healer in many instances—especially so we've noted in America where police shootings are more prevalent—the officer recovering from the deepest of depressions, perhaps not always returning operationally, but certainly able to function at a desk job."

John had been slouching in his chair, but Marjorie's news caused him to almost slide off it.

The sight was so comical she couldn't help but laugh. "John, John ... in your wildest dreams do you *really* believe you and Michael qualify as level three contenders?"

"Well, er ... no. I don't even consider myself a level one."

Marjorie grew serious. "*Now hold on.* This is your first shooting where an offender has died, right?"

"It is."

"Then you're stage one whether you like it or not. And that's how I'm going to write up my report." She cautioned him with the lift of one brow as he started to protest. "For you *not* to be stage one means you have psychopathic tendencies, in other words no empathy ... is that what you want me to put in my statement?"

"If you're asking me what empathy I have or had for Sergey being put down like the mongrel dog he was, well I can tell you, I *am* a psychopath, because on the empathy scale where he's concerned I'm not sure I register anything at all."

Marjorie cocked her head as a warning. "A word of advice. If and when you're questioned by your superiors, *do NOT repeat what you've just said to me.* Play the game and admit all police shootings are a tragedy. Work on the fact that in this instance it was unavoidable and saved lives. Like I explained, play the right cards and you'll come out of this ok."

John's eyes met Ballard's, but no support was offered, rather a resigned shrug indicating there was no choice but to wear Marjorie's assessment on the chin. "Think about it Johno, at least this approach gives us a slim *chance* at remaining operational."

An acquiescing grunt of submission erupted from John, aware he needed to quit while still ahead.

Marjorie began writing copious notes in her folder, but was interrupted as the conference room door burst open, with Ken, Bobby and Susan charging in. Without any apology they covered the last steps to where Ballard and John were sitting, flushed in the face and out of breath. Realising an operational necessity was afoot, Marjorie rolled her chair back to afford the detectives more space.

Gulping air, Ken blurted, "We think Igor's downstairs. He's demanding to see both of you."

Confused, John uttered, "Igor! The Russian? Downstairs in the foyer?" There was a heavy dose of incredulity in his voice.

Susan took up the commentary. "We knew you were both in a meeting with Marjorie when we got the call from reception. Thinking it best not to disturb you, Ken went down instead."

"And Igor's *still* in the foyer?" John continued to have difficulty getting his head around the announcement.

Ken did his best to fill in the blanks. "In disguise mind you ... and a bloody good one at that. He's dressed as an old man, glasses, beard, raggedy clothes, walking stick and all. I've seen the identikit photo and all I can say is, disguise or no, if this guy *isn't* Igor then I'll hand in my resignation."

Ballard evaluated the situation, demanding of Susan, "Did you bring your car in today?"

Susan's ringlets bobbed. "Yes, it's in the carpark."

Ballard looked to John, aware that what he was about to ask wouldn't be to his partner's liking. "Great. So it's only Ken that Igor saw, not yourself and Bobby?"

They nodded as John tensed, convinced he knew what was coming.

"Susan, I want you to get in your car and park in Spencer Street, just down from our building. Bobby, you hang about on the footpath near the entrance and *try* to look unobtrusive. John and I will go and see what this is all about. Igor will have some diabolical escape plan so there's no chance we'll be able to arrest him. When he's about to leave we'll phone you both. Do your best to keep him in sight until John and I get in the Bentley and take over. John's car is too obvious with all its aerials, and if Igor gets picked up in his Aston Martin, the Bentley's the only thing that will match its speed."

The pained expression on John's face grew in intensity.

"Under no circumstances are you to approach this guy." Ballard's eyes were fierce. "Ken, while Susan and Bobby are waiting for our call, ring Tim and have him scramble a team on the road who can move in—assuming we haven't lost him—and hopefully arrest this bastard. Also give Tim a full description of Igor's disguise so his guys have *some* idea who they're looking for. As well, have Tim arrange for PolAir to be overhead. Are we clear what has to be done? Any questions?"

Although disappointed he wasn't to be in the hunt, Ken confirmed along with Susan and Bobby that they were up to speed. Turning, all three raced to the door.

John addressed Marjorie who was listening in, fascinated. "Sorry about that, but as you can see, Igor's a big fish we need to reel in."

She appeared perfectly at ease. "I'll get started on your reports. I've got enough to make a solid recommendation, and don't worry John, it *will* be favourable ... but please don't go punching any more detectives. There's a limit to how much protection the AC can offer you guys."

Catching her last words, Ballard and John collided at the conference room door in their haste to get to the lift.

With the descent seemingly in slow motion, John punished the ground floor button for no apparent reason other than to settle his nerves. "Mike, to front up like this, Igor must be sporting bloody gigantic cahoonas. And you're right, he'll have some devious plan that'll blow up in our face should we try to arrest him."

Ballard was tight lipped. "I know this is a big ask of Susan and Bobby, but everything is happening so fast there's no alternative to ensure the bastard stays in sight until we're able to tail him in the Bentley ... assuming he goes by car. By the time we're done with him in the foyer, Tim's team should be almost on the road, backed up by PolAir and hopefully between them they can pull off the arrest of the century."

Reaching the ground floor, John's shoulder collided with the opening door due to his impatience to exit the lift. Ballard grabbed his arm. "Take it easy. We're here to *listen*, and keep the bugger with us for as long as possible."

John dropped his head, sheepish. "Yeah, sorry, it's just that this is—"

Ballard cut in. "I know Johno. But let's see what he wants

first before jumping in the deep end."

They headed over to the lounge area of the foyer where a number of sofas and armchairs were positioned for use by the general public while they waited to be attended to. Sitting with his back to them was an old man with grey, matted hair. Dressed in shabby clothing, with both hands resting on the crook of a walking stick propped between his knees, Igor was hunched forward as though in considerable arthritic pain.

Moving in front of him, the detectives assessed the man, each concluding Ken was indeed on the money. In spite of the sheer brilliance of the disguise, it was apparent Igor hadn't bothered to wear contact lenses, the returned steel-like gaze proof positive this was indeed a key member of The Board, an elite tactician and expert assassin.

Not bothering to shake hands, Ballard requested, "You asked to see us?"

Igor remained seated, unperturbed by the psychological imbalance posed by the two detectives towering over him. His penetrating gaze morphed into one of mild amusement. "As you'll have guessed I have limited time, after which, should I *not* walk out the front door, many of your brethren will die."

Despite wishing he had resisted the urge, John checked around him but saw nothing out of the ordinary, assuming the proposed threat would originate externally.

Desperate to retort '*but we'll take you down with us*', Ballard answered, "We're still waiting."

Igor's increasing amusement accentuated his crow's feet. "Actually, I'm here to do you and your department a favour."

A snort of derision escaped John's lips. Levelling a measured stare at John, Igor continued, "The Ndrangheta are becoming a thorn in our side, and as such my ..." he hesitated, choosing his words with care, "my organisation has decided ..."

"You mean The Board, or as you prefer to call them, Cobet." Ballard thought it best to clarify proceedings.

"Yes indeed. My organisation has decided this inconvenient group needs to be taught a serious lesson. That said, we've questioned why we should soil our hands when your police force is perfectly equipped to do the dirty work for us."

Again John couldn't contain himself. "So you're classifying the Ndrangheta as a mere inconvenience?"

A dismissive, almost imperious wave of Igor's hand, which was clothed in a moth-eaten mitten, preceded, "They're Italian, we're Russian. But let's not waste time obfuscating." He pointed to his watch, a battered timepiece with a scratched face and a well-worn leather band, the thoroughness of the man's disguise as expert as anything created by a Hollywood costumer. "Ndrangheta have in their possession two cannisters of highly refined nuclear waste. I'm aware you've been asking yourselves what *can* they ... or more to the point ... what *will* they do with this material?"

He paused, enjoying how he was building tension, Ballard and John resisting the urge to expedite the Russian's delivery, remaining silent in fearful anticipation of what they were about to hear.

Igor didn't fail them. "Ndrangheta intend to pollute your Thomson Reservoir with this radioactive waste, rendering over sixty percent of Melbourne's current domestic water supply useless should your government fail to pay a substantial sum of money."

Both detectives stiffened, their worst fears realised. While Ballard felt obligated to go through the motions, his gut told him Igor wouldn't risk arrest by inventing such an outrageous story were it not true. "How do you know this?"

The Russian struggled to his feet, the acting so convincing that Ballard had difficulty linking the figure before him with the supreme athlete who less than four months prior had clambered up the container crane at the docks so surefootedly. Reading the detective's mind, Igor looked at him sideways, as if questioning his sanity. "How do I know this? The Ndrangheta are our enemy, it's my business to know everything they're doing."

In an attempt to claw back at least some psychological advantage, Ballard took a risk. "Rumour has it you're playing both ends against the middle."

The steely eyes grew even colder, then relaxed, once more exercising their neighbouring crow's feet. "Ah, so you *have* been chatting with Vincenzo. Lovely man. Smart too. Say hello to him for me next time you meet." He gave an exaggerated, almost theatrical sigh, enjoying every moment of his pantomime. In a heartbeat he turned serious. "No, we've no interest in stealing cannisters of nuclear waste, that's for others to squabble over. Our overriding objective is to destroy your storage facility. Something made significantly more difficult now your military have taken control."

Despite every effort not to, Ballard's mouth slackened, amazed at Igor's depth of knowledge regarding current police activities and strategy; not to mention his cavalier attitude while standing amongst dozens of detectives as they crisscrossed the foyer.

Covering for his partner momentarily lost for words, John demanded, "We need details! When and how are the Ndrangheta going to pollute the reservoir?" The question came out stilted, the Russian's bombshell still sinking in.

"I *was* hoping your surveillance teams in the Yarra Ranges

might have located the cannister for us by now. Alas they haven't had any luck." He clicked his tongue in disgust. "Sloppy surveillance by any standard, but we live in hope."

Again Ballard's mouth slackened at the Russian's breadth of knowledge, his surprise replicated by John who managed to recover first, re-asking, "We're still waiting ... *when and how*? And what are they going to do with the second cannister?"

Hooking a thumb towards him while addressing Ballard, Igor quipped, "My, my, your colleague here is *very* persistent. I'll give him that much."

The Russian's jocular manner proved too much for John, Ballard having to place a calming hand on his partner's arm lest he destroy any chance they might have in determining what Igor's real intent was.

In a flamboyant sweep of his arm to inspect his watch, the rapid movement out of character with his old man disguise, the Russian exclaimed, "Must rush, time's money." Without a backward glance he shuffled towards the automatic doors, confident he was untouchable; at no risk of being arrested, his arrogance generated a howl of rage from John.

"The shithead's messing with our heads Mike, and he's doing a bloody fine job of it! So ... do we believe him?"

Wincing, Ballard declared, "What choice do we have?"

Spinning on their heels, both men raced through the turnstiles and punched the lift button to take them to the carpark. Predicting John's request, Ballard thrust the Bentley's key into his partner's hand while he snatched up his mobile, speed dialling Susan's number.

She answered on the first ring. "I can see him Michael, he's walking south along Spencer Street towards the Southern Cross station. Bobby's tailing him just in case he takes the train."

Having piled into the Bentley, John fired the V12 before launching out of the parking bay and heading down to ground level, the GT's tyres protesting on the smooth concrete surface.

Bracing himself against the door, Ballard responded. "Good thinking Susan, he may well do that—"

A pause from the young detective was followed by a hurried, "*I take that back*, he's ... he's stopped and is now on his mobile." Susan's voice was upbeat as it came through the speaker system, delighted at the prospect of being a key player in shadowing Igor. Ballard slipped his mobile into his coat pocket, no longer needing to hold onto it.

Impatient at the delay of the metal security barrier's slow retraction into its recess, John floored the accelerator the instant it was safe to do so. Weaving between traffic, a narrow gap allowed him to head up the Latrobe Street tram tracks where he jumped the red light, swinging hard right into Spencer Street. Ballard braced his forearm against the door. "Easy tiger ... he's just up ahead, on the far side of the street. After our chase down at Geelong he knows what this beast looks like. We don't want to spook him. Susan's got this covered."

John swung into a no-standing zone, hunching over the steering wheel, his concentration redlining.

Ballard got back to Susan. "What about the SOG team and PolAir, have you heard from Ken?"

"I have. He's given Igor's details to Tim who claims a team will be on the road within ten minutes ... that was five minutes ago. As for PolAir, it's on the way back from the Yarra Valley ... but it's still twenty minutes out."

John grunted, "The SOG will be in a Balkan which is no match should he be picked up in—"

"*Say again Susan.*" Ballard cut his partner short.

"A black Mercedes van has just pulled up—"

"*Shit.*" John thumped the steering wheel in frustration. "We're stuffed Mike."

"Not necessarily Johno. At least it's not the Aston Martin."

Susan maintained a running commentary. "He's got in and ... and ..."

"AND?" Both men shouted at once.

"The Merc has U-turned and is heading south along Spencer ... I'll keep track of them, hanging back so I'm not spotted—" She broke off before claiming, "*Get in Bobby, get in!*" Another pause was followed by, "Bobby's with me. I'll give him the mobile while I drive."

Bobby came on the line, breathless from what would have been a mad dash across Spencer Street. "Jeez, boss. The bastard's one jump ahead of us every step of the way."

John pulled away from the curb, cursing a taxi driver who cut in front of him. "Are you armed?"

An affirming chorus followed.

"Ok, keep the van in sight. We'll stay behind you for the time being." Ballard hesitated. "As you haven't got much to do at the moment Bobby, keep this line open while you ring Tim on *your* mobile to find out where he's at. Leave that line open as well."

John considered Ballard's light-hearted jibe, smiling at the mental image of his protégé having a mobile in each ear. Seconds later, Bobby was heard in rapid fire discussion with Tim.

Ballard laughed. "He's not the only one working two mobiles Johno. Give me yours. I need to contact Ken and have him notify the AC of Igor's warning."

John reached inside his jacket, his eyes remaining focussed on the traffic around him; he handed over his mobile, steering one-handed. Seconds later Ballard had Ken on the line. He detailed the threat posed to Melbourne's water supply and for the AC to coordinate a response, advising Surveillance to focus their efforts on the Thomson Dam, ensuring they were backed up by SOG personnel at all times.

Having voiced his dismay at the alarming news, Ken disconnected. Taking back his mobile, John stated with more than an air of despondency, "Christ, can you imagine the utter chaos were the Thomson ever to be taken out? And focussing on our immediate issue, now we know the death squad have picked up Igor, any arrest will have to be via Tim's guys. The problem with that is he won't be able to match their pace in the Balkan." He struck the steering wheel. "I don't hold out much hope we're going to—"

"Tim and his crew are on Spencer Street! They'll be coming up behind you." Bobby's voice was sharp with excitement.

Susan came back on, her enthusiasm infectious. "The Merc has turned right into Flinders Street and it's jumped the red light."

"*Do the same, do the same.*" Bobby urged Susan on. Seconds went by before Bobby cried, "Mike, I'm convinced he's heading for the Burnley Tunnel!"

John decelerated hard, the GT's carbon ceramics working overtime. Ballard shot a confused look towards his partner as passing motorists tooted their anger at having to swerve around the Bentley.

"Think about it Mike, if the van *does* take the tunnel, our best course of action is to rip up Flinders and turn right into Kings Way which has an on-ramp to the tunnel. This'll put us in *front* of Igor."

"Good thinking my man. It's a wonder the death squad didn't do that in the first place ... perhaps they've changed their mind regarding where they initially wanted to go." Ballard switched focus. "Bobby, the second you know for sure the van's taking the tunnel, contact Tim. Have him go via the King Street on-ramp. And let us know if anything changes."

"Roger that."

John looked across at Ballard, amused at how excited Bobby and Susan were at getting out of the office and away from their endless grind of brief preparation. The first against Deputy Commissioner Salisbury arrested at the Melbourne Club, suspected of being part of The Board's Australian cell; the other briefs against Igor and Tatiana Olegovich, the latter having unceremoniously despatched her Russian husband over the balcony in their Toorak mansion, the husband a Board cell leader.

After glancing in the rear-vision mirror, John twisted in his seat for a better look. "Bloody hell, Tim's just pulled up behind us."

Ballard peered around, the front of the gunmetal-grey Balkan looming large in the rear window. "Wait here. I'll nip back and update Tim. Toot if we have to move out." Scrambling from the confines of the GT, Ballard met Tim who had alighted from the Balkan, a ten-shot Smith &Wesson pistol strapped to his thigh, his communications mike anchored at the corner of his mouth.

The SOG commander wasted no time. "Fill me in."

Ballard began a rapid-fire update, detailing how it was thought Igor and several of the death squad were driving into the Burnley Tunnel, the King Street on-ramp the most direct route to head them off. He was interrupted as John leapt from the GT, bellowing, "The tunnel, it's on!"

Tim raced back to the Balkan, shouting over his shoulder, "Get going! We'll be right behind you."

CHAPTER
14

Ballard slid onto the GT's Mulliner leather seat in one fluid motion, the door closing beside him with a satisfying thud as John accelerated into the traffic. The Bentley's acoustic-suppressing windscreen and glazed side windows minimised the brutal growl of the six-litre V12 as John floored the accelerator, the twenty-one-inch Pirelli tyres gripping the road like glue.

Ballard noted the sheer delight on his partner's face. "It's good to see a man enjoying his work—"

"Christ, why wouldn't I? I'm driving a bloody rocket ship worth nearly four hundred big ones, and today we have the real possibility of nailing this damn Russian once and for all."

Ballard agreed while casting a cautious eye on the side mirror. "That's great John, but remember, that bloody great grey thing behind us is nearly eight tonnes and doesn't have a lot of acceleration. Its top speed is a hundred and thirty klicks with a tail wind. We don't want to leave Tim and his crew in our dust."

John wasn't convinced as he swept left into Flinders Street, choosing the tram tracks for a clear pathway ahead, surging hard towards Kings Way. "Why not? Think of us as their forward scouts."

Watching out for oncoming cars as his partner drifted the GT onto Kings Way, Ballard reached forward, activating the Bentley's navigation system to bring up a map of the surrounding area. "Maybe so, but we need to be mindful that Igor's with his goons who could take us out without breaking sweat."

Concentrating on his driving as he wove between slower vehicles, John did his best to pretend he hadn't heard. Grinning, Ballard spoke into the GT's Bluetooth mike. "Bobby, are you there?"

The reply through the speakers was instant. "Yes boss."

"An update if you will."

Loud throat clearing preceded, "Susan's doing a fabulous job keeping the Merc in sight without getting too close. We've managed to get the rego number, but it'll be a stolen plate for sure ... do you want to write it down?"

John leaned forward, snarling at the mike, "While it's a fact that we're older than your damn parents, laddie, I'm sure if we repeat the number several times aloud it just may well stick in our foggy grey matter—*get on with it.*"

It was all Ballard could do not to laugh as Bobby blurted, "Oh ... er, righto ... One-golf-echo-eight-foxtrot-lima. Do you want me to repeat that?"

Sarcasm dripping from each syllable, John snapped, "Yeah, why not."

"One-golf-echo—"

Ballard grinned. "Bobby, Bobby, it's ok, he's pulling your leg."

Chortling laughter from Susan could be heard in the background.

Undeterred, Bobby added, "The traffic at the moment is at a crawl, we're level with the Power Street off-ramp and the Merc hasn't taken it, so they're definitely committed to the tunnel."

Ballard studied the thirty-one-centimetre navigation screen, analysing where the King Street on-ramp for the tunnel would position them in relation to the current location of the Mercedes van. "At this rate we're a certainty to be in front of the buggers." Glancing over his shoulder he was surprised to see the Balkan so close behind, reasoning that motorists would be keen to steer clear of the intimidating vehicle bearing down on them, its headlights flashing and siren blaring.

Checking the mirror, John commented, "That's some driving back there. I must compliment the guy when all this is over."

Ballard backhanded him. "Keep your mind on the job. The last thing I need is to have to explain to Robert why his very expensive plaything has been dinted. Speaking of the ex-army colonel, thank God he can't see what we're doing to his prized possession."

Not bothering to reply, John wove his magic through the traffic, seizing gaps where he saw them, the end-result a rapid descent into the tunnel proper. As he thrust his sunglasses to the top of his head, the Bentley's Bi-Xenon headlights came alive. Flicking a glance to his right he merged seamlessly into the tunnel's nearside lane, a check of the mirror satisfying him that the Balkan had done the same.

"So what now Mike? Do we drive at this pace and wait for the death squad to catch up so Tim can attempt to stop them while hopefully not creating havoc in the tunnel, or do we wait until we're out on the freeway where there's a bit more wriggle room?"

Ballard hesitated, looking back to confirm the Balkan was still with them. "It's a hard one John. Attempting anything in the tunnel could be disastrous for other motorists, as well as difficult for emergency services should we need them."

The monotonous flash of the strip lighting overhead was hypnotic as the two men grappled with what they should do.

"Back off Susan! The bastards are shooting at motorists."

Bobby's panicked voice caused John to decelerate.

"Bobby, Susan! Are you alright? What's happening?" Ballard was rigid in his seat, fearing the worst for his two detectives.

His voice high-pitched, Bobby exclaimed, "We're ok. I don't know if they spotted us, but the death squad are shooting out the tyres of the vehicles around them ..." There was a lengthy pause. "Over there Susan! Take the gap. *TAKE THE GAP!*"

A stream of profanity echoed over the speakers from both detectives. "Mike, it's utter chaos here. Cars are sideways and have run into each other, basically all three lanes are blocked off. We're stuck. We can't go any further. It's clear this is Igor's plan to stop anyone following him."

"Where's the van now?"

"It's pulled up twenty metres ahead of the logjam ... *Christ—*"

"What is it?" Ballard silently cursed their remoteness from what was unfolding behind them.

"An Aston Martin ... Susan, is that Igor's? ... *yes, it is!* Boss, Igor's wheels have stopped alongside the van and Igor has just hopped out and got into the passenger seat of the Aston Martin. He's taken an automatic rifle with him. Both vehicles are now heading in your direction. You should see them—"

"Bobby, hang up your phone to Tim. I need to contact him."

Without waiting for a reply, Ballard speed dialled Tim's number.

The SOG commander got in first, having overheard Bobby's last comments, his voice filled with tension. "Mike, I need you to keep driving and leave this to us. I'm up here in the turret. When either the Merc, the Aston Martin or both show up I'll take out their tyres and my lads will do the rest. By the time either of those vehicles get here all the traffic in front of the pileup should have driven past us. That'll give us an empty stretch of tunnel to deal with these bastards when they get alongside."

John shook his head and shouted into the mike, "Pull up beside us Tim and have one of your lads hand over a spare rifle! At present all we've got by way of weapons is our respective willies, and mine isn't shooting too straight these days."

Determined his request should be acceded to, he checked the mirror before stabbing the brake, forcing the Balkan to do the same, pulling up alongside. Lowering the driver's window, John reached out and took the assault rifle offered by the SOG member in full tactical gear.

Atop the turret, Tim bellowed down to them. "Now get the hell out of here and let us do our job!"

Grinning up at him while throwing a salute, John left the window down as he accelerated forward. "If Tim thinks we're going to ride off into the sunset while all this action is unfolding, he's got another thing coming. I'll maintain a hundred metres in front of him Mike and no more."

Ballard grunted as he familiarised himself with the weapon. Leaning across he rehearsed pointing the barrel out the open window, John hunching forward to provide him additional room. "This is going to be bloody loud in your ears John. It fires twelve rounds a second."

John turned to him, wide-eyed. "*Oh great*. Then make it worthwhile, ok?" He fixed his gaze on the rear-vision mirror as Ballard twisted in his seat, staring out the back window, both taking in the tunnel behind them which was empty of vehicles except for the Balkan a distance to their rear.

Stiffening, Ballard declared, "Here comes the van. So Igor's letting the heavies clear a path for him."

John involuntarily slowed but was urged on by Ballard who insisted they maintain a healthy distance from the action. "We don't want to get in Tim's way."

Grudgingly John sped up, swearing under his breath while Ballard reached across, resting the barrel of the rifle on the leather trim of the open driver's window.

The Mercedes van approached at high speed in the right-hand lane, eighty metres behind the Balkan. Despite the distance to the Bentley, the chatter of automatic gunfire being laid down by Tim in a lethal wave of 5.56millimetre NATO rounds could be heard echoing in the confines of the tunnel.

At first the barrage appeared not to slow the van's progress, but in what seemed like slow motion, the vehicle lurched to the left before completing a full three hundred and sixty degrees slide as it passed the Balkan, finishing up twenty metres ahead. So focussed were Ballard and John on the immediate spectacle, they didn't spot the Aston Martin approaching from the rear, its front passenger window open with Igor firing up at the armoured vehicle's turret. Tim failed to respond, possibly reloading after emptying his magazine into the van.

Hitting the brakes in one tortuous scream of smoking

rubber, the Aston Martin passed the stationary Mercedes at what John estimated to be forty kilometres an hour, Igor firing a continuous burst, shattering the van's windows and screen, eliminating any possibility of the survivors divulging Board secrets.

John roared his anger. "The murderous bastard! He *has* to be taken out Mike." Without waiting for a reply, he slammed the Bentley into reverse, backing up in a cloud of burning rubber as Tim reloaded and unleashed a fresh burst at the Aston Martin which began accelerating away from the Balkan.

Ballard squeezed off a barrage as the Aston Martin shot past, Igor thankfully not returning fire, having also emptied his magazine. John braked hard, pinning Ballard against his seat, the latter moaning, "Don't ask me how John, but I missed taking out the bugger's tyres."

His face animated, and with a maniacal chuckle, John quipped, "In that case I feel a *need for speed* coming on." Planting his foot, the GT's eight hundred newton metres of torque hurled the vehicle forward, the Aston Martin now at least four hundred metres ahead.

"What the bloody hell do you think you're doing? Come back you damn fools!" Tim's voice thundered out of the ten-speaker audio system as though he were in the vehicle with them. Ballard looked at John whose eyebrows were raised, questioning whether the SOG commanders order should be obeyed, only to be rewarded with a terse, "Go for it Johno, what have we got to lose?"

Licking his lips, John steered the GT into the centre lane of the tunnel, the V12 howling its pleasure. He leaned towards the mike. "Er Tim ... think of us as your forward scouts. Get hold of PolAir and see if they're able to track the bastard. We'll maintain our distance behind Igor ... *I promise.*"

"Don't give me that bullshit you dopey bastard. You're going to get yourselves killed at this rate." Tim barked an order to one of his team to find out the location of the police helicopter. "Ok, keep your heads down and stay on the line. We'll follow you as best we can."

Ballard checked his weapon's magazine, noting he only had five rounds left. "Somehow we got out of that unscathed Johno. Well done."

"I heard that!" Tim's voice roared over the speakers once more. Ballard made a zipping motion across his lips. "Ok, let's see if this beast can make any inroads on the Aston Martin."

A moan of frustration escaped Tim.

No sooner had Ballard uttered his challenge to John than they emerged into bright sunshine, the tunnel now behind them. The Aston Martin was still four hundred metres ahead in the left lane. "So he's choosing to stay on CitiLink rather than take the Burnley Street exit." Ballard was tense, straining forward in his seat.

In stark contrast, John was relaxed, focussing on his driving, hands light, ten to two on the steering wheel as the digital speedo climbed past two hundred and forty kilometres an hour, the deserted three lanes as smooth as any German autobahn. A frown crossed his brow. "I'm beginning to think your target practice on the Aston Martin may have been partially successful Mike. We're definitely closing the gap, and for a vehicle capable of well over three hundred, the driver up there is either having engine troubles or Igor has asked him to slow down so we can catch him ... and we know what could mean."

Overhearing the chatter, Tim came over the speakers.

"Don't get any closer you two. I wasn't going to say this but Kathryn and I are getting married in a fortnight, and as her big brother she wants you to give her away. Michael—be sensible and *don't* cock things up by getting yourselves killed. And for your information, PolAir should be overhead any second. They've been given the Aston Martin's description, but the only trouble is there's nobody onboard the chopper equipped to take on Igor."

Tim's declaration regarding his sister stunned Ballard, but he thrust the announcement to one side. "Ok Tim. We'll update you as we go. How far back are you?"

"We should be out of the tunnel in the next thirty seconds. Where are you?"

"Crossing the Yarra near Scotch College—"

"Didn't I tell you something's wrong with the Aston Martin?" John thrust an accusing finger in front of him. "It's possible you punctured the petrol tank or a radiator hose or something."

John was perplexed as the Aston Martin was now a mere two hundred metres in front. Without warning it pulled sharply off the freeway and into the service lane, coming to a complete halt. Seconds later the passenger door was flung open and Igor stepped out, still clutching the assault rifle, no longer feigning an old man demeanour. Casually watching the approaching Bentley, he wasn't in any hurry, the driver joining him, also carrying an assault rifle.

John stood on the GT's brakes, the vehicle sliding to an eye-popping halt in the service lane. "Here we go again Mike. A bloody Mexican standoff with this guy holding all the aces, knowing he can shoot our eyebrows off at this range should he choose to."

Ballard relayed the current situation to Tim who ordered,

"We'll be there in less than a minute. Stay in the car. PolAir's above you and can track those two if they make a run for it."

Seemingly carefree, Igor went to the boot of the Aston Martin with the driver who extracted what turned out to be a grappling hook and a coil of rope.

"*YOU'VE GOT TO BE SHITTING ME.* They just *happen* to have one of those in the boot?" John sat open-mouthed, stunned at what he was witnessing.

Ballard strained forward. "Tim, you'd better step on it. The guys are making a run for it over the sound wall—"

"They're what?"

"You heard me. I'd say thirty to forty seconds will see them on the far side. Considering the athleticism Igor displayed down at the docks, this'll be a piece of cake for him."

A stream of profanity erupted from the speakers, with Tim shouting at his driver to continue putting his foot down. Watching in disbelief, Ballard and John saw the driver swing the grappling hook in ever-increasing circles prior to letting it fly up and over the top of the sound wall. A retraction of the excess rope and several hard yanks saw Igor clambering up the side of the wall like a mountain goat. Having discarded his assault rifle, he reached the top in record time. Following closely behind him, the driver made heavier work of the climb, and was halfway up when Igor leaned out and callously shot him in the head with a handgun. Dropping like a stone, the driver crumpled at the base of the wall, Igor retracting the rope and confiscating the hook before disappearing.

John was speechless, and while not surprised at Igor's brutal actions, he was enraged by the casual manner in which the Russian had eliminated any chance of the death squad members being captured and divulging intel that may impact The Board.

The high-pitched whine of jet engines overhead heralded the arrival of PolAir. Peering through the Bentley's sunroof, Ballard and John watched as the chopper hovered above them before commencing its tracking of Igor's movements on the far side of the wall. At the same time the Balkan slid to a halt alongside, Tim scrambling from the vehicle with two of his team, Ballard and John doing the same from the GT. The SOG commander approached while his officers sprinted ahead towards the Aston Martin, flinging grappling hooks over the wall and clambering up the side, their rifles strapped to their backs.

"Michael, John, your work's done here. And thanks for not getting yourselves killed. Go back to the office and I'll update you later as to whether we've caught the bastard." His broad grin expressed his heartfelt relief that his colleagues were unharmed. Hopping onto the Balkan's running-board he was driven forward to the stranded Aston Martin. Grasping the rope, he effortlessly scaled the sound wall, disappearing over the top.

Ballard checked his watch. "My, my Johno, would you believe it's just turned 3 p.m. Isn't it amazing how much fun can be jammed into a few short hours?"

Glancing up again, both men saw PolAir peel off to the west, dropping lower, hopefully advising Tim and his team where they should be looking, the intel minimising the risk the officers faced against the elite Spetsnaz soldier who would stop at nothing to remain at large.

Feeling bone-weary, Ballard and John slumped back into the Bentley's form-hugging seats, the adrenalin rush now dissipating, leaving them exhausted but grateful they had survived; at the same time they were angry that their objective of arresting Igor was as unresolved as ever.

Firing the motor, John nudged Ballard on the arm, his look questioning.

Ballard responded. "To the office, Jeeves—slow and steady if you will. We've had enough excitement for one day."

Ignoring him, John planted his foot, the GT responding willingly.

CHAPTER
15

Greying, bushy eyebrows hooded the AC's commanding blue eyes which were locked onto Ballard's and John's, the latter wilting under the senior officer's steadfast gaze. The time was 3.45. "Yet again you ignored the advice I gave you this morning, going about your business with the subtlety of two raging bulls."

Robert Mayne couldn't contain a snort of amusement.

Not done, the AC added, "Thankfully the debacle in the Burnley Tunnel resulted in little more than a bunch of angry drivers and a shit load of insurance claims ... but it *could* have ended in a bloodbath—it appears the gods were on your side." The brutal stare was maintained, even Ballard having difficulty absorbing the laser-like scrutiny, aware how close he and John had come to receiving a departmental disciplinary charge.

In an attempt to restore a modicum of dignity while presenting a spirited defence, Ballard blurted, "With Igor such a prize, sir, and limited time to assemble an immediate SOG team, I made a personal decision to track him until Tim's forces could be engaged to take over."

The AC's following words were a relief to the detectives' ears. "It may surprise you to know that in your shoes I would have done exactly the same. It's just galling that the bugger keeps slipping through our fingers."

John flicked a relieved glance at Ballard before mumbling, "Thank you sir. Nothing like this will *ever* happen again."

The AC's seat protested as he lurched forward, his forefinger stabbing the tabletop to emphasise his point. "Detective, I suggest you *not* make statements you cannot possibly keep."

A louder snort escaped Robert, the ballistic expert making no attempt to hide his mirth while John's shoulders rose in a 'who me' gesture, convincing the AC of the detective's total lack of sincerity.

Clearing his throat, the senior officer gazed around the table, taking in his audience. To his left Bernard sat soaking up the vibe of the briefing, also enjoying the exchanges. Alongside him, Jordan was busily scribbling notes in his folder, Ballard assuming the soldier was about to address the gathering. Assistant Commissioner Gerhart Müller sat to attention to the AC's right, his fingers interlocked, a thoughtful expression in place, keen for the briefing to progress to more pressing matters. To Müller's left, Ken's demeanour made it clear he was praying he wouldn't be called upon to contribute, but having been prewarned, he knew that to be a futile wish. Alongside him, and in total contrast, James Patterson exuded abundant self-confidence. Like Robert Mayne, he was amused at Ballard's and John's discomfort, having winked at both men moments prior. His shoulder almost touching the ASIO agent's, Robert sported yet another outlandish bowtie, a jade-green masterpiece, by all accounts one recently added to his collection.

Waving a hand towards Jordan, the AC directed, "I'm glad

you could make it back on such short notice. I'd like an update on the current status at the storage site, and also your technical team's efforts in cracking the remaining files on the iPad."

Looking sharp in his army uniform, Jordan got straight to the point. "All of the resources I requested ..." he cracked a wry smile, "except the attack helicopter ... are in place. The barrack quarters that I had some doubts about considering the remoteness of the location are working fine, so on that front we're up and running. The chief of army is negotiating with the State Government regarding the duration of the occupation." He appeared momentarily perplexed. "I'm hearing on the grapevine that the Government is contemplating establishing a permanent community nearby. It'll have facilities such as housing, shops, a post office, a bank, recreational amenities, even a pool and a cinema—all the prerequisite infrastructure to maintain a permanent civilian workforce. This will be separate from the Ouyen township due to the area's inadequate rental accommodation, and what can only be described as the location's basic services. I get the distinct impression the town's residents are hell-bent on keeping the status quo. As for the army, it will continue to rotate troops through the base making the site a permanent fixture. All this of course is subject to the world's nuclear waste being secured in the medium to long term."

The concept of a small rural town springing up in close proximity to the army base highlighted to all present the measures the State Government was willing to adopt to secure the enormous revenues on offer.

Ballard raised his hand, with the AC nodding his way. "Sir, during our discussion with Igor, he made it clear *stealing* the cannisters was not The Board's priority ... rather destroying the storage site was. This despite him being fully aware of the military muscle and hardware now in place. John and I didn't consider his comment to be an idle threat." Ballard swung his attention to Jordan. "In *your* opinion, what sized force and what weaponry would The Board need to employ to realistically overwhelm your defences?"

Jordan paused, pinching the bridge of his nose as he reflected. "We believe they have two options. The first would be to flood us with personnel and equipment, upwards of fifty to seventy well trained, highly equipped elite soldiers, assuming they weren't picked up first on our radar and taken out with artillery and anti-personnel mines. The second option, and the one most likely to be adopted is the Trojan horse technique. This is where a small number of personnel infiltrate the compound seizing key hostages, or conversely smuggling key hostages in with them, attempting to convince my troops to open the storage site. I've personally instructed all the soldiers stationed there as to what their response must be should that situation eventuate—"

"And that is?" John asked with a degree of trepidation.

Jordan didn't mince words. "We're soldiers, we follow orders. Those orders are not to open the site to unauthorised personnel, even if the chief of defence or the prime minister are being held hostage, pure and simple."

John blinked several times as he digested the statement, with the AC breaking the uncomfortable silence. "Perfectly correct. So Jordan, be on the alert that The Board haven't given up on their original objective. A lot of money is at stake, and we all know that's what drives them." Changing subject, he asked, "And the iPad?"

Jordan was all over the request. "I know Michael pointed out that The Board isn't interested in stealing cannisters, but one of the files we cracked indicates there's to be a very important shipment out of Melbourne. While it doesn't specify what the cargo will be, on the face of it the cannisters have to be a possibility even though The Board didn't initially steal them."

"The ship's name?" The expectation on the AC's face was shameless.

"Unfortunately not listed, but we may get lucky if we crack more of the files."

"So no mention of when this mysterious ship is sailing?" The AC's expectation remained high.

"Yes, that *was* listed … in five days."

The AC turned to AC Müller. "That's got to narrow down the possibilities. Gerhart, could you follow up with Surveillance? Here's hoping we get lucky and get those damn cannisters back."

The counter terrorist commissioner accepted the instruction with a brief nod.

Reaching forward, the AC scooped up his mobile to make a call, barking, "Yes, send him in."

Within seconds a young man in civilian clothing entered the room; he was escorted by a uniformed officer, who after delivering the guest, turned and left. Settling at the far end of the table the young man appeared self-conscious, in sharp contrast to his rugby player physique and good looks. The AC put everyone's curiosity to rest. "I've invited Mr Trent Silverwood, a senior technical specialist with Melbourne Water along to provide us with expert advice as to how Melbourne's drinkable water is supplied."

Ballard whispered in John's ear, "In biblical terms, Trent means torrent … rather apt wouldn't you say?"

John's inscrutable look didn't go unnoticed by the AC who waved an acknowledging hand towards the specialist. "By way of explanation Trent, we've called you in here to advise us on a number of technical issues. As a law enforcement agency, we have to be on the front foot should a terrorist attack ever occur here in Victoria—whether it be against our electricity supply, our transport systems, our airports, or even our drinking water. By understanding more fully how these services operate, we as a police force are better equipped to defend them."

Ballard directed an innocent head turn towards his partner who picked up on his meaning, silently acknowledging the cunning ploy the AC was adopting to learn all he needed to know about Melbourne's water storage without divulging it was under threat.

Trent was nervous, acutely aware that he was the only civilian in the room. Taking stock of those present, he reached forward and grasped his glass of water, gulping nearly half the contents in one draught. Wiping his mouth with the back of his hand, he declared, "Yes, my manager explained you wanted information on the mechanics of how we supply the community with clean, drinkable water, and the processes we have in place to drought-proof Melbourne." Appearing hesitant, he asked, "Shall I begin?"

The AC smiled disarmingly. "Yes, please do. Remember young man, you're amongst friends here."

Trent eyed the group, and despite the AC's reassuring words, it was clear he didn't share the senior officer's assurance. "By way of history, Melbourne received its first piped water from the Yan Yean Reservoir in 1857. Subsequent prolonged drought periods necessitated constant increases and improvements to Melbourne's water storage, and in 1888 a large area of the upper Yarra Valley was reserved for that very purpose. The expansions continued over the next one hundred and thirty years, with the Thomson Reservoir completed in May 1983—this included the Thomson-Yarra tunnel which is three metres in diameter and thirty-five kilometres long. The reservoir itself is twenty-three kilometres in length, with a surface area of 2,230 hectares."

John watched as the faces around the table changed from interested to fascinated. He noted with amusement that even Ballard was caught up in the avalanche of statistics.

Realising he had won over his audience, Trent wound up his delivery. "The Thomson Reservoir has a capacity equating to sixty percent of Melbourne's total water storage, potentially holding a mind boggling 1,068 billion litres, or to put it another way, 428,000 Olympic swimming pools. This is four times the capacity of our next biggest reservoir.

Unable to contain himself, John blurted out, "And just as well Trent, because the time Michael spends under the shower is bloody outrageous."

Several sniggers erupted around the table, with the AC adding dryly, "Thank you for that piece of trivia John, and I won't bother asking how you happen to know this."

More laughter ensued. Robert rocked forward in his chair. "So what's the Thomson's current capacity?"

Trent's reply was instant. "One hundred percent. Most people don't know this but it's only ever been full four times. As I said, its sole purpose is to drought-proof Melbourne, allowed to fill in wet years so it can supplement the other reservoirs during times of drought."

Ballard caught Robert wincing, the ballistics expert processing the devastating impact should the reservoir be taken out of commission. Considered glances rippled around the table, all happy to leave the general thrust of the briefing to the AC. "So breaking this down to my level Trent, the Thomson Reservoir acts as a giant bucket supplementing Melbourne's water supply. Were it removed from the mix for any extended period, and for whatever reason, what would the effect be on Melburnians as a whole?"

Scratching his blonde mop of hair, Trent took his time to reply. "There are multiple variables at play here. If this were to occur during a prolonged drought period, immediate stage four restrictions would be implemented and life would be pretty grim for everyone. Depending on the length of time the reservoir was out of action, this may lead to *critical* water shortages, and despite the desalination plant at Wonthaggi working overtime, Melbourne's population, and industry in general would be subjected to ongoing draconian water restrictions. In fact, many vital industries would have to shut down, the majority permanently."

Thoughtful, the AC asked, "What's the desal plant capable of generating annually?"

"One hundred and fifty gigalitres, that's approximately one-third of Melbourne's yearly requirement."

"Is that a best-case scenario?" It was clear the AC was dubious of anything that private enterprise and government officials claimed, distrustful of their impartiality.

Trent hesitated, torn between his loyalty to the organisation employing him, and the reality of what the desalination plant could produce. "One hundred and fifty gigalitres is achievable providing the infrastructure holds up, but all complex systems fail at some point, requiring significant maintenance and repair. The reality is the plant was built as a short-term buffer to help Melburnians get through a dry period until the next winter, it's *not* a solution for multiple years on a continuous basis."

"Hmm." The AC inspected the ceiling, contemplating his next question. "Back onto the Thomson Reservoir, where does the water flow once its released?"

Again Trent was up to the task. "The Upper Yarra, then Silvan Reservoir, all via a nineteen-kilometre tunnel."

"Can the tunnel be opened and shut as required?" While assuming it was a rhetorical question, the AC asked anyway.

"Indeed it can."

"How long does that take?"

"Only a matter of minutes. I'm told ten to fifteen on average."

"Are there personnel onsite to do this around the clock?"

"No, but experienced staff *can* be available within the hour." For the first time a fleeting shadow of misgiving crossed Trent's face, alarmed at the direction the questioning was heading.

Sensing the young man's disquiet, the AC attempted to reassure him with a manufactured smile. "We're merely exploring all the options Trent. That way we can develop and test strategies which best address a potential catastrophe."

Still spooked, the Melbourne Water expert declared, "I'm not sure that there's much more I can add, other than to state the obvious. Without clean, drinkable water, Melbourne and its associated industries would shut down, as I said, many permanently."

Having rung to call the uniform officer back into the room, the AC flashed another benevolent smile towards Trent. "Thank you for your time and the excellent presentation Trent. Let's pray nothing untoward ever eventuates, but it would be foolhardy for us in our role as law enforcement not to prepare for such an eventuality. Again, my sincere appreciation for your time, and please pass on my gratitude to your manager."

Aware he was being dismissed, Trent hauled himself to his feet, then, with a nervous nod to all present, he allowed himself to be escorted from the room.

The moment the door shut the AC sighed long and hard, running his fingers through his hair, clearly disturbed by what he had learned. Like twin lasers his eyes locked onto Robert's. "I know I'm going to regret this Robert, but ... you're up next to detail what the impacts would be should these bastards release this damn material into the Thomson."

As Robert climbed to his feet, James raised a hand. "Kevin, before Robert gets underway, I need to inform you that I spoke with Vincenzo Ricardo prior to the meeting. He gave me some disturbing news that the Italians were less than truthful regarding what they included in their two cannisters. Not only is there U-235 in them, but there's ten kilograms of Caesium-137 as well."

Robert's whistle of shocked surprise drew everyone's attention, nobody quite sure why his features had suddenly tensed. Matching Robert's disquiet, Bernard's brow developed even more lines than usual, the retired CIA operative bracing for the worst.

The AC was in no doubt that a bombshell was about to be delivered. "I guess I don't need to ask whether James' revelation heralds more bad news Robert?"

The ballistics expert didn't hold back. "Indeed you don't sir. If Caesium-137 *is* in the mix, and released into the Thomson, then Melburnians are in deep doo-doo for a very long time." He checked around the table. "A mere twenty-seven kilograms of the stuff was released into the atmosphere after the Chernobyl explosion in 1986. Despite that low amount, high densities of radioactivity settled for a one-hundred-kilometre radius around the site. Further afield, dangerous levels of 137 were detected in northern and central parts of Scandinavia. Moreover, in a number of Swedish lakes the 137 content in the fish exceeded the legal limit for human consumption until 1992, and it's still a health risk today. It's been quoted by expert scientists that just four teaspoons of 137 exploded in a dirty bomb would contaminate an area of sixteen square kilometres."

Taking out his handkerchief he blew his nose noisily while everyone took in what he had just disclosed. "Moreover, while the half-life of 137 is only thirty years, Trent made it very clear that if the Thomson was out of commission for even a couple of years the impact on Melbourne and its population would be devastating." He began ticking the points off on his fingers. "For a start the desal plant would be in overdrive with a mad scramble to build several more, their completion not for several years, even if the builds were fast tracked. Secondly, the public would be justifiably distrustful of their drinking water, so much so they wouldn't want to drink or shower in the damn stuff for fear of getting seriously ill or dying. Businesses would collapse and there'd be a mass exodus out of Melbourne. Property prices would tank and the economy collapse—"

The AC raised a hand to halt the flood of misery pouring forth. "Ok Robert, we get the picture, and even if a fraction of what you're suggesting occurs, it'd result in an economic disaster that would take decades to recover from, if ever. So tell me, how *would* the Ndrangheta release this ... this 235 and 137 into the water?"

Robert's grim smile was more a baring of teeth. "Very carefully, that's for sure. While the cannisters remain sealed they're nuclear-bomb proof. My guess is that after donning appropriate protective gear they'd unbolt the access cap then thermal lance the welding to free the lid, but not remove it. That way they wouldn't be exposing themselves to the radiation. *Then*, if it were me, I'd wind a shitload of high-grade detonating cord around the seal of the lid along with several wads of C4. After floating the container out into the reservoir near where I knew the exit tunnel was located, I'd blow the whole shebang to kingdom come. Water would flood the container—what's left of it that is—along with the cannister, which by this point would be breached, causing a second minor explosion as the 137 reacted with the water. A cloud of hydrogen gas would be created, along with caesium and hydroxide ions that would spread far and wide, all highly toxic. As well there would be dispersion of massive amounts of radioactivity for God knows how many kilometres in every direction. Depending on the depth of water, which I'm assuming with the reservoir at a hundred percent full would be over a hundred metres near the retaining wall, you'd have a cannister still emitting these nasties for a bloody long time."

Groans of despair erupted around the table, everybody looking to one another, many unsure what the next steps should be. The AC pulled the briefing to order. "In about forty-five minutes the Chief and I will front the minister to explain what we're doing about this impending disaster ... and it won't make for a pleasant discussion." He turned back to Robert. "Dare I ask, is there a magic bullet that rids the water and soil from radiation pollution?"

The gloomy expression on Robert's face would have

been comical had the subject matter not been so critical. "Unfortunately not. In a nutshell, radioactivity can't be *removed* per se, rather it has to be concentrated and contained. Some success has been achieved with small volumes of water artificially contaminated with micro-carbon carboxymethyl cartridge units to filter out the radionuclides, but never on the scale we would need.

"God knows how many birds and small animals drink from the reservoir despite the security fencing. They in turn would pass the contamination into the human food chain, along with the fish in the reservoir, were they eaten. Regarding the water, it can't be siphoned onto land as it would pollute the soil, and even if it didn't, the sheer volume involved would make that option impossible. Sir, I confess I'm out of my technical depth on this one. Much cleverer brains than mine may have a solution, but I *do* know we're talking many years, possibly a generation before we overcome this disaster should it occur."

The AC's jaw muscles flexed. "Well then, we'll just have to prevent it from happening in the first place." Turning towards Gerhart he commanded, "Call up Tim and have him send as many of his team to the reservoir as he can spare. Also, we have no choice but to inform Melbourne Water's senior management that if the tunnel from the Thomson is currently flowing water into the lower reservoirs it must be shut off, *immediately*, and remain shut until further notice. Tell them we have a credible threat of the water being polluted, just don't tell them by what."

Addressing Jordan, he added, "The Chief and I will demand the minister contact the chief of army requesting military personnel be provided to surround the reservoir until these bloody cannisters are located and entombed in the storage site.

It's just our bad luck the damn lake is twenty-three kilometres long." He shook his head as he envisaged the number of military troops required for such an arduous task. "James ... Bernard, any online intel your contacts can provide on the whereabouts of these cannisters would be welcome right about now. Follow up on the satellite imagery with Robert and also with surveillance." The two men accepted the challenge, aware how crucial their efforts may prove to be. "Gerhart, you'll need to be onsite at the reservoir to coordinate things. The last thing we need is for all these groups to be charging about, falling over each other."

He turned to Ken who literally shrank in his seat. "Young man, I hear you have a rather impressive handle on profiling. You've exactly two minutes to give us your thoughts on what's going through the heads of this Ndrangheta mob, and the probability they're about to attempt to extort the Government out of a sizeable chunk of money."

Proving to Ballard and John's amazement how he could think on his feet when pressed, Ken got down to business in record time. "The first question is where does Igor fit in with this mob, and is he a credible source? It would seem he's playing both sides of the fence, so anything's possible. Yes, the satellite imagery showed one of the trucks with a container heading towards the reservoir, but is it a dummy, has the cannister already been offloaded somewhere else and the container empty? What's to stop the Ndrangheta pretending to still have the cannister inside as they float it in the reservoir while demanding a ransom. If they pull off the bluff, they'll have the money and *still* have two cannisters to sell to the highest bidder."

Ken's left field thought bubble had his audience sitting up

and taking notice, especially John, who was viewing his charge through appreciative eyes. Reverting to old habits, Ken took a mini gulp of air before continuing, the scarlet of his cheeks creeping down his throat. "While this is a proposition that has to be considered, it doesn't help us right now because with the stakes so high we can't take the risk that they may or may not be bluffing. I'd suggest Surveillance recheck the imagery to see if there are any time gaps when the cannister could have been offloaded to another vehicle, or hidden somewhere while enroute to the reservoir."

Shrugging, having divulged that piece of advice, Ken prepared for the next. "No question Ndrangheta are ruthless enough to do what's being suggested by Igor. If nothing else they have a reputation to uphold. Should the Government refuse to pay the extortion demand they'll *have* to blow the cannister, assuming there *is* one inside the container. This will send a clear message to authorities around the world that when they make a threat, they mean business. It was a Yank by the name of Brian Jenkins who wrote, 'Terrorists want a lot of people watching, not necessarily a lot of people dead'. This holds true for the very reason that if *too* many die, those who are left, namely the very people they wish to influence, well, they'd be even more against the terrorists than they already were. Polluting the reservoir with 235 and 137 won't kill too many people, but it *will* make the world sit up and take notice, pressuring any future government to pay up and not risk putting millions of lives in turmoil for decades."

The AC grunted. "Thank you Ken, your time's up. In a nutshell, what you're telling us is the Ndrangheta are a mean bunch of pricks who shouldn't be messed with. I'll take your advice and have the satellite imagery rechecked to see whether they offloaded the cannister on the way through. Thank you, that'll be all."

Ken slumped back in his seat, his brow moist, grateful he had survived the intense scrutiny of his peers; all the while John maintained a supportive stare in his direction.

The AC scanned his audience. "Ok, you know what to do. Remember, we're all on a tightrope without a balancing pole on this one. One false move will bring everyone and everything crashing down around us. So let's get out there and prevent a catastrophe."

Everyone scrambled to make their escape, with Ballard and John as keen as anyone, but to no avail as the AC cut short their attempt to flee. "Michael ... John, just a moment if you please." Both detectives caught the other's eye, shrugging as they remained in their seats. "You'll be wondering why I've requested you to stay back." An amused twinkle occupied the AC's eyes.

Ballard thought he would play along with the AC's apparent good mood. "A pay rise, sir?"

Focussing on John, the AC asked, "Not even close. Your thoughts Detective Senior Sergeant?"

Without hesitation, John shot back, "A promotion, sir?"

Pretending to be exasperated, the AC got down to business. "I've read Marjorie's initial report and unsurprisingly she claims that after an appropriate time off you'll both be fit to resume normal duties—"

"How much time off?" John's look of alarm matched Ballard's.

"The timing couldn't be worse under the circumstances, but let's make it until I can arrange another interview with Professional Standards, hopefully within the next day or two."

His intense scrutiny of John spoke volumes.

"Whenever you can schedule that meeting sir will be fine by John and myself. We're more than happy to sit in the sun for a while." Ballard knew his tongue-in-cheek declaration wouldn't be believed by the senior officer, but he posed it anyway.

Glancing at the wall clock, the AC growled, "Get out of here you two, and for Christ sake keep out of trouble. Do you think you can manage that just this once?"

Two brisk salutes were aimed in his direction.

CHAPTER
16

The growl of the Bentley's motor, as smooth as the day it was built despite the punishment dished out earlier by John, reverberated in the confines of Natalie's garage. Just as Ballard switched off the motor and grabbed his briefcase from the back seat, Natalie burst through the side door and flung her arms around him.

"I'm glad you didn't get home any earlier my sweet. I had Kayla and Josh put on the roast and prepare the vegetables after school because I was tied up at work until nearly six. To make matters worse the traffic in Hoddle Street was absolute bedlam." She peered sideways at him, her face a mask of secrecy. "Guess what? ... Tim and Kathryn are inside and they've got some exciting news for you—"

"They're bringing the wedding forward because Kathryn's pregnant." Ballard's sardonic throwaway had Natalie assessing him through narrowed eyes. "Well actually, you're half right."

"So my sister is *half* pregnant?"

"*Noo*, but I'll let them give you the news, and Michael, *please* act surprised. They're both sitting in the lounge like nervous teenagers."

"Tim a nervous teenager?" Ballard was disbelieving, well aware of the dangers the SOG commander had faced throughout his career, including the recent encounter with Igor mere hours earlier, the outcome something he needed to discuss at length with the inspector when he could manage a private moment.

Not bothering to explain further, Natalie led him inside. Placing his briefcase near the hallstand, Ballard poked his head into the kitchen, Natalie having disappeared into the lounge. "Two budding chefs in the making I see."

Tea-towel in hand, Kayla took the empty bowl that Josh had finished rinsing. "Hi Michael, I just hope my gravy isn't too lumpy." She became conspiratorial. "I want to prove to Mum I really was listening when she showed me how to make it."

Grinning, Ballard quipped, "If it *is* lumpy, just squish it through a strainer ... I won't tell."

Picking up on the subterfuge, Josh shook his head, his eyes rolling in his head.

The scorn on Kayla's face was well practiced. Leaving the teenagers to settle their differences, Ballard entered the lounge to see his sister and Tim sitting together on the couch holding hands. Natalie was alongside them, curled up in an armchair; all were in deep conversation. Tim sprang to his feet and pumped Ballard's hand while Kathryn air-kissed her brother's cheek.

Natalie's subsequent stern look at Ballard was loaded with caution for him to take seriously what he was about to hear, and for once not allow his humour to run amuck. Maintaining a straight face, Ballard directed his attention towards the couple. "Natalie tells me you've got something of great importance to discuss."

Tim cleared his throat, uncharacteristically nervous. "We do Michael. Kathryn and I are getting married ... next Sunday."

Ballard pretended to be confused. "Yes, I know that, but what's the important news you wanted to talk about?"

"*Michael.*" Natalie almost jumped out of her chair, admonishing Ballard for ignoring her advice.

Not done, Ballard added, "So I'd be correct in assuming the undue haste is because this is a shotgun wedding ... my question is, who's holding the shotgun?"

Natalie shook her head in exasperation, secretly amused by the exchanges.

Coming to Tim's rescue, Kathryn was on the front foot. "Michael, *I'll* be holding the shotgun if you don't agree to give me away." In an unexpected mood change, her lip trembled. "With Mum and Dad gone you're the only family I have left."

The display of raw emotion snapped Ballard back to serious mode, the reminder of his parents' deaths a harsh reality; his dad dying from a stroke, and his mother from a car accident, the memories ripping the scab from a wound he believed had long since healed. Reaching forward, he squeezed her hand. "Sis, it'll be my honour. So where are the nuptials to be held?"

Blinking back tears, Kathryn attempted to keep her emotions in check. "We loved where you and Natalie had your wedding, so we decided to have ours at Rupertswood too."

"*Really*?" Ballard couldn't hide his surprise, and noting Natalie's reaction it was clear the decision was a popular one.

Tim rallied. "Yes, hence the rush. We spoke to Margaret who's still the manager out there, and it was either next Sunday due to a cancellation or we had to wait another six months—"

"By which time the baby bump would be nigh on impossible to conceal—"

"Michael ... *enough*!" Despite her outburst, Natalie's eyes crinkled as she leaned down and gave Kathryn a hug. "How many guests?"

Again Kathryn was hesitant, to the point of being embarrassed. "We don't want any great fuss, something intimate, close friends only." She paused. "Thirty, forty at the most, and we apologise for the late notice, all this has happened so suddenly."

Ballard opened his mouth for another round, but the challenging look on Natalie's face silenced him. Reaching forward, he shook Tim's hand. "Congratulations young man, you're taking on a handful—"

"*Michael!*"

"But saying that, she's the most loyal, loving, capable person I know, and should you ever strain a muscle, her physiotherapy skills will get you going in no time."

Blushing, Tim muttered, "I've called on her expertise more than once already."

Unable to help himself Ballard shot back, "I'll bet you have."

The appearance of Kayla and Josh prevented Natalie from giving Ballard a well-deserved jab.

"Dinner's served." With a theatrical flourish of hands ending in a synchronised bow, the teenagers straightened up before leading the way into the dining room where plates loaded with roast lamb, a variety of vegetables and steamed greens were already in place, along with carafes of water and orange juice, plus two piping-hot gravy boats filled to the brim.

Sidling up to Kayla, Ballard asked, "Any need for the strainer?"

A vigorous shake of her head ensued. Ballard drew back Natalie's chair, and settling, she shook out her napkin, spreading it on her lap before announcing, "I'm very impressed. So all my hard work has finally paid off."

Kayla's smile was one of contentment, while Josh was less certain, looking to Ballard and Tim for any sign he should join in and accept the compliment. He chose to do so anyway.

For the next hour conversations ebbed and flowed as they tucked into their meals, finishing with sliced fruit and ice cream for dessert. Afterwards, the teenagers were excused to start their homework, each uttering their good nights while Natalie and Kathryn volunteered to wash the dishes, speculating Ballard and Tim had important work matters to discuss.

Choosing adjacent armchairs, Ballard posed the question he had been desperate to ask all evening, despite assuming the answer after noting Tim's subtle headshake when they first greeted each other. "Igor?"

With a roll of his eyes, Tim confirmed what Ballard already knew. "The bastard literally vanished. Even PolAir lost sight of him amongst all the houses and back yards. By the time my guys and the uniforms arrived to do a house to house it was a lost cause. I can't believe I'm saying this, but in a way I'm glad we *didn't* corner him because there'd be a heap of dead homeowners on our conscience right about now. Anyway, my 2IC took over until he was told to hotfoot it along with his guys up to the reservoir.

As disappointed as Ballard was, he had to agree, any arrest of Igor needed to be on their terms, away from the public who would have been caught up in the crossfire of the ensuing mayhem. For the next ten minutes Ballard gave Tim a detailed rundown of the threat posed by Igor to the Thomson Reservoir.

Shaking his head in disbelief, Tim confirmed his agreeance with the AC's demand that the majority of his team should support the military in guarding the reservoir, all under the coordination of AC Müller. "We've no choice *but* to take this seriously because the Ndrangheta are bloody ruthless enough to do what they claim."

"Exactly what Ken said, and the AC has no misgivings that if it happens, high profile heads will roll, including his own."

Tim was reflective. "Which as we know isn't fair. After all, it was the damn government who chose the low-key security approach in the first place ... and look where that got us."

"So in a nutshell Tim, we're fighting on two fronts as James outlined —The Board, which remains hell-bent on taking out the storage site, although Jordan has made that nigh-on impossible, and secondly, the Ndrangheta, believing they're in for a massive payout should they pull off their threat against the Government."

Grimacing, Tim was conscious of the predicament that the politicians and senior police now found themselves in should the demand be made. "And another fact of life Mike—were our pollies to go cap-in-hand to the federal Attorney-General, he won't be amenable with any cash handout after forking over a billion for the Parliament House cockup."

Ballard appeared apologetic. "Tim, I'm sorry. Here I am busting your chops with work problems when you and Kathryn should be on a high, planning your wedding." He shrugged off his previous tribulations. "What can I say ... so you're both taking the plunge? With you as her husband I couldn't be happier for Kathryn, and like I've said many times, you've a loyal one there, and tough as nails to boot."

Tim's earlier nervousness was gone. Now fully relaxed, he was grateful he had Ballard's blessing. "Thanks Mike, and I promise I'll do everything in my power to make her happy."

Ballard laughed. "Just make sure she does the same for you. She can be a stubborn young filly at times, so you'll have your hands full." Again, unable to help himself he added, "Figuratively speaking, that is."

Grinning, Tim looked up, welcoming Kathryn and Natalie into the room, Kathryn cautiously asking, "Tell me you've both solved the department's problems ... at least for the time-being?"

Tim was in two minds as to how frank he should be, blurting out, "If only it were that easy—"

Ballard chopped him short, determined to ensure work issues were suspended for the evening. "Yes ladies, done and dusted, never to be mentioned within these walls ever again."

Both women scoffed, aware they would never be told the complete truth as a consequence of their menfolk being involved in complex cases that had to remain secret to ensure the safety of innocent lives.

The next half hour was spent swapping wedding plans, with Natalie careful not to impose her wishes on how it should unfold, rather, subtly slipping in what had and hadn't worked for her and Michael. "The best news is you'll have Margaret with you all the way. She's a professional through and through, and she'll make sure everything runs like clockwork."

Ballard watched on, praying Natalie's optimism and Kathryn's carefully evolving plans wouldn't be disrupted by either The Board or the Ndrangheta. He promised himself he would do whatever it took to make certain the day was as perfect as it should be.

CHAPTER
17

"Well the bastards gave it a bloody good crack!" The attendees in the Critical Incidence conference room chose to remain silent, fully aware that when the AC was in one of his foul, take-no-prisoner moods it was best to say nothing until invited to do so. Delwyn, sitting alongside Ballard and John who had been recalled from their days off, cast a brief glance at the two detectives, praying neither would venture into treacherous territory. To John's left, Tim caught the superintendent's cautioning stare, smiling at her misgivings that the detectives may at some point inadvertently say or do something to further infuriate the AC.

All in the room focussed their attention on the wall screen, which displayed a live shot of Jordan in combat fatigues that were uncharacteristically filthy, his face unshaven and covered in grime—it was evident the storage site had been attacked. The AC asked the burning question on everyone's lips as he stood at the designated spot in the room so his image would be projected back to the lieutenant colonel. "Jordan, have any of your troops been injured?"

After taking a generous swig from his field flask, the officer wiped his mouth with a grubby sleeve, his voice booming loud and clear over the room's multiple speakers. "No casualties, but three have shrapnel wounds to their arms and legs. Thankfully their body armour did the trick and protected their vitals."

The AC was visibly shaken. "Only if you have the time … are you able to take us through what happened?"

The lieutenant colonel was out on his feet with fatigue, but he pressed on. "Just before dawn our radars picked up twenty-five incoming drones three kilometres out."

A number of concerned mutterings erupted around the conference table.

"No sign of nearby choppers, vehicles or armed personnel?"

"None at that point, the drones were on a pre-set flight path, GPS locked onto our position. We engaged them when they came within range with our three Raytheon multi-spectral lasers which thank Christ we'd installed less than twenty-four hours earlier. These units lock onto incoming targets—the nuts and bolts of how they work I won't go into other than to say the lasers take out the electronics in the drones. Our particular units are fifty- kilowatt systems, so their maximum range is limited to a kilometre. We've subsequently inspected the drones we destroyed and each had a payload of just over two kilograms of C4, all with wireless detonators."

The mutterings became a chorus of outright shock. Jordan overheard the outburst, nodding in agreeance with the justifiable outrage. "Yes, fifty-plus kilograms of C4 detonating inside the camp would have wiped us out."

Unable to contain himself, John called out, "How many drones did you end up shooting down?"

"Twenty-three."

The blunt statement hung in the air. "What damage did the remaining two cause?"

"Thankfully they exploded before they got too low, but the shockwave knocked out several huts, and a number of vehicles were damaged by flying debris. The shrapnel that caused the injuries to my soldiers came from metal shards embedded in the packs of C4. While it was bloody chaotic at the time, it could have been a hell of a lot worse." His measured tone failed to hide the inner rage bubbling beneath the surface, his attempt to suppress his fury largely unsuccessful.

"I'm assuming what you've told us so far was only the beginning of the attack?"

Jordan took another mouthful from his flask. "It's clear the plan was to flatten the base with the C4 then land two choppers with heavily armed personnel onboard to gain entry to the site. My guess is this would have been achieved by executing whoever was still alive in the camp until the security staff inside the complex crumbled and let them in."

"Two choppers you say … so what *did* happen?"

"We launched RBS-70 missiles the second we knew the incoming choppers were part of the assault. There were no survivors in the subsequent wreckage, which was just as well because the fifteen onboard were armed to the back teeth, and while they wouldn't have been a match for our soldiers one-on-one, again I stress that if the drones had done their intended job the outcome would have been catastrophic."

The AC was impressed and it showed. "Congratulations Jordan. Please pass on our appreciation to all your troops for doing such a fantastic job. Hopefully this proves to our Spring Street residents that there's a need to have a permanent military presence at the site which is well equipped. In short, it's going to be *our* Fort Knox, requiring appropriate and ongoing protection. One more question before you go, how long will you need to sort out the damage to the camp?"

Jordan cracked a weak smile. "Two to three days should do it. The RAEME team are already here and getting stuck in."

"Thanks for taking the time, Jordan. You look beat. Get something to eat and a well-earned rest." A chorus of best wishes generated a weary smile from Jordan as his image disappeared from the screen.

Moving back to his chair, the AC focussed on Robert for several seconds before demanding, "Goddamnit! What the hell is going on in this world when military attacks are now orchestrated via bloody drones!"

For the first time that Ballard and John could remember, Robert appeared reticent to take centre stage, not having prepared for this left-field scenario, but he rose to the occasion, nonetheless. "Drone technology has developed to the point over the past ten years that the military had no option but to take it seriously. It was obvious these devices could and would be used as delivery platforms for reconnaissance and assaults on the enemy. Jordan was correct to add air-defence lasers to the camp's arsenal. And yes, that much C4 going off would have wiped out all the personnel, the vehicles and the weapons—in fact, most of the infrastructure. It'd be a miracle if *anyone* was left alive to be used as a bargaining chip."

"But doesn't someone have to be within range to guide these things to their destination?" The AC was confused.

Robert attempted a half smile. "Try upwards of a hundred kilometres away and more, carrying payloads of five, ten, even fifteen kilograms while travelling at speeds of 120 kilometres per hour. Many of the more sophisticated units employ fuel injection to provide electric power to each of the motors, thus vastly increasing the drone's flight range. As Jordan said, these things can be programmed to fly to exact locations and land within a metre or so of their intended target."

The AC struck his forehead with the heel of his hand. "God forbid, The Board, the Ndrangheta, and now bloody drones dropping packs of C4 out of the damn sky. No wonder retirement is becoming more and more appealing."

Nobody in the room believed a word of his lament, aware the greater the difficulty the stronger his resolve would be to meet the challenge head on. His ensuing comment underscored that reality. "After I've briefed Command, my next call will be to the Minister to ram home the necessity for a permanent military presence up there. If this episode doesn't convince the bastards, then nothing will."

Once more Robert was in the AC's sights. "Changing subjects, any luck with the satellite imagery and whether the truck hauling the container stopped off somewhere to unload the cannister?"

Again Robert failed to display his usual self-confidence, aware how critical the question had become should a demand for money be made by the Ndrangheta. It was clear he was dreading the horrific repercussions were the intel he provided proven to be incorrect. "Sadly, there *are* time gaps in the footage. Certainly long enough for the container to have been driven into a secluded area and the cannister offloaded. I'm still determining why these gaps exist, but they're there." His look was disturbed, as though he were personally responsible for the breaks in continuity.

"So should the container find its way into the reservoir,

there's no way we can advise with any certainty whether or not there's a bloody cannister inside?"

Continuing to look and feel wretched, Robert's reply was reduced to a weak shrug. To his relief there was a knock at the door and Peter walked in. A round of applause echoed throughout the room, everyone relieved their colleague was up and about and seemingly on the mend.

"Apologies sir, this was the earliest I could get here. They kicked me out of the hospital later than I'd planned."

Springing out of his chair, the AC shook Peter's hand, the energetic pumping causing the superintendent to wince in mild pain, despite it being his left shoulder that was injured. "Sorry Peter. I'm assuming you've been cleared medically to return to light duties?"

"Indeed I have, and from what I hear a lot has been going on which I'd like to get my teeth into." He dared Ballard and John to say otherwise, and was rewarded with open grins from his colleagues, happy to see their partner back on his feet.

As usual, John went one step further. "And about time you stopped lolling about chatting with sexy nurses ... you need to get into some *real* work."

The AC took up John's cheeky segue. "Indeed Peter, I want you to liaise with Robert. Finding these cannisters is paramount, and the satellite imagery is our only hope of locating them. Robert will fill you in on the possibility one of them may finish up in the Thomson Reservoir, and what the implications would be if that scenario materialises."

After scribbling a note in his daybook, he added, "Post-updating Command and the Minister, my next port of call is to brief Damien Harcourt, the federal Attorney-General's representative. He needs to know we're facing another ransom demand which will be every bit as unrealistic as the one we experienced during the Parliament House siege." He gritted his teeth. "And I've no doubt how *that* conversation is going to play out. Oh, and for everyone's information, AC Müller informs me at least a hundred military personnel will be supplementing Tim's officers who are already at the reservoir, but even with those numbers the expanse of the waterway means there'll be significant gaps along the shoreline where a cannister could be smuggled into the water."

Tim took up the AC's offer to share his thoughts. "You're correct sir. Were there three hundred soldiers they wouldn't fully cover such a vast expanse of water. I've asked my 2IC to instruct each of the military to patrol one kilometre either side of their allocated position. That way we'll come somewhere towards effective coverage. Each soldier will be armed and equipped to remain self-sufficient in the bush for a minimum of three days, after which they'll be relieved by a fresh, fully kitted contingent. The army's using this deployment as a training exercise for their troops, but they're mindful of the seriousness of the circumstances and the imperative that the container *not* make it into the water. Of course, all this assumes Igor hasn't sent us on a wild goose chase and the cannister is in a completely different location."

The AC turned to Delwyn. "On another matter, you and your staff have had a pretty torrid time of it at the site sorting out the murdered security contingent. How's your team holding up?"

As always, Delwyn's pragmatic, no-nonsense approach came to the fore. "It was certainly harrowing, no doubt about it, but as I pointed out to them, this is part and parcel of working in Homicide. Only in this instance there were considerably more bodies involved than at most crime scenes. But thanks for asking, sir. The bottom line is they got on with the job as they're trained to do."

The AC showed his appreciation. "As for the briefs they're preparing, at least Sergey's can be put to bed, with Igor's now taking on a new urgency. How close to finalisation are those for Vladimir and Tatiana?"

"All done. They've been filed electronically with the Supreme Court's Criminal Division, and all I can say is the RedCrest system has proven yet again to be as slow and convoluted as we all know it to be, but we got there in the end. Bobby's the case manager for Tatiana, and Susan for Vladimir. Due to the detailed video footage of Tatiana heaving hubby over the balcony of their mansion in St Georges Road there shouldn't be too much trouble getting a solid conviction for her. Vladimir, on the other hand, as the financier for the Note Printing Australia robbery and the Parliament House siege, well, that's a different kettle of fish. We've pinged him for a Section 3A constructive murder charge on those two issues, which I admit is a long shot. It'll mean our prosecutor, Inspector Ian Simpson, will have his work cut out getting that one over the line. If we lose those charges, and it's fifty-fifty at best, we'll get Vladimir on a swag of lesser associated offences. What isn't in doubt is bagging him for incitement in Tatiana's husband's murder. While I'll never lay claim to a slam dunk for *any* hearing in the Supreme Court, I'm confident on this one. Both of these nasty individuals will be going to jail for a very long stretch, and not before time." A headshake confirmed her conviction.

The AC was pleased that at least some progress was being made to bring the long-term offenders to justice. He waved a hand at Tim. "You'll need to liaise with the judge hearing the cases regarding courtroom security so we don't wear another cockup like we had with Tatiana."

Ballard and John eyed one another, cheeks ballooning, the image of Tatiana threatening to drive a hatpin into the brain of one of her security guards in the County Court still a painful memory. The fact neither detective could prevent her from exiting the building was a humiliation for which they hadn't fully come to terms with. The SOG commander agreed to the AC's request, also keen to ensure there wasn't a repeat of the embarrassing incident.

A reflective rubbing of his jaw—the AC's customary gesture that the briefing was coming to an end—was chased by a gruff, "Ok, folks, tread carefully on this one because we're entering a critical phase that'll blow up in our faces if we're not on the ball."

His caution ringing in everyone's ears, there was a mad scramble for the door. Bracing his hands against the table, John began hauling himself to his feet, stopping when Ballard nudged him, pointing towards the AC.

In an exaggerated twist of his head, John pretended to ascertain whether the AC's gun-barrel gaze was meant for anyone else. Turning back, he perpetuated the charade, stabbing his chest with a forefinger while his eyebrows arched in the universal 'who me?' question.

The AC was having none of it, clearly not in a humorous mood. "Yes you, Henderson. Sit down." Rubbing plate-sized hands over his face in a weary gesture, the AC continued. "Professional Standards are giving me a bloody hard time ... anyone would think they've a personal axe to grind." He sighed. "*Of course*, silly me, perhaps it has something to do with you punching out one of their detectives."

John sought moral support from Ballard, but none was forthcoming. "I didn't hit him all that hard—"

"Hard enough Henderson, hard enough." The senior officer appeared in two minds how he should proceed, but decided the direct approach was the most practical. "It would seem they're hell-bent on benching you two, making you permanent desk jockeys."

A howl of anguish escaped John's lips before he could bring his emotions under control. "Surely they don't mean ..."

"Yes, they do mean ..." The AC's eyes blazed, but his expression suggested his anger was directed towards Professional Standards. "I'm in the middle of a goddamn crisis and a bunch of ... of ... *desk jockeys* are doing their best to rob me of two of my most senior and experienced detectives. Well, it's not going to happen." A clenched fist struck the table with such force that Ballard was in two minds whether structural damage had been inflicted on the woodwork. "As I said yesterday, I want you two to take formal leave for a few days while I sort this damn mess out at Command level. Make sure wherever you go you can be back here within a couple of hours. I'll be in touch to keep you up to speed." His forefinger pointed accusingly towards the door. "Now make yourselves scarce so I can get on with it."

Not needing further encouragement, the two detectives scrambled to their feet, each mumbling their thanks on the way out.

"Of *course* I can take a day or two off Michael, even three for that matter. I've heaps of leave owing. I just hope Sonia can do the same. We got on so well in Italy, and Hobart will be every bit as much fun as walking the streets of Venice ... *really it will.*"

Raising an eyebrow, uncertain how genuine Natalie's enthusiastic declaration was, Ballard added, "I need to apologise in advance darling, this holiday will have to be a short one, a couple of days at the most. The AC wants John and I close by so we can be back in the office within hours should it be necessary."

"And will it be?" The uncertainty in Natalie's voice stabbed deep into Ballard's psyche.

He glanced over at John who was at his desk, his mobile clamped to his ear, in deep conversation with Sonia. "I'm certain we'll have more than enough time to explore Hobart's renowned treasures." No sooner had he uttered the words than his partner gave him a thumbs up, confirming Sonia was free to join in on the trip. "Good news Nat, Sonia and John have agreed to tag along." He wrenched the mobile from his ear, Natalie's cry of delight the culprit.

"That's wonderful, I'll start packing—"

"Er, as I said, it's only going to be two or three days."

"I know Michael, but we women need to look our best."

"Sweetheart, you could wear a hessian bag and rubber boots, and have mud on your face, and still look a million dollars."

Natalie chuckled. "Rose coloured glasses Michael—rose coloured glasses." With a further laugh, she was gone. John came over, a huge grin in place. "Sonia's tickled pink, and she insists that even though she's coming up to five months, an hour's flight to Tassie won't trouble her one little bit." Despite his words, a shadow of doubt remained.

Ballard scoffed at his concern. "You needn't worry, Sonia's as fit as a fiddle, and remember this Johno, Russian women work in the fields up to the very last day. Good God man, some of them give birth *in* the field, then after tucking the baby on a hip they continue digging up potatoes."

"Very funny. And I'm sure Sonia will be delighted to learn she's being compared with Russian women who spend their life toiling in the field."

Ballard thought for a second, then shot back, "Believe me, it's no insult being likened to Russian women. Have you seen some of those lady tennis players?"

John pursed his lips. "Hmm, yes, I take your point."

"Ok, now that conundrum is settled, let's see if my travel agent Dave can pull off one of his miracles and get us a flight for tomorrow morning, as well as some decent accommodation." Snatching up his mobile he made the call and minutes later a 9.15 a.m. flight was locked in.

Looking across the room, both men saw Delwyn approaching, appearing tired but as always, supremely determined.

"The AC rang to see if you'd left yet. He wanted to know where you were going. I mentioned you thought Hobart might be on the cards. He jumped on that and *suggested* ..." Delwyn's expression made it clear the suggestion was more a directive, "he *suggested* you two might like to call into Hobart's police headquarters during your travels and have a chat with Deputy Commissioner Wayne Johnston who's heading up their Special Response and Counter-Terrorism Command. Apparently, the AC's had numerous discussions with Johnston who's becoming increasingly nervous that The Board may be targeting the Hobart docks, just as they have here in Melbourne and Sydney. The boss wants you to give Johnston a sitrep regarding what's going down in our patch, and the things he should watch out for."

Ballard looked hard at John, straight-faced. "We managed

to pinch a few hours away from our better halves in Venice, so I'm sure we can do the same in Hobart."

Delwyn dropped her head in resignation. "Heavens above, I shudder to imagine what romance actually looks like to you two."

Puffing his chest out in a pigeon pose, John boasted. "I have it on excellent authority that Michael and I are regarded as top-shelf catches, our partners have told us so many times."

Delwyn's head shaking increased. "It just goes to show, love really is blind." In a farewell gesture, she waved a hand in their direction as she returned to her office.

CHAPTER
18

Leaning across the aisle in the Boeing 737 Max, with Sonia sitting to his left, and Ballard and Natalie to his right, John whispered to his colleague, the whites of his eyes showing, "Isn't this the same model that had so much trouble a bit back, with two of the bastards falling out of the sky?"

Checking neither Sonia nor Natalie had overheard John's concern, Ballard pointed overhead. "As soon as the seatbelt sign goes off, let's play musical chairs so the ladies can sit together, then I'll fill you in on the details."

John rolled his eyes, not sure which was worse, a barrage of statistics from Ballard or the fear of a mid-air failure. Turning to Sonia who was sitting with her eyes closed, also a believer that aviation was very much against nature, John kissed her on the cheek. "All's well in the bub department?"

Placing a hand on what could be described as a beginning baby bump, she responded, "Yes, all good. But there's no question the kicks are getting stronger, here, feel this." She took John's hand and positioned it on her stomach. Concentrating, he suddenly drew his hand away before replacing it, astonished at the force of the baby's movement. "It's a boy, with a kick like that, it's a boy for sure."

Sonia's brow knitted in mild concern. "Would you be disappointed if it's a girl?"

"Are you kidding me? A mini you ... what's not to like." Sonia's brow returned to its former serene state.

The moment the seatbelt light went out, accompanied by the universal chime, positions were swapped with Sonia joining Natalie.

Aware what was to come, John declared in an attempt to avert the inevitable flood of technical jargon, "I'm feeling much better now that we've levelled off."

"Nonsense, in a nutshell, it was the MCAS that caused the two crashes."

Rolling his eyes, John moaned, "Ok, I'll bite, what's the MCAS?"

"It's the plane's Maneuvering Characteristics Augmentation System. It literally flew the two planes into the ground. Putting it another way, it acted against its own *raison d'être.*"

John's eyeroll went all the way to the back of his head. "I knew this was coming."

Grinning, Ballard elaborated. "The very reason the augmentation system exists is to prevent planes from stalling and subsequently crashing. Paradoxically this is exactly what it forced them to do."

Fearing the answer, John demanded, "Just tell me the damn fault's been rectified."

"Indeed it has. The MCAS is now connected to the *two* angle-of-attack sensors prewarning pilots of an impending stall. Prior to that, the system was connected to only *one,* which beggars belief. Equally as important, the automated correction instigated by the MCAS has been reduced to one activation, not endless repeats. These changes, along with a host of others now make this one of the safest planes in the air. Trust me Johno, I have this on rock solid authority. You could chip your tooth on it."

Grumbling, and still far from convinced, John professed, "I'll agree with you when we get this thing down on the tarmac." Hunching closer, he became conspiratorial, his face gloomy. "Are our worst fears about to be realised Mike?"

Realising what his partner was referring to, Ballard checked that Natalie and Sonia were in deep conversation before admitting, "Marjorie's report is in our favour, so that's a plus, but there's no denying Professional Standards are out to make a point." He grinned, surprising John considering the criticality of the matter. "Let's not forget, punching one of their own on the proboscis wasn't your most constructive career move—"

"The bastard deserved it."

"No argument from me, but these groups get a might testy when someone has the balls to push back at them." The grin widened. "They take it as an affront to their professionalism."

"*Professionalism!*" John's outburst was sufficient for Natalie and Sonia to break out of their heart-to-heart. Waving a reassuring hand, John added, "Mike, the guy I knuckled couldn't find loose change in his own pocket. It's clear he's never had to make a split-second life and death decision, and Sergey wasn't the sort of guy you dillydally with."

"Very true Johno, however you have to admit, old sins cast long shadows, and we've been pushing the envelope to the max over the past six to eight months. Something had to give."

"Do you think the AC will be able to pull a rabbit out of his hat and keep us operational?"

Ballard considered his partner. "If anyone can do it, he can.

After all these years I'll wager he's got a kitbag of favours to draw from." He gave John a playful punch on the arm. "Now, enough of that. We're on days off, remember?"

Leaning across the aisle, he waited patiently for Natalie to finish what she was saying, not wishing to interrupt her animated discussion with Sonia, assuming it was to do with Kathryn's wedding preparations. Seeing Sonia pointing, Natalie broke off, demanding of Ballard, "Is what you're about to ask me more important than your sister's matrimonial plans Michael?"

Shrinking back in mock dismay, Ballard offered, "Not if you believe it isn't, my darling."

Both women laughed, with Sonia declaring, "Not very convincing Michael. No, we were discussing your speech, considering how you've been allocated best-man duties."

Scratching the back of his neck while concocting a suitable reply, he finally said, "I'm very honoured to be offered such an important role ... and as for my speech, I'll just wing it on the day."

Natalie scoffed. "You'll do nothing of the sort. The speech you gave at *our* wedding was marvellous, and I expect one equally as impressive for your sister. Heaven knows the dramas you've put her through over the years."

While the comment was meant to be light-hearted, it caused Ballard's features to tense as he recalled the life and death hostage crisis in his home at the hands of Parnell.

Recognising the trauma that the incident still caused him, Natalie drew breath. "I'm sorry Michael ... I didn't mean to open old wounds. I was referring to when you two were young and on your parents farm in Bordertown—"

Ballard held up a reassuring hand. "It's fine Nat. I know

what you meant. And yes, I *was* rather brutal in the pranks department, but Kathryn survived and has always given as good as she got."

Natalie agreed. "Yes, she's told me a number of things you both did to each other, and quite frankly it's a wonder either of you survived into adulthood."

Ballard was curious. "So the wedding's next Sunday? Are you *sure* my sister isn't pregnant—?"

"No Michael. It's purely a practical decision. They didn't want to wait another six months because there's a strong rumour Rupertswood is to be bought by the Salesian College and won't be available for receptions anymore. When they heard that, they chose to play safe."

Natalie's declaration saw Ballard's brow crease, his marriage to her a perfect moment in time, and now one that the inexorable march of progress was threatening to impinge upon. Nodding his understanding of his sister's actions, he smirked, "So I shouldn't joke about this being a shotgun wedding in my speech—?"

"You most definitely should not."

Natalie's indignation saw Sonia smother a laugh as she placed a hand on her arm. "I'm sure he's only kidding." She fixed Ballard with an extended stare. "You *are* kidding, aren't you Michael?"

Ballard made a zipping motion across his lips. "I'll be a model of propriety."

Realising his joke had run its race, Ballard glanced up as he heard the 'Fasten Seatbelt' chime. Nudging John, he asked, "Ever been to Hobart's airport?"

A shake of his partner's head was all the encouragement Ballard needed. "Well my friend, you'll notice a stark difference between it and the Singapore and Rome airports we went through on our trip—their annual passenger movements being sixty-eight and forty-two million respectively."

Realising there was to be no escape, John enquired against his better judgement, "Ok, how many pass through *this* little establishment we're lobbing into?"

"Two and a half million."

Not wishing to show his surprise, John let himself down. "*Really*? Christ, more people go through the Maccas café in Bourke Street. It's a wonder the airport breaks even. How many passengers use Sydney and Melbourne?"

"Forty-two and thirty-seven million."

"Now that's more like it, and without doubt the reason we had to zig zag in the line at Tulla for so long to check in our luggage—"

"Exactly what I've said so many times to Nat!" Ballard's outburst had both ladies staring his way, his following claim directed towards Natalie. "John agrees with me, darling, there *has* to be a better way to process passengers than this infernal backwards and forwards zig-zag nonsense."

Natalie shook her head in despair. "John, please don't get Michael fired up on airport passenger movements."

Sheepish, John admitted, "Too late, but I'll try to think of something different to occupy him." A sudden pocket of turbulence drove all thoughts of commuter movements from his mind as he white knuckled the armrests of his seat. He turned to Ballard. "One of the safest planes in the sky, eh?" The question was a full blooded accusation.

"Yes Johno, we're as safe as houses."

"Even during a bloody earthquake?" A deep-throated moan followed.

John snatched his and Sonia's luggage from the fastmoving carrousel with the same enthusiasm an Australian rugby player would tackle a New Zealand opponent. Catching Ballard's raised eyebrow, he shot back, "I didn't want to wait another damn circuit considering I missed the cases the first time around."

Sonia placed a hand on his arm. "It's fine John, we're on holidays remember?"

He encircled her waist, planting a kiss on her cheek. "And don't you let me forget it."

"Oh, I won't."

After signing up for their hire car, and with the luggage squeezed into the boot, Ballard and Natalie sat in the back of the Mazda Astina while John weaved his way out of the carpark. Beside him, Sonia busied herself by entering the address for the Hobart Casino into the navigation system.

Natalie gave Ballard's hand a firm squeeze. "I couldn't be happier Michael. This is going to be every bit as much fun as any of our overseas trips." She reached forward and tapped Sonia on the shoulder. "Isn't that right?"

Uttering a sigh of relief at having mastered the technical challenges, Sonia turned in her seat. "Talk about the fab four, I haven't been this happy since ..." She struggled for the appropriate words. "Well, since I don't know when."

Taking his eyes off the road for a second, John quipped, "Pretty soon it'll be the fab five."

"Hmm, that may cramp our spontaneous lifestyle a bit, but it'll be worth it."

In the back seat, Ballard mouthed a silent 'spontaneous?' at Natalie, wide-eyed, not for an instant believing his partner in crime for over twenty years could ever be described as spontaneous. Natalie elbowed him with an accompanying stern look, cautioning him to say nothing that would spoil Sonia's optimistic outlook for the future. To change the subject she professed, "I've never been to the Tassie casino, I can't wait to see it."

Taking that as his cue, Ballard offered a historical update generating a sigh from John. "It opened in February 1973 and was Australia's first legal casino. It's seventeen storeys high and is dodecagonal in shape—"

John thumped the steering wheel in frustration. "Here we go again, and I'm silly enough to ask, what in hell's name is a dode … dodecag … thingy shape?"

Registering yet another warning look from Natalie, Ballard answered, "Twelve sides. Apparently it's still the tallest building in Hobart, and has a revolving restaurant at the top."

Sonia rubbed her stomach, only this time it wasn't to feel her baby bump. "Yum, count me in. What about you Natalie?"

"Revolving or not, I'll be there with a bib on."

John honked a wayward driver who was having difficulty deciding which lane he preferred. *"One or the other dopey."*

The driver finally settled on the left lane, offering John a fixed glare as they passed.

Sonia placed a calming hand on his thigh. "Let's not upset the locals darling. We've all the time in the world."

Minutes later they approached the Tasman Bridge, with John choosing the middle lane.

Ballard peered out the window. "Piers 18 and 19." His tone was sombre, recalling as a teenager his father's unwittingly graphic description of the bridge collapse in January 1975, the cause the bulk carrier Lake Illawarra losing control late at night and crashing into the two piers. "Just a horrible tragedy all round, seven motorists died, along with five crewmen ... the Illawarra sinking within minutes of the bridge's roadway collapsing onto its upper deck."

Natalie and Sonia voiced their sorrow, agreeing how horrific it must have been for all concerned. John commented, "I remember seeing footage of the two cars perched on the edge of the broken section, their front wheels in mid-air."

Ballard grunted in response. "Yep, a Monaro and a Kingswood station wagon. I bumped into a retired Hobart copper years ago who was one of the first responders. He told me how the driver of the Kingswood crawled back inside to retrieve his pay packet from the front seat ... apparently it had his week's wages in it."

"*You're kidding*!" John checked over his shoulder, causing Sonia to extend a cautioning hand on his knee. Returning to his primary task of getting everyone safely to the hotel, he apologised. "Sorry darling, but talk about desperation."

Ballard agreed. "Yeah, the copper wasn't too thrilled at the guy's antics, that's for sure. He also mentioned the only thing that prevented the Monaro from going over the edge was the automatic transmission gouging into the bitumen. The husband and wife inside were very lucky indeed."

"Bloody hell. I wonder if the driver took out a tatts ticket afterwards?" John was amazed at how close they had come to a horrible death.

Twisting around to address Natalie and Ballard, Sonia summed up her heartfelt wish. "Let's pray a tragedy like that *never* happens again."

The dulcet voice of the navigation system interrupted their contemplative thoughts, guiding John through the relatively traffic free streets of Hobart's CBD and onwards to the casino's undercover car park. Alighting, they hefted their bags from the boot and with their luggage trailing behind them they entered the hotel foyer.

After signing for their adjacent rooms they headed for the lifts, John patting the substantial pillar in the middle of the floor as he went past, the structure one of the primary support columns. He nodded his approval, confirming that it appeared sturdy enough to bear the weight of the building.

Natalie called out, "Come and take a Captain Cook at this view." Without waiting for Ballard and John, the two ladies diverted towards the floor to ceiling glass windows overlooking Sandy Bay and beyond to the CBD, the Tasman Bridge in miniature in the background. The two men joined them.

"You can see why they built the Casino on this spot," Ballard waved a hand to encompass the expansive vista. "What a fantastic location to watch the Sydney to Hobart yachts cross the finish line."

John humphed. "Bloody waste of money if you ask me. They're just a bunch of filthy rich sailors showing off."

Ballard laughed. "Your just jealous because you get seasick on even the smallest of waves. God, what would you be like on one of those boats as it was tossed about coming down the east coast in rough seas?"

John clarified what his reaction would be. "Soiling my Bonds big time. Christ, I was having kittens when we went out into Port Phillip Bay on your motor cruiser to rescue Delwyn and Marjorie."

Attempting to salvage the conversation into something resembling a holiday, Natalie broke in. "Michael, when you said we'd be staying at the casino, Sonia and I did a bit of snooping on Google and there's a shot tower down the road that we'd like to take a look at."

John's eyebrows headed north. "To me shot tower is code for a bloody lot of stairs ... am I correct?"

Unable to resist, Sonia offered, "A mere three hundred. Absolutely nothing compared to what you managed when we climbed St Peter's Cathedral at the Vatican. That was five hundred and fifty-one."

John rubbed both thighs. "And I'll *never* forget it. Ok, time to check out our rooms."

The instant Ballard and Natalie entered their suite, a squeal of delight erupted from Natalie. "*Wow.* It's the same view as downstairs in the foyer, but this time from the sixteenth floor! What a clever hubby you are." Throwing her arms around him she hugged him so hard he was left gasping.

"Careful Nat. At my age my bones are quite brittle, and my heart isn't what it—"

"Stop being silly, you're the healthiest fifty year old I know."

"How many *do* you know?"

A mischievous flutter of lashes followed. "I've bumped into one or two in my time." Unzipping her case she hung up several outfits before taking Ballard's hand, dragging him to the door. "No time to waste. Sonia's as keen as I am to see the shot tower. It's quite famous. When it was built in 1870 it was thought to be the tallest in the world." She shook her head. "It turns out it wasn't, but it's still one of the highest in the southern hemisphere."

"I can't wait to see John's face when you repeat all that in the middle of our climb."

"Perhaps I shouldn't, I don't want to upset him—"

"If you don't, I will."

Natalie pushed him into the corridor, with Ballard pretending to stumble, clutching his back like an old man. As if by telepathy, Sonia and John appeared at the same time, all four crowding into the lift, Ballard pressing the ground floor button.

Natalie touched Sonia's arm. "What did you think of your view?"

"It was fabulous—"

"Yes ... the same as downstairs, but better. I can't wait to see all the city lights from up there tonight."

Even John was impressed, indicating so to everyone's surprise. Holding a hand against the edge of the opening lift door, he stood aside as Sonia and Natalie stepped out. Just as Ballard moved to follow, he shouldered him out of the way, re-joining Sonia, encircling an arm around her waist.

Natalie rolled her eyes. "You men, deep down you're nothing more than a bunch of naughty children."

CHAPTER
19

As they left the hotel all four glanced skyward, noting the high cirrus clouds scudding across a picturesque azure canvas. Approaching the hire car, Sonia and Natalie chose to sit in the back, leaving Ballard to ride with John.

Gunning the motor, John swung onto Sandy Bay Road. "Three hundred steps you say?" His growled question wasn't directed to anyone in particular.

Reaching forward, Sonia wound a lock of hair at the nape of his neck between her fingers. "And it's comforting to know you'll be beside me all the way."

John's reply was another growl, albeit one that had inherent affectionate overtones.

The eight kilometre trip to the shot tower was short, less than ten minutes, with John finding a parking bay in a nearby side street. Exiting the car they strolled towards the sandstone, three storey building, the shot tower at the far end rising an impressive fifty-nine metres. The overall image was that of a giant steam locomotive, the chimney overstated to a ridiculous degree.

Natalie nudged Sonia and whispered, "Talk about boys and their phallic symbols."

Pretending not to hear, John craned his head as they got closer. In a whinging, petulant schoolboy voice he moaned, "This isn't turning out to be a bloody holiday at all. It's a ... a ..."

"A chance to work off a few extra pounds Johno?" Ballard's suggestion caused Sonia and Natalie to grin at one another.

Entering the gift shop, they were struck by its old-world charm. A number of tables and chairs were positioned off to one side for weary tourists once their climb was complete, perhaps with a cup of tea in hand, or spoiling themselves with a plate of scones topped with jam and cream, the patrons mindful not to spill anything on the snow-white, starched table cloths.

A diminutive lady with grey hair and a positive expression greeted them from behind a wooden counter stacked with travel brochures; alongside were miniature models of the tower. "Good morning everyone. I take it by how healthy you all appear to be you'll have no trouble making the climb?" The moment she uttered the words she spotted Sonia's maternity bump and hesitated. Laughing, Sonia put her mind at ease. "Don't worry, I'll be fine ... my fiancée will be with me. I promise you won't need to call an ambulance."

Digesting Sonia's words while analysing John's growl of trepidation, she informed them of the ticket price, and once the transactions were complete, she pointed towards the door that led to the tower.

On entering, John did a double take. First, he glanced down at the vat of water where the lead pellets were collected, then upwards to the platform high above from where the molten lead was released. "You've got to be kidding me! If I climb up there I'm a monty to suffer a nosebleed." Looking around he discovered he had been left to his own devices, everyone now engrossed with a series of photos on the walls depicting the tower's history. Beneath each, written in meticulous cursive handwriting were step-by-step details as to how the tower was built, and what the process was to make the lead shot.

Ballard winked at Natalie and Sonia. "Ok ladies, lead the way, we'll be right behind you ... won't we Johno?" Yet another moan from the lanky detective was the ever-predictable reply.

Surprising everyone, and defying popular belief that pregnant women should take things easy, Sonia surged ahead with Natalie close behind. With a bow and a sweep of his arm, Ballard offered for John to precede him to the circular stairs, which appeared to spiral upwards towards Heaven.

With his partner trudging in front of him, Ballard commented, "Earlier I consulted Google and found out some fascinating facts about shot towers. Did you know they were invented by William Watts of Bristol and patented by him in 1782?"

Through gritted teeth John hissed, "No I did not, and nor do I care."

Grinning, Ballard poked him in the back to hurry him up, both falling behind the ladies' impressive pace. "Prior to that, shot was made in moulds, and as you can imagine it was labour-intensive and very inefficient. Young William came along and revolutionised the process by building a tower much like this one. At the top he poured molten lead through a copper sieve—as it fell, the air pressure formed the lead into perfectly round spheres which cooled in the vat of water below. The final product was then checked for roundness and polished with graphite to lubricate the individual shot ... damn ingenious don't you think?"

Exasperated, John came to an abrupt halt, with Ballard bumping into him. "Now either I stand here listening to your rantings, or I continue on up these infernal steps ... providing you button your lip. I can do either one of those two things, but I won't do both."

Making a zipping gesture across his mouth, Ballard pointed a finger skyward. "Consider it done my good man, now onward and upwards."

Reaching the top of the stairs they moved to the outside balcony which encircled the tower, John choosing not to look down despite being encouraged to do so by Sonia and Natalie who couldn't help giggling at his discomfort. Taking advantage of the pollution-free air Tasmania was renowned for, they worked their mobiles overtime, capturing shots of the Derwent River and beyond to Mount Nelson.

Sonia spontaneously hugged John, clearly enjoying every aspect of the holiday so far, her pleasure matched by Natalie who stretched up on tiptoes to kiss Ballard's cheek. "It's so nice to see you and John relaxing. You both needed to unwind considering what you've been through over the past few months."

In a miracle of timing, and in abject defiance of her words, Ballard's mobile sprang to life, causing him to wince when he saw who the caller was. Nudging John, both men moved to one side. "Well Pete, at least we got a few hours of our getaway in before work encroached to liven things up."

Not bothering to apologise, Peter got down to business. "Check out the twenty-four-hour news channel tonight. You'll see a repeat of the Premier and the Chief's second press conference which went some way to explaining how things went so wrong regarding the transportation of the cannisters, along with the security contingent being murdered, and to top things off, two of the cannisters going missing."

"Christ, what brought all this on? I'm assuming the press got wind of what really happened and threatened to blow the whistle?"

A terse laugh followed. "Correctamundo! It was a case of get in first or be buried alive."

John leaned closer so he could hear both sides of the conversation.

"How did it go down?" Ballard wasn't confident, unsure how such an appalling disaster could be presented in a positive light.

A whistle of amazement preceded Peter's next revelation. "If I hadn't seen it with my own eyes, I wouldn't have believed it. The Premier put the blame of poor security squarely on the various countries demanding to provide their own personnel. While he commiserated over their fate, he pointed out that none of *our* security were involved. What he didn't elaborate on was the train driver and the engineer copping it in the neck."

John was astounded. "You can't be serious."

"It gets better. He then slipped in the fact ... well, he had no choice come to think of it ... he fessed up that two cannisters were missing, but get this, he convinced the press that with the remaining shipment now locked away inside the site, it won't be long before the other two are located and secured. He claimed *that* fairy tale was based on solid intelligence. Then, without a shadow of shame, he repeated how the government took charge, securing the site and its surrounds with the military. He then boasted, yes *boasted*, how effective the security detail was in repelling the drone attack. Following that exposé, he reminded everyone of the untold billions the venture would secure for Victorians over the coming decades, and the benefits that would flow from such a cash injection. To my way of thinking, greed has now outweighed human life in the minds of the press *and* the politicians. Let's say it wasn't their finest hour—the pollies as well as the press I'm referring to."

He drew breath before continuing. "To the media's credit, the Chief was asked some pretty hairy questions, but he was so caught up in the Premier's rhetoric he went along with the fantasy that finding the two missing cannisters was a done deal."

Ballard shook his head. "Please tell me the possibility of the Thomson Reservoir being polluted wasn't mentioned?"

"Not a word. Even the Premier in full flight couldn't have hosed that one down."

"How did the AC take the news?" John already knew the answer but felt he had to ask.

"Incandescent rage would be putting it politely Johno. Even I learned a few new swear words."

Ballard checked that Natalie and Sonia were still engaged taking photos. "Anything we need to do?"

"Hell no. It's just that I didn't want you turning on the news and having a heart attack. Oh, and the AC still wants you to meet up with DC Johnston to discuss Hobart's ports."

Ballard laughed. "We'll slip that in somehow during one of the girls' shopping trips. By the way, how's the shoulder coming along? I imagine triage nurse Diane is taking good care of you?"

John's snort almost drowned out Peter's startling confession. "Actually, she's moved into my place so she can keep tabs on any post-op infection. I have to admit I'm getting used to all the attention."

"And I'll bet she's getting her fair share of attention in return."

"Yeah, righto John, I'm sure Pete's been a perfect gentleman." Ballard's grin was from ear to ear.

"Ok, you two, if I can't have a sensible conversation then I may as well hang up."

"Pete … we're thrilled for you, especially Nat and Sonia. We can't wait to give them the latest news."

Peter carried out his threat.

Ballard and John stared at one another, still digesting how the Premier managed to pull off such an audacious briefing without being torn apart by the press. Scratching the back of his neck, Ballard suggested, "Perhaps we should leave this as having been a social call from Pete, putting to rest any concerns Nat and Sonia might have."

John was in total agreement. "Sounds like a plan."

"Hmm, so what's this *plan* you two are cooking up?" Approaching, Sonia placed an arm around John's waist, her gaze hesitant. Eager to pass on Peter's romantic news, John's revelation had both women gobsmacked.

"So, Diane's *moved in* … to Peter's apartment?" Natalie couldn't believe what she was hearing.

Ballard followed up with, "Ain't love grand?"

"It certainly is, and don't you two do anything to discourage it." Natalie was emphatic, stabbing a stern finger at both men.

The sightseeing over, they made their descent, John grumbling that his quads were on fire. Re-entering the reception area, they thanked the ticket lady before emerging into warm sunshine. Aware the day's activities had been predetermined by Natalie and Sonia, Ballard and John stood dutifully to one side, waiting for the next announcement.

"As we're so close, we thought a drive up Mount Wellington would be a pleasant interlude." Natalie swivelled around, pointing at the almost 1,300-metre-high mountain in the distance.

"You did say *drive*?" John leaned down, massaging both thighs.

Sonia laughed. "Yes John. We're not planning on scaling the east face armed with ropes and pitons if that's what you're thinking."

John's brow creased while Ballard smacked his forehead with the palm of his hand. "Very impressive Sonia. I didn't know you had a mountaineering bent."

Natalie leaned across and whispered in John's ear, "Pitons are metal spikes hammered into crevices in the rockface and used as leverage by rock climbers."

John pretended he was being unfairly picked upon before heading back towards the hire car, his demeanour exaggerated hound-dog. Smiling, Sonia caught up, linking her arm in his as she kissed him on the cheek.

Natalie grinned. "Perhaps I shouldn't have stirred him quite so much."

Ballard scoffed. "Nonsense. He's a big boy, and believe me he's up to it."

With everyone in the car, John set off, not requiring Sonia to enter their destination in the GPS as road signs were spaced sufficiently to guide them towards the summit. The twists and turns in the road were sufficiently taxing to generate intense concentration as John expertly negotiated the bends, attacking the task with rally-driver fervour.

Checking her mobile, Natalie exclaimed, "Well, knock me down with a white feather … I never knew that."

Leaning across, Ballard peered over her shoulder, "What's that, darling?" hopeful she had discovered details which would send John's blood pressure soaring.

"Doctor Google says that Charles Darwin climbed the

mountain one afternoon in 1836, so you're in good company John."

Grunting his reluctant acknowledgement, John concentrated on his driving, refusing to be drawn into the jesting raging around him.

To his chagrin, Natalie wasn't anywhere near being finished. "Oh goody. Apparently close to the summit there's a tourist spot called The Chalet. If we pull over there it's just a short walk to the Organ Pipes which were formed during the Jurassic period when Tasmania was separating from Antarctica. The rock itself is dolerite which means—"

"Which means Superman can't fly anywhere near it." The smirk on John's face showed he had resigned himself to the reality a cross country hike was now on the cards.

"Very funny John, but I said dolerite, not kryptonite." Natalie was happy to see he was at last getting into the swing of the holiday, with Sonia's smile showing she was equally pleased, if not a tad relieved.

Reaching the signpost pointing towards The Chalet carpark, John nosed into one of the empty spaces, ogling a gunmetal-grey Lamborghini parked nearby. "Now that's the car we *should* have hired."

Ballard was amused, ever conscious of the magnetic allure high performance sports cars held for his partner. "Had we more time we could have come over on the *Spirit* and brought the Bentley, then you'd be in your element."

"Not on your life, buster." Natalie was adamant, her eyes flashing. "I've heard too many horror stories linked to the Bass Straight crossing—I want to *enjoy* my holiday, not spend my time over here recovering from seasickness."

Sonia joined in. "I'm with you. I couldn't think of anything worse than being tossed about in a ship all night, then having to recuperate when we should be sightseeing." Taking John's hand once he had locked the hire car, she hauled him away from the very expensive distraction. "We're here to discover nature darling, not drool over how fast a ton and a half of metal can hurl itself from nought to a hundred."

After heading along the path for less than ten minutes they came to a small fenced off clearing. Towering majestically overhead were the Organ Pipes, the vertical fluted column's soaring a hundred and twenty metres skyward."

"Will you look at that silly bugger, he's going to break his damn neck." John's accusing finger pointed to a lone climber halfway up the cliff face, his progress slow but steady.

Their hands covering their mouths, Sonia and Natalie watched on, concerned for his safety.

"I know climbers do it because of the challenge, but it still amazes me why they take such risks." Natalie shook her head as she and Sonia moved closer to inspect the wonder of nature before them.

John elbowed Ballard. "They might have balls, but rock climbers don't have any bloody brains if you ask me. And if something goes wrong they expect others to risk their necks saving them. I mean it's a past-time which serves no worthwhile purpose whatsoever."

Ballard considered his partner for several seconds. "I agree, but clearly there's something in the human psyche that drives us to push boundaries. If we humans hadn't taken risks over the millennium we'd still be scrabbling about in the dirt and living in caves." He shrugged. "We certainly wouldn't be experiencing the pleasure of driving Bentleys or Lamborghinis."

John washed both hands over his face, his expression thoughtful. "You just may have hit the nail on the head."

Having taken photos from every conceivable angle, Natalie and Sonia returned from the safety barrier, satisfied they had secured lasting memories of a wonder of nature which was an attraction for tourists from around the world.

Sonia took John's hand once more, dragging him along the path towards the car, calling over her shoulder, "Onwards and upwards to the summit."

Natalie was in awe. "Incredible! He's like putty in her hands. Who would have thought the day would come when a beautiful lady was able to tame such a wild, unpredictable alpha male."

"Steady on Nat. Wild and unpredictable might be overdoing it a smidge ..." He hesitated. "No, on second thoughts, recalling some of his exploits when we patrolled the streets of St Kilda all those years ago—yep, back then wild and unpredictable summed him up pretty much to a tee."

Arriving at the summit car park, John sat fixated, arms locked, knuckles white on the steering wheel. "Are you guys seeing what I'm seeing?" Incredulity had his voice rising two octaves. "That's bloody snow out there!"

Sonia was ecstatic. "How wonderful! I haven't seen snow in years. Come on, darling, the cold air will be good for you, it's bracing." Without waiting she bolted from the vehicle, scooping up a handful of snow and fashioning it into a ball. Fronting the rental with John still inside, she deliberately aimed at the windscreen, hurling the missile with surprising accuracy.

"Where does she get all her energy?" John addressed Ballard and Natalie who were watching the spectacle from the back seat, not expecting an answer and knowing little or no sympathy would be offered.

To underscore the point, Natalie blurted, "Thank your lucky stars you have a fiancée with so much get up and go, buster ... as well as the strength of character to put up with you."

Spinning around, John noted the twinkle in Natalie's eyes, but he realised she was also deadly serious. Sensing this was his marching orders, he hopped out and joined his fiancée, each throwing snowballs at one another like carefree teenagers.

After trooping along the concrete path, they entered the Pinnacle Observation building, appreciating the welcome rise in temperature; even so, John's hands remained firmly thrust inside his trouser pockets. Uttering their delight, Natalie and Sonia rushed to the massive glass window overlooking the stunning views of Hobart and the Derwent River, their mobiles at the ready. The scenery was breathtaking, affording a sweeping vista stretching at least a hundred kilometres. Their frenzy of photo taking eventually satisfied, they returned to where Ballard and John were standing, both men impressed by the spectacular view.

Natalie checked her watch, surprised it was already 2.00 p.m. "Now, for our next adventure ... Sonia and I have decided we'd like to check out the shops at Salamanca Place." Noting the men's pretended interest, Natalie scoffed at their pitiable acting. "Fully aware you lads would be bored senseless, Sonia and I, and against our better judgement I might add, have decided you both deserve a get-out-of-jail card. This means you're free to meet with whomever it is you've already planned catch up with."

Despite their protestations, John and Ballard were impressed by Natalie's intuitive presumption.

Scoffing, she added, "Don't give me that *how-does-she-know* stare. It doesn't take a brain surgeon to figure out that despite being on holidays you're still in touch with work ... and most likely this one is an excuse to contact *someone* down here who's involved with your current investigations."

Wincing at the accuracy of her declaration, Ballard glanced towards John, both deciding honesty was their best option. "As a matter of fact, our AC has suggested we have a chat with one of Hobart's deputy commissioners—"

"The *chat* won't require you to go operational like you did in Venice, will it? Gliding past Sonia and I in one of those rubber speed boats full of tactical soldiers armed to the teeth, all the while pretending you were checking out gondolas?" A shadow of concern flitted across Natalie's face, her look matched by Sonia.

Both men held up defensive hands, with Ballard declaring, "No Nat, you have our word, this is nothing more than an intelligence sharing exercise." Ballard turned to John, "I'll ring the DC to set up a meeting, and with any luck he'll make time for us while the ladies stroll the market in town. My guess is we'll be back at the hotel around five." He moved to one side.

Sonia reached out and touched John's arm. "That'll be perfect. And as luck would have it, our trip coincides with the Dark Mofo festival down in Shed One at the waterfront."

With heightened trepidation John asked, "And what's the Dark Mofo festival?"

Attempting without much success to keep a straight face, Sonia responded, "Oh it's a bunch of artistic people putting on high-brow shows for the public's entertainment—"

John's moan was followed by a chuckle from Sonia, who hastened to clarify. "But the reason we'll be going to Shed One is to take part in the food festival which includes every dish imaginable. You'll be in culinary heaven, my darling."

John was upbeat. "*At last*, the holiday's on the up and up."

Ballard returned, mobile in hand, the contact with the Counter Terrorism DC an obvious success. "Indeed John, the holiday *is* on the up and up. The DC said he'll fit in with us. I said we'd be there in about forty-five minutes. We can drop Nat and Sonia off on the way."

Natalie smiled coquettishly. "We're so glad we can be out of your hair while you men do what's necessary to ensure we women remain safe." She appeared embarrassed the instant she uttered the words. "I'm sorry Michael. That was meant to be in jest, but somehow it came out all catty."

Ballard gave her a hug. "Not to worry. John and I know how difficult our work can be for you both, and we're forever grateful for your understanding. In all honesty, we couldn't do what we do without your backing."

John surprised everyone, including himself. "I'll second that. The comfort and support you both give us is ... is beyond words. I still pinch myself when I think how lucky Mike and I are."

Both women hugged their partners, onlookers assuming something significant was afoot ... and they were right.

CHAPTER
20

Hobart's police headquarters was in sharp contrast to Victoria's modern, glass and concrete, thirty-nine-floor skyscraper. The cube-shaped, cream-coloured, ten-storey edifice in Liverpool Street projected uninspiring solidity, but scant else.

"You're sure the DC's ok with us parking inside?" John asked Ballard as he waited at the lights to turn into Argyle Street.

"He is indeed. I gave him our reg number and he said he'd pass it onto security."

Swinging left, then left again into the carpark entrance, John lowered his window and spoke to the smartly dressed security officer. "Detective Inspector Michael Ballard and Detective Senior Sergeant John Henderson to see Deputy Commissioner Johnston. He's expecting us."

The security guard stood to attention, falling short of saluting his visitors whom he assumed must be very important to be meeting with the senior officer. "Yes sir. Please park on this level in bay forty-six. I'll ring Mr Johnston and let him know you've arrived. He contacted me earlier and said he would personally escort you to his office." His expression suggested he hadn't come to terms with the attention his visitors were receiving from a deputy commissioner.

Throwing his own salute, John winked as he raised his window. Slipping the car into gear, he began negotiating the tight turns around the carpark's pillars. "That's a first, being addressed as *sir*. Has a nice ring to it don't you think?"

Ballard backhanded his partner, a grin forming. "And if you can ever resist the urge to knuckle Professional Standards detectives, you just may land a promotion and make the *sir* a reality."

John snorted. "In your dreams, buddy boy. That's the *last* thing on my bucket list." He shook his head. "Pretty surprising to have a DC collect us in person though."

"*Over there.*" Ballard pointed to the allotted parking bay.

Alighting from the vehicle, they closed their doors just as an authoritative voice boomed, "Good afternoon gentlemen. I'll hold the lift for you."

Jogging over, they piled in, the door held by a diminutive police officer in full uniform. Despite his slight stature, the DC's demeanour suggested he was accustomed to being in charge. He shook their hands, the grip firm but not aggressive. "Wayne Johnston, pleased to meet you."

Ballard and John introduced themselves, the officer sporting a lopsided smirk. Punching the tenth-floor button, he said, "AC Thompson has told me quite a lot about you two, including some of your more infamous exploits, one of them being firing military grade weapons at bad guys out of a diving helicopter. *Mother of God.* I'm in two minds to have him authorise a secondment for you both over here, my troops could do with a bloody good shake up." As the lift door opened on the allocated floor, he directed, "To your left."

Entering his office, both detectives were impressed by the bird's-eye view across the CBD to the waterfront, the vista including Constitution Dock.

"That'd have to be a distraction when the Sydney to Hobart yachts come in." John couldn't resist the light-hearted dig, at the same time spotting the framed citations decorating the wall.

The DC laughed. "I do my best to turn my back on the action John, other than an occasional peep over my shoulder." He pointed towards a table and chairs off to one side, a set of glasses and a water jug in place. "Please take a seat, we have a lot to discuss."

It was plain to see he was cut from the same cloth as their AC. Polite but authoritative, clearly intelligent, and someone who didn't suffer fools. Both detectives felt at ease, knowing they could speak freely with none of the new-age political correctness that made hardnosed discussion and decision-making nigh on impossible.

As soon as everyone settled the DC got down to business, an open folder and a gold pen close at hand. "Kevin tells me you have a number of very nasty players who are making your lives hell at the moment, and my concern is there's nothing stopping them spreading their tentacles to my neck of the woods."

John looked to Ballard, more than happy for his partner to take the lead. Hunching forward, Ballard opened with, "Sir, we've—"

The DC cut him short. "Before we get underway, let's drop the *sir* and replace it with Wayne ... are we clear?"

Both detectives accepted that this was a directive, not a suggestion. Ballard continued, "Wayne, you'll find it hard to believe some of the intel we're about to pass on, but bear with us because unfortunately we're not exaggerating. For starters we're tackling an elite group of Russian criminals who operate out of Moscow with cells in most western countries, and certainly one in Melbourne. They go by the name of The Board, the Russian derivation being Cobet. Their targets are high profile hits that secure them large sums of money and equally exorbitant ransoms. The group is made up of ex-Spetsnaz soldiers, Russian politicians, diplomats, high-profile criminals, and undoubtedly a whole series of corrupt businessmen and IT specialists. The full-skills gamut you could say. In Victoria alone they've been responsible for a robbery on our Note Printing Australia building, a siege on our state parliament, and recently they attempted to smuggle in a billion dollars' worth of drugs through our Geelong port."

The DC was a study of concentration, which heightened at the mention of the smuggling operation in Geelong. "Yes, I'm aware of these incidents, but the media coverage was ..." he hesitated, "lacking any specificity."

Ballard continued. "What's been covered even less, due to our department and the Government not wishing to pass on any more information than necessary, is The Board's recent attempt to destroy the nuclear waste facility near Ouyen. And the buggers damn-near succeeded. The elite ex-Spetsnaz soldier leading each of these criminal ventures was Sergey Alistratov."

It was the DC's turn to move forward in his seat. "The operative word I'm told being *was*. Kevin detailed how you had to put the bastard down before he could blow the tunnel and kill not only yourselves, but a heap of workers." He was both disturbed yet impressed at the same time. "Your department and the Government should be very grateful for your actions."

The snort from John was loud and laced with meaning. "Try telling our Professional Standards Command that our efforts were noteworthy."

The DC burst out laughing. "Yes, Kevin also mentioned your *run-in* with one of their detectives. I wish I'd been there to see it. We need Professional Standards monitoring our actions, no doubt about it, but a lot of their detectives are just damn pen pushers who've never had to make a snap life-and-death decision in their lives."

Ballard and John checked one another, now appreciating the bond which existed between their AC and the senior officer for so much of their professional life to have been discussed.

Pushing on, Ballard explained, "One angle The Board pursued was successfully blackmailing our Ports Minister during the letting of a contract with our Melbourne docks. As a consequence, our ports are figuratively a swinging barn door, allowing contraband to move in and out of the country at will. We believe we've been partially successful in curbing the illegal movements due to a recent source of intel that has proven to be very accurate, but the pressure from The Board on the minister resulted in him taking his own life."

Ballard glanced at John, both concealing the truth that the minister was in fact in witness protection, with his so-called suicide arranged by Ballard and John to fool The Board into believing he was dead, thus protecting the minister's wife and children, who for their own safety needed to believe he was deceased.

"A stroke of luck led us to the new intel—a consequence of securing an iPad which lists a host of illegal activities that The Board is, or will be, embarking upon."

The DC's eyebrows shot skyward.

"Clearly we need to be selective as to which activities we focus on so we don't overplay our hand—"

The DC was intrigued. "Yes, that makes sense so The Board won't suspect you have the iPad."

"It's a long story how we came to acquire it, but despite the files being encrypted, which the army is helping us crack, it's proving to be the difference between us winning the battle against The Board and open anarchy."

The DC rubbed both hands over his face. "Christ, if the public only knew."

"That's exactly what we've said many times." John reconfirmed in his own mind how perilously close-to-the-bone law enforcement in Australia was operating.

The DC inclined his head. "Your Premier and Chief Commissioner gave a press conference today stating several nuclear cannisters have been … *misplaced*." The emphasis on the last word matched his troubled expression.

Ballard replicated the look, indicating that he and John had been at several briefings to discuss the matter. "While the reinforcement of the storage site by the military has proven to be a major success, the loss of the two cannisters could quite literally blow up in our face."

"The Board's doing?"

Ballard was decisive. "Unfortunately not. A competitive group with an Italian pedigree dating back to the 1800s is in direct competition with The Board. They call themselves the Ndrangheta." He waved a hand at John. "What would you say Johno, these bastards are proving to be every bit as ruthless and capable as The Board?"

John agreed. "Without doubt, and then some. As Mike said, they're the group who stole the two cannisters so we're waiting for the inevitable ransom demand. Unfortunately, the federal Attorney-General won't be forking out cash any time soon—"

"So the billion-dollar ransom rumoured during your Parliament House siege wasn't a myth?"

Ballard and John were unsure how to respond.

"Don't worry, Kevin told me some time back how that episode backfired big time on the Government. And truth be known, in the AG's shoes I'd also be leaving my hands in my pockets regarding any new demands. Generally speaking, shelling out money in these circumstances *may* solve the immediate problem, but it creates many more intractable challenges."

Ballard breathed a sigh of relief, not having to falsely deny a ransom demand had been paid during the Parliament House siege. "Another complication we have is there's an operative here in Australia who's not only as skilled militarily as Sergey was, but is an actual Board member. We can't be certain, but it appears he's playing both sides regarding his group and the Ndrangheta. His name is Igor Greshnev, and he's a very nasty piece of works."

The DC was genuinely surprised. "Hmm, that complicates matters. So what you're saying is we have two competing criminal groups, both wanting dominance in Australia, specifically in our ports so they can move contraband whenever they feel like it. I'm assuming at present they're focussing on the Melbourne and Sydney ports, but inevitably Hobart may be targeted. Is that a fair assumption?"

John stepped up to the plate. "I guess this depends on what the two groups believe they can move through your Tassie docks. Your population is what ... a quarter of a million in Hobart ... half a million in the whole of Tasmania?"

The DC nodded as John pushed on. "While drugs are always a possibility, you'd think for either of these groups to take any significant interest down here there'd have to be something else they could bring in, move out, or get their claws into." He waited expectantly and the DC didn't disappoint. "Most people don't know this but Tasmania exports around 80,000 tonnes of aluminium ore each year."

The revelation had Ballard and John openly surprised.

"Add to that, 210,000 tonnes of manganese. Of course, there's our meat, seafood, wood, paper and timber products. On the flip side we *import* 360,000 tonnes of alumina and a whopping 630,000 tonnes of fine metals." The DC poured himself a glass of water, offering to fill two more glasses. Ballard and John declined, still intrigued by what they were hearing. "So you see, our ports are significantly busier than most people believe, not to mention the wine and dairy products we export, but for the life of me I can't see any angle where criminal groups could make *serious* money from these activities."

John was far from convinced. "Oh, believe me Wayne, if they put their mind to it, they'll find a way. I can't tell you how they'll do it, but once they figure out the means they'll set about blackmailing, threatening and extorting their way to making a profit. The reason I say this is because if I'm not mistaken, the Port of Melbourne is a major hub for freight in and out of Tasmania. As a consequence, this *has* to be a drawcard for The Board and Ndrangheta."

The DC could only shake his head. "Yes, thank you John. That gem of advice has cheered me up no end. And you're right, the Port of Melbourne *is* a major transit point for us." He gave an exaggerated sigh. "I thought my role in counter terrorism was difficult enough, but from what you've just told me we're moving into a whole new realm of criminality, and it won't be limited to dealing with outlaw bikie gangs and would-be extremists."

"That's for sure Wayne, and speaking of which, we know for a fact The Board aren't shy in using the bikie gangs for low-level drug distribution, standover tactics and the odd murder, so that bunch of crooks still remain in the frame. And of course, there's Wrest Point."

John noted he had no problem gaining the DC's full attention. "Where there's a casino there's money laundering. It's not out of the question both groups may view Wrest Point as such a backwater it suits their purpose ... no offence Wayne, but it *could* be an avenue for them so it has to be considered."

Ballard winced, aware he was about to add further to the DC's unease. "I'm afraid John's hit the nail on the head how these organisations operate, and please don't think we're here to teach you how to suck eggs—"

"Don't worry, I'm here to learn. Go right ahead, but before you do that, do either of you know the origins of the saying ... to suck eggs?"

John's eyes did a substantial roll, while Ballard sensed the DC was taking a momentary reprieve from the onslaught of bad news. "Actually I've no idea Wayne."

John growled out the corner of his mouth, "That'd be a first."

The DC chuckled. "Neither did I until I checked up on it. Apparently, hundreds of years ago most elderly people had either very bad teeth or none at all. So, to get their protein they would poke a hole in the end of a raw egg and sucked out the contents."

Ballard grinned at John who was shaking his head. "So you see Johno? It's not just me who comes up with these gems."

John's groan had the DC roaring with laughter, witnessing firsthand the camaraderie between the two detectives. "I'm sorry Michael, you were about to say ...?"

"Should either of these groups target Tasmanian ports, or any other major facility, they'll focus on anyone with authority and influence, doing what's necessary to intimidate that person or persons in order to gain a foothold. As they did for our Ports Minister, and to a lesser extent, John and my families. Add to that list one of our deputy commissioners who was arrested a few months back while attending a Board cell meeting, the group knocked over in The Melbourne Club in Collins Street no less."

The DC's previous mirth evaporated. "*Christ.* I heard about the arrests, but I didn't know one of your DC's was involved in the shenanigans."

Ballard kept the commentary flowing. "The DC's to be presented with full charges in the near future, but closer to home, when Sergey was looming large, my wife was threatened and her two youngest had to spend a period of time with their grandparents. On top of that, John's pregnant fiancée was one of the hostages in the Parliament House siege."

"*My God.*" The DC's eyes bulged, each revelation rocking him to the core.

"We also have a Russian *femme fatale* by the name of Tatiana Olegovich in the mix. Thankfully she's now back in custody and her trial's coming up soon. Her claim to fame is having family links to one of the senior Board members, and just for fun she pushed her Russian diplomat husband to his death off the balcony of her Toorak mansion. Furthermore, she arranged for our Ports Minister to be buried up to his neck at one of our beaches with the tide lapping up to his chin. That was an unsubtle warning for us to back off from questioning him over corruption issues associated with the port tender process."

"*Jesus Christ*! Kevin wasn't kidding when he said crime in Victoria was getting complicated." The DC attacked his scalp, his fingers disappearing among steel grey hair which was inordinately thick for someone his age.

John maintained the flood of disclosures. "And that's not the half of it. After we arrested Tatiana, Sergey had our homicide superintendent and the force's psychologist captured and beaten senseless in retaliation. Then they were stripped naked and imprisoned in a shipping container charged with C4 which they dumped into Port Phillip Bay. Michael and I were forced to arrange for Tatiana to be freed from the women's prison or the container would be blown up with the ladies inside. We had no choice but to release Tatiana. Once she was clear of the prison we were given the location of the container which by then was out in the middle of the damn bay. This meant we had to rescue the ladies using Michael's sports cruiser, Sergey demanding police vessels were not to be used. Then in a blatant display of intimidation to remind us who was running the show, and what *could* have happened, he blew the container to kingdom come the moment we cleared the area. So you can understand how after all these threatening instances against our work colleagues and family, putting the bastard down in the tunnel has our Professional Standards assuming we were hell-bent on exacting revenge."

The DC was speechless for several seconds before snarling, "*Tell 'em to get stuffed.*"

"My sentiments exactly, Deputy Commissioner."

So incensed was the DC he didn't object to his rank being used.

Adopting a tag team approach, Ballard took his turn. "So from all this it's obvious what we're up against. The only advice we can give you Wayne is to get your police minister to check on current or impending tenders regarding the ports to see whether there's any fishy business going on, no pun intended, and whether or not the minister responsible is under any form of coercion. And yes, we know firsthand how difficult *that* task will be."

The DC nodded his understanding, his gold pen flashing as he scrawled a series of notes.

Ballard pushed on. "You'll have informants within the bikie gangs, so see whether there's any unusual activity amongst their members. As John indicated, your isolation and limited population numbers are in your favour, but out of sight and out of mind can also be a magnet for The Board or even the Ndrangheta to consider this as a sleepy hollow and ripe for the picking."

Ballard took a breath, allowing the DC to digest the cascade of intelligence flooding his way. "John and I are certain the two cannisters of nuclear waste are earmarked for a more political target overseas than on our mainland, or even here in Tasmania."

The look of relief on the DC's face was profound. "Well, that's the first piece of positive news I've heard from you two."

Mischief never far from John's repertoire, he added, "Have we mentioned the death squad?"

The DC's expression darkened, speaking volumes. Grinning, John elaborated, "I'm not sure about Ndrangheta, but The Board have a group wherever they operate who do the mopping-up when things go belly-up. By way of example, when Tatiana heaved her husband over the balcony, a black Mercedes van pulled into the driveway and the body was collected, the blood washed off the cobblestones and all traces of the dead diplomat erased within minutes."

"How do you know all this?"

"We had the mansion under full camera and audio surveillance. It'll make interesting viewing for a jury when this gets to the Supreme Court, that's for sure."

Ballard took over. "So Wayne, you can see the degree of sophistication these groups apply to everything they do." His eyes narrowing, he weighed up his next comments. "It's clear our AC wouldn't have asked us to brief you if he didn't trust you implicitly. What I'm about to say is classified and can't leave this room, but it may give you some confidence. The Board can and will be beaten."

The DC went to take another drink of water, then changed his mind, replacing the glass on the table in front of him with studied care. "Go on."

"A CIA agent we've had dealings with in Venice has contacts in Moscow as high as the Kremlin hierarchy. He now has credible intelligence that The Board is about to hold a top-level meeting in Moscow to discuss a number of crucial issues. One of the items on the agenda will be how they're going to tackle the competition they're running into with the Ndrangheta. The agent wants representatives from key Western countries to assemble in Moscow prior to the conference taking place. His own elite special forces will conduct the raid."

Showing astuteness, the DC questioned the practicality

of such a venture in the heart of Moscow. "But the Russian Government, surely they wouldn't allow this to happen under their watch?"

"Great point, and here's where The Board's success and reach into all levels of society, including within Russia, has backfired on them. It appears The Board's gotten way too big for its boots and is now a direct threat to the Government. It's no surprise the Russian president wants the threat removed. He dare not ruffle feathers within his own power base because he hasn't a clue who he can trust. That being the case, he's happy to allow us to clean up his mess on the proviso he takes full credit for being tough on crime. From that point on he can suss out who's who, and life in the Kremlin will return to normal."

Deciding he did need the water after all, the DC took a long drink. After swallowing he confessed, "No wonder Kevin said all this was far too complex to discuss over the phone. I really appreciate you both taking the time. I'm also damn impressed as to how well you're on top of things. Yes, you can have your big-time crooks and spies, I'm content to plod along here and pray we really are out of sight and out of mind, as you put it."

Sensing the DC was at briefing overload, Ballard looked to John before offering an apology. "I know all this has been scattergun, but you're right, there have been times when we've felt overwhelmed, and these missing cannisters are a real-and-present danger for us. We *have* to get them back."

Closing his folder, the DC parked his gold pen on top, his intelligent face a study of concentration. "Again, thank you gentlemen. All I can say is I see why Kevin holds you in such high regard—"

"Damn shame he never lets on." John couldn't help himself.

The DC remained serious. "Trust me, I've no wish to blow smoke at you, but I'm in your debt concerning the intelligence you've passed on. Forewarned is forearmed as they say. Make sure you extend my best wishes and thanks to Kevin when you see him next."

Everyone arose as one, each satisfied they had achieved what they had set out to accomplish.

CHAPTER
21

The gothic banquet held annually in Shed One at Salamanca Place, Hobart, is a signature evening event associated with the Dark Mofo festival. It features an orgy of food and beverages, the delicacies sold by an eclectic mix of stallholders, and to demonstrate how popular it is, up to 18,000 people attend each night.

Entering the venue, the two couples spotted the long lines of tables crammed with food and patrons. John licked his lips in anticipation, grinning foolishly at his companions. "Now this is *my* kind of outing."

They began making their way along the stalls, checking out what was on offer, the smell of exotic foods, the buzz of the crowd, and the festive atmosphere of enjoyment proving to be intoxicating. Sonia linked arms with Natalie, while Ballard and John maintained a keen eye on a staggering array of steaks being cooked on portable BBQs. They finally settled on a painfully thin man in blue overalls who was wielding tongs over an electric grill crammed with cuts of choice beef in the final throws of being seared to perfection. Signalling to the ladies that they had found their gastronomic nirvana, they placed their orders, having to opt for side salads instead of their preferred char-grilled vegetables. As compensation, they smothered their steaks with copious quantities of BBQ sauce.

Nearby, Natalie and Sonia decided upon sizeable helpings of sautéed snapper, each serving accompanied by generous portions of mixed salad. Armed with plastic utensils and a bundle of serviettes, they hunted for table space large enough to accommodate four people. A number of patrons noting their plight, shuffled closer to make room for them. Almost tipping his plate into their lap, John apologised, thankfully recovering his balance at the last moment. Everyone tucked in, Ballard and John finding the going tough despite their steaks being soft as butter, wishing they were armed with traditional serrated knives. Sonia chewed thoughtfully on a morsel of fish before confessing, "This may not be Venice, but I'm having every bit as much fun." Planting a lingering kiss on John's cheek, she left behind her Estée Lauder calling card. Nobody bothered to inform him he was now sporting perfectly shaped crimson lips on the side of his face. Natalie nudged Ballard, then leaning across, whispered in his ear, "One good turn deserves another Michael. Let's pretend after our meal that we're all bushed from today's sightseeing and that we should head back to the hotel. I feel I need to come up with an appropriate reward for you after arranging our holiday for us."

"Why ma'am, I do believe you have me at a disadvantage, unable to refuse your generous offer."

Unaware of the devious machinations unfolding alongside her, Sonia sat mesmerised by the festive atmosphere in the room. "It's incredible we don't have something like this in Melbourne. I guess the Queen Victoria Night Market is as close as it gets, but the venue there is more open and ... and, not as *civilized* as this." She squared her shoulders to validate her point.

Polishing off the remnants of his steak, John chewed methodically, all the while hinting he would respond. After swallowing hard, he changed his mind.

Ballard took up the challenge. "When we get back to Melbourne Sonia, we'll fire off an email to the Lord Mayor, demanding she come down here to check the place out."

Desserts followed, all different to suit personal taste, but each comprising obscene quantities of mouth-watering calories. Dabbing her lips with a serviette, Sonia appeared hesitant. "John ... Michael ... earlier on I was chatting with Natalie about tomorrow's activities." Again, she displayed indecision. "I'd like to visit Port Arthur." Then in a rush she added, "I know it might not be the cheeriest place to go on a holiday, but my mother's aunt was one of the victims of the shooting in '96, and I've always promised myself I'd go there one day and pay my respects ... if that's ok with you both?" She held her breath, hoping for a positive response.

John hugged her. "Of *course* we'll drive down there. In fact, earlier on today Michael and I discussed we should do just that."

Sonia gave a weak smile. "You're such a terrible liar, but I do love you for it."

John shook his head. "I simply can't imagine how terrible it must have been for your folks, or for you for that matter with your mum's aunt dying so brutally." He squeezed her against him once more, not sure what else to say or do.

"When I was young, Auntie would come and visit for Christmas and Easter. I used to sit and listen to her stories about life, what I'd face growing up, things to expect as an adult. I learned heaps about human nature from her … she was very wise."

"And then you met me and all your expectations were surpassed." John's attempt at levity was just the tonic Sonia needed.

"Actually yes my darling, you've proven yet again how right she was—good men are gold, and should *never* be allowed to escape." She clasped his arm with both hands, having no intention of letting him go while he in turn flushed from the neck up.

Their meals complete, they drove back to the casino, blissfully content, all ready for a relatively early night, agreeing to head off to Port Arthur straight after breakfast.

Natalie reached up and whispered in Ballard's ear the moment they entered their room, "I feel a bubble bath coming on, it was so thoughtful of you to book a room with a spa."

"Will it be safe after such a big meal?"

"I passed my lifesaving course at school. You'll be safe in my hands."

And safe Ballard was, with bubbles up to his chin, and Natalie snuggling against his chest, a stab of desire coursed through his body as he caressed her silky-smooth skin. Almost purring with contentment, she pressed back against him, her hands wandering to all the right places, the warm water a soothing balm.

Twenty minutes later, so as to avoid the inevitable hazard of their skin turning to that of an old prune, they dried off with the enormous white towels before retiring to the king-size bed, deliciously warmed by the electric blanket. After declaring how much they loved each other, they were asleep within minutes.

CHAPTER
22

Located on the Tasman Peninsular, the scenic township of Port Arthur is a scenic one and a half-hour drive south east of Hobart. With a tiny population of just two hundred and fifty, its humble beginnings were that of a timber station in 1830.

The penal colony commenced operation in 1833 and continued for forty-seven years, all under the auspices of the British Empire; the colony one of eleven correctional facilities located throughout Australia. The prison and immediate surrounds covered 146 hectares, and was the final destination for the most hardened of British criminals, along with repeat offenders, and even those whose crimes were as trifling as a stolen loaf of bread.

Unlike other penal stations which inflicted harsh physical punishment on the inmates, Port Arthur chose the 'Separate Prison Topology' approach, pursuing psychological discipline. Good behaviour was rewarded with extra food and other benefits, whereas bad conduct resulted in minimal bread and water rations, together with the forced wearing of a hood for visual deprivation, along with a compulsory silence regimen.

While it was believed this would encourage the prisoners to self-reflect on the error of their ways, the reality was it sent many completely mad, forcing the powers that be to rethink their tactics. By any measure the penal colony was not a pleasant place, with over seventy-five thousand inmates sent there and seven thousand never leaving, dying as a result of the harsh treatment and brutal conditions.

Sitting alongside John in the hire car, having just relayed the avalanche of facts and figures, Ballard slipped his mobile back into his shirt pocket. "I tell you what Johno, compared to Port Arthur, today's prisons are a bloody holiday camp."

Overhearing the comment from the rear seat, Natalie concurred. "I remember doing a school assignment on Port Arthur, and you're right Michael, those poor inmates suffered terribly, many of them for the most insignificant of crimes."

John cast a glance over his shoulder. "The fact that seven thousand died is proof it wasn't somewhere you'd want to finish up."

Sonia joined in. "And to think all this was still going on less than a hundred and fifty years ago."

There was quiet contemplation in the car as John passed through the township of Sorell, motoring along the Arthur Highway. Peering at the GPS he announced, "Another forty minutes, folks."

The banter in the car turned light-hearted, with Ballard and Natalie doing their best to distract Sonia from what would be an emotional few hours. But it was something she was determined to do as a sign of respect for her aunt.

As predicted, forty-five minutes later they entered the township of Port Arthur, no one daring to blink for fear of missing it. After pulling up in the historic site's car park, they stepped out, Ballard and John arching backwards, their hands pressed on the small of their backs.

Natalie scoffed, "Check them out Sonia, you'd think they had one foot in the grave and—" She broke off, conscious the mention of graves was not the most appropriate topic of discussion.

Sonia's expression was tense, but her response was reassuringly positive. "You don't have to tiptoe around me ... *truly.* This is something I need to do, and while I'm sad about Auntie dying under such tragic circumstances, I have to keep everything in perspective."

Natalie linked her arm in Sonia's. "You're a brave lady. Was your aunt in the Broad Arrow café when the shooter burst in?"

Sonia nodded. "Yes she was, so let's make that our first stop, then we can move on and enjoy the rest of the day sightseeing."

With their tickets bought, and after seeking directions as to where the remains of the café were, they headed along Jetty Road. John's arm was firmly encircled around Sonia's shoulders as he pointed towards the memorial garden and reflection pool off to the left. Out of respect for the fallen, no signs depicted its location. A wooden cross stood starkly at the rear of the garden on which was fixed a metal plaque; it bore the names of the twelve persons slain.

Sonia approached, reading down the list. After several seconds she spotted the name that she was searching for. Reaching out she touched it, silently reflecting on the horror associated with that fateful April day.

Everyone stood back, affording her the time she needed. Almost a minute passed before she spun around, her eyes shining with tears. Forcing a weak smile she declared, "Enough sadness, let's explore what this place has to offer."

And explore they did, fascinated by what they saw, yet never far from the realisation as to how brutal the convicts' existence must have been. Freezing cold in winter, boiling hot in summer, these factors alone contributing to such a high death toll.

For a change of pace, Sonia pointed up at an arborist high in the uppermost limbs of one of the enormous gum trees. Despite the visible safety harness and ropes, John shuddered, mesmerised by the agility of the man as he trimmed dead limbs with a small chain saw. "Jeez. I hope he's getting appropriate danger money for risking his neck." They stood watching in awe as the man went about his work, Natalie mouthing "pollarding" to an amused Ballard.

As they turned to head towards a ruined building, Ballard's mobile rang. Tempted to ignore it, he checked the screen then breathed a sigh of relief, thankful he hadn't disregarded the call. It was from the AC. Motioning for John to accompany him, they moved a short distance from where Natalie and Sonia were standing, still intrigued by the agility of the arborist.

"Good afternoon, sir, I'm assuming this isn't—"

"I need you and John back here by 1700." The demand couldn't have been blunter, and the tone in the AC's voice caused Ballard to stiffen with alarm.

"May I ask what's happened—?"

"A ransom demand has come through. Peter received a call from Igor." There was a minimal pause. "How this bastard gets our mobile numbers is beyond me. The claim is for one-and-a-half billion—yes, I know, it's a bloody crazy figure, but there you have it."

"Has the federal Attorney-General been contacted?"

"Yes, and Igor has given us an 1800 deadline, but before I

go into that, where are you both now?"

"Port Arthur ...with Natalie and Sonia."

"Standby." The AC barked several instructions then was heard in an intense conversation for almost thirty seconds. "I'm on another line with Deputy Commissioner Johnston. He'll be sending the Westpac Rescue chopper down to pick you both up. Expect it in the next ten to fifteen minutes—"

This time it was Ballard cutting the AC off, angry he and John were being ordered back for no apparent reason. "Excuse me sir, while I understand the urgency of the ransom demand, why is getting us back to the office so important? It's not like we can resolve the situation."

The AC rattled off further orders in the background prior to replying. "The container has been driven into the Thomson Reservoir, so we have no choice but to assume the cannister is inside—"

"*Jesus.* How did that happen? Where were the soldiers?"

The reply was instant. "Two of them were shot. Nothing was heard so silencers were used. This opened up several kilometres of shoreline without guards. Surveillance checked out the location and reported that a forklift was driven into the water and the container floated out—the forklift's still in the drink. They've subsequently spotted the container drifting towards the retaining wall. Now it *may* be filled with concrete, or this could be the real thing. We just don't know, but we can't take the risk. I've been in touch with Silverwood from Melbourne Water and he's confirmed the pipeline out of the Thomson has been shut off."

"I still don't understand what we ..."

"Included in the ransom demand is that you, John and myself be seen on the wall of the reservoir by 1700 hours or the container will be lit up. This is Igor's way of jerking us around."

Ballard felt John stiffen beside him, his ear against the mobile. Glancing at his watch, Ballard saw it was 2.15 p.m. "But that only gives us …"

"Three hours and forty-five minutes to get here." The AC's voice was a low growl. "This is how we're going to do it. As I said, DC Johnston is arranging for you to be picked up at Port Arthur, and I've just been told the chopper should be there in about ten minutes. It was already down your way. From there you'll be flown to Hobart Airport which should take about twenty minutes. The Gulfstream jet which the Hobart police lease from time to time is being fuelled and will be ready to fly you to Moorabbin Airport … another hour and fifteen based on that thing's top speed. PolAir2 will pick you up from Moorabbin and fly you to the reservoir, *another* thirty minutes. According to my maths, this has you both here at the reservoir between 1700 and 1730 hours. I'm adding some leeway for changeovers between flights." He was heard clearing his throat. "This gives us a bit over half an hour to come up with something positive before showtime. A piece of cake really."

"Bugger me, this is cutting things very fine!" It was clear John didn't share the AC's optimism regarding the travel times.

"John, never underestimate the reliability of modern transport." The AC wasn't in any mood for self-doubt, but his tone softened as he added, "I can't promise there won't be any danger, but Igor has us over a barrel … so tell me now if you don't want in …"

Ballard looked at John, his partner's expression positive. "You already know the answer to that, sir."

"Yes, as I thought. Ok, *should* the cannister go up we'll

be evacuated immediately. The military have already been pulled back from the shoreline because the very reason they were there is now null and void. Tim has sniper teams moving into position around the dam wall wearing that woolly mammoth camouflage shit they put on. As well, personnel with radioactive protection clothing will be on site to measure radiation levels should things get ugly. That way we can positively determine whether the bastards really did light up a cannister or it was one gigantic bluff."

Ballard was confused. "I'm assuming Robert's description of how the cannister could be breached was put to Igor to determine if this is for real and … ?"

"Good point Michael. Peter claims Igor took great delight in detailing how the cap was unbolted and the welds cut. So appropriately placed C4, as Robert suggested, will undoubtably rupture the cannister, then God help us all." It was evident he was agitating to end the call. "Please apologise to Natalie and Sonia for me … and I don't need to tell you this *must* be kept secret. Make up whatever yarn you like, but they can't be told the truth. Now I need to negotiate a way out of this mess with the Attorney-General, but I'm not holding my breath. I'll see you both up at the wall." Without further comment he was gone.

Ballard pocketed his mobile, checking that Natalie and Sonia were still out of earshot. "Clearly Igor's using us as targets to put additional pressure on the Attorney-General. After all, one-and-a-half billion is one-and-a-half billion, and Igor will pull every lever at his disposal to get his hands on that much money. So Johno, we're on our own with this one, and it's clear the AC believes we have no option but to play along. The stakes are too high to do otherwise. The thing that amazes me about all this is whether Igor is acting for The

Board or Ndrangheta. If the former, then *somehow* The Board has pinched the cannisters off the Italian mob." Frustrated, he checked the time. "Now for the hard stuff. We've got to come up with a story that doesn't give the game away."

They approached Natalie and Sonia whose faces were drawn, aware something of significance was afoot. Doing his best to remain nonchalant, Ballard took Natalie in his arms and kissed her, John doing the same with Sonia.

Natalie demanded, "Ok, what's going on? Spit it out you two." Sonia's expression was equally distrustful.

Swallowing, Ballard confessed, "John and I have been called back to work—"

"*Today … now?*" Sonia alarm caused John to flinch.

"In the next few minutes." John pointed skyward. "There's a chopper coming to pick us up."

Both women caught their breath, realising the call was more serious than they first thought. To Ballard's relief, John blurted out an excuse that contained an element of truth. "One of the bad guys we've been tracking has demanded we be present when he attempts to negotiate a deal. Apparently we're the only police members he trusts. Our AC has indicated this is something too important to pass up. He sends his apology."

Far from convinced, Natalie queried, "What, so you don't have any choice?" Her eyes bored into both men.

They shook their heads, with Ballard replying, "None at all, and as the AC said—"

"*I know, I know … it's too important to pass up.*" Sonia finished the sentence for him.

Reaching into his pocket, John gave Natalie the hire car key, with Ballard adding, "You have another day down here in Tassie, so go mad in the shops and we'll see you tomorrow night when we pick you up at Tullamarine."

John gave Ballard an expressionless glance, praying his partner's optimism was on a solid footing.

"Why does it feel like we're not being told the full story?" Natalie was still uneasy. "I mean a chopper being flown in to pick you both up. That's pretty unusual wouldn't you say?"

John came to Ballard's aid, desperate to throw in a degree of levity. "Obviously because you're mere women we knew we couldn't concern you with the actual truth. That's because some truths are too true to be told, so this was the best excuse we could come up with in the short term."

Both women punched him several times on the arm, the full-on assault only halted by the sound of an approaching helicopter. Gazing skyward the tiny spec grew larger, the words 'Westpac Rescue' and 'Police' coming into view.

Ballard nodded to John. "Our chariot awaits, old son." Grasping Natalie by the shoulders, he stared into her troubled eyes. "I'm so sorry darling. I wish there was another way, but there isn't. Now there's nothing to worry about, this is simply routine police work. I'll see you tomorrow evening at the airport."

Eyes glistening with tears, Natalie didn't chance her voice, her hug strong and prolonged, fearful John's light-hearted words had more than a degree of validity in them.

John's departure was equally emotional, his hand on Sonia's baby bump his last contact with her. Turning, both men sprinted towards the chopper which had landed on the open expanse of grass near one of the historical buildings, the blades still spinning.

CHAPTER
23

The ascent wasn't as brutal for John as it had been in Malcolm's Eurocopter, this going some way to settling his nerves. Both women waved from the ground, their faces partially covered by one hand to deflect the cloud of dust generated by the spinning blades.

"Bloody hell Mike, I don't know about you, but leaving Sonia like this was the hardest thing I've ever had to do. It felt like one of my arms was being ripped off. And it has to be hell for both of them not knowing what we're up to."

Ballard looked at his partner before staring out the window. "Ditto my friend, and yes, Nat's pretty shaken up as well. All I can say is something damn positive had better come of this. Prayers aside, you know what this is turning into, don't you?"

John inclined his head. "Yeah, we've replaced one bad arse Russian with another, and this prick's proving to be just as vicious, if not worse … I'll go so far as to say he's a whole *level* worse."

Speaking into their mikes they thanked the pilot for his prompt lift-off before settling back, reflecting on what lay ahead. While the Kawasaki BK 117's cabin wasn't as refined

290

as Malcolm's chopper, it's cruising speed of 262 kilometres per hour meant the AC's estimate of twenty minutes to reach Hobart's airport was achieved with two minutes to spare.

By contrast, after pounding across the tarmac and scrambling into the executive jet, the interior of the Gulfstream G550 *was* in Malcolm's league, and with a top speed of nine hundred and forty kilometres per hour, it was clear it was going to put the estimated flight time to Moorabbin to the sword. Sitting in the plush side-by-side seats, both men's lanky frames were able to stretch out, Ballard quipping, "Don't get *too* comfy Johno. PolAir will seem like a T-model Ford when we have to change horses."

Grinning, John retorted, "Don't spoil it for me."

Reclining back, they luxuriated in their surrounds until Ballard's mobile shattered the tranquillity. He saw it was from Peter. "Hi Pete, you'll never guess where ...

"The AC's wife's being held hostage at her home by the death squad! Igor rang me fifteen minutes ago to drop the news." Peter's voice was raw with emotion. "Clearly the bastard's pressuring the attorney general to come good with the money."

Watching Ballard, John saw the colour drain from his partner's face, ageing him ten years in as many seconds. Leaning across he demanded, "What is it?"

Ballard switched the mobile to speaker while out of the corner of his mouth he hissed a repeat of Peter's message. He then asked, "What's the AC doing about it? And doesn't it strike you as odd that Jean would be held hostage at her home, and not taken somewhere secret?" He pictured in his mind's eye the AC's wife, toughened mentally over the years by her marriage to the senior officer, but despite this, terrified by what she was now confronting.

Peter broke Ballard's thoughts. "The trouble is we're all up here at the reservoir. When I passed on Igor's demand, the boss didn't hesitate. Assuming Jean was still at home, he got on the blower and ordered Tim to send his best team over to take the bastards out—"

John drew breath as Ballard blurted, "Christ! That's one hell of a risk."

"It is, but he gave detailed instructions how the guys could get onto the property around sunset without being seen. At this time of year sunset's just after five. He told them where to find the spare key for the back door. There's no doubt he was giving unequivocal authority for the death squad to be shot on sight—there wasn't to be *any* negotiation."

Ballard's lined countenance turned to despair. "Pete, while it's a remote possibility, there's a chance Nat's two youngest may be in danger. I need to ring them." He checked the time. "They'll be close to coming out of class. I have to warn them not to go home, rather to go straight to their grandparents."

"Mate, do what you have to do. I'll ring you back when I have more info." He disconnected.

Agitated, Ballard speed dialled Kayla. The number rang but diverted to voice mail. "Kayla, this is Michael. There's no time to explain. *Don't* go home to the townhouse this afternoon. Take Josh with you straight to your grandparents. *This is very important.* Ring me when you get this."

Tense, Ballard tried Josh's number. To his relief the teenager answered, confirming he and Kayla were still at school. Ballard repeated his request. "I haven't time to go into details Josh, but you and Kayla are *not* to go home. Use the credit card I gave you and ring for a cab to take you to your grandparents as soon as you finish school. Call me when you get there." Satisfied his request would be obeyed to the letter, he hung up.

"Christ John, more and more I'm convinced Igor has to be put down just as we did for Sergey, and to hell with Professional Standards."

Agitated, John agreed. "My sentiments all along. And you've done the right thing Mike, while there's bugger all chance Igor would target Kayla and Josh as part of his threats, we can't be too careful. Are you going to let Natalie know?"

Ballard bit his lip, hesitant. "No, I'll ring her after Kayla and Josh have arrived at their grandparents. If I call her now she'll want to ring the kids, and I don't want *anything* to delay them."

John stretched out in his seat, washing his hands over his face. "A gutsy move by the AC. Speaking of Professional Standards, they may well be interviewing the boss when all this is over." He shook his head in an attempt to clear his thoughts.

Ballard wasn't so sure. "They'd better not try or he'll eat them for breakfast. The death squad is a terrorist organisation, and as you know John, after the bloody cockup in the Lindt Café in Sydney, the rules of engagement regarding terrorists with weapons holding hostages has changed *dramatically*."

John's eyebrows climbed. "God, let's pray our guys don't miss."

Twenty minutes later, as the Gulfstream commenced a nerve-jangling descent from its cruising altitude, Peter rang back. "PolAir's on the tarmac Michael. How long before you land?"

"Wait up, I'll ask." Ballard spoke into his headset and was informed it would be wheels down in eight minutes. He passed on the estimate.

"Good. This means you should be here on the wall in a little over half an hour." He paused, obviously checking his watch. "Worst case you'll be touching down twenty past five." He took a breath. "I spoke to Tim who's somewhere in the bush near the reservoir wall with his troops. He said his guys in town have conducted surveillance on the boss's home and saw no movement inside for thirty minutes. Taking a chance, they used the emergency key and went in. Nobody was home, but a couple of chairs were overturned in the lounge. By all accounts the death squad have taken Jean to a location where they have more control over proceedings. That's *not* what the AC wanted to hear."

"How's he holding up?" Ballard couldn't begin to imagine the anguish the senior officer must be experiencing.

"Surprisingly well on the surface, but he's bleeding inside. To a degree his negotiations with the AG are a blessing in disguise, he needs to be doing something, *anything* to keep him fully occupied. He's certainly showing he's a tough old bastard, able to operate under these circumstances." Peter grunted. "Between you and me, the Attorney-General's holding firm on the money as we thought he would. While he's genuinely sympathetic with the AC's plight, he isn't budging, and he's insisting on being kept in the loop so he's up to speed with what's going on here as well as with Jean."

The Gulfstream captain's voice came over the public address system, warning his passengers to remain seated and to fasten their seatbelts. Overhearing the announcement, Peter wrapped up. "You two have things to do. I'll see you in thirty."

As Ballard thanked his colleague, a text came through from Kayla indicating she and Josh had arrived at their grandparents and had spoken to their mother. Displaying the text to John,

Ballard breathed a sigh of relief, knowing he had no choice but to make a call. "I need to put Nat's mind at ease."

Speed dialling her number, he opened his mouth to greet her only to be beaten to the punch.

"*Michael, what's going on? I have a right to know!*"

Ballard swallowed, realising there was to be no sugar-coating. "The AC's wife has been captured by Russian criminals—"

"What? Jean?"

"Yes. I'm sorry we don't have many details, but for safety's sake I took it upon myself to make sure Kayla and Josh went to your parents—"

"Thank you for thinking of them Michael." There was a pause. "*Has* there been a threat made against them?"

The fear in Natalie's voice cut through Ballard like a knife. "No darling, I promise. I'm merely playing it safe."

"Sonia and I want to come back today."

"Nat, even though there's been no threat against either of you, it'll make John and my lives a whole lot easier if you two remain in Hobart, knowing you're out of harm's way. *Please* come back tomorrow as planned, the issues here will be resolved by then."

John made a gesture that he wanted to speak to Sonia.

"Sweetheart, everything's under control, trust me. Now John wants to talk to Sonia. Is she with you?"

"Michael, *please* be careful. And ring me as soon as you can when you're free. I love you." She paused. "Here's Sonia.

John snatched the mobile from Ballard, and for the next two minutes he did his best to reassure Sonia that neither he nor Ballard were in any danger. Reluctantly he disconnected, his brow lined. "Bloody hell Mike, that was tough going. God this is hard, and getting harder."

Ballard agreed. "It is Johno, but it pales into insignificance when compared with what Jean and the AC are going through."

Their sombre trains of thought, racing at a million miles an hour, were broken by the Gulfstream wheels touching down. Bolting from the executive jet over to PolAir, they hurriedly shook hands with the pilot before strapping in, doing their best to get used to the noisier environment, and as Ballard had predicted, the far less salubrious surrounds. Unlike at Port Arthur, this pilot didn't waste any time, the fierce ascent causing both men to white knuckle the edge of their seats.

Adding to their discomfort, they were informed via their headsets that a twenty-knot headwind was going to make the trip interesting. Ten minutes in, John confessed through gritted teeth, "Our pilot may call this *interesting*, but I call it shitting myself, and I don't mind admitting it."

Laughing, the pilot glanced over his shoulder. "There's some bottled water near your feet. Take a drink, it'll settle your stomachs."

"Or have us throw up." Despite this, John took the advice and swigged several nervous gulps before offering the bottle to Ballard who copied his partner.

Below them the roads were packed with early homeward-bound traffic, most with their headlights on, the ribbons of light mesmerising as the detectives mentally steeled themselves for what lay ahead. Both feared Igor would find himself in an untenable position when it became clear no money was forthcoming; a predicament in which he would have to act, not only ordering Jean to be harmed in some way, but blowing the cannister rather than backing down, thus maintaining his self-proclaimed aura of invincibility.

CHAPTER
24

In what seemed much less than thirty minutes, but on verifying was five minutes more, their attention was drawn to the mind-boggling image of the Thomson Reservoir ahead of them. While they had seen photos of the dam many times, viewing it for real was a jaw-dropping experience. The two-lane roadway snaking across the top, together with the expanse of bluestone that covered the entire earthen wall to prevent erosion, and the massive spillway off to the left were breathtaking in their scale. Behind the one-hundred-and-fifty-five-metre-high retaining wall, and stretching ahead for more than twenty kilometres, the sheer expanse of water was spectacular.

John whistled softly. "Now I can see why it was nigh on impossible to effectively secure the shoreline. Christ, you'd need a thousand troops, and even then there'd be hefty gaps between each one."

Ballard agreed, taking in the panoramic vista which under normal circumstances would be a tourist's delight, the incredible view accentuated by their elevated height. But unlike carefree sightseers, Ballard felt a veil of dread envelop him, experienced enough to know Igor was a professional criminal who currently held all the aces.

As they flew closer, the gunmetal-grey exterior of a Balkan armoured vehicle became visible, parked midway on top of the dam wall. Nearby were marked and unmarked police cars, with PolAir2 to one side, its rotors stationary. Figures were dotted throughout the area, some in uniform, others in plain clothes, and many in SOG fatigues.

As PolAir banked to make its approach, one of the uniform officers moved away from the parked vehicles, indicating where the pilot should land, his arms waving furiously. While the directions failed to match the finesse of an experienced airfield marshall, the officer got the message across in his own unique way. On landing, Ballard and John thanked the pilot before scrambling from the cabin, spotting Peter jogging towards them, his expression far from encouraging.

Moving away from the high-pitched whine of the jet engines as they wound down, Ballard and John met up with the superintendent who didn't waste any time. "It's hitting the fan guys. Igor's ratcheting up the pressure big time. I've just got off the blower from him. He's threatening to cut off Jean's fingers if the AG doesn't come up with the money by 1800."

"*Christ.*" John clamped both hands on top of his head, incandescent rage boiling over as he glanced about him, as though attempting to locate the Russian himself. "Where do you think the shithead's hiding?"

"We don't know. Hell, he could be sitting in a penthouse anywhere in Australia for that matter. I've contacted Intelligence and Covert Support to see if they can triangulate his position via his and my mobile, but as he's certain to be using a cypher phone, the encryption on those things means there's bugger-all chance anything of value is going to come of it. PolAir2 did a flyover of the entire area just before to see if they could pick up any thermal images of people hiding—not much use mind you if they're crouching under a Mylar blanket. Either way there was nothing that could be passed on to Tim and his troops who are scattered all over the shop.

"What we *do* know is the bloody container is for real. It's out there floating pretty damn low in the water, so there's *something* heavy inside." Snatching a small pair of binoculars from his jacket pocket, he thrust them towards Ballard. "Take a look to the left of the outlet tower." He pointed to the circular concrete structure extending vertically from the surface of the water, fifty metres from the dam wall.

Focussing, Ballard let out a confirming grunt before handing the binoculars to John. "Yep, large as life. It doesn't mean the cannister's inside, but you're right, the container's low in the water."

Peter nodded. "We've flown a drone over it fitted with an infrared camera to pick up any heat being generated. Our theory being if the cannister *is* inside and the lid's unbolted with the welds cut, there *should* be heat coming from the bloody container … that said, we didn't get a positive reading. Now while nothing showed up on the camera, considering the potential for contamination," he waved an expansive hand in the container's direction, "we just can't *assume* the cannister isn't inside."

John glanced at his watch. "Seventeen thirty. Christ, we haven't much time left for … for *anything*." He shrugged, frustrated at the sheer hopelessness of the situation. "The main issue now is Jean's wellbeing. You say we haven't a clue where she's being held?"

Peter shook his head, heavy with grief. "Igor sent me a

photo of her. She's inside one of their Merc vans. Clearly this gives them flexibility to move locations at will. The word's out to uniform patrols to KALOF any suspicious vans parked in nearby suburbs. We stressed the patrols aren't to approach but to let us know. Either way it's pretty futile ... it's like searching for a needle in a haystack."

John was incensed. "God, the pressure the AC must be under, his wife about to be maimed, and the AG tattling in his ear and refusing to budge on the ransom demand."

They stood gazing across the expanse of water, agonising over the AC's dilemma.

Sighing once more, Peter confessed, "I wanted to give you guys a heads-up before you met up with the boss ... Oh, I forgot, Assistant Commissioner Müller left half an hour ago with some of Tim's team to check out a possible sighting further up the shoreline. The moment the AC arrived Müller made it abundantly clear he wanted to pass full control back to him."

John went to clap his partner on the shoulder but stopped just in time. "How's the wound coming along?"

Peter's look of despair was one of 'in the scheme of things John, it's irrelevant'. Blinking hard, John acknowledged his partner's point of view.

As they approached the AC, despite the emotional strain he was under, it was evident he was very much in command. With machine-gun rapidity he barked orders to the personnel around him. At the same time, with his mobile glued to his ear, he relayed to the Attorney-General the latest developments. He registered Ballard and John's arrival while saying, "Sir, we can't be certain the cannister *isn't* in the container. We've used infrared in an attempt to determine if there's any heat being generated, a sure sign of nuclear waste, but we haven't been able to ascertain anything conclusive." He went silent. When the senior officer did respond it was clear the AG had been asking about his wife. "We know the death squad have her, we've been sent photos. No, it's impossible to know where she's being held ... we believe she's inside a van, but where the van is ... yes, yes, I understand. If I were in your position the decision would be the same. Thank you, sir." His eyes haunted, he disconnected.

Turning, he greeted Ballard and John. "Sorry to drag you away from ..."

"Sir, it's a non-issue. We're just distraught about Jean's situation. She's a lovely lady, and as brave as they come."

"I appreciate that Michael. As I've said many times, our beloveds don't sign up for any of this crap. *We* do, but certainly not them." His expression was measured, but below the surface a barely controlled rage was about to explode.

Ballard decided the only meaningful assistance he could offer was to provide direct support. "Sir, if and when Igor rings back I'd like to speak to him."

The AC accepted the suggestion. "I agree Michael. You and John have a history with the guy, and you *may* be able to convince him that it's futile to harm Jean. Surely all this posturing is a giant bluff to see whether the AG will weaken ..." His voice trailed away, clearly not convinced of his own words.

The detectives shuffled their feet, helpless to relieve the agony the AC was experiencing. Registering their dilemma, he cleared his throat before demanding, "Stick close by gentlemen, and should any of you conjure up a plan which may help resolve this damn mess, please let me be the first to know."

Ballard continued his focus on forward planning. "I see you

have personnel here with meters to measure radioactivity in the water should the container go up."

The AC nodded. "Yes, Trent Silverwood contacted me to confirm the tunnel feeding the Thomson River and the downstream reservoirs has been shut off, so if the reservoir *does* become contaminated, at least it'll be contained."

Peter's mobile burst into life with an incoming message. He opened it and clicked on the attached video, curious yet fearful. There was general shuffling for position, the AC afforded the best vantage point.

The video was of Jean, astonishingly calm under the circumstances, sitting facing the lens, steadfast, defiant. On closer scrutiny she appeared unhurt, although her Bette-Davis hairstyle was dishevelled. Ears straining, they listened to her message, their hearts in their mouths, her words gut-wrenching.

"Kevin, I'm fine. These men are demanding I ask that you pay the money or I'll be hurt. *Don't do it.* I told them no amount of threats would make you change your mind. You'll do what's right. I've been married to you for too many years to know you'll weaken. I love you with all my heart and these *... these rotten animals can go and—*" A vicious wrench on her arm lurched her sideways out of vision as she cried out in pain, the video ending abruptly, shocking everyone.

The AC visibly stumbled, Ballard and John grabbing an arm each to support him, his normally tanned features drained of colour. In a guttural, almost primeval roar, he bellowed, "*I'm going to kill those bastards!*"

Unlike idle threats people make when aggrieved, the detectives knew the AC's declaration of war was as certain as the morning sun rising.

Peter's mobile chirped. Checking the screen, apprehensive, and registering that no number was displayed, he mouthed it was Igor. Reaching out, Ballard took the phone, switching it to loudspeaker as he watched the AC recover from his outburst. Taking a punt, he declared, "Igor, this is Michael Ballard."

"Michael my friend, it's so good to hear your voice. In case you were wondering, I've been ringing your colleague Peter because I didn't want to disturb your Hobart getaway with John and the ladies. *That* would have been poor form of me."

A chill ran the entire length of Ballard's body, but ignoring the deliberate psychological baiting, he got down to business. "John and I and the Assistant Commissioner are here on the wall as you requested. We know your men are holding the AC's wife hostage. I'm here to beg you as one professional to another not to harm her. You won't achieve any better outcome by hurting her. All it will do is treble our resolve to track you down." Ballard waited, fearful he may have gone too hard too soon.

The extended silence was less than five seconds, but it felt like an eternity. "Hmm, my request is very simple Michael … instruct your Attorney-General to transfer the money … *all of the money* … I've already given the account details. After all, your federal Reserve Bank's RITS system is really quite efficient, not like the old days, so transferring one-and-a-half billion is nothing more than a few key strokes. As you know, we discovered *how* effective it was when the money was moved during our fun times at Parliament House." The humour in his voice was disarming, but just as quickly his tone reverted to pure evil. "Now, initiate the transfer and I give you my word your city's water supply won't be polluted. On top of that, the lovely Jean will still be able to lift up her grandchildren for a kiss. You have until 1800 hours. Not one second longer." He disconnected, his words echoing in everyone's ears.

Checking their respective watches, everyone noted they had twenty minutes before the deadline. The AC barked a series of orders to nearby officers. "Have the two chopper pilots prepare to take off. Peter, give Tim a call and have him and his troops move back from the reservoir and take cover. This's assuming the bloody cannister *is* going to light up."

To another officer he demanded, "Tell the guys with the radiation suits and the Geiger counters to get ready, then have them get down behind something solid." The officer headed off in a panic.

The AC glanced about him. "I'm assuming those chaps have the *appropriate* equipment for the job?"

Ballard blurted out unnecessary facts in the hope of diverting the AC's mind from the horrible reality confronting him. "Yes, they' all have scintillation detectors ... capable of picking very low levels of radiation."

The senior officer assessed his inspector, his expression unreadable. "Hmm, thank you Michael. I knew I could rely on you to provide—"

There was a sudden massive thump, along with a shock-wave of scorched air that instantly had everyone ducking. John snarled, "The prick's set off the charges early."

Peering around the vehicle they were behind, they witnessed a gigantic plume of water rising from the reservoir's surface, a cherry-red ball of flame at its base. Chunks of container and what appeared to be rock or concrete arced through the air, with one sizeable piece landing on the roadway, narrowly missing two officers who were flat on their stomachs. As though in slow motion, further pieces of metal and debris began tumbling back down, the ball of flame gone, replaced by a black mushroom cloud of smoke expanding into the evening sky.

The sound of the choppers firing were heard, the rotors slicing through the air. The detectives scrutinised the AC, painfully aware of the renewed anguish he must be suffering, knowing the monsters had in all probability enacted an unspeakable atrocity on his wife of thirty-two years. Ballard rested a hand on the senior officer's shoulder. "I promise you we'll get the bastards."

The AC wasn't able to speak, his eyes moist. He moved away to marshal his emotions. Seconds later he was on his mobile, presumably calling the AG.

Peter swung into action. "Right. I'll go and see what the team make of the radiation levels, if any."

Ballard held up a cautionary hand. "*Don't* go near the water. Let the guys come to you." The superintendent agreed, his expression grim.

To John, Ballard ordered, "Get hold of Tim. See if he saw anyone or anything, and if not, tell them not to hang around. For safety reasons he and his troops need to be well back from the water, just in case."

For the next ten minutes there was a hive of activity, then Peter returned with a questioning expression. He approached Ballard who wasn't sure what to expect. "Zip, niente, nichts, rien—"

"Ok, ok. I get it."

"No, you don't, that's the point, there's *no* radiation in the water. The whole thing was a gigantic con." Peter was having difficulty comprehending the situation. "Obviously the guys will carry out more tests. They have an inflatable which they'll use to get nearer the point of the explosion, but Mike old son, I think we've hit the jackpot."

Both grinned at one another like schoolboys. Approaching the AC, they saw him still on his mobile. Suddenly he dropped to his haunches, his head bowed, then slumping forward, he collapsed onto his knees.

They rushed over, lifting him to his feet, noting with alarm a single tear rolling down his cheek. He looked at them, dazed, "It's Jean. She rang me. *She's free.* They let her go."

He resumed his call. "Where are you now?" There was silence before he stressed, "You need to get to a doctor as soon as you can. Have the lady call an ambulance. Yes, yes, you *know* I love you. You were very brave. I'll ... I'll see you soon." Choking with emotion, he disconnected.

Alarmed at hearing that Jean required an ambulance, both detectives feared the worst. Unable to utter the words, 'Is she injured?' they waited for the AC to respond.

In a daze he whispered, "She's fine, they let her out of the van unharmed ... then they just drove off."

"Where is she now?" Ballard was confused.

"Apparently somewhere in Essendon. She knocked on the door of a nearby house and asked the lady who answered if she could use her phone. Her only injury is her shoulder. You saw what happened in the video when one of the goons yanked on her arm. She's not sure whether that popped her shoulder or not, either way she said it hurts like hell. She's now waiting for an ambulance."

His focus was on Ballard, his expression appreciative. "While we'll never know, your words with the bastard *may* have convinced him of the futility of harming Jean. We're both very much in your debt."

Ballard was grateful for the AC's words, but far from convinced his exchange with Igor had any significant influence on the Russian's subsequent actions.

Peter reached out, relieved at the excellent news, shaking the AC's hand, pumping it longer than need be. "Well done, sir. Mike and I commented earlier how impressed we were you could remain so functional under the circumstances. This has been a first-rate lesson for each of us, demonstrating what true grit and courage is all about, and of course I'm including Jean in that. What an amazing woman. You chose well, sir, that's for sure."

The AC acknowledged the praise and added, "I've always known how mentally strong she is, but to stare down thugs who are about to cut your fingers off . . ." He searched for the appropriate words. "I'm certain I couldn't have addressed a camera with such strength and ... and *dignity*."

With a deep breath he returned to the matters at hand. "Ok, now tell me, are we going to turn green in the next day or two?"

Peter grinned from ear to ear. "It's good news all round, sir. No one's been injured, and to this point there's no readings showing *any* radiation. It's been one bloody great hoax, and had you weakened, and no one could have blamed you or the AG if you had, we'd have seen a heap of money go into an untraceable account so The Board or perhaps even Ndrangheta could go on doing what they do."

The AC brought his three detectives into his confidence, gesturing for them to come closer. "Let me tell you something, just between us. The last conversation I had with the AG had him within a cat's whisker of capitulating. He openly admitted the Federal Government wastes as much money as the ransom demand every few months on pointless projects that go nowhere. He agonised over Jean's predicament, quite separate from the catastrophe should the reservoir have been polluted. He said he didn't know what he would have done if it was *his* wife being held captive."

Ballard and John contemplated how close Igor had come to pulling off his contrived act of treachery.

John scratched the back of his neck, his brow furrowed. "I'm not convinced the bastard's all that fussed about the money. Don't get me wrong, he'd have taken it with open arms, but you heard the tone in his voice. He was toying with us—there's something else at play here, I just don't know what."

Ballard considered his partner. "You might be right Johno. Blowing the container was a clear warning to us he *could* have polluted the reservoir had he wanted to. The fact he didn't, hints that the cannisters are destined for bigger things. The other aspect I don't understand is how Igor is managing to operate within both camps. As we know, The Board's hell-bent on blowing up the storage site, while Ndrangheta was focussed on the cannisters, with Igor a main player in both groups. To my way of thinking that's a ballsy move fraught with danger, and despite his smarts, it may well get him hung, drawn and quartered, *literally*."

The AC concurred, while not bothering to show the slightest concern for the Russian's health. Checking several texts on his mobile, he discovered one of them was from Assistant Commissioner Müller. Half-smiling, he commented, "Gerhard will be back here in the next twenty minutes or so. He heard the explosion and wants to know what happened. He can liaise with Trent Silverwood to determine what's to be done with the bits of container in the reservoir. As for me,

I'm done here, I need to get back to Jean. I'm assuming you three will want a lift in PolAir?"

"Oh great." John smacked an open palm against his forehead. "Just to end the day's fun, let's drop down on top of a bloody thirty-nine-storey building in windy conditions."

The AC growled. "Suck it up son, there are far worse things in life … as you've just witnessed."

CHAPTER
25

Once more encapsulated in a state-of-the-art cocoon of high-tech steel and plexiglass, held aloft by five composite rotor blades beating the hell out of the air in a fundamentally inefficient aerodynamic manner so as to defy gravity, Peter, Ballard and John found themselves rubbing shoulders with the AC as they travelled at more than 240 kilometres an hour towards Melbourne.

Less than ten minutes into the trip the senior officer removed his headset and took up his mobile. His first call was to the Chief Commissioner. The three detectives slipped off their sets and leaned in, engaging in unashamed eavesdropping.

The AC observed them through narrowed eyes while speaking. "Yes sir, the container was a blatant try-on. Let's face it, had *we* been the crooks we'd have given it a crack too. Uh-huh, I agree, Igor had nothing to lose. What's not so great is my detectives' belief the two cannisters are bound for a far more sinister undertaking which we're working to determine. Yes sir, their recovery *is* our first, second *and* third priority." The AC shuffled more upright in his seat, his face softening. "That's correct ... yes. I appreciate you asking. Unharmed save for a dislocated shoulder. Hmm, I doubt that'll hold her back. I am, very much so, not only relieved but *very* proud." A cheeky wink was directed at Peter. "Yes, I agree, I did choose well. No question sir, I'll be sure to pass that on. Yes, I'll keep you informed. I'm ringing him now." He lowered his mobile to his lap and viewed his audience with a sardonic smile. "It's reassuring to know the Chief has his priorities in order, ascertaining that the Thomson's okay *before* raising Jean's plight ... he got there in the end though." The thinly veiled sarcasm was enjoyed by all.

His next call was more agreeable, the Premier enquiring about Jean's welfare upfront before moving onto what was proving to be a political nightmare for him. "I agree, Premier. We dodged a bullet on this one. Yes, I plan to, perhaps not as many personnel, but still a physical presence at the reservoir in case this was a smoke screen to make us drop our guard and the Ndrangheta do still have the cannisters."

Glancing at one another, the three detectives were angry with themselves that the euphoria of the moment had them failing to recognise another attack against the reservoir was still a possibility.

The AC's laugh was humourless. "No, Premier, I'd advise against that. It'd be premature for another press conference right now. Once we locate the two cannisters you'll have more than enough good news to share around. Hmm ... without doubt. As I agreed with the Chief Commissioner, this has to be our primary focus. Yes sir, thank you, I'll pass on your regards. Correct ... some of those key players are with me right now in PolAir. Sorry about the background noise. Goodbye Premier."

Rolling his eyes, the AC double-checked he had ended the call before commenting, "He sends his thanks for a job well done. He's also bloody toey about this whole affair and wants to call a press conference as soon as possible, and you heard my reply to *that* gem of political suicide. Needless to say, the Chief and the Premier are acutely conscious of the political ramifications if this thing goes belly-up."

"I'll bet neither had any suggestions as to how we go about *finding* these cannisters."

John's caustic riposte saw the AC raising an eyebrow. "No John. It's exactly why they *fund* our police force ... to do just that, locate the cannisters."

Chastened, John's cheeks flushed, much to the enjoyment of Ballard and Peter. The drone of the jet engines was a backdrop to everyone's private thoughts until they were broken by Peter's mobile springing to life. Answering, his face lit up. "Jordan, to what do I owe this—*you what*? Hold on." He switched his mobile to speaker. "Go for it."

"Who's with you?"

"AC Thompson, Michael and John. We're in PolAir in case you have trouble hearing us."

"Hello gentlemen. Good news ... we've cracked another two files on the iPad and one of them is *very* interesting indeed. Cast your minds back to the Wallenius Wilhelmsen shipping line and the *Themis*. Yes, the very same ship that offloaded at the Geelong port all those John Deere tractors with drugs stuffed in the tyres. One of the files on the iPad has indicated a specific cargo is to be loaded onboard the *Themis* prior to it heading to Sydney to drop off a consignment of Toyotas. From there it's setting sail across the Pacific to the west coast of America—"

Peter's grip on his mobile tightened. "This cargo... would I be correct in guessing what it may be?"

"You would indeed be correct. With two cannisters of nuclear waste on the loose, I thought it prudent to pass on that this *might* be the means by which The Board is moving them out of the country."

Ballard lowered his head towards the mobile. "Jordan, we've discussed amongst ourselves how Igor's somehow involved in both camps. What's confusing about your info is the timing because the attack on the train was at least eight weeks after Igor lost the iPad in the drink at Swanson Dock. Up 'till now the iPad has only listed criminal activity specific to The Board, yet the raid on the train was carried out by the Ndrangheta."

Their bent heads crammed closer as Ballard continued, "Is it possible that The Board originally planned to steal the cannisters, but the Ndrangheta muscled in and beat them to it? In which case the question now is, has The Board *really* got the cannisters back, and have the drivers of the trucks and anyone else who happened to be in the way been fed through a woodchipper? If so, it would appear The Board's original plan has been restored. What's more, it's quite likely The Board's encouraging Igor to be involved with Ndrangheta so hiccups like this can be ironed out before they get out of hand."

Jordan's silence said it all.

The AC took up the commentary. "Jordan, your team's discovery means we have to assume the cargo *is* the cannisters, and by default this will be the most probable way we recover them. A great job all round! Pass on our appreciation to your technical team. I assume you've already checked the *Themis'* departure date?"

A slight pause followed. "The size and importance of these

ships is such that their movements are recorded online to the minute. She heads out of Webb Dock tomorrow at 1900."

Emitting whistles of surprise, everyone was mindful how much had to be done in a short space of time. The AC finished up with, "Jordan, the hard work your guys are putting into this is very much appreciated. It's giving us the chance to get a step ahead of these bastards. We'll take it from here, but if you come across any further intelligence … well, you know what to do." He slipped his phone into his coat pocket.

Ballard looked up from his mobile, having searched the *Themis's* itinerary online. "It says here it can carry up to 3,500 vehicles across its thirteen decks. Five hundred Toyota Highlander SUVs are being offloaded here in Melbourne, and then the same number is being dropped in Sydney. After that the ship's off to the land of the Stars and Stripes." He peered closely at the screen. "Christ, the clearance above the cars is less than thirty centimetres, and they're parked side by side, front and back, again with a thirty-centimetre clearance all round. I'll let you work out the logistics of searching amongst *that* lot." He paused again. "Ok … the *Themis* has three adjustable decks where special cargo can be stored, so my guess is that's where the cannisters will be located if they *are* onboard. The worrying aspect is the nuclear waste is potentially destined for somewhere in America, and we all know that won't be for the country's greater good." He took in the equally concerned faces around him.

Ever practical, the AC declared, "We'll have time later on to contemplate where the cannisters are destined. For the moment let's focus our efforts on locating the suckers. John, ring Tim and have him report for a briefing tomorrow morning at 0600 hours with at least ten of his remaining crew on standby. Michael, have Delwyn organise a search warrant for the *Themis*. We need it ready for the morning. Thank Christ we have night courts that make emergency approvals a hell of a lot easier. Peter, I've had second thoughts. Let's secure Jordan's assistance and all the military muscle he can provide. They can form a protective perimeter around the *Themis* because if the word gets out that we're hot on the trail of the cannisters, the death squad are going to switch into overdrive. Finally, let's get James Patterson in on the action. Ask him to attend the briefing. I'm sure ASIO would love to be in the mix." The AC cocked his head to one side, a thought springing to mind. "John, when you speak to Tim, make sure he organises personnel armed with those heat-sensing Geiger gizmos ..." He sought a response from Ballard, smirking, and wasn't disappointed.

"Scintillation detectors."

Endeavouring to keep a straight face the AC checked his watch, noting it was after 7 p.m. "Folks, clearly you're going to be dragging people back to work on this one, but the prize is so great no stone can be left unturned. I have a senior contact in Maritime Border Protection who I trust isn't in The Board's pocket. I'll prewarn him there's *something* illegal that we believe is being loaded onto, or is already on the *Themis*. He doesn't need to know the exact details other than his people should be there, after all, monitoring prohibited cargo is one of their key roles." He laughed. "Can you imagine the egos that'll be dinted when we run roughshod over these high-profile groups during the search?" He hesitated. "Oh, one more thing, I need to contact the Ports Operations manager, I'm assuming there's an afterhours number ... no, strike that, I'll make the call in the morning. I don't know who he or she is, but it's prudent they only get a last-minute warning in case The Board does have that individual in their pocket. The same goes for the *Themis*'s captain. One minute his ship's offloading drugs at Geelong, the next thing cannisters of nuclear waste are being loaded onboard right under his nose. Hell, the question has to be asked whether *he's* on The Board's payroll." He took in his colleagues, about to reveal an uncomfortable truth which on consideration was highly credible. "You do realise that if Jordan *is* correct regarding the cannisters, then the goldmine of information gleaned from the iPad will come to an end?"

Ballard was on the front foot. "What you're suggesting is we'll have drawn from the well one time too many."

"Exactly. Surely The Board knows by now we have a reliable source of intel on their movements, and a lost iPad would have to be one of the culprits … assuming Igor has fessed up about losing it, which on second thoughts is not a certainty." The AC rubbed his hands over his face. "Ok, have I missed anything or anyone?"

Peter joked, "I've a feeling you've made a fair crack at covering everything of importance, sir. My one question is how does Igor know our mobile numbers and so much about our personal movements for Christ's sake? There's *got* to be a snitch in the department on the take, and that person has to be pretty damn high up the line. Dare I suggest someone who's a buddy of our Deputy Commissioner Salisbury?"

If Peter's question was designed to focus the AC's mind, he succeeded far beyond his expectations. "If it's the last goddamn thing I do I'm going to make sure that bastard remains behind bars!" The intensity of anger in the AC's voice didn't surprise the three detectives, the decades-long hostility between the two senior officers was legendary. The subsequent linking of Salisbury to The Board verified the AC's belief that the Deputy Commissioner was a dirty cop of the worst kind, his involvement with the group over time costing multiple civilian and police lives. For the AC this was the ultimate betrayal to the organisation he loved, whose very existence was to protect the public and their property—an ideal he would defend to his death.

John's fear that PolAir's landing on the police headquarters building would be a nerve-jangling reality proved correct. The prevailing northerly, gusting at over twenty-five knots tested the young pilot's substantial skills. He had to make three separate approaches before setting the Leonardo down on the helipad—all onboard heaving sighs of relief. Despite swallowing several times after the landing, the AC quipped, "Well that was pretty routine."

John turned to Ballard, his cheeks flushed. "Now you know why I'll never consider becoming a senior officer, not that I ever had the chance. Gallivanting about in this bucket of bolts is enough to convince me that being a lowly senior sergeant will do me just nicely."

Chuckling, the AC rubbed his hands together. "Collectively we can be more than grateful things went our way tonight, however, you're all experienced enough to know our grip on this situation is still bloody tenuous. So go home, get some rest, and I'll see you in the morning. If we're as lucky as we were today, by tomorrow night we should have two nuclear cannisters back under our control." Adding as an afterthought, "And a mightily pissed off death squad breathing down our throats."

Yawning widely, and following it with an extended stretch as he sat in the passenger seat, Ballard eyed his partner who had pulled up in front of Natalie's garage, the engine switched off. "Now come on Johno, you're every bit as knackered as I am … are you *sure* you won't kip down in the spare room?" Tongue-in-cheek, he added, "Nat's really quite fond of you … I'm sure she wouldn't mind."

Grunting, John scratched at his five o'clock shadow. "Yeah, but nah. I appreciate the offer but the drive home will clear my head. Jesus Mike, the more I think about what could have gone wrong today—"

Ballard was sombre. "But it didn't John, and that's all that matters. Any win against this mob has to be grabbed with both hands. I don't need to tell you there's going to be plenty more days when things *won't* fall our way."

John heaved a theatrical sigh. "How right you are, boyo. Yep, tomorrow's going to be a bundle of fun." Firing the motor, he waited for Ballard to climb out before reversing into the street, his hand waving royally from the window as he drove off.

Letting himself into the hallway, Ballard switched on the lights, noting how quiet the townhouse was without Natalie and the children to greet him. Placing his keys on the hallstand he headed for the kitchen. Considering the contents of the fridge, he poured himself an orange juice. Then slumping on a bar stool, he drank half before dialling Natalie.

"Michael, where are you … and John? Are you both ok? And what about poor Jean? Tell me she's not hurt. Have you eaten?"

"Nat darling, I'm in the townhouse, I'm fine. John's driving home even though I offered for him to crash here. The best news of all is Jean's safe and unharmed." Ballard decided not to go into the details of her shoulder. "Now, what else was on your list?"

"Oh, thank God Michael. I'm so relieved, and the other concern was, have you eaten?"

"No, not yet, but don't worry, I'll rustle up something, I'm a big boy—"

"Hmm, don't I know it, but that aside, there's herb bread and some minestrone soup in the fridge. It'll take ten minutes tops in the microwave."

"Ah, still taking care of me despite the six hundred kilometres between us … sounds great."

"Michael, just a moment, I'll let Sonia know she can ring John."

Ballard listened to the women's muffled but excited conversation before Natalie rejoined him, breathless. "I'm back, and while I'm not silly enough to think you can give me specifics, is whatever you were doing now over? Sonia and I have been worried sick."

Ballard swallowed a mouthful of juice, weighing up what he could and couldn't say. "Nat, I'm sorry we had to leave you both so melodramatically, but John and I were never in any danger, and we aren't now. It was nothing more than plain old boring policework."

"Please don't give me that! You *never* have boring days, and as I've said so many times, you tell me everything is all ok then I find out otherwise."

Ballard did his best to steer the conversation. "Kayla and Josh will be in seventh heaven at their grandparents, so you don't have to worry on that score."

"Too true! I rang them earlier and they were deep in a game of chess with Dad. It was all I could do to get them to take time off to talk to me."

Ballard felt relief, picturing normality. "Nat, I promise John and I will be at the airport to pick you both up, so don't fret, we *will* be there." He laughed. "Remind me again what time you land?" He heard rustling in the background as Natalie dug into her bag. "5 p.m. Michael, and don't be late." The tension in her voice eased, which was music to his ears.

"Darling, go mad in the shops with Sonia and we'll see you tomorrow evening. And don't forget … I love you."

"Ditto, my handsome man."

CHAPTER
26

The tension in the Critical Incident conference room could be cut with a knife, everyone acutely aware that any slip-ups while at the *Themis* would cost lives and careers. The AC, showing no obvious signs of fatigue from his ordeal twelve hours earlier, focussed on Tim who was sandwiched between James and the Lieutenant Colonel. "I take it your 2IC is holding down the fort at the reservoir?"

"He is indeed. He's also ensuring there are regular tests of the water for any traces of radioactivity. So far everything's indicating negative."

The AC muttered his relief at the news. "Is your second team ready for the search on the *Themis*?"

"Yes sir. I have twelve personnel, plus myself."

"If the containers *are* on the *Themis*, then the death squad will already be there, or not far away. As a precaution, while your team is searching the decks, Jordan will establish an outer security cordon." The AC turned to the Lieutenant Colonel who needed no encouragement to detail the firepower he had at his disposal.

"Like Tim, I'm playing safe with numbers, deploying a

mini platoon of fifteen troops. They'll be armed with M4A1 Carbines and Heckler and Koch MP7 submachine guns. The carbines are equipped to fire stun grenades if required. We also have two Balkan's on loan from Tim with turret-mounted heavy machine guns." He flashed an appreciative grin at the SOG commander. "Finally, and if necessary, we can take out any vehicles the death squad turn up in using our M72 LAW rocket launchers."

With a studied gaze, the AC evaluated the Lieutenant Colonel's declaration while whistles echoed around the table at the lethality of the weaponry being used. "Thanks, Jordan. Let's pray this doesn't degenerate into World War III, but if it does, then it's clear you're more than prepared."

Jordan shrugged. "As you know, sir, I was present during the attack at the storage site, so I'm aware of this group's capabilities. Tim asked that my troops be miked up and in communication with his team so we can coordinate proceedings, especially if things turn rough."

The AC agreed. Holding up what everyone assumed to be the search warrant, he turned to Delwyn sitting to his left. "At least if the raid turns sour nobody can claim we weren't legal."

Delwyn met his gaze. "Ken requested the warrant cover two days so we won't be hampered by time constraints." The faintest of smiles appeared. "And as I've never seen inside one of those floating carriers, I'd like to come along with you sir, if I may."

While the request was polite and wisely sought, Ballard and John had no doubt the Superintendent would be coming rain, hail or shine. Grinning at her, they were rewarded with an unsubtle wink. The AC caught the exchange. "Good work arranging the warrant. And yes, both you and I have personal reasons for wanting to be at this shindig. No, you're more than welcome." Tapping his pen against his daybook, he declared, "On a personal note, Jean's doing fine. Her shoulder's been reset, and in spite of instructions to recuperate in hospital for a day or two, she's demanding to get back home."

There were universal expressions of heartfelt relief and best wishes.

Getting back to business, the AC's eyes scrutinised the table. "I don't need to remind you to keep your vests on while at the dock. It's certain that things are going to get ugly down there."

Swivelling in his seat, he addressed Bernard who was sitting alongside him, the Texan taking in the briefing details with his familiar calculated expression. He was clearly impressed by Tim and Jordan's firepower. "Bernard, I believe you have intel applicable to the raid?"

The drawled response was measured. "I do indeed Kevin. Firstly, Bernard junior has picked up online chatter that while it's heavily coded, reinforces our belief *something* of significance is occurring at Webb Dock. If it *is* the cannisters, then as you claim, there's no question the death squad will be playing a considerable part in those proceedings."

Heavy in thought, he sipped from his cup. "The second thing is my CIA contact, Vincenzo Ricardo, flies into Melbourne tomorrow at 1100 hours. He wants to update you all personally regarding his interrogation of Maxim Dabylov. The guy's been *very* cooperative ever since his arrest in Venice."

John nudged Ballard with his foot as Bernard continued. "Despite being a longstanding Cobet member, Maxim's decided his best and perhaps only chance of remaining alive is to spill the beans on the group's closely guarded secrets. For that he's accepting protection from the CIA rather than being cast out by Vincenzo who wouldn't hesitate to inform the wrong people the guy has divulged all.

"Long story short, Cobet's top-level meeting in Moscow is set for early next week to discuss a number of matters which you all know about. Vincenzo will fill us in on the details, but in essence this appears to be the best chance we'll ever have to crush Cobet once and for all."

Peter, who had been silent up to this point raised a question for the AC as well as Bernard and James. "With Igor being a senior Cobet member, it stands to reason he'll be at the meeting in Moscow. The calls I received from him yesterday didn't have the lag time you get when made from overseas, so that indicates he was in Australia as of 6 p.m. For most bigtime criminals, leaving the country requires avoiding the major airports. For Igor however, who can come and go as he pleases as a result of his expert disguises and armed with the very best forged passports, I recommend we monitor passengers flying anywhere near Moscow over the next few days."

All three men agreed, with James adding, "Leave that to me, and while it'll be nothing less than chasing a ghost, I have identikit photos of his known disguises which I'll circulate to all our international airports. You're right though, it's definitely worth a shot."

The AC chose to bring the briefing to a close, asking, "Tim, what radio channel are we operating on?"

"Thirty-two."

The AC studied him closely. "I'm guessing you as much as anyone here is hoping this raid is wrapped up today?"

Tim remained silent.

"Forty-eight hours to your wedding on Sunday is cutting

things a wee bit fine I'd have thought. I hope Kathryn's not too stressed by your absences?"

Blushing, Tim responded, "It's all under control, sir, and I'm expecting yourself, Peter, Delwyn, Michael and John to be at Rupertswood by 1400 hours on Sunday."

Grinning, the AC responded for the invitees. "Thank you for reminding *each* of us in case we'd forgotten. I can assure you we'll be there with bells on."

Becoming serious, he addressed the room. "Folks, we now have an opportunity to hit The Board where it hurts. As much as I hate acquiescing to politicians, the current crisis we face with these cannisters, while overwhelmingly a public safety issue, is equally a political imperative which if handled badly will bring down the Government. You're all experts in your fields, so if anyone can pull this off, collectively you can. Go with the very best of luck from me and stay safe."

CHAPTER
27

Never one to miss an opportunity to showcase his driving skills, John braked aggressively, swinging hard left off Webb Dock's Tiger Drive before accelerating along Wharf Road which ran parallel with the water. One hundred metres ahead, the orange-red hull of the *Themis* loomed large, its huge access ramp protruding at forty-five degrees from the stern, anchored onto the dock by its sheer weight.

Ballard craned his neck, searching for the best place to park. "Let's not get too close John, remember, this time we're mere spectators. If this show lights up, our Smith & Wesson's will be as useless as water pistols compared to the firepower Tim and Jordan have at their disposal. No, for once we watch from a distance and keep our bloody heads down." Still searching he jabbed a forefinger towards a vacant spot among hundreds of parked Toyota SUVs. "Over there!"

Reversing, John positioned so the *Themis* was in a clear line of sight to their right, while maintaining full view of the Balkan parked at the intersection with Tiger Drive on their left. Their chosen position proved the perfect vantage point to witness everything that might go down without being in the way, aided by two Sony binoculars with digital zoom, the glasses extracted from John's 'goodies' bag, which he took to every stakeout.

With the deep throb of the *Themis* turbines a background drone, they opened their windows slightly, taking in the blended aroma of diesel fumes and stagnant seaweed, all accompanied by the intermittent beeps from the giant mobile container cranes in the distance. Ballard remarked, "Aha! I see Jordan's parked the second Balkan across the access ramp to stop anyone going in or out of the ship. If they *are* contemplating escape, they'll change their mind once they see the muzzle of that damn machine gun pointing at their privates."

John hummed his agreement while sweeping his binoculars along the wharf, focussing on the military personnel spanning the full two-hundred-metre length of the ship. At the far end of the wharf, off to one side, an untidy group of fifty or so men outfitted in high-vis vests stood dejectedly, some of them smoking, others on their mobiles, all far from happy at being dragged from their work. "Do we know who those guys are?"

Ballard refocussed his binoculars. "I'd say some are *Themis* crew. Would you believe only a handful are needed to operate a ship this big—eight to ten on average, along with the captain and perhaps an officer or two."

"Are you serious? For something as huge as that bloody great monster?"

"As for the others, I'd say they're the drivers offloading the SUVs. I checked on Google earlier and it said that to load 3500 vehicles they need around a hundred and seventy drivers to do the job. Shuttling back and forth, the vehicles are driven on and strapped down in less than forty hours." He pointed towards the group. "As you can see, for this exercise, to drive the five hundred vehicles off requires only a fraction of that number."

A soft whistle escaped John's lips. "Private enterprise, eh? If only our governments were that efficient." He focussed on three self-important seagulls strutting along the wharf, as confident and cocky as any group of young sailors on shore leave. Glancing behind him at the breakwater near the mouth of the Yarra River he joked, "In all the times you've gone past in your motor cruiser with Natalie, would you have *ever* believed you'd be on a stakeout fifty metres away, searching for nuclear waste cannisters?"

"Not in a million years, my friend."

On the far side of the *Themis*, on the opposite wharf, a second ship was moored beneath four red cranes, each busily loading containers onto the vessel's deck. The skill of the crane drivers was evidenced by the precision with which they positioned their cargo.

Ballard was about to speak but cocking his head he stopped short, instead taking note of the police radio. "Clearly Tim's team have begun sweeping the ship." His comment was a result of the SOG members cross-checking each other's position on the multiple decks, and what point their search was at. "Believe me Johno, with the equivalent of thirteen soccer fields to inspect, the task won't be easy. Christ, the death squad could be hiding anywhere inside that damn thing." He tweaked the radio's volume as he listened to Tim announce he had two suspicious containers in sight, requesting those in his team with detectors to report to him midship on the eleventh deck.

John was about to emit a euphoric cry when his mouth dropped open in surprise. "Bugger me Mike, can you believe it? That's the AC driving past with Delwyn sitting beside him like Lady Muck ... *and* ... *and* Pete's in the back." He glanced at his partner, more than a trifle miffed. "Talk about timing, and how come *they* get a close up squiz at proceedings and we're left sitting out here like naughty schoolboys?"

"That's because we *are* naughty schoolboys. Professional Standards told us so."

John huffed his disgust, his eyebrows drawing together. "Stuff 'em. And don't ever tell me rank doesn't have its privileges."

Ballard watched as the three officers walked up the ramp, all wearing their vests. He addressed his partner, his gaze thoughtful. "You know something Johno? I'm proud of you. Here we are on yet another stakeout and you haven't complained once about having to wear *your* vest. This has to be a first for ..."

"Holy Christ, here they come!" The distress in John's voice prickled the hairs on the back of Ballard's neck. "Mike, take a look! Four vans approaching along Tiger Drive, and they're not bloody sightseers."

Ballard swung his binoculars, confirming four black Mercedes were travelling at speed towards the Balkan parked at the intersection. Snatching up the mike he bellowed. "Jordan, Tim, approaching Merc vans along Tiger Drive are death squad personnel! Respond."

Jordan's reply was controlled, calm even. "I'm in the lead Balkan. Yes, we've seen them. If they don't stop, we'll take them out."

Both detectives sat spellbound, glued to their binoculars as the heavy machine gun mounted in the turret of the Balkan fired a warning burst across the front of the leading van, now only fifty metres from the armoured vehicle.

Undeterred, the vans accelerated and were met with a barrage of gunfire resulting in the lead vehicle slewing sideways on blown tyres. Men dressed in black military fatigues leapt out, and positioning themselves, began firing automatic weapons at the Balkan, one launching a shoulder-mounted missile that disintegrated harmlessly off the armour plating. Undamaged, the three remaining vans accelerated past the Balkan, and swinging left, headed towards the *Themis*, the trailing vehicle suddenly lurching sideways, it too suffering blown tyres. The remaining two Mercedes kept coming until the rear van spectacularly erupted in a ball of flames, struck by an M72 rocket fired from the Balkan, cartwheeling end over end, almost finishing in the water before coming to rest on its roof.

Soldiers leapt from Jordan's Balkan, crouching beside it, engaging in heavy gunfire with death squad members who were sheltering behind their respective vehicles. The third van struck by the rocket continued to burn, now a blazing inferno with no chance of survivors.

A second explosion directed the detectives' attention towards the remaining van that had roared passed them, also hit by a rocket, this time fired from the Balkan parked near the *Themis* ramp.

The group of men who had been standing impatiently at the far end of the wharf had long since scattered, falling over themselves, scrambling to seek what cover they could without success. The soldiers guarding the ship remained crouched on one knee, their weapons levelled along the wharf.

"Mother of God! ... can you believe all this?" John remained open-mouthed as he and Ballard took in the carnage erupting in front of them. "The stupid idiots didn't stand a chance ... they were on a bloody suicide mission!"

Ballard disagreed. "Perhaps not Johno. I'm thinking they didn't know about Jordan and his troops. I think someone inside the ship tipped the death squad off when Tim's team began the raid, therefore assuming twelve SOG guys were all the death squad would be up against. He'd have thought a full-on assault with perhaps fifteen or so men would get the death squad through any resistance Tim could mount. The guy was trapped *inside* the ship, unaware Jordan and the combined firepower he was able to unleash was waiting for this lot on the *outside*. Had he known this he'd never have allowed his guys to come in so gung-ho. This now raises the question ... is the shithead still hiding on the ship?"

Tim and five of his team were seen running along the wharf towards the closest burning van, flames illuminating the interior. Weapons levelled, they approached with caution, fanning out so as not to present a group target. Their vigilance was rewarded as a lone figure struggled from the burning wreck, armed with an assault rifle. He squeezed off a burst in their direction while lying prone. A barrage of shots rang out and the man dropped his weapon, blood pooling around him on the roadway.

Seconds later the continuous chatter of gunfire near the Balkan at Tiger Drive ended, Ballard and John assuming the attackers had all been shot. Acrid, black smoke spiralled into the sky from the destroyed vehicles, tainting the light breeze as several SOG personnel armed with large volume extinguishers extracted from the fire bollards dotted along the wharf began spraying the dying flames.

Deciding it was now safe, Ballard and John left their vehicle and approached Tim who was coordinating proceedings with his team. From the far end of Wharf Road, Jordan and several of his soldiers were seen heading their way at a brisk trot. In the opposite direction, the AC, Delwyn and Peter were spotted coming down the ship's ramp, all hurrying towards them.

Once together as a group, Tim reached out and pumped Jordan's hand, each man grinning foolishly, the SOG commander commenting, "Thank Christ your guys were here. We had enough on our plate *inside* the ship."

Jordan's shrug indicated it was business as usual. The AC, together with Delwyn and Peter, also shook Jordan and Tim's hands, the relief on their faces palpable.

"Nobody injured?" The AC was having difficulty comprehending how so many of the death squad could be neutralised without any fatalities among the police and army personnel who had fought so bravely. Jordan and Tim did their best not to be over proud, stating their troops' respective training and body armour had saved the day. Not wishing to dampen the euphoric mood, but knowing he had little choice, Ballard set about explaining his theory that someone on the ship had tipped off the death squad, generating the armed response. "If this is true then he or they must still be on the ship."

Delwyn turned, scanning the wharf in the direction of the men who had reassembled into a ragtag bunch, all clearly shocked at what had just occurred, a few of them hesitantly approaching, curiosity overcoming their obvious concerns. They were ordered back by one of the soldiers.

Delwyn dipped her chin in their direction, posing, "He *could* be amongst that lot."

John beat Ballard to a reply. "I don't think so. If he was outside the ship he'd have known about Jordan's reinforcements, along with the Balkans, warning the death squad what they were up against. That lot has proven in the past they're not suicidal. No, as Michael suspects, I reckon the guy's still onboard."

Ballard appeared undecided. "The question now is, what's he going to do? Enough noise has been generated out here for him to know the game's up, so he'll remain in hiding if he knows what's good for him, which is a problem in itself."

The AC took control. "Tim, did you confirm any radioactivity near the containers?"

The SOG commander nodded. "No doubt about it, the detector lit up like a neon sign. We haven't broken the seals on the containers yet to confirm it's the cannisters, but I'm certain we've struck pay dirt."

The AC couldn't hide his delight, now able to inform the Chief Commissioner and the Premier that the eagle had landed. "All that's left for us to do now is to find whoever's onboard and get the cannisters up to the storage site. Jordan, your thoughts?"

The army officer didn't hesitate. "I'll have two of our heavy carriers driven in from Watsonia to collect them." He turned to Tim. "If I may, I'll hang onto the Balkans as escorts front and rear of the convoy."

Tim waved a nonchalant hand. "Be my guest."

"As backup, I'll also take along two troop carriers, so without sounding overconfident, I'll guarantee by 1700 hours today these cannisters will be secured at the site."

The AC's smile widened. "Brilliant." Turning to Delwyn and Peter he laughed. "Sorry to do this to you, but under Tim's protection I'm leaving you both in charge to calm down a very irate captain, and at the same time try and find out if he has any links to The Board. All the while coordinating Forensics, the coroner, possibly the fire brigade ... you know the drill ...

Call your respective teams down here to help."

Despite the senior officers holding each other in the highest regard, Delwyn couldn't resist a slight dig in his direction. "Er, yes, I *do* know the drill, sir. I'm sure Ken, Bobby and Susan will be tickled pink."

Peter rubbed his wounded shoulder. "Looking forward to it. A bit of sea air will do me the world of good after being cooped up in hospital."

The AC grew serious. "For God's sake, keep your heads down. We don't know for sure if there *is* someone still hiding on the ship, but we have to assume it's a possibility. Tim, get your 2IC back from the reservoir as soon as you can to take over. I'll arrange for PolAir to make the transfer … you have a wedding to prepare for. This gives you the rest of today once you're freed up here, as well as all of tomorrow … not a lot of time I'll wager. On that note, we'll see you out at Rupertswood on Sunday, dressed to the nines."

With a shake of the SOG commander's hand, the AC turned and directed his attention towards Ballard and John, commanding, "Walk with me, gents."

John eyerolled Ballard as they followed the senior officer along the wharf, neither sure what was in store for them.

"Before coming down here this morning I had a quick chat with Bernard. He gave me a heads-up as to what tomorrow's briefing with the CIA agent is all about. It appears the big-daddy meeting of The Board is to be held either Tuesday or Wednesday next week, Moscow time."

John's expression begged the question, 'And this affects us how?'

The AC gave the detectives both barrels. "You, Michael and myself will be on a plane to Moscow come Monday morning."

CHAPTER
28

John's stunned expression matched Ballard's perplexed look, each breaking stride, unable to fully digest what they had just been told. John sought urgent clarification. "Moscow? Moscow Russia? I … I thought that rumour was a joke. I never believed *we'd* be going."

"Yes, Moscow Russia. Which I believe at this time of the year is a balmy nineteen, perhaps twenty degrees during the day, dropping to eight or so at night. So, pack a jumper or two." The AC was clearly enjoying stringing the detectives along.

John wasn't about to give up. "And the *real* reason we're going there?"

The AC became serious. "Think back to the end of World War II when Eisenhower, Churchill and Stalin carved up Europe between them. Well, if the raid on The Board is successful, there are going to be a lot of very nasty Russians who'll be going to prison for a long, long time—in some cases forever. Guess who *we've* been allocated by the powers that be … in this case the CIA?"

Ballard didn't bother to draw breath. "Igor."

"Correct. And all of us have an interest in bringing that

bastard back to face justice … Jean very much included. As soon as I get back to the office, I'll set the extradition papers in motion from this end. Bernard believes the Politburo is so keen to get rid of these bastards there won't be any hold up from them."

John dragged fingers through his hair. "I assume I'm going in place of Peter because of his shoulder?"

"Got it in one. Operationally he's not ready for a twenty-one-hour flight, or the rigour of who knows how many sleepless nights."

John added, "Don't get me wrong boss, I'm in boots-and-all, along with Michael." He was rewarded with a confirming grin from Ballard.

The AC extracted the key to his car from his jacket pocket. "Lots to do gentlemen. You'll need to break the news to your better halves. Where are they by the way?"

Ballard responded. "Still in Hobart. They'll be flying into Tulla around—" he checked his watch, "about two hours from now."

"Well then, finish up what you have to do at the office then take the rest of the day off. I'll flip you a text an hour before the briefing tomorrow with Vincenzo. After that, pray nothing gets in the way of Tim and Kathryn's wedding on Sunday. Rupertswood is a lovely old mansion … as you well know Michael."

"I do indeed, sir." Changing the subject, Ballard asked, "How *is* Jean after her ordeal?"

The AC's eyebrows did a full rotation. "All I can say is she's a damn sight chirpier than I would have been. After lunch she's off to the physio. The Department's arranging a driver for her. Christ, it owes me that much."

The detectives agreed.

Appraising them both, the AC quipped, "You two showed remarkable restraint today by not rushing about and getting involved in the action. Maturity suits you." The twinkle in his eyes defused the sarcasm.

Ballard checked out his partner, praying John wouldn't blurt out that he had been seconds away from T-boning one of the death squad vans as it sped along Wharf Road "I'm told it comes with advanced years, sir."

Two hours later, Natalie flung her arms around Ballard's neck, refusing to let him go until she was convinced that he was in one piece. Sonia replicated the action with John, her pregnancy in no way hindering the vigour in which she greeted him. While trekking to the baggage carrousel, both men apologised for leaving the ladies to contend with their cases at the Hobart airport.

Sonia scoffed. "I'm only pregnant John, not an invalid."

"I, er … don't I know it …" Joking, he enquired, "I hope you got the money back on our tickets, they *were* refundable after all."

Halting progress, Natalie stepped in front of Ballard, defiant, falling short of thrusting both hands on her hips. "Yes, we *did* get the refunds, having rung the airline yesterday, and that brought Sonia and I to the conclusion that perhaps you'd both *predicted* something at work would drag you away from your loving partners. Were we correct?"

Spluttering, the two detectives thought seriously about defending themselves, but wisely declined, their orchestrated shrugs a sign of total capitulation, with John muttering, "Guilty as charged, Your Honour."

"Ah ha! Sonia … the next time we go on holidays with these two, let's get together beforehand so we can plan an alternate itinerary, just in case." They winked at one another, enjoying the pitiable expressions on their men's faces.

As if by telepathy, Ballard and John held off disclosing their impending Moscow trip until everyone had ordered sandwiches and a cup of tea at their favourite boutique café in the airport. With their suitcases beside them, and having devoured most of their meal, Ballard knew details of the trip couldn't be postponed any longer.

"*Moscow!*" The synchronised cries of disbelief from the two women drew unwanted attention from other diners.

John did his best to calm the situation, unaware he was making matters much worse. "*You're* shocked, how do you think *we* feel?"

Glaring at his partner, Ballard silently commanded him to take no further part in their ensuing attempts to calm two very distressed ladies who had abandoned their sandwiches and cups of tea. "It's only for a few days."

"When are you leaving?" Natalie's sense of alarm was mirrored by Sonia, who clung onto John's arm for reassurance.

Ballard's look of desperation was amplified by John's helpless shrug, along with an uncharacteristic absence of a pithy retort. "At this point we believe Monday."

"Will it be dangerous?" Natalie spat out the words, throwing her serviette onto the table in exasperation. In an aside to Sonia, she confessed, "Why am I even bothering … of *course* it'll be dangerous. *Nothing* these two do is *ever* run-off-the-mill." Pausing, she appeared embarrassed, realising her tantrum wasn't helping Sonia, who remained silent, having paled considerably. "Darling, just ignore me. They know what they're doing." Desperate to be convinced by her own words, her expression changed to resolute.

Contemplating what the news meant for both ladies, an uncomfortable silence descended on the table.

Keen to make amends, John introduced a topic he knew would calm the tense atmosphere, or so he thought. "The good news is Michael and I will be here for the wedding."

This time it was Sonia's turn to deep probe. "Will Tim be going to Moscow as well?"

Although John's laugh wasn't his most convincing, he accepted it had to do. "Lord no, it's just the AC, Michael and myself. And the purpose is to bring back a prisoner." He turned to Ballard to verify he hadn't divulged more than he should, rewarded with the faintest of nods.

Realising their men had no option but to comply with departmental orders, Natalie and Sonia relented, agreeing the wedding would be a lovely distraction and an opportunity to forget about the stresses of work, if only for a few short hours. Natalie squeezed Ballard's hand. "I'm popping out to Rupertswood tomorrow morning to help Kathryn finalise the setting up of the tables. Margaret and her staff do a fantastic job, but as you know Michael, Kathryn's very much cut in your mould, everything has to be just so." She stared pointedly at him. "And it's not hard to see why, growing up with you." Addressing everyone, she concluded, "Kathryn won't be happy unless she's added her personal touches."

Light-hearted conversation ensued: how suited Tim and Kathryn were for each other; where they might go for their honeymoon; what Ballard would say in his speech; and Sonia mischievously asking John whether he was also giving one. Almost spitting out the last of his sandwich, he shook his head, declaring he would leave that to the professionals and pointing to Ballard.

Their snack over, both men checked the time, keen to leave the airport before the evening peak hour. Grabbing a suitcase in each hand, much to the protestation of the ladies, they headed out of the terminal to their respective vehicles, parting after a warm hug between Natalie and Sonia.

Having settled in the Bentley, Ballard felt Natalie's reassuring hand on his thigh, the smile on her face a welcome relief. "You poor man. Here you are fighting horrible men, and if that isn't hard enough, you have me banging on and making your life a misery. I'm so sorry darling."

Ballard leaned across, kissing her on the lips. "You'll be proud of me ... and John also. Since we left you yesterday, we haven't put ourselves in a single dangerous situation. So there, we're maturing after all."

Natalie's expression changed to one of open wickedness. "I hope your newfound maturity hasn't affected your cheeky side because I checked earlier and it'll be two hours before the kids get back from Mum and Dad's."

Ballard fired the motor, the growl of the V12 proof positive there was indeed no time to waste.

CHAPTER
29

A text appeared on Ballard's mobile just as he was swallowing the last of his chicken and salad sandwich, the snack cobbled together minutes earlier, and while it lacked Natalie's deft touch, it was all he needed after a hearty breakfast earlier. Before leaving home to support Kathryn, Natalie had given him a lingering hug as appreciation for not misplacing his naughty side. Smiling at the memory, he checked the wall clock, noting it wasn't yet 11 a.m.

As was the AC's norm, the text was to the point. '*The briefing is at 1200 hours.*'

Dialling John's number, it rang once before he answered. "Yeah, I got it too. I'm on my way. I'll see you at the office."

Scribbling a note for Kayla and Josh who had popped out for a milkshake, Ballard apologised that their evenly poised chess game would have to wait until he returned. Already in his suit, pre-empting the notification from the AC, he was in the Bentley in record time, the Saturday morning traffic in Toorak Road heavy but moving. Stepping from the lift, Bobby was the first to greet him. "Bloody hell, boss. I've seen more than my fair share of shoot-ups on TV, but they weren't a patch on what went down at Webb Dock. It must have been incredible watching it live." Ballard looked across at Ken and Susan who were in furious agreement. "Let's just say John and I checked out the action from a safe distance, leaving everything to the professionals—which Tim and Jordan are, *big time*. It's a lesson for all of us to know when *not* to poke our noses into a situation which could have ended with a bunch of our people injured or killed."

Bobby spotted John approaching. Guessing the topic of conversation, John addressed his crew. "And just as well the public don't witness that side of life very often, if ever." Echoing the AC's words in the chopper he added, "*We* get paid to clean up the mess which Delwyn tells me you all did rather well."

The three detectives were taken aback by the compliment from their boss, something John offered sparingly. As he often expressed to Ballard, 'Too much praise and the buggers get complacent'.

Hamming it up, Bobby made a pretext of taking his pulse, checking he hadn't misheard. At the same time Ken and Susan reached out with the backs of their hands, feeling each other's foreheads, searching for any signs of fever.

John's growl was half-serious. "Now tell me, is the brief for the DC ready?"

They pointed to the bulging folders on their desks, with Ken claiming, "Done and dusted, and the electronic copy has been submitted into RedCrest. We're waiting for a date from the County Court. Unfortunately, the brief against Igor is another matter, it just keeps growing, but we're on top of it."

The grunt from John could have been taken as discontent to the untrained ear, but Ken knew it to be tacit approval.

The lift doors opened and Delwyn stepped out, briefcase

in hand. Heading over, she asked her senior detectives, "Are we good to go?"

They flashed a half grin, with John joking, "We certainly are, after all, what else would we rather be doing on a sunny Saturday morning?"

Delwyn gave him a questioning look. "I know we're a tad early, but let's head on up anyway."

Doing their best to ignore Bobby's puppy-eyes at being left out of the briefing, they elected to take the stairs. On arriving at the conference room, they found it vacant.

John settled into his favourite chair. "So other than us, the AC, Peter and Vincenzo, who else is coming?"

"I asked the same question yesterday, but the AC was tight-lipped." She laughed. "What I do know is Peter's spitting chips at missing out on the trip because of his shoulder. By contrast, the AC's peeved because he may not get back in time to give evidence against Salisbury. *God, he hates the guy for betraying the department*! But the lure of hauling Igor back here to jail is just too great. Oh, and another thing, you two were right."

John puffed out his chest, however, the look on his face indicated he didn't know why.

"There *was* a whistle-blower on the *Themis*. Tim's team did another search of the ship, deck by deck. The guy was found hiding in one of the SUVs. He was challenged, and as appears to be the *modus operandi* with these lunatics, he came out guns blazing and had to be put down." The beginning of a satisfied smile emerged. "I can tell you there was some pretty horrific damage done to a number of vehicles, and the captain was more than a tad narky at the fact. Apparently bullet holes aren't covered under their insurance policy." The smile developed into a throaty chuckle.

"Do you think the captain's in on the action?" Ballard inclined his head; unsure how successful Delwyn had been in her grilling of the naval officer.

"Pete and I questioned him for almost an hour, and we brought up the drugs shipment at Geelong Port for good measure. If he *is* involved with The Board, he's hiding it very well. So no, I don't think so." Changing subjects, she asked with a developing smirk, "Did either of you see the chief and the Premier's press conference last night regarding the cannisters?"

John nearly exploded, beating Ballard to a reply. "*Did I see the press conference?* Christ, after ten minutes I had to turn the bloody TV off… the self-congratulatory crap from those two was nauseating. You'd have thought it was them who took on the death squad and not Tim and Jordan. Speaking of Jordan, I'm assuming the cannisters are now tucked away safe and sound in their rightful place at the storage site?"

Delwyn laughed. "Yep, like bugs in a rug. Apparently, where the tunnel was damaged by the explosion, they've already cleared away the rubble and repaired the roof. Isn't it amazing what can be achieved in a short space of time when truckloads of money are at stake?"

Several minutes later, John's 'who else is coming' question was answered. The door opened and the AC entered, resplendent in full uniform. Next, Bernard ushered in Vincenzo, closely followed by Jordan, Peter and James.

Ballard and John had been turning over in their minds the mental image of the CIA operative, wondering whether their high-octane interlude with him had overplayed their recollection of his features, but that was short-lived. The instant they saw him familiar memories flooded back: the heavyset frame commanded respect due to his height and build being similar to Bernard's; the jet-black hair swept back from a broad, but lined, forehead; strong, even teeth that enhanced his smile; and intelligent eyes that missed nothing. It was all there, evoking an aura of confidence throughout the attendees. In reality, Vincenzo was a younger version of Bernard, the two men's presence filling the room.

On spotting Ballard and John, Vincenzo broke protocol and rushed over, wrapping Ballard in a rib cracking bear hug, followed by a European kiss on both cheeks. He turned to John, about to repeat the same welcome.

"Stay right where you are, boyo. None of that kissing shit for me, ok?" John was adamant, waggling a forefinger, nevertheless the twinkle in his eye was unmistakable.

Roaring with laughter, Vincenzo gave John a vice-like, double-handed grip. Turning to the AC, he apologised. "I'm sorry Kevin, but I *am* Italian after all, and let's face it, these two guys saved my life, along with those of my men. I owe them."

The AC dropped his head. "For Christ's sake, don't remind them because they'll hold you to it."

Once everyone was settled, the AC got down to the point of the briefing, nodding a greeting to Vincenzo. "Welcome to Australia. I'm told you're here to detail how the threat of The Board may well be coming to an end."

Sitting calmly with his fingers interlocked and his hands resting on the table, the larger-than-life figure took in his audience. "The criminal reach of The Board, or as I prefer to call them, Cobet, is more extensive and insidious than we ever imagined. Their annual revenue from crime is approaching that of a small country. Luckily for us, but at the same time unfortunately for them, this group now has a significant competitor, the Ndrangheta. So much a competitor, Cobet is holding a crisis meeting in Moscow either Wednesday or Thursday this coming week to decide what to do about it. Also on the agenda will be what tactics are required to take out your nuclear waste site, their first concerted attack having been so effectively repelled by Jordan's troops."

The Lieutenant Colonel responded to the compliment with an appreciative smile.

Vincenzo ran a forefinger along one eyebrow, appearing introspective. "I stress you need to keep at the forefront the destruction of the storage site, it being a key objective for Cobet. How do I know all this? Well, the senior Cobet member we arrested in Venice … a gentleman—and I use the term loosely—a gentleman by the name of Maxim Dabylov has decided it's in his best interest to tell all, after some gentle persuasion that is."

He paused. There was no doubt from his steely gaze that the 'gentle persuasion' may not have been fully compliant with the Geneva Convention. "There's to be upwards of ten to fifteen Cobet members at the meeting, the head of the snake so to speak, plus an unknown number of security. I don't have to explain the difficulty this poses in terms of mounting a raid to capture everyone alive, especially after hearing about your adventures at Webb Dock yesterday."

A wave of mutterings did the rounds, with John whispering to Ballard, "I'm not sure about you Mike, but his definition of what constitutes an adventure might be a smidge out of whack."

"And here's where it gets both interesting *and* fortuitous for us. The CIA have always had contacts at the senior level within the Central Committee which sits above the Politburo, without which there'd have been a third world war decades ago. Now, while the Russian president is, to put it mildly, power mad, unlike the Chinese guy, he's happy to be a big fish in his own pond. In the past, Cobet has served his purpose, doing a substantial amount of the dirty work he didn't want or need to know about. Fortunately for us, Cobet has gotten too big for their boots and now the President wants them gone. So why involve the CIA you ask?

"The simple answer is that while the President appears all powerful, the Central Committee operates very differently to our democracy. In a nutshell, the President's not certain who his true friends and allies are any more than he knows who's about to stab him in the neck. It's an understatement to say he has a host of powerful enemies, so he's decided to outsource the task of getting rid of Cobet to us. All this with the proviso his hands remain clean, and he gets all the credit for eliminating a criminal organisation, which is giving Russia a worse name than it already has." He sat back, glass in hand.

Ever practical, Peter queried, "This Maxim character, what's the chance he's spilled his guts to Cobet, warning them of the raid ... and I'm assuming he'll be at the meeting?"

Vincenzo took his time, giving the question due consideration. "He most certainly will be, and yes, dropping us in is always a possibility, but to do that would be to sign his own death warrant. He *knows* I'll put the word out that he's talked, and he's seen what his organisation is capable of doing to traitors. No, in my mind he's not prepared to risk torture of that measure, aware it would also be inflicted upon his family."

Delwyn was curious. "With so many to arrest, and with their own security squad on standby to protect them, how many special forces will you need to execute the raid?"

Vincenzo had the answer ready. "Yet another excellent point. As Michael and John will recall, my Gruppo di Intervento Speciale, or GIS teams, are elite soldiers. The Central Committee is allowing me to land an Alenia C-27J Spartan troop carrier ... specially fitted out at the CIA's expense I might add ... at the Chkalovsky military airfield northwest of Moscow. Onboard will be thirty of my team, along with their equipment which I can assure you is comprehensive." This time Vincenzo's pause was longer, again affording everyone time to process what he was relaying.

Not to be left out, Ballard asked, "Accompanying your team, how many of the Russian special forces will be tagging along?"

Vincenzo's grin was replaced with a number of firm nods. "*Bullseye*. The Central Committee has arranged for ten of their Spetsnaz soldiers, along with their colonel to be part of the assault." Without any display of bravado he claimed, "Fortunately, along with Bernard, I speak fluent Russian, so I'll be able to instruct the men when to duck and when to shoot."

There was the slightest of delays before everyone realised he wasn't joking.

"So, this brings us to the spoils of war. Your arch nemesis Igor will be in the mix, and Kevin has made it crystal clear he's destined for an Aussie prison. And after the trauma he put Kevin's wife through a couple of days ago I can understand why."

Everyone noted the AC's poker face, his only outward emotion the repeated rippling of his jaw muscles.

Vincenzo continued, "Bernard and I, and by default the CIA, have tabs on Anatoli Demyan who happens to be a pseudo-uncle to Tatiana Olegovich, a rather nasty piece of work that I'm told you have in custody for multiple unsavoury crimes."

Ballard switched his focus to Bernard who appeared unmoved at the mention of Tatiana's name, yet the detective was mindful of the pain the Texan must be experiencing, only now aware that Tatiana was his daughter, a fact he had been oblivious of for more than thirty years.

Vincenzo wasn't finished. "There are a number of other key Cobet hierarchy who the CIA will be bagging, Maxim being one of them despite the Italian Government kicking up a stink, claiming he should be theirs. To maintain his cover and any future intel we may glean from him, we need to arrest him exactly as we will be for his brethren. Great Britain and France also have their requests in, but the Central Committee will be taking the lion's share, meaning the Russian President can put behind bars those he believes were out to dethrone him."

Vincenzo shrugged as he drew breath. "So … realistically, despite our caper having more holes in it than a Swiss cheese, I still have every faith we'll deal Cobet such a tremendous blow that it'll be fatal. Of course once this lot's sorted out we'll have to contend with the Ndrangheta. But that's a battle for another day."

Glancing at the AC who was listening intently, Vincenzo announced, "Now for the housekeeping aspect of this escapade. I've arranged first-class tickets for Kevin, Michael and John to—"

"You're bloody kidding me?" Shaking his head in disbelief, John blurted, "If my fiancée *ever* finds out I've flown first-class to *anywhere* without her I'm dead meat."

Vincenzo barked a delighted laugh. "You forget a number of things my friend. Firstly, we're operating under the CIA slush fund, and while not unlimited, it's pretty damn extensive. Secondly, it's a twenty-one-hour flight with one stopover. I need you all wide awake when you arrive. Last, and just as importantly, first-class travel is a damn nice way to fly."

John didn't have any comeback, mouthing the words 'first-class' to Ballard while doing his best not to catch Peter's jealous eye. Recovering, he asked, "And our accommodation when we get to Moscow?"

"Hmm, that's where standards drop somewhat. It'll be at the Chkalovsky airbase. I'll pass all the details on to Kevin, as well as the tickets. Travel light because you won't be in Moscow for very long. Oh, and your flight back will be in a chartered jet with Igor handcuffed to the undercarriage."

This time everyone did laugh.

"When do *you* fly out?" Ballard was curious as to Vincenzo's agenda, staggered at what the agent had to accomplish before the raid.

"First up I have another briefing with some of James' senior brethren, another reason for my trip out here to your sun-drenched land." The ASIO officer acknowledged the room with a brief nod. "Then at 1800 hours today I'm off to Venice aboard an Emirates flight—which by the way is the airline you'll be flying. The next time I see you will be at the Chkalovsky military airfield in Moscow on Monday. So, I guess there's nothing more to say other than good luck gentlemen."

John smacked his forehead. "Monday! Thank God ... that'll give me more than enough time to brush up on my Russian."

Vincenzo looked across at Bernard, his eyes crinkling, the slightest head shake visible. "You're absolutely right. Aussies *are* a breed of their own."

CHAPTER
30

The Rupertswood mansion, completed in 1876 and the birthplace of 'The Ashes' cricket urn, was the former residence of Sir William Clarke, a baronet of significant influence in Victoria. The building was then, and remains today, a magnificent example of the famed Italianate style, its most imposing feature a thirty-metre tower overlooking a circular, gravel driveway. Entering the grand foyer, visitors are drawn to the Victorian tessellated tiles underfoot. Lifting their gaze, they are free to marvel at the six stained-glass windows, considered to be among the finest examples in the world. Stepping forward, a visual reward in the form of a magnificent staircase boasting a polished walnut handrail greets them, sweeping upwards to the first-floor bedrooms, and what were once the servants' quarters.

Having famously entertained the Duke and Duchess of York, who later became King George V and Queen Mary, as well as Dame Nellie Melba, not to mention the English cricket team, Rupertswood also played host to Natalie and Ballard's wedding.

Sitting beside Natalie at Kathryn and Tim's bridal table in the mansion's impressive ballroom, with its six-metre-high ceiling and ornate cornices illuminated by elaborate brass lights, Ballard reflected on having stood at the exact same spot while delivering his own wedding speech. Guessing his thoughts, Natalie commented, "And an impressive speech it was too, darling." Leaning forward she beamed at Kathryn who was sitting to Ballard's right. "My dear you look simply gorgeous. Tim's a very lucky man."

Wearing a stunning Christina Rossi ivory crushed silk and antique lace gown, Kathryn nudged Tim who was taking in the guests while sampling a glass of champagne, looking resplendent in his navy tuxedo, starched white shirt and burgundy bow tie. She proudly repeated Natalie's claim. "I've been reliably informed *you're* a very lucky man, but on reflection I believe it's *me* who's won the lottery."

Ballard rolled his eyes, pleading, "Cut it out you two. I know you've booked the bridal suite upstairs, but try to hang on for just a few more hours."

Natalie's elbow was swift and direct. "Michael, they're *newlyweds* for heaven's sake."

Agreeing, Ballard added, "I'm fully aware of that, Nat. Didn't I give away the wedding rings during the celebrant's rather extended ceremony, everyone packed into the foyer like sardines as a result of the downpour outside?"

Raising his own glass of sparkling water, Ballard toasted Tim's parents, Frank and Muriel, who were contentedly watching proceedings. Seated to Tim's right, they were too far away to converse with, but the gesture was appreciated and reciprocated, underscored by their smiles, synonymous with parents delighted that their son had married well.

Turning to Kathryn, Ballard insisted, "Feel free to tell Tim I *also* think he's a lucky guy."

Kathryn's eyes glistened as she squeezed his hand, her emotions such she had to compose herself before replying. "Michael, you already know this, but I'm going to say it anyway. Not only have you been a wonderful brother to me, but you filled the void when Mum and Dad died. As much as I miss them, you've shown me the love and affection they would have heaped on me. I can't thank you enough for that. And your concern for me was front-and-centre when that horrible man held me captive. You risked your life to save mine and suffered horrible injuries doing so."

His own eyes moistening, Ballard felt overwhelmed by his deep-seated affection for his sister. "After that rather formal exposé, just keep doing what you've done so far in life sis, that's all I can ever ask." Glancing at her right cheek where her captor had struck her so forcefully with the barrel of his Glock, he noted the scar was barely visible. Knowing words would only get in the way, brother and sister sat in comfortable silence. Looking on, Natalie admired the incredible bond between them, choosing to remain in the background.

Gazing out into the room from the recess of the bay window where the bridal table was positioned, Ballard found it to be the perfect vantage point to view everyone present. On the far right near the dance floor, the grand piano was being played superbly by the pianist Kathryn and Tim had chosen to provide the musical backdrop, the volume audible but not intrusive, unlike most wedding receptions.

Performing a visual sweep, Ballard concluded the festivities were indeed an intimate affair, which Tim and Kathryn had insisted upon. The five evenly spaced, circular tables spanning the room were occupied by close friends and family, their animated faces warmly lit by elegant candlelight.

The table to Tim's right contained his closest SOG work colleagues, and Ballard didn't need to be a lip reader to know what the discussions were about, the group exclusively from his elite squad. Close by, and almost immediately in front, the neighbouring table was a fascinating mix of police members and their wives. The AC and Jean, her bandaged shoulder concealed beneath her creme ensemble, were in deep discussion with Peter and Diane who in turn included John and Sonia in their spirited conversation. Sitting opposite, Delwyn and her partner Rachel were playing a listening game, smiling often, suggesting to Ballard that the AC had begun recounting one of his many tall tales from an illustrious career.

At the three adjoining tables, the guests were a grouping of Kathryn's and Tim's closest friends, their average ages causing Ballard to feel every one of his years. The buzz of chatter and laughter within the room proved the wedding couple had chosen their guest list to perfection, the well-considered seating arrangements adding to everyone's enjoyment.

Professional in their black pants, white starched shirts and bow ties, the wait staff were busily serving three choices of entree which Natalie inspected with a skilled eye. "Ok Michael, I'll make this easy for you. Would you like the rockmelon bruschetta with goat's cheese and prosciutto, the chicken and spinach dumplings, or the shakshuka, which is egg poached in a smoky, spiced tomato sauce?"

Totally perplexed, Ballard waved a questioning hand at John who was gazing in his direction. As their eyes met, both men produced an exaggerated shrug. Lifting his chin in acknowledgement, Ballard guessed Sonia was repeating the very same options Natalie had just offered him. "Nat, as I've said on many occasions, one of the downfalls of modern society is excessive choice, but even so, I think I'll settle on the chicken and spinach dumplings, mostly because it's the only entrée I can pronounce."

Smiling, Natalie acknowledged the waiter who had been waiting patiently, holding the tray for their inspection. After everyone had been served, Ballard tucked in, his immediate reaction heralding that his choice was the right one. Natalie chose the rockmelon bruschetta, each morsel savoured, the individual flavours tantalising her taste buds. By contrast, Ballard's methodical mastication proved to be nothing more than a necessary preamble to him swallowing his food. Staring at him, Natalie shook her head. "Darling, you're meant to enjoy your meal."

Cocking his head to one side, Ballard asked, "Ah, so you're assuming I'm *not* enjoying it?"

"Well, no, not by the speed by which you're gulping it down."

As Ballard was about to spear his second last dumpling he spotted Margaret, the Rupertswood manager. Petite, in her early fifties, her blonde hair was styled in a short bob. She had been a godsend for his and Natalie's wedding, ensuring everything was arranged to perfection. Smiling at them both as she approached, she spoke with Kathryn and Tim before turning back to them. "Is everything to your liking? Gosh, it seems like only yesterday when you two were the stars of the show."

Unable to resist, Ballard commented, "Yes, perfection all round. So you mean we *aren't* the star attraction tonight?"

Shaking her head, Margaret eyed Natalie with amusement. "Nothing has changed I see, just how I like it." With a broad smile, again directed towards Natalie, she was off, wandering the tables, her eagle eye verifying all was as it should be, conversing with her staff as required.

Leaning closer, Natalie commented, "She still runs a tight ship."

Ballard agreed. "Hmm, it would appear so."

Having stopped playing, the pianist switched on background music to pre-recorded versions of his own compositions. Approaching the bridal table he spoke briefly with Tim and Kathryn before addressing Ballard. "The groom is ready for the speeches. Would you like me to make the announcement?"

Swallowing his last mouthful, then chasing it down with a gulp of apple cider, Ballard agreed. "Why not, now's as good a time as any."

Natalie squeezed his hand for reassurance as the pianist did his best to gain everyone's attention. Realising it was a lost cause, Ballard rose and tapped his glass with a fork. The pianist thanked him before heading back to the piano, relieved Ballard had succeeded in drawing the guests' focus.

Looking around, Ballard opened with an age-old joke. "Well, thanks to you lot I've just cracked my glass." The obligatory titter among the gathering indicated the ice had been broken. "Folks, how often have we attended a wedding and thought, hmm, I'm not so sure this marriage will go the distance?"

There were general whispers of agreement, along with a few hesitant faces, unclear where the speech was heading. Turning to Kathryn and Tim, Ballard's beaming countenance said it all. "Well, we can be assured that's not the case here tonight. Kathryn has found her prince charming, and Tim his beautiful princess. Now you may be surprised to know I'm rather protective of my young sister." More tittering. "So, when she told me she'd met this great guy and thought he might be the one, I was instantly on the alert. Then she mentioned he was a police officer."

Deliberately hesitating, he saw some of the guests turning to one another, again uncertain of the speech's intended path. "At this news I was concerned that Kathryn may be getting into a relationship that would face greater tribulations than most. When I asked who this mystery man was, and she told me it was Tim, well, I was even *more* worried ..." Pausing yet again, Ballard milked the crowd, which was now openly bemused. "Worried the marriage wouldn't happen fast enough."

A roomful of relieved laughter and general whoops resulted, along with much table thumping ensuing from the SOG contingent. "Not that I needed to worry. These two are very much in love, and by my reckoning they always will be. This being the case, while life's inevitable problems will surely surface, they'll be ably resolved by two people fully equipped to handle anything that's thrown their way. So, on behalf of my wife and I ... I offer the married couple a heartfelt toast to their future together." He raised his glass. "To Kathryn and Tim." The gesture was reciprocated throughout the room, followed by a resounding burst of applause.

Plonking down, Ballard leaned across and kissed Natalie on the lips, generating a fresh round of revelry. Cupping his face, she stared deep into his eyes. "Textbook as always, darling."

All attention turned to Tim, who whispered in Kathryn's ear before rising to his feet. "Let me begin by stating the obvious. Speeches come naturally to Michael, unfortunately that's not the case for me. Having said that, I hate it when grooms *read* their speeches. I've always believed marriage is such an important occasion that words should come from the heart." Another round of applause burst from the SOG table, the police members getting into the spirit of the occasion in more ways than one. Tim placed a gentle hand on Kathryn's shoulder as she smiled up at him. "Meeting Kathryn has changed everything for me. She's literally transformed my *view* of the world. While I love my job, Kathryn is a major factor now in everything I do, so for the first time *ever* I have a healthy work-life balance." He directed his next comment to the AC, claiming almost guiltily, "Don't worry, sir, I'll still be giving my job my absolute all."

"Son, you'd damn well better!" The growled response generated widespread merriment.

Tim threw a salute towards the senior officer before turning back to his bride. "So darling, my promise to you is that *every* day of our marriage will be better than the one before. This is my solemn pledge." Leaning down he planted a lingering kiss, resulting in rapturous applause, followed by calls for more.

The speeches over, the wait staff moved into top gear, serving the main course with military precision. Their formal tasks behind them, Ballard and Tim were free to enjoy their meals. Grinning at one another, each appreciated the camaraderie that existed between them.

Tucking into his herb-crusted chicken and rice, with sautéed apricots and broccolini, Ballard leaned across and inspected Natalie's grilled rack of lamb, steamed asparagus and scalloped potatoes. "All good?"

She gave him a 'you should have asked me *prior* to my taking a mouthful' look, but responded anyway, mumbling her words as she dabbed her mouth with a napkin. "Just delicious."

Kathryn poked Ballard with her elbow. "Here I was thinking you'd have gone with the lamb Michael, for old times' sake, considering how you used to slaughter and butcher a sheep each week on the farm for Mum to cook."

Grimacing, Ballard remembered back to how the task was thrust upon him the moment he turned fifteen, a fact of life on farms, and something his father expected of him without question. "Sis, as you well know, eating lamb seven days a week was enough to put me off it forever, but Mum managed to cook it in so many different ways it was never boring. Remember her favourite saying, 'you have two choices of meals in this house, take it or leave it'?"

Kathryn uttered a throaty laugh as she recalled life on the farm where choice was purely mythical, and day-to-day existence, while regimented, was more than enjoyable.

Finishing his last mouthful, Ballard whispered to Natalie that he was going to work the room as she had suggested earlier, indicating this would free her up to pass on motherly advice to Kathryn. He got to his feet, pretending to ignore her prolonged gaze which was a direct warning for him to behave himself. Grabbing a spare chair, he settled between Tim and his parents, congratulating them on having raised such a fine son, and what would surely be an even finer husband. Grateful of the praise, they chatted for several minutes about married life and its various aspects, then Ballard indicated he should move on so he wouldn't be accused of favouritism.

His next stop was the SOG table, the police members sitting more upright as they interacted with what was in essence a senior officer. "Having a good time, guys?"

Their chorused, "*You bet*," brought a satisfied grin to Ballard's face.

After requesting they take special care of their boss over the coming weeks because he might be a touch distracted, Ballard moved to the AC's table. He held onto Jean's hand, feeling surprisingly emotional, almost as if she were his mother. "It's so good to see you Jean. You're an inspiration to us all. Are you on the mend?" He pointed to her shoulder.

An impish grin preceded, "What shoulder?"

A ripple of laughter circulated around the table, with Ballard giving the AC a helpless shrug. "Talk about one of a kind."

Speaking to Peter and Diane, he asked the charge nurse if Peter's wound was on the mend. She assured him everything was progressing well, with no sign of infection, highlighting it was constantly itching, a sure sign it was healing.

Five minutes of chit chat ensued with Delwyn and Rachel, both congratulating him on his speech while passing on their relief it wasn't as long as the one he had given for his wedding. Not entirely sure he had received a compliment, he thanked them, and was rewarded with a wink from Delwyn. Leaning closer, she whispered, "Have you told Natalie about your trip to Moscow?"

Glancing at John who was in deep discussion with Sonia, he grimaced, "Yes, Nat *and* Sonia as a matter of fact, and I can tell you it didn't go down well."

Rachel joined in, the merest hint of a twinkle in her eyes. "You can hardly blame them Michael. One minute you're abandoning them in Hobart, the next you're gallivanting across to the other side of the world. I asked Delwyn what it's all about but she wouldn't tell me. Any chance you might elaborate?" The tone of her question was such that despite being a senior police officer herself, she was aware Ballard wasn't in a position to pass on sensitive information. Grinning, she accepted the status quo.

Ballard dragged his chair over to Sonia and John. "I take it your meals were to your liking?"

John rubbed his stomach, more than content. "I'm thinking about attending one of these slap-up wingding's *every* week."

Sonia took in her fiancé. "You do know it'll be *our* wedding in the near future, and you can eat all you want then."

Ballard was mischievous. "I hope that's not the only reason you're getting married John."

Opening his mouth, John's response was delayed as he decided on the most appropriate retort. Placing a hand on Sonia's swelling baby bump, he declared with feeling, "Certainly not. I've got important responsibilities heading my way, and above all, a wonderful woman to spend the rest of my life with."

Taken aback by his partner's profound reply, it was Ballard's turn to be temporarily lost for words. "Wow! The perfect answer my good man."

Sonia squeezed John's hand. "He *has* changed for the better, don't you think Michael?" Her look of contentment said it all.

Shaking his head, Ballard was about to move back to the bridal table when he noticed one of the male waiters gesturing to him. Excusing himself, Ballard approached the man who was standing off to one side. As he drew nearer, something about the waiter's stance set off alarm bells, a sudden chill traversing the entire length of his body.

Standing before him, wearing identical attire to the other waiters, while sporting blonde hair and a neatly trimmed moustache, both of which Ballard knew to be false, was a nightmarish apparition ... an apparition in the form of Igor.

CHAPTER
31

Feeling weak at the knees, and with all colour draining from his face, Ballard's mind went into overdrive. Glancing over at the bridal table he was relieved nothing appeared to be amiss—Natalie and Kathryn still chatting, and Tim fully engaged with his parents. Checking the AC's table behind him, the senior officer, along with Delwyn, John and Peter were curious as to what the waiter's issue might be, but it was obvious they had no idea who he was.

Ballard felt panic well inside him which he did his best to control, his mind exploding with multiple scenarios. Was Igor alone? Did he have a weapon? What chance was there to overpower him before he injured or killed someone? What was the best course of action now the Russian had shown his hand?

It was obvious Igor was exploiting the drama; however, his opening words belied his facial benevolence, which was akin to an amusing yet wicked uncle. "*Michael, Michael. I so* enjoyed your speech, but I'm here on a more important matter. Taking back the nuclear cannisters yesterday was a step too far. Now I *thought* we had an agreement—you and your colleagues and your respective families would remain unharmed providing your department didn't get too much in our face."

Ballard felt lightheaded at the situation confronting him. On the one hand normality was swirling all around, yet a professional terrorist belonging to a brutal criminal organisation was standing before him, smiling as he threatened his work colleagues, family and friends. Ballard didn't bother asking what the Russian wanted, aware he wouldn't have to.

Proving how in tune he was with Ballard's conflicting thoughts, Igor added, "I'm busy for the next three or four days, but afterwards we really do need to have a sit-down, you and me." In the blink of an eye, any semblance of good humour evaporated, his features setting like stone. "The wellbeing of all your families depends on it."

The trickle of ice running down Ballard's spine became a tsunami.

Waving a hand towards the SOG table, Igor cut to the chase. "Now it may have crossed your mind that those fine officers over there could rush me, pinning me down, allowing you to get all hot and sweaty and read me my rights." The grey eyes projected unspoken cruelty. "My advice to you is if I don't walk out the front door in the next few minutes..." he leaned in towards Ballard, "this place will light up like the fourth of July, and a lot of innocent lives will be lost, including those dearest to you. *Am...I...clear?*"

Ballard maintained a fixed stare at his antagonist, realising any form of verbal engagement was futile. Igor was on an ego trip and nothing was going to stop him from enjoying himself to the fullest. Reaching out, the Russian patted Ballard's cheek, causing a number of those nearby to look up in surprise, unsure what could possibly warrant a waiter to act in such a familiar way with one of the principal wedding guests.

At this point, John realised something was very wrong. Shoving back his chair he approached, his expression part curious, part aggressive. Ballard held up a cautioning hand, causing Igor to chuckle before declaring, "My, my. The dynamic duo together once more." His voice low, he ordered, "Rein him in Michael, we don't want a tragedy unfolding at such a joyous occasion, do we?"

"Need a hand Mike?" John assessed the situation in seconds, recognising Igor despite the Russian's low-key disguise.

Answering for Ballard, Igor joked, "No problem here John. I was informing young Michael that we all need to sit down later in the week and hammer out some ground rules. But for now, I'm a busy man and must be off."

Ballard saw John tensing, as though about to make a move, but he stopped him in his tracks. "Keep your cool John, I'll explain everything later."

Igor uttered another throaty chuckle, clearly enjoying every second of the dramatic situation he was inflicting upon both detectives. "Sound advice Michael. As I said, I'll be in touch." Pivoting on his heel, he walked calmly towards the door.

Moments later, Margaret hurried over, confused. "Michael, did my waiter do or say something to upset you? One of my staff told me you were talking to him for quite a long time." Her brow was furrowed, distressed there may be an issue requiring her intervention.

In a muted voice Ballard explained, "Margaret, that pretend waiter was... *is* an extremely dangerous criminal."

Despite drawing breath, she was professional enough to hide her misgivings from nearby guests who were oblivious to what was unfolding around them.

"He's here on a matter I can't discuss. What's more he won't be taking any further part in tonight's proceedings. Please don't approach him, just allow him to leave."

Margaret did her best to understand what was going on. "I had a call after lunch from one of my top waiters indicating he was sick, but he said he'd found a reliable replacement. He sounded very distressed at the time, something I put down to his illness, and then this chap ... he said his name was Eric, he turned up here less than an hour later. He fitted right in ... he certainly knew what he was doing. Things were so busy I was just grateful he was able to help out. I told him I'd sort out the paperwork after the shift was over."

Ballard looked at John, both fearful of the fate of the waiter who had rung in sick. Doing his best not to alarm Margaret, Ballard asked, "Could you give me the waiter's phone number and address so I can have someone go around and check that he's ok?"

Despite Ballard's innocent words, apprehension crossed Margaret's face. She did her best to bring herself under control. "I'll ... I'll go and get it. Michael, John, I'm *so* sorry this has—"

"Margaret, please believe me, *none* of what's happened here is your doing. On the contrary, the criminal world we operate in has encroached on *you* and your staff. When the guests have all gone I'll explain everything in more detail. In the meantime a few of us need to use your smoking room ... it won't be for long. There are some issues we need to discuss."

Margaret did her best to remain calm. "Of course, take your time. I'll have one of my team turn on the lights ... would you like any refreshments—?"

Ballard touched her arm. "No, nothing like that. We just want a private spot for a quick chat. And Margaret, thank you for being so understanding."

She made a concerted effort to appear in control as she headed for the door.

Ballard drew John closer. "Have the AC, Pete and Delwyn meet Tim and myself in the smoking room. Make up any story you like so as not to alarm the ladies. I'll go and extract Tim, hopefully without spooking Kathryn and Nat."

John's growl was from the heart. "Will do Mike. Jesus, doesn't this prove that come hell or high water we *have* to put this bastard behind bars before something tragic happens to our loved ones?"

"My thoughts exactly."

The Rupertswood smoking room is world famous. It was where Lady Clarke burnt the bail after her staff lost a friendly match with the English cricket team, placing the subsequent ashes in a tiny urn, the vessel now secured behind glass at Lord's. The room itself exuded a brandy and cigar ambiance due to the antique furniture strategically positioned throughout, along with the oversized double-hung windows adorned with heavily brocaded damask drapes. Heirloom paintings hung on all four walls, illuminated by ornate chandeliers which cast a warm glow over the entire room, everything coalescing to create a sense of abundant wealth.

Entering, Peter and John plonked on one of the leather sofas, while the AC, Delwyn and Tim settled into wingback Chesterfield armchairs. Ballard took a fourth, and spinning it on one leg, sat facing everyone.

Appearing and sounding agitated that his wife's aggressor had been in the same room, the AC demanded answers. "Ok Michael. What did that bastard want?"

With a sweep of his hand Ballard brought John in on his reply. "We both agree that Igor is furious because we denied him his major payday at the reservoir, then adding insult to injury we swiped the two cannisters right from under his nose. That undoubtably makes him appear less of a poster boy in the eyes of The Board, and he's hell-bent on making us suffer because of it."

John was confused. "But why go to all this trouble just to warn us we're treading on his toes? Christ, he could have rung you or Peter on your mobiles and said the same thing."

"Ego John, as well as a giant power play. He's reaching out and grabbing us by the throat, warning us that he can get to us at any time and any place, including our families. That's full-on intimidation. I'm afraid his coercion is the beginning of a more sinister phase we now find ourselves in ... a phase in which we're up to our armpits in complications."

A fragile silence descended on the room, broken by the AC barking, "All the more reason that we arrest this prick in Moscow before something disastrous happens." Checking his watch, he declared, "Come to think of it, the bugger may be hopping on a plane tomorrow about the same time we are." His bark grew harsher. "It had better not be our flight!"

Nobody laughed.

Ballard broached Igor's threat that he would 'light up' Rupertswood. "There's no question he knew by threatening us we'd fold and not arrest him. He gave away it's most likely a ruse by stating he wanted to speak with us at the end of the week. But can we take the risk?" It was clear everyone was agonising over the decision that had to be made—continue on with the reception or have all the guests vacate the building.

Again, the AC cut to the chase. "I agree Igor used the threat as a safety net for himself, but you're right Michael, we can't be certain of that. Tim, as inconspicuously as you can, have your comrades in arms," he waved in the general direction of the ballroom, "have them leave their table in a staggered manner so as not to alarm everyone, then give them the basics that there may be an explosive device somewhere in the building. There are ten guys so they should be able to toss over all the rooms in about fifteen minutes. A couple will need to check outside as well, just in case."

Ballard posed a complication the officers may face. "We'll need to bring Margaret in on this because some of the rooms will be locked. Igor's skilled enough to unlock any one of them in seconds, so we can't assume because they *are* locked that he hasn't been inside."

The AC agreed. "Good point." He looked up as there was a timely knock on the door and Margaret poked her head in. The AC waved her over, summing up the situation and the need for the SOG officers to gain access throughout the mansion.

To her credit Margaret didn't panic, partially reassured by the AC insisting it was a precautionary measure and nothing more. Reaching out, she handed Ballard a piece of paper. "This is my waiter's address and his mobile number. I've already rung but it went to voicemail."

Ballard did his best not to show his concern. "Ok Margaret, I'll follow this up and let you know."

Glancing over her shoulder several times she left the room.

The AC went through the required actions. "Tim, get your chaps on the move. Delwyn, ring a couple of your team and have them attend at the waiter's address to see what Igor's been up to. We all know he's not the sort to leave loose ends, so I'm not holding out much hope for the poor bugger's health."

Ballard imagined in his mind's eye the young officers walking in on what surely had to be an execution-style killing. "In the meantime, sir … John, Pete and myself will do our best to work the room so the guests continue thinking there's nothing out of the ordinary happening. We'll come up with a cock-and-bull excuse like a dropped napkin or something so we can check under their tables in case Igor's wired up one of those." He gave Peter and John a resigned shrug. "Come to think of it, all this shouldn't be too hard to pull off."

Everyone raised their eyebrows in unison, aware they were about to undertake tasks approaching mission impossible. The AC stood up, flexing his shoulders to relieve tense muscles. "Well then, let's get to work."

As predicted, within twenty minutes the respective responsibilities were completed without anything suspicious being discovered, everyone able to relax, reassuring their partners all was well. Despite this, Natalie was having none of it. After completing her circuit of the room, having chatted with various guests, she took Ballard aside and demanded, "I *know* something's going on Michael, so please tell me what it is."

As Ballard was about to respond, he was saved by the pianist inviting Tim and Kathryn onto the dance floor for the bridal waltz, the guests encouraged to join in at the end. Eyeing Ballard with a fixed look, Natalie let him off the hook as they mingled with the other guests, clapping the newlyweds as they began their dance, each gazing lovingly into the other's eyes.

"Romantic, isn't it?" Ballard encircled Natalie's waist with an arm while waving John and Sonia over, both couples standing together, the distress of the previous thirty minutes now at the back of the detectives' minds. It was Sonia who broached the issue of their trip to Moscow. "You'll ring me, won't you?"

John pretended to be nonplussed by the request, but it wasn't convincing. "Of *course*, darling. You *know* I will ... once during the day and twice at night."

Natalie's eyes posed the identical question, prompting Ballard to reassure her. "That's a ditto." Leaning down he kissed her on the lips, a lingering and emotional embrace, all thoughts of what the next few days would bring thrust to one side, his immediate focus centred on what he must do to keep his wife and her children safe.

CHAPTER
32

For anyone prepared to pay an exorbitant sum of money, flying First Class with Emirates is an experience not to be missed, something John was mindful of as he settled back in the spacious surrounds of his luxurious suite. To his right he watched Ballard take full advantage of the two hundred centimetres of legroom available as he stretched out in his ample leather seat. "Hey Mike, the hostess just told me my damn chair can give me a bloody massage ... that *can't* be right—can it?"

Ballard leaned forward so he could better see his partner, as well as the AC to John's left across the aisle; the senior officer having bagged the window seat, his privacy partition still in the open position. "If only the girls could see us now Johno. Can you imagine what they'd say if we'd taken up the spa offer in the airport lounge before we took off?"

While the AC couldn't hear the exchanges between his detectives, he guessed the general thrust of their conversation. Shaking his head, and with a wry smile he buried himself in his work which included forwarding numerous texts and emails to police members back at the office.

As the A380-800 levelled off at its cruising altitude of 13,000 metres, Ballard unbuckled his seatbelt and plonked down on the ottoman in John's suite. "This sure beats Kingsford-Smith's experience when he crossed the Pacific in 1928 in the *Southern Cross*."

John's head slumped forward as he agreed how pampered they were compared to the pioneers of long-haul flights all those years ago. "Hard to imagine what they went through. Christ, *our* biggest worry is whether our fold-down beds are comfy enough ... which I'm reliably informed they are."

Chuckling, Ballard got to his feet. "Come on. There's a couple of issues we need to discuss with the boss."

Crossing the aisle, Ballard checked that the suite directly in front of the AC was vacant before propping on the senior officer's ottoman, John content to lean against the partition. "Sorry to interrupt you sir, but I've an update regarding the waiter shot in his home. Susan has just texted that after confirming he was indeed shot, street CCTV shows someone looking horribly like Igor arriving at the property, knocking on the front door then leaving twenty minutes later."

The AC cursed aloud. "The ruthless bastard, he has *no* regard for human life. I know I sound like a broken record, but we *have* to stop him and his cohorts. What I cannot fathom is how he knows the *details* of all these people ... the poor waiter for instance?"

John muttered under his breath, "At least now with Vincenzo on the warpath we've got our best chance of putting him away for a very long time. We've seen him in action, and self-doubt isn't in his DNA."

Lounging back in his seat, the AC gazed at his detectives. "Be that as it may, we're dealing with a shitload of conflicting elements here. Look at the players ... there's Kremlin contacts popping up throughout this caper, with the President lurking in the background. As well there's a bunch of Spetsnaz soldiers and a team of Italian special forces all armed to the back teeth, everyone thrown together, along with a CIA agent and three Aussie detectives in the mix who are totally out of their depth. To my way of thinking that makes for one hell of a political cockup if this shindig goes belly-up."

John grunted. "We can only live in hope. Thankfully Vincenzo has arranged for us to be picked up when we land in Moscow at ..." A bemused stare preceded, "Christ, when he mentioned the name of the airport it sounded more like a damn swear word."

"Sheremetyevo International." Ballard saved the day. Following up he added, "Google lists the Chkalovsky military airbase as fifty-four kilometres due west, less than an hour's drive."

John checked about him. "I guess it'd be too much to expect the barracks at the airbase to have this degree of luxury on tap."

The AC's barking laugh drew the attention of a passing flight attendant who acknowledged his good mood. "'Fraid not John. So appreciate all this indulgence while you can. I'm certainly going to." He pursed his lips. "I guess I shouldn't be casting doubt at a time like this, but how good *is* this Vincenzo character?"

Ballard was emphatic. "Like we said, we saw him in action in Venice. The bugger's ice cool under pressure ... doesn't second guess ... and according to Bernard who's worked with him for years, he's our best, perhaps our *only* chance of bringing The Board down."

"And what's the probability that those being arrested won't be replaced by a younger more ruthless bunch of thugs?"

Ballard flicked a millisecond glance towards John which didn't escape the AC; both detectives realising the past few days had taken a toll on their boss, his apparent indecisiveness something they hadn't experienced before. "Sir, we'd be kidding ourselves if we thought there weren't understudies waiting in the wings. But the guys in charge are psychopaths … control freaks of the tallest order. By my reckoning they'll do everything and anything to remain in power, so training up replacements isn't something that would figure highly on their to-do list. Any newbies will have to fight among themselves for a year or two until the new pecking order is sorted out."

John agreed, with the AC admitting, "Scrub that last question, I'm just tired—"

"And for good reason I might add." John was on the front foot in defence of his boss.

Grinning, the senior officer joked, "Thank you John. Even so, perhaps it best if it wasn't broadcast that I let my guard down."

John made a zipping motion across his mouth.

"Ok, I'm going to skip dinner and have a snooze for a few hours until we get to Singapore. I suggest you two do the same …" He cocked his head to one side, a smirk materialising. "But I'm forgetting, you're both much younger than I am." He slipped his mobile into the breast pocket of his shirt before closing his laptop and waving the detectives away.

Back in Ballard's suite, the two men kept their voices low, with John admitting, "Well, you don't see that too often … in fact I don't think I've *ever* heard the boss express self-doubts."

Ballard ran his hand along the leather armrest of his seat.

"Igor taking Jean as a hostage has knocked him for six. If he ever lost her he'd never recover, all those years together, that makes for an incredible bond." He took in his partner. "Just as it'll be for yourself and Sonia."

Grinning like a schoolboy, John whispered, "I sure hope so."

Each of their respective dinners, which were of a standard akin to fine dining at a classy restaurant, came and went, followed by two movies, one of which John shared with Ballard by synchronising their screens.

Ninety minutes after landing, and back onboard a second A380 for the next leg, the flight attendants fussed about as they made up their beds, with John and Ballard choosing to don the monogrammed cotton pyjamas provided. Stretching out, they were asleep within minutes—the soothing background hiss of the air-conditioning aiding their slide into a deep slumber.

After what felt like only minutes, Ballard was woken by John shaking him on the shoulder. "Wakey wakey my good man. The AC's already up and about. Christ, he's a bundle of energy for someone his age."

Peering through one eye, Ballard inspected his partner prior to checking his watch, noting it was just after 4.00 a.m. Moscow time. This meant they had just over an hour and a half before landing. Grabbing his clothes and toiletry bag, he strolled to the rest room with the opportunity to take a short but invigorating shower. Emerging twenty minutes later, shaved, fully dressed and hair combed into a semblance of normality, it was John's turn, keen to experience the mind-bending novelty of showering while flying at 13,000 metres.

A filling breakfast of free-range scrambled eggs, waffles and a piping hot pot of tea prepared all three for what lay ahead.

Feeling his phone vibrate in his pocket, Ballard checked the screen, reading a text from Vincenzo. '*Your arrival time is 5.45 a.m. Will pick you up myself and drive you to the Chkalovsky airfield. Make the most of what's left of your first-class flight! V.*'

Showing the text to the AC and John, Ballard appreciated Vincenzo's sense of humour as he reminded his partner that accommodation at the airfield was going to be bare-bones basic. Pretending to be unfussed, John shrugged, resigning himself to the reality of barrack life in a Russian military airfield base.

Feeling the tension mount as they reflected on what they were attempting to achieve, they were cognisant how difficult it would be for Vincenzo and his team to arrest elite criminals on their own turf without a massacre ensuing, thus creating an international incident.

CHAPTER
33

Sheremetyevo International Airport in Moscow was originally built as a military airfield. After an extensive and costly transformation, it has become the busiest commercial airport in Russia, and the fifth most utilised in Europe, with four of its six terminals reserved for international travellers. Exceeding sixty million passengers annually, along with more than 500,000 aircraft movements, it is now an airport that competes successfully on the world stage.

Landing on the main east-west runway, the A380 completed its taxi to the terminal, the massive jet engines winding down. Peering out the AC's window, Ballard and John took in the two main rooflines of the airport; one structure resembling the grey, forbidding sarcophagus that covered the Chernobyl nuclear power plant, the other a gigantic replica of the Louvre's glass pyramid.

"Will you check that out. These Ruskies sure don't do things by half." John was open-mouthed at the spectacle.

Ballard sized up his partner's mood, "Now John, do *not* forget that this is Russia. So for Christ's sake try not to antagonise any of the officials. Most of them would think nothing of locking you up for something as trifling as a decent sneeze."

A mischievous grin preceded, "Mate, while I'm on Russian soil I'll be a model citizen ... *promise*."

Ballard shook his head in frustration, muttering, "You'd better ... for all our sakes."

Having taken Vincenzo's advice to travel lightly, they compared each other's carry-on luggage as they repacked their toiletries, John quipping, "I never thought I'd be visiting another country bringing only a couple of pairs of underpants, a change of socks and a damn toothbrush."

Ballard gave him a dubious sideways glance. "Methinks that's a wee exaggeration Johno. I very much doubt Sonia would have let you out the front door if that was all you'd packed."

The AC approached, overhearing Ballard's comments. "Speaking of front doors, Vincenzo has just texted me. We're to wait onboard until all the passengers have disembarked, then a hostess will escort us to the rear exit where he'll meet us on the tarmac."

John was impressed. "Bloody hell. No battle through Customs? The bugger must have some clout."

The AC agreed, "You'd better believe it. He'll have pulled strings to keep us as invisible as possible. Now John, in case you've forgotten, we're in Russia, so don't go punching anyone who happens to annoy you."

"Mike's already read me the riot act. Like I said, it's 'Yes comrade, no comrade, three glasses of vodka comrade'."

The AC unleashed a cobalt-blue stare at Ballard. "Do you believe him?"

Ballard laughed. "Like I've always said, this guy can be

impulsive, but he's damn smart. He knows when the odds are stacked against him."

John pulled at his ear, unsure whether or not he had been complimented.

It was almost twenty minutes before a smiling flight attendant approached and asked them to follow her, which they did, passing through Business Class, the cocktail lounge, then along the lengthy aisle in Economy. Ballard chuckled. "Don't forget Johno, your first-class experience is about to dim in your memory bank faster than you can say Vladivostok."

The AC studied his detectives, his look that of a father unclear if his hyperactive children would behave themselves when it was needed.

Descending the rear steps, they spotted Vincenzo propped against a grey, camouflaged GAZ-2330 Tigr armoured jeep. With legs crossed and arms folded, he cut an impressive figure in his military fatigues.

Spotting them he strolled over, shaking the AC's hand. "Pleasant trip?"

"Yes thank you Vincenzo, but you've spoilt us for any future long-haul flights."

"Ever thought of joining the CIA?"

The AC looked hard at the operative. "Perhaps a decade or two ago I might have considered it."

Vincenzo turned to Ballard, pumping his hand like a long-lost friend. "*Ah ...* but *you're* not too old. It's worth contemplating, so don't dismiss the invitation outright."

Ballard pretended not to have heard. "Hello Vincenzo. Good to see you again."

A mischievous smile formed as the agent fronted John, his arms widespread, pretending he was about to hug him—at the last moment he stopped short. "Oh, I remember, no embracing. I'm glad you could make it."

"What, and miss out on twenty-one hours of non-stop pampering?" John hooked a thumb over his shoulder at the A380 towering behind him.

Vincenzo laughed, then in the space of a millisecond he switched to all-business. Pointing to the jeep he invited them to climb aboard. Once inside he addressed the Spetsnaz driver, uttering a brisk order in Russian, prompting the soldier to perform a tyre-protesting U-turn on the tarmac as he headed towards the exit checkpoint. The guard at the gate, armed with an automatic weapon, strolled around the jeep, assessing each occupant until he came to Vincenzo's window. The CIA agent flashed his identification. As if by magic the boom gate swung up and they were on their way.

The passing countryside was heavily treed and picturesque, their journey skirting north of Moscow. Twenty minutes into the trip a number of towns were entered with everyday folk going about their business, oblivious to the significant intent of the occupants in the military vehicle. Vincenzo maintained a tour guide patter throughout the journey, refraining from any discussion regarding what they were planning to achieve, Ballard putting this down to the driver not being privy to what was about to unfold in the coming hours.

The overwhelming first impression of the Chkalovsky airfield was the vast array of military aircraft, several taking off as they arrived, the air vibrating from the sheer power of the huge jet engines. The terminal itself was compact, the façade a combination of yellow-and-blue painted brick, fronted by manicured lawn areas, the grassed sections dotted with numerous miniature ornamental pines.

Vincenzo turned to face them. "Michail here will show you to your quarters." He gave the driver a playful pat on the shoulder. "It'll give him a chance to practise his English."

Michail flicked an emotionless glance at his passengers in the mirror, both hands ten to two on the steering wheel, his beret glued to his head. "Good morning." His accent was heavy with Slavic inflection.

The three policemen greeted him back, John nudging Ballard, amused that the salutation, while welcome, was fifty minutes late. As they pulled up in one of the parking bays, Vincenzo confirmed that their watches were set to Moscow time. "There'll be a briefing at 1130 hours. This gives you just over an hour to settle in. I'm assuming you had breakfast on the plane?"

John studied the CIA agent. "Yes we did, and I'm presuming once we've finished our lunch, steaming hot towels will be dispensed via silver tongs, much the same way as we experienced on our flight?"

Vincenzo threw back his head, roaring with laughter. "But of course John, this *is* Russia after all. It's a very civilised country."

Checking into their rooms, Ballard was pleasantly surprised at the standard of accommodation. While compact, it sported a single bed, an adequate wardrobe, a wall-mounted bench, a chair and a TV. The bathroom had a toilet, a shower and a small basin, above which was a mirrored vanity unit.

A tap on the door, when opened, revealed John leaning laconically against the jamb. Entering the room he claimed, "Far from first-class Mike, but it could have been a damn sight worse."

Ballard pointed to the sole chair as he plonked down on

the end of the bed. "What do you make of Vincenzo's take on things?"

John's cheeks ballooned. "For a guy about to put an axe through a bunch of crooks who are running rampant worldwide, he's a bloody cool customer. He sure *appears* to know what he's doing. Christ, he must be on top of things … after all, we're here in the middle of Russia with backing from the highest level of government, so that has to count for something."

Ballard agreed. "One way or the other we're going to find out within the next—"

A sharp knock on the door had Ballard snatching a glance at the wall clock which showed 10.40 a.m. Perplexed, he opened the door to find Michail standing to attention, his expression apologetic. "*Izvinite*. The meeting is now. Follow me."

Before he could stop himself, John shot to attention, throwing a roundhouse salute. Elbowing him in the ribs, Ballard grabbed his mobile from the bench where it had been charging, Vincenzo having provided the appropriate adaptors. "Has our assistant commissioner been informed?"

Michail grew even more ramrod straight. "*Da*, in meeting room."

Not surprised the AC had taken a jump on them, Ballard and John followed Michail through a bewildering array of corridors. Stopping at a door bearing a sign reading *Konferents-Zal*, Michail knocked on the door, and swinging it open, stood to one side, indicating for both men to enter.

They proceeded into a large room, two of the walls bristling with digital screens, none of them active. A bulky conference table and chairs dominated, with Vincenzo and the AC side by side at the head.

Vincenzo invited them to take a seat. "The reason I've called you all together this early is to go over the spoils of war once more." He didn't appear embarrassed by his dramatic statement. "Clearly Igor's your primary focus, and as I said when I was in Melbourne, I hope you throw the book at him and he *never* gets out of jail. He's certainly guilty of enough serious criminal offences to have him put away for good."

"That's providing we *do* get him." The AC was steadfast in not wanting to be caught up in the hype the raid would be anything but a total success.

Vincenzo assessed the senior officer with eyes displaying the respect the AC had earned over a lifetime of fighting crime. "I have to admit Kevin, you may be right. So far Igor's outfoxed us at every turn, and for a very long time." He shrugged, angry with himself for succumbing to anything resembling negative thoughts. "*Assuming* things eventuate as we pray they will, Igor's your man. The CIA however, are dead set on snaring Anatoli Demyan. He's caused the FBI and CIA endless headaches over the years, and despite Bernard's insistence that back in his day Demyan was more valuable to them in terms of intel by remaining free than being in jail, that's now come to an end."

His brow furrowing, he added, "I'm also aware, as you all are, that with Tatiana groomed by Demyan throughout her formative years, it's turned her into a very dangerous *femme fatale*, and being Bernard's daughter, this adds a considerable degree of complexity to proceedings."

Everyone agreed, having listened to the heart-wrenching revelation by the Texan of the incredible circumstances that led to him discovering he was Tatiana's father.

"The French DGSE ..." Vincenzo threw to John, challenging him.

Without hesitating John responded with a grin, "Directorate-General for External Security, the equivalent of the CIA and MI6."

Vincenzo clapped his hands, clearly impressed. "*Bravo, mio buon uomo.*"

Guessing he had been complimented, John confessed with mock humility, "Michael reminded me what DGSE stood for during the flight."

Vincenzo laughed. "The French have their eyes set on a former diplomat of theirs who defected to Russia almost a decade ago. At some point in the past five years he crossed over to the bad guys and became a member of The Board."

"His name?" Ballard was curious.

"Claude Garnier. He has an accomplished eye for the ladies and made the fatal mistake of bedding a senior French politician's young daughter. Hence Garnier's diplomatic career was over before it ever really began. As he'd been a regular attaché to Russia in his first year or so, it made sense for him to make it his permanent home, his wife and children having cut him loose."

Vincenzo ran his fingers through his hair. "So that's the CIA, the DGSE and you Aussies catered for, which leaves the Italians, the English and the Russian President. I can tell you my countrymen are none too pleased with Maxim Dabylov cavorting about like the wealthy playboy he purports to be on the island of Giudecca just off Venice. Especially as he insists on flaunting his bloody great mansion while being part of an international crime syndicate. That state of affairs doesn't sit well with the Italian Government, even though most of *them* are crooks in their own right. The CIA will arrange for his and his family's witness protection on the understanding the

Italians can get to him whenever they wish to."

He moistened his lips. "So, on to the Brits. MI6 have insisted on collaring Aleksei Agapov who has on multiple occasions slipped into Britain on fake passports and poisoned two of their top scientists. This piece of gossip has been supressed by the English Government because they don't want word getting out that their borders are basically a gaping hole."

Leaning back in his chair he took a huge breath, as though about to deliver a speech. "So last, but certainly not least, we come to the Russian President. Like the president before him, he's an ex-colonel of the former KGB, also a seventy-plus-times billionaire, and now President for life." He grinned. "However long that life may be after him taking over the Ukraine foray. Understandably he's taking the lion's share of the spoils from this raid."

The AC grunted an acknowledgement, fully aware of the politics at play.

"My sentiments exactly Kevin. So as we know, like all Russian presidents, this guy's sole purpose in life is to remain in power. Now The Board, while it also has significant self-interests, has served the President's purpose by being his personal vacuum cleaner, sucking up and disposing of anything or anyone that's a threat to him. To clarify this, the FSB, or Federal Security Bureau, is responsible for safeguarding the Russian population. The FIS, the Foreign Intelligence Service handles overseas espionage. Both organisations have latitude in their operations that you guys, and even the CIA would die for, but there are limits as to what they can get away with. Even the GRU can only push the envelope so far."

John looked puzzled. Vincenzo helped him out. "The Glavnoje Razvedyvatel'noye Upravlenije or GRU. Their primary purpose is to gather intelligence on foreign militaries, among other nefarious activities that are far from legal."

John gasped. "Don't even *think* about asking me to memorise that bloody mouthful!"

Again Vincenzo roared with laughter. "So, getting back to business, The Board is another beast altogether when compared against these groups. It goes without saying they are *very* conscious of the need for presidential protection. For this they've been willing to do his bidding when things get really messy for him, thus ensuring the umbrella of protection he provides remains open for them—*until now.*"

He rubbed a hand across his jaw, his intelligent eyes narrowing. "The CIA's intel has it that The Board is no longer happy with the President on a number of fronts, as I mentioned, the least being his disastrous extension of the incursion into Ukraine, the ongoing international sanctions cramping their style. As a result there's a push within the group to distance themselves, perhaps even knock him from power, and as you can imagine that's not a positive career move in this country. Consequently the President has decided The Board must go, and he's happy for us to orchestrate this—with provisos of course. Namely, that he gets all the accolades of a successful operation, plus he bags the remainder of the members other than those already mentioned. On top of that, and more importantly, should things turn nasty his hands are to remain clean."

Vincenzo sat back, glancing at the wall clock before inviting comment. Ballard and John deferred to the AC who wasn't slow on the uptake. "Vincenzo, a lot of what you know about this meeting has come from Dabylov. I brought this up with you back home, but I'm going to raise it again—is he playing us for suckers?"

Vincenzo rocked forward. "A good question then, and just as valid now. Nothing's ever certain in this line of work, but I'll bet my career Dabylov still loves his wife, despite his repeated dalliances, and there's *no* doubt he adores his children. He knows full well that if he falls foul of the CIA, their chances—his wife and children that is—of reaching another birthday are zero should The Board ever get wind of what he's told us. No, he's rock solid and mentally prepared to enter witness protection with his family ... and as an added incentive he gets to keep most of his ill-gotten gains."

The AC wasn't fully convinced, looking to Ballard and John to see if they had any queries, with Ballard adding, "And they say crime doesn't pay. Now you may well cover this in a few minutes, but how many of the top-level Board members are going to be at this meeting?"

Vincenzo could barely contain himself as the question was being asked. "Let me say first and foremost, this meeting we are having now is the 'who gets what' part, and our subsequent meeting will be the 'how are we going to do it' bit. That being the case, my major and some other key players are on standby, coming here in fifteen minutes. To answer your question Michael, let me confirm that this gathering of The Board is going to be the queen-bee of their get-togethers. Everyone will be there. It's clear they're still hell-bent on destroying your nuclear waste site as you know, with plans for a similar one or two to be built in Italy, their sticky fingers in the honey pot. Now, with the Ndrangheta poking their nose into proceedings, it's an irritation that has grown into a full-blown crisis, so the meeting will also focus on how that thorny issue can be resolved. Like I said, this is the first time I can ever remember where all The Board members will be present. As such, this is our one, and realistically the most probable chance of crippling them for good. Just yesterday Dabylov updated his estimate to say there should be twelve to fifteen Board members present."

He studied his audience. "Any further questions?" As none were forthcoming, he added, "Good, now onto the 'shoot-'em-up' part." Taking his mobile he forwarded a text. "The major in charge of my GIS team …" Once more he eyed John who responded without hesitation, surprising Ballard and the AC.

"Gruppo di Intervento Speciale. I've been practising in the mirror so I wouldn't embarrass myself." John was chuffed he had got it right.

Vincenzo placed a hand on the AC's shoulder. "Don't let either of these two out of your sight."

The AC's gruff humph made it clear what his thoughts were in relation to that gem of an idea.

"As I was saying, the major in charge of the GIS team, Major Gallo, is about to join us. He was onboard the inflatable when we arrested Dabylov. So Michael, John, you've already met him. Furthermore, the Spetsnaz commander, Captain Lebedev will be attending, representing his ten-man team. I'm told his English is better than mine, so that's a bonus." He grew serious, almost tense. "Finally, Colonel Volkov from the FSB is sitting in, and I'm praying he'll report back to the President that the raid is highly achievable."

It was obvious from Vincenzo's mood change that for the assault to proceed, Colonel Volkov had to be convinced of its likely success before permission would be granted. No sooner had this realisation sunk in for the policemen than there was a knock on the door and three very different individuals entered.

Leading was the GIS major, Ballard and John recognising

him immediately. He was followed by a Spetsnaz soldier in uniform, the five stars on his epaulettes confirming his rank of captain. Finally, dressed in a drab dark suit and with a manner to match was the FSB colonel, the garb and deportment reminding Ballard of a World War II Gestapo agent. All three settled around the table, the Colonel deliberately separating himself by several chairs.

Vincenzo went through the introductions with a minimum of fuss, keen to detail the finer points of how the raid was going to be performed for the Colonel's benefit. He opened with, "Major, just confirming that you have fifteen personnel in your strike team? And captain … ten in yours?"

Sitting to attention, the Major verified this was the case, with the captain stating his squad number and readiness in what could only be described as an Oxford-educated voice, astonishing both Ballard and John.

Vincenzo addressed the FSB officer. "Colonel, as you know, the meeting of Cobet is to be held in the FSB headquarters building at 24 Kuznetsky Most, Moscow, on the second floor in Conference Room 206 tomorrow morning at 0900 hours. As is always the case, the room is fitted with video surveillance and audio, which I'll demonstrate in a moment.

"Next door, Room 205 will be the launching point for my team under the command of Major Gallo, along with Captain Lebedev's squad. You've arranged for a series of monitors to be installed in 205 so every aspect of the conference room can be observed, assisting the teams to determine when and how they should launch their assault."

The Colonel's face was expressionless, the only indication he was remotely interested, or even alive for that matter being an occasional blink. Ballard glanced at John, both realising

Vincenzo was describing the raid in excruciating detail so the Colonel had no option but to accept he was receiving a complete briefing as to what was to take place.

Having maintained his composure at the Colonel's apparent indifference, Vincenzo coolly assessed the Colonel's demeanour, fully conscious an unsubtle power play was afoot. "Ok Major, as this will be an assault conducted in close quarters, please describe how you intend to capture alive the Cobet members while neutralising the armed security personnel who will be in the room with them."

With typical Italian self-assurance the Major got to work. "The door to the conference room will be guarded on the outside, so the first task will be to take out those personnel positioned in the corridor. We'll determine the number by deploying a snake camera under our door. Once we've established how many and what weapons they're carrying, I'll notify Captain Lebedev. He, along with two of his team dressed in Russian military uniforms so as not to generate suspicion, will approach from the far end of the corridor, engaging the guards in conversation, drawing them away from Door 206. Then, using their GSh-18 semi-automatic pistols they'll take them out. Assuming the guards are wearing body armour, the pistols will be loaded with vest-penetrating ammunition ... all this in case head shots aren't viable, and of course silencers will be used." He paused to allow the scenario to play out in everyone's minds.

The AC looked towards Ballard and John, and despite his impassive expression, the merest head shake was akin to a five-minute monologue.

The Major continued, "Again, presuming the entry door is locked, we'll breach it with a ram at the exact moment the room's lights are extinguished to maximise the impact of the five M84 stun grenades we'll deploy. One of our team will be in the circuit breaker room at the end of the corridor in radio contact to throw the switches at the precise moment. This has already been tested by Captain Lebedev, with the circuit breakers labelled so there won't be any mistakes. We've decided on five stun grenades as the dimensions of the room are substantial, twelve by twenty metres, with an eight-metre-high ceiling."

Surprised at the size of the conference room, John asked Vincenzo, "You estimate there will be up to fifteen Board … er, scrub that, Cobet members at the meeting?"

"As I mentioned, Dabylov believes it *could* be as few as ten, but he's confident it'll be nearer fifteen. With those numbers we estimate possibly ten additional armed personnel will be stationed inside the room, so the teams could be facing as many as twenty-five personnel."

The Major wasn't concerned. "Along with Captain Lebedev's team who will be in Room 205 with us, my team will enter wearing night vision and protected by hi-tech composite metal foam vests. We've tested these and they're fully effective against 7.62 ammunition." He checked his audience to confirm everyone was up to speed, but needn't have bothered. "From the monitors in 205, we'll have calculated where the guards are located in the conference room before we breach. We plan to neutralise them within five … at the very most ten seconds of entry using Heckler & Koch MP7 submachine guns fitted with thirty-round magazines, each loaded with vest-piercing ammunition. We can't be certain, but it's likely the guards will be wearing the equivalent of our vests, either way we'll apply headshots where we can as the primary option. We won't be using silencers so as to maximise noise and confusion during the kill phase."

Again the three policemen shook their heads, and in spite of their experience in dealing with criminals of every persuasion throughout their careers, they found the direct, dehumanising manner in which the military regarded enemy combatants to be confronting, yet in a perverse way, reassuring.

Lifting a hand, Ballard asked, "I understand how Captain Lebedev will be able to move his squad into position in the FSB building prior to the meeting without raising suspicion, but how does the Major get his troops into Room 205 undetected?"

With the faintest twinkle in his eyes, Vincenzo chose to put the FSB officer on the spot. "Colonel, perhaps it best if you describe how this will be achieved."

Appearing to ignore the request, the concentration of six pairs of eyes dissolved his staged indifference. Clearing his throat and annoyed at being put under scrutiny, in a heavily accented voice he explained, "Our building has access tunnels allowing entry to select floors, including level two. The assault team's equipment has already been taken to 205."

Ballard smiled, because if looks could kill, Vincenzo's family would already be making funeral arrangements.

The Colonel continued, "Russian uniforms have been provided for the GIS soldiers. They'll enter 205 in small numbers, and at irregular intervals several hours before the meeting begins. Once the Cobet members are in place, the second-floor corridor will be sealed off from other staff in the building. As this has been standard practice for previous Cobet meetings, it won't appear suspicious."

He sat back, his fixed stare at Vincenzo challenging the agent to ask anything further of him.

Grinning openly, Vincenzo thanked him before turning his attention to his Australian counterparts. "Kevin, Michael, John … tomorrow morning we'll be locked away in a surveillance van provided by the Colonel. It'll be parked alongside the FSB building which is opposite Lubyanka Square. Onboard monitors will access the live feed of 206, exactly as we have here, including audio." Swinging around, having scooped up a remote, he pointed upwards and two of the wall monitors sprang to life. Displayed were live shots of Room 206, observed from either end. It caused John to exclaim, "*Jesus Christ. Check the place out!*"

As the Major had described, the room was large, the entire ceiling an elongated concave painted in a pale blush-rose, duplicated to great effect on the walls. Ornate terraced cornices encircled the ceiling. A feature of the cornices was a decorative horizontal border of inlaid onyx marble that matched the fourteen demi-columns spaced evenly around the walls, each topped by an ornate gold frieze. Hanging midpoint from the ceiling was a spectacular multi-tiered crystal chandelier that added to the room's grandeur. Beneath it, and occupying pride of place, was a highly polished timber conference table capable of hosting twenty guests. The accompanying redwood chairs were highly detailed with ornate carvings, and featured velvet padded armrests and seats. On the far wall, behind the head of the table, the Russian coat of arms was emblazoned on a floor-to-ceiling tapestry, which as much as anything set the tone of the room.

A chuckle from Vincenzo redirected everyone's attention. "Yes, it's hard to imagine that this spectacular chamber will become a killing field." His words were a harsh reminder of what was at stake, and the brutal actions necessary to achieve a positive outcome. "Any questions?"

Ballard was first out of the blocks. "I see there are three entry doors. I'm assuming the double doors at the foot of the table are the ones leading in from the outside corridor? If so, where do the two side single doors at the head of the table go?"

Mischievously, Vincenzo smiled at the Colonel, not bothering to reply, causing the officer to unleash another look of disgust at being forced to provide an answer. "They access a separate corridor and will be bolted shut on the far side as is always the case whenever Cobet meets." Driven to a caustic aside, he added, *"Which I said before."*

It was evident the Colonel wasn't going to make any further contribution without putting up a spirited defence. John decided it was time to throw a curve ball. "What's the contingency if everything turns belly up, *despite* all this forward planning?"

This time Vincenzo was on the front foot, eager to respond, but a blunt, "We shoot them all," from a stone-faced Colonel silenced the room.

John demanded an explanation. "What, even the Cobet members?"

The Colonel glared at his Australian irritant, regarding him with open disdain, not bothering to reply, which had Ballard placing a subduing hand on John's arm to prevent him from exploding. Vincenzo stepped in with a much needed clarification. "Despite wanting the Cobet members to be taken alive for intel purposes, we can't afford for *any* of them to escape. So yes, a decision will have to be made at the time whether or not to take them all out—but I stress, that will be a last resort."

Vincenzo thanked the Major and the Captain for their

contribution, the Colonel a deliberate omission from his acknowledgements. "Ok, in summary, and assuming the assault goes to plan, the following Cobet members will be arrested and escorted back here to the airbase for the authorities to fly them to their respective countries for prosecution. In no particular order that includes Anatoli Demyan for the CIA; Aleksei Agapov for MI6; Maxim Dabylov for the CIA and the Italians so he and his family can enter witness protection, and hopefully provide us with ongoing intel; Claude Garnier for the DGSE; and for our Aussie contingent, Igor Greshnev. And let me say, a nastier bunch of professional criminals you'll never wish to meet."

This time he did involve the Colonel. "By default, the remainder of the Cobet group will be arrested by Captain Lebedev and his team, and as the FSB building has its own prison, this will simplify placing these offenders behind bars."

Ballard studied Vincenzo to determine whether his direct reference to the FSB prison was an unsubtle backhander, heralding back to darker times when the KGB were at their most ruthless. The twinkle in the CIA agent's eyes could be read to mean a multitude of possibilities, however the expression on the Colonel's face made it plain as to what his belief was. Ballard winked at the Italian who lifted his chin in recognition.

"Now, if there are no more questions, I wish you and your squads every success. Please pass on my gratitude for their efforts to this point, and for their undeniable bravery. Believe me, I know how complex and dangerous their mission will be in the morning, but I have every confidence in their ability to achieve our objective."

There was a shuffling of chairs as the Colonel, the Captain

and the Major made to exit the room, the latter two officers shaking Vincenzo's hand. Turning, they followed the Colonel who was already at the door. The AC, Ballard and John remained seated due to Vincenzo indicating for them to stay. Raking fingers through his hair, a tuft remained cocked sideways as he studied the policemen. "Well, is the Colonel onboard with us?"

John appeared in two minds as he cursed under his breath. "One thing's for sure, he's a right smart arse. He'd be what ... late thirties? All I can say is a kick in the nuts to sort him out wouldn't go amiss."

Vincenzo was amused at the intensity of John's loathing of the man. "My sentiments exactly. The trouble is, *he* ... or rather his bosses have the President's ear, so that's a reality we have to contend with."

The AC summed up Vincenzo's initial question. "There's no doubt the Colonel's happy for your team do the heavy lifting. What astounds me is his openness regarding how Cobet operate with impunity under the protection of the FSB. It's as if Cobet has been filling a Black Ops role for them, but now that they've bitten the hand that feeds them they have to go."

"Spot on Kevin, at least with FSB's approval we've got a real shot at putting them out of business—made much easier I might add by having the head of the snake presented to us on a plate by the Russian Government." He sprang to his feet. "Come with me. I've got something to show you."

CHAPTER
34

Minutes later they were in the airfield's projection room, the AC, Ballard and John ensconced in the front row. Vincenzo propped behind a laptop, and after pulling a small object from his pocket he held it aloft. "If someone had told me thirty years ago I could store 2 terabytes of data on a device this tiny I'd have told them they were insane."

John concurred, "Thirty years ago I wouldn't have had a damn clue what a terabyte was ... still don't come to think of it."

Inserting the flash drive into the laptop, Vincenzo entered a number of keystrokes then activated the projector. Spinning sideways in his chair he announced, "What I'm about to show you are filmed assaults by my squad, similar to what they'll be undertaking tomorrow morning. Without blowing my trumpet they've perfected the art of surprise when entering a room where heavily armed combatants are present. In particular, they've mastered what to do at the doorway the split-second they breach the room. The ensuing three to five seconds determines the success or failure of these types of operation. Their technique enables the maximum number of rounds to be fired without shooting each other in the process. Take a look."

The screen came to life and the policemen sat riveted as they watched three separate breaches, in awe at the timing and coordination of the soldiers—from the point they attacked the door with a battering ram, to the initial release of the stun grenades, then the actual entry where one group went in low, firing their weapons, while the second team shot above their heads.

Ballard performed mental arithmetic, coming up with, "By my reckoning the two entry doors into Room 206 are wide enough to allow three soldiers to go in low, side by side, with three above them, six firing simultaneously. The rate of fire of a Heckler & Koch is sixteen rounds a second, so in the first three to four seconds of breaching the room they could unleash upwards of four hundred rounds. Providing they hit their targets I'd think that would just about do it."

Hearing the assessment, John almost fell off his seat. "Christ. Talk about a bloodbath."

Vincenzo's eyes were like flint. "And as I said, it couldn't happen to a more deserving bunch of bloodthirsty *bastardi*." The ferocity of his outburst had his audience eyeing him in momentary surprise.

Thinking back to what he saw on the monitors in the conference room, Ballard still wasn't convinced about the effectiveness of the ram against doors as solid as those in Room 206. He broached his concerns with Vincenzo who tapped his temple with a forefinger. "Ah, Mr Ballard ... your question is an excellent one. When I first saw the live footage of the room, I too had my doubts about one person breaking the lock."

He switched off the projector and retrieved his memory stick which he slipped into his pocket. "We've redesigned our existing ram in the airfield tool shop. It's been extended and now has additional handles." He beamed like a proud father relaying news of a healthy newborn. "It's become a four-person ram, and with the adrenaline flowing as it will be at the point of entry, I'm satisfied one blow will do the trick. We've tested it on mock-up doors weighted to simulate those in 206 and fitted with a similar lock mechanism. Nonetheless, it's a serious point you raise."

Ballard outwardly agreed, but deep down wasn't persuaded, Vincenzo's words of how critical the first seconds would be after the breach echoing in his head. The AC also had his doubts as he raised a separate issue. "Vincenzo, I'm still coming to terms with the problem of the damn doors. What's your team going to do once they burst into the room and toss in the stun grenades should an armed guard be sitting or standing either side of the doors? Yes, you'll know via the cameras if they are there or not, but *if* they are, won't two of your initial six-man team need to move forward and around the doors to take them out? This will break up the three-by-three, high-low formation." He was apologetic. "I know that's a bit of a mouthful, and not delivered as succinctly as I would have liked, but you get my drift."

Vincenzo clapped the AC on the shoulder. "I do indeed. And yes, we've discussed this at length. The doors are too thick to shoot through, so the team member on the left and right of the three going in low will reach around the door near where each guard is and deploy a defensive grenade to take them out."

Puzzled expressions abounded, causing Vincenzo to grin. "Yes, aside from stun grenades, very few people know there are such things as offensive and defensive grenades. Each are identical, except the defensive grenade doesn't release shrapnel. To ensure we don't kill the Cobet hierarchy, the defensive grenade's shock wave will take out the guard without seriously injuring those sitting further away at the table."

Vincenzo's comment triggered a concerning thought for Ballard. "Speaking of those Cobet members at the table ... up 'til now we've focussed on their bodyguards, but won't the Cobet men be armed? Christ, that could mean upwards of twenty or more shooting back at your team."

To Ballard's surprise Vincenzo didn't appear at all concerned. "During Dabylov's interrogation he revealed a very interesting fact. Weapons for Cobet members at these meetings are banned."

"You're kidding me, why?" John sat to attention.

"Dabylov said it's a rule enforced in all meetings as a result of a pretty nasty shootout a couple of years back which left five or six of them dead, a consequence of someone not happy with a particular decision. What does that tell you about this bunch? Since then only trusted security guards are permitted to carry weapons. So on that point the cards have fallen our way."

The AC pressed on. "Changing subjects. The Colonel made it clear the room is fitted with cameras and audio, therefore won't Cobet be suspicious and have them turned off before the meeting gets underway?"

"Not part of the FSB rule book Kevin. The latitude afforded Cobet is on the proviso their meetings are recorded for the Central Committee's scrutiny. Common sense dictates Cobet must be conducting separate clandestine meetings if they're plotting something they don't want the committee to know about. As a consequence, tomorrow's meeting will be limited to discussing tactics linked to their next operation, such as wiping out your nuclear waste site, and what they have to do to bring the Ndrangheta to heel."

He leaned forward conspiratorially. "Speaking of the *other* meetings these bastards have that the Central Committee are none the wiser of, one of the first things I've instructed the Major to do once the shooting stops and everyone's handcuffed, is to confiscate each of their mobiles. They'll be labelling as to who they belong to and taken to 205 where my technician will begin analysing them." He raised an explanatory hand at John's questioning stare. "Yes, I *could* wait until we all get back here, but that may be too late. A number, text or email, especially on Demyan's or Igor's mobiles may point us in a particular direction, so I don't want to waste hours before discovering a vital piece of intel was missed and key personnel have fled the country." He smiled. "I'd suggest you'd be aware in my line of business it's essential to have access to highly skilled technicians. *You* probably call them geeks. Well, my geek is a damn clever geek."

The AC's expression indicated his total agreeance with the steps being taken by Vincenzo, while John took his time computing what he had just heard. After due consideration he turned to Ballard, suggesting with a half-smile, "You know what Mike? I think this guy just may have things under control … as much as anyone can when faced with such a complex and unpredictable operation."

Ballard agreed, despite the trepidation gnawing at the back of his mind. He was conscious that any action against Cobet in general, and specifically against criminals as sophisticated and treacherous as the two principal Russians involved, could lead to unforeseen outcomes, and not good ones at that.

Checking his wristwatch, Vincenzo declared, "And now

I believe it's time for lunch in this establishment's very ..." he searched for the appropriate word, ending up with a compromise, "*efficient* mess hall."

Without question the mess hall was indeed efficient, but the first-class pods in the A380, the Windsor Hotel in Spring Street, Melbourne, or even Pelligrini's Café in Bourke Street it was not. After due analysis they settled on the Vareniki, which Vincenzo explained were Russian cheese dumplings accompanied by a rather stolid dollop of sour cream. "They'll sit in your stomach like mini bricks until your digestive juices give up trying to ignore them and get to work."

"Oh well, with that for a recommendation I can hardly wait." John took a sip of his scalding hot tea to prewarn his stomach what it was about to encounter, grimacing at the prospect.

The AC glared at his senior sergeant. "For Christ's sake, stop whining and eat your damn food."

Vincenzo grinned at the AC's no-nonsense, fatherlike command.

All about them, airmen, soldiers and support crew were tucking into their meals, their initial curiosity overtaken by the need for sustenance before getting back to work. Vincenzo explained what they would be doing after lunch. "I've reserved a set of wheels for a trip into Moscow. I'm going to take you to Lubyanka Square so you can see for yourselves the FSB building and to get a feel of the place."

Thoughtful as he chewed on the last of his dumpling, John responded, "Vincenzo, we're in your capable hands. Ain't that so Mike?"

Just short of gagging on his final mouthful, the result of insufficient lubrication on the last piece of undercooked dough wreaking havoc in his throat, Ballard could only blink and nod at the same time, tears forming just as the food broke free and headed south. He finally managed a rather hoarse, "Count me in."

Again, the AC contemplated his two detectives, his face deadpan as he shook his head.

Vincenzo's commentary was enlightening, if not disturbing as they sat in the jeep gazing across at the Neo-Baroque FSB building, its façade of yellow brick denoting a site where untold atrocities were once unleashed, with question marks remaining as to whether or not they were still occurring.

"It was built in 1898 on the exact spot where Catherine the Great once headquartered her secret police in the late 1700s."

John's head spun around on hearing this, stage whispering to Ballard, "Christ, they're all a bunch of bloody savages … the lot of them. And still are to my way of thinking."

Observing him in the rear vision mirror, Vincenzo agreed. "Yes, I fear the repression against so-called dissidents is ongoing, but the torture techniques are far more sophisticated these days." He extended an arm, his forefinger an accusing pointer. "Notice anything specific about the top floor?"

They peered up at the building, with the AC claiming, "No windows."

"*Correct.* And for good reason. That's where the prison's located, along with the torture chambers."

John's mouth dropped open a second time.

"It's believed between 1938 and 1952, upwards of 35,000 people passed through the prison, with very few of them coming out alive. And here's some statistics for you to digest: the FSB has at its disposal more than 66,000 uniformed staff,

4000 of them being special forces troops. It also employs 200,000 border guards … all this for a population of 150 million. Doesn't that strike you as a government with more than its fair share of paranoia?"

There was collective headshaking, everyone cognisant of the incredible contrast between the oppressive restrictions that were incumbent on Russian daily life and the general freedoms enjoyed by all Australians.

Vincenzo's forefinger changed direction. "We'll be parked over there in the surveillance van. As soon as the bullets have stopped whizzing we'll go in. I've arranged for two armoured personnel carriers equipped with all the necessary 'boys' toys' to transport our prisoners back to the airfield."

"Boys' toys?" John was curious.

Vincenzo smirked. "Those beasts are 7.2 tonnes each, armed with remote weapon stations firing 12.7 millimetre Kord machine guns. They're also fitted with 30 millimetre AGS-17 grenade launchers. The remote-controlled turrets have normal and thermal-imaging cameras and laser range finders. On top of that they have enough armour plating to counter any attack launched from shoulder-mounted missiles."

John's head slumped forward, a habit he was repeating more often during his time in Russia. "Yep, I'd say that constitutes 'boys' toys' … big time. Any chance we can catch a ride in one?"

Vincenzo smiled but didn't respond.

Appearing thoughtful and sounding appreciative as he sat in the passenger seat alongside Vincenzo, the AC commented, "We're all very grateful you're spending this much time with us. Being over here without your guidance would have been, well, daunting to say the least … no, I'll go so far as to say nigh on impossible."

There was an extended chuckle. "For my Aussie mates, nothing's too much trouble." He leaned forward and fired the motor. "Time to go. We don't want to draw unnecessary attention to ourselves."

For the next twenty minutes he took them on a whirlwind tour of the streets near the Kremlin. First up he pointed out the Grand Palace, then he showed them where the President had installed his helipad, adding that close by an oak tree planted by the astronaut Yuri Gagarin was now fully matured. They drove past Cathedral Square near the Moscow River, everyone awestruck by the sights, yet fully appreciating the acute contradictions of a country where excessive wealth was the norm in privileged enclave's, while millions of ordinary Russians remained locked in abject poverty, their only solace a plentiful supply of vodka.

Driving back to base, Vincenzo glanced at the AC. "Kevin, I need to borrow you for half an hour to go over the extradition papers for Igor. They have to be signed by both of us to ensure there are no legal roadblocks." Over his shoulder he added, "As for you guys, you've the rest of the afternoon off. I recommend an early dinner though because we'll be up and about at 0400 hours tomorrow morning."

He slowed down for a wayward driver. "For the remainder of the afternoon I'll be going over final details with my assault team, along with the Spetsnaz captain so we don't finish up treading on each other's toes when the action kicks off. I also need to confirm individual flights for the respective prisoners and their escorts." He flashed another grin. "We don't want the wrong bad guy turning up in the wrong country, do we?"

All shook their heads, painfully aware of the complex issues the CIA agent faced to achieve arrests, which if successful would become folklore throughout enforcement agencies. No one volunteered to trade places with him.

Arriving at the airbase, Vincenzo parked in one of the empty bays. Switching off the motor, he hunched around, his forearm propped against the back of his seat. "Thankfully we're in pretty good shape. We've prepared as well as we possibly can for unforeseen eventualities, and my men have proven they can adapt in the blink of an eye, so I'm confident of success ... but not overconfident." He was keen to project a positive mindset towards his audience, and despite the obstacles facing him, he succeeded.

"Michael, John, I'll see you both in the morning." He turned back to the AC. "Ok Kevin, let's knock over this paperwork."

Everyone alighted from the vehicle, the AC accompanying Vincenzo inside. Watching the senior officers disappear through the front door, both detectives shrugged, aware the pointy end of the operation was fast approaching.

CHAPTER
35

John gave Ballard a firm nudge on the shoulder. "Mate, I couldn't sleep so I figured if I couldn't then you shouldn't either."

Peering up at him from his bunk, one eye open, Ballard demanded, "What kind of loopy logic is that?"

Grinning, John sat on the end of the bed. "Oh, just that when I rang Sonia last night she said to say hello. She mentioned you were a good friend and I should appreciate what you do for me."

"So you took that as permission to wake me up ..." Ballard reached out and squinted at his wristwatch propped on the side table, "*fifteen minutes early?*" Relenting, he added, "As a matter of fact Nat sends her regards as well. She wanted to know when we'll be coming home. I said we should be flying out this afternoon, or perhaps tomorrow morning."

John agreed. "Yeah, Sonia the same. I said I wasn't sure but I thought it would be today or tomorrow."

Ballard swung his legs over the side of the bed. Bending forward he anchored both elbows on his knees. Rubbing his eyes with the heel of both hands he added, "I guess it'll be what it will be. Now get out of here so I can have a shave and shower. I'll see you in twenty. No doubt the boss is already up and pacing his room."

Feeling the tension rising, John gave Ballard an amiable shove on the shoulder. "God I hope this doesn't turn ugly. Think of it Mike … if *we're* nervous, what the hell must the Major, the Captain and their crews be feeling? I mean we've faced some pretty hairy situations over the years, but what they're attempting later on is something else."

Ballard agreed as he pushed his partner towards the door. "Twenty minutes, now go."

As soon as John departed, Ballard got to work, shaving and showering, and with three minutes to spare he left his room. Turning to his right he knocked on the AC's door which opened immediately. "All good to go sir, John will be out in a—"

As though overhearing him, his partner stepped into the corridor, his hair wet and slicked back behind his ears. "I hope you two weren't thinking of starting without me."

Muttering under his breath, the AC locked his door before heading towards the canteen, the two detectives trailing behind him, nudging each other to settle their fraying nerves.

Arriving in the mess hall, the AC turned to them. "I've a feeling today is going to be a long one, so tuck into whatever's on offer."

Resisting the urge to salute, John couldn't help uttering under his breath, "*Yes* Dad."

The AC refrained from commenting, but his returned glare commanded that the retort be the last joke until the day's events were over.

It didn't take them long to discover Russian military breakfasts were no more exciting than midday meals. Leaving the servery, their trays contained a bowl of porridge, and floating on top was what could only be described as a swollen, severed finger, masquerading as a sausage. Alongside the bowl was a glass of tea, a plastic container of milk, two slices of Russian bread, and a small spread of a dubious substance purported to be butter.

Settling at their trestle table, John looked across at Ballard, alarmed at what he was about to consume. Defying the AC's previous directive regarding jokes, he repeated Fabio's immortal words, *"I canno' believe it's no' butter,"* even managing a mildly successful Italian accent.

Ten minutes in, Vincenzo arrived, slipping alongside the AC. When questioned he indicated he had already eaten. His mood change from the carefree tourist guide of the day before to the ruthless, special forces officer he was now presenting couldn't be starker. This was a professional CIA agent under immense pressure to succeed, something demanded of him by his bosses in Langley, Virginia. As such, he was determined that nothing would get in his way, the consequences of failure too great to contemplate.

Ballard pondered why the CIA were leaving everything to one man, not allowing a 2IC to shoulder at least some of the workload, thereby reducing the possibility of Vincenzo making a mistake due to his punishing schedule. Nothing obvious came to mind, other than the necessity to keep knowledge of the mission limited to as few personnel as possible, in so doing, ensuring Cobet didn't get wind of the attack on their meeting. Again Ballard worried the reach of the criminal group was so advanced and tentacle-like that a forewarning of the assault was still a distinct possibility. He kept his fears to himself.

Vincenzo sipped from the glass of tea that John offered as an excuse to get rid of it. "The Major, the Captain and their teams have already left." He glanced at his watch as did Ballard, both men noting it was just after 0500. "They'll group in Room 205 and double check all their equipment. From this point on the Major is in command of the assault. We'll be in the surveillance van monitoring everything that happens in 206. Throughout the operation I'll be in radio contact with the Major."

Vincenzo's detailed relaying of the necessary actions didn't require a response, it was more a verification in his own mind that everything was progressing as planned.

"When do we head off?" John continued to chew on a piece of bread with minimal enthusiasm.

"Meet me outside in fifteen minutes." Despite the direct reply, it was clear Vincenzo's mind was elsewhere. "I'm about to call the Colonel to make sure he'll be contactable should we need him." After another gulp of tea the agent sprang to his feet, giving a reassuring wink before departing the hall.

Staring after him, the AC was apprehensive. "The poor bastard. Now *that's* a man under a shitload of pressure." His statement supported the detectives' own beliefs.

The trip into Moscow was mostly in silence, broken occasionally by John making bland comments about passing scenery, or that he hoped his breakfast sausage wouldn't react too badly later in the morning. Vincenzo laughed, appreciating having Aussie humour on tap to keep his mind from what was to come, even if only for a few minutes. Traffic was almost non-existent, with the surveillance van's headlights making less and less impact on the road's surface as dawn broke over the horizon.

On either side of their vehicle, in large capital letters were the words INTER RAO UES. An accompanying flame-red logo of the earth depicting the Russian continent encircled by fingers of fire was positioned above the company name. When questioned by the AC, Vincenzo replied, "It's an electricity generation and distribution company that operates throughout Russia. Sporting that livery will allow us to park near the FSB building for an extended period without drawing suspicion. Everyone will think corrupt company executives are inside doing a deal with the Government. And as you can see, the van's windows are heavily tinted to prevent prying eyes."

While Ballard wasn't totally convinced of Vincenzo's premise, believing company executives would be travelling in something more upmarket than a van, new and shiny though it was, he accepted this was Russia, and besides, the CIA agent had more pressing concerns to contend with.

Circling Lubyanka Square, Vincenzo spotted the perfect location to park near the headquarters building. "To guarantee a reliable radio signal we need to be within a hundred metres of Room 205 ... ideally sixty to seventy." Gazing upwards at the second floor, he commented, "This should do it."

Scrambling into the rear of the van they took up position on the bench seats, with Vincenzo drawing a hinged utility shelf across his lap before attacking an iPad keyboard. Within minutes the two monitors on the van wall sprang to life. Not long after they were looking at live footage of 206, which at just after 0700 hours was empty. No one complained about the wait, mindful of the tension that would be mounting among the attack teams, their imminent actions shaping as a life-and-death dogfight.

Satisfied he had adequate eyes on proceedings, Vincenzo tested his radio contact with the Major, again happy all the equipment was operating as it should be. Relieved, he leaned back against the side of the van while addressing the AC. "Kevin, you may be wondering why I've gone to so much trouble to remain remote from 205? Put another way, why I'm not coordinating the attack from inside the room?"

The AC deliberated on his answer, curious but not wanting to offend. He settled for a simple, "Yes, but I'm sure you've got a valid reason."

Vincenzo took a deep breath. "God forbid that the raid should turn against us … but if it does I need to be sufficiently removed so I can coordinate immediate support personnel."

John lurched forward, not sure what he was hearing. "And you have them on standby?"

A faint smile flitted across Vincenzo face. "As I said yesterday, I've arranged for two carriers to be close by to escort the prisoners back to the airbase. What I didn't mention was I have fifteen special forces soldiers onboard *those* units to back up the Major and his squad should things get nasty."

"Where are the troops now?" Ballard's curiosity mounted, concerned two armoured personnel carriers parked on a city street may draw unwanted attention.

"Need I remind you Michael, this is Moscow. Military vehicles are as common here as London's black cabs. The carriers are two streets away, and can be onsite within a minute if necessary."

John joined the question-and-answer session. "Is the Major's aware of these troops?"

"He is indeed, and despite him claiming he has ample firepower at his disposal, I insisted the reserves be in place … and no, it wasn't as a consequence of any doubts I might have about him or his troops' abilities."

The three policemen respected the life-and-death decisions

Vincenzo was making, impressed how calm he was as he faced the crucial phase of the operation less than an hour away. Their admiration for the CIA agent was in sharp contrast to their own misgivings as to how successful the assault would be.

Time dragged on as they watched pedestrians strolling past, most of them carefree, very few bothering to even glance at the van, with several displaying only a passing interest. Seemingly from nowhere, one came up and face cupped, peered through the tinted glass. Under his breath, his face centimetres from the pedestrian's, John hissed, *"Piss off shithead."*

Vincenzo flashed his perfect smile.

In a low voice John claimed to Ballard, "I know I'm repeating myself, but those guys in 205 aren't lacking balls. I'm not sure I could handle what they're about to do."

Overhearing him, Vincenzo scoffed, surprising the detectives. "Horses for courses John. Have you forgotten being aboard a certain billionaire's chopper and firing automatic weapons at a bunch of Ndrangheta henchmen armed with rocket launchers? I'd say that's a damn sight scarier than sitting in your office wading through mountains of paperwork."

Both men reflected on Vincenzo's words, neither convinced that what his soldiers were about to undertake matched anything they had ever confronted in the bravery stakes.

It was the AC, along with Vincenzo, who first noticed movement in 206 on the monitor. Two women entered from the corridor, each pushing a trolley laden with water jugs and glasses which they distributed along the length of the table. A third woman, also steering a trolley, headed for the small table positioned against the side wall, unloading what on closer inspection were plates of food, mostly sandwiches, and two trays containing an assortment of cakes. Ballard and John hunched forward, careful not to block Vincenzo's view, the latter speaking into his mike with the Major who confirmed all was in readiness. No sooner had the agent finished his exchange than a fourth trolley was manoeuvred through the door, this one laden with enough bottles of alcohol to quench the thirst of fifty drunken sailors on an all-day bender.

"Bloody hell Mike, I'm having second thoughts about this mob." John did his best to maintain a serious demeanour. "With this much catering on tap I'm tossing up whether I should apply for a part-time position with them."

"Count me in Johno."

The AC transferred his gaze to Vincenzo, silently apologising for his wayward sons. All the while the four staff chatted amongst themselves, their Russian accents pronounced, and while heavy to the ear, the Slavic tones were in sharp contrast to their youthful appearance.

"What are they saying?" Ballard was hopeful something of value might be gleaned that could assist the major, but Vincenzo put a sword to his optimism.

"While there isn't a direct translation, it goes something along the lines of 'How is it dull, boring old men can eat and drink so much? No wonder they're so fat'."

Ballard was disappointed. "I guess it was worth a shot."

The four staff left the room as a group, silence descending once more. The men sat watching, apprehensive.

Counting the chairs around the table, John voiced the obvious. "Thirteen ... the other seven have been propped against the wall." He looked to Vincenzo whose expression was thoughtful.

"Hmm, no doubt about it, certainly not as many as I'd hoped." He arched back, gazing at the roof of the van, assessing what the numbers meant. "At least the amount of food dropped off suggests we're still on track for the key players to be there." He froze, his eyes glued to the screens.

Five men in Russian military uniforms entered, strolling casually alongside the table. Midway, they placed down their folders then perused the displayed food, all laughing at something before turning and taking their seats.

"*Christ,* check out the ribbons on those guys!" John was staggered. "Which begs the question, why the hell would the President agree to his top brass being part of Cobet?"

Vincenzo was matter of fact. "Many of their clandestine actions require military planning and resources for them to succeed. All covert of course."

The AC was excited, uncharacteristically bullish. "So … five present and eight to go." His enthusiasm mounted, clearly itching for the action to begin.

No sooner had he uttered the words than a stream of men entered the room, all wearing business suits. Behind them were armed men in special forces fatigues adorned with distinctive Vietnam-era, tiger-striped patterns. They split up either side of the table, two positioning along each wall as well as one left and right of the entry doors.

Vincenzo made his thoughts known. "Those two will need to be taken out first."

The three policemen were silent, almost forgetting to breathe, mesmerised by what they were witnessing. In a move startling his colleagues, John thrust a forefinger at the left-hand monitor. "Check out Dabylov!"

Ballard peered closer at the screen. The Russian was on his own and appeared disturbingly uncomfortable.

Vincenzo snorted. "Hmm, not good, it's clear he isn't

handling this well, despite insisting he attend the meeting. He claimed that for him not to be there would be a death sentence. I just pray he can keep it together for a few more minutes."

The Cobet members settled around the table, the two chairs at the head remaining empty. Conversations erupted but were so entangled, interpretation was impossible. John nudged Ballard on the arm, worried Demyan and Igor may have chosen to avoid the meeting. "Perhaps they got wind of something."

Vincenzo wasn't entertaining the possibility. "Those two didn't get to where they are without giant egos and a sense of drama. You'll find their going to make a grand entrance, it's in their—" He stiffened, and for good reason, his words prophetic. Like conquering generals the two men entered the room and strode to their seats, their heads held high. Dressed in dark business suits, their manner was nothing short of imperious. Underscoring the authority they commanded, everyone in the room sprang to their feet. A prolonged round of applause echoed throughout, nobody daring to sit until Demyan and Igor had taken their places. It was obvious the two were revered by most, and without question, feared by many.

What proved surprising to Ballard and John, having dealt with Igor for so long, was Demyan assuming the lead. Calling the meeting to order in Russian, his voice was a deep timbre, strong and commanding. With an imperious wave of his hand, he signalled to a nearby guard who stepped forward and grabbing the head of one of the seated men in a vice-like grip, snapped his neck in one vicious wrench. The man slumped forward, face down on the table, his arms limp by his side.

All in the van, including Vincenzo, gasped at the spectacle, words choking in their throats, their shock similar to those of the room's attendees whose darting glances signalled their fear that they may be next.

Recovering first, Vincenzo hissed, "There you have it. Intimidation 101. No discussion, no warning, just a premeditated action to keep The Board members on a knife edge. This is the sheer terror by which Demyan and Igor rule."

The horrified silence in 206 was broken by Igor addressing the group in Russian. Ballard turned to Vincenzo to ask what was being said but saw he had recontacted the Major, the exchanges rapid and staccato. Thirty seconds passed before Vincenzo was able to update the detectives. "The Major has deployed the snake camera. There are three guards outside in the corridor. He's passed this onto the Captain who'll now play his part." He broke off, once again in contact with the Major, more rapid-fire exchanges taking place. His brow furrowed and his eyes grew intense, setting off alarm bells for his audience.

John whispered to Ballard, "Jesus Christ Mike, can you believe how ruthless these bastards are?"

Ballard nodded, glancing at the AC who sat expressionless, his body coiled like a spring, aware the success or failure of the operation hinged on this next crucial phase.

Almost a minute passed before Vincenzo startled everyone by punching the air. "*Fantastico.*" There was no need for interpretation, the CIA agent gleeful. "We now have three dead guards in the corridor."

He was back on the mike. "*Quando entri?*" A pause was followed by, "*Che dio sia con te.*"

Three worried faces presented to him, with Ballard asking, "I got the *Quando entri* bit, but what was the *Che dio*-something or other?"

Vincenzo didn't take his eyes from the monitors. "I asked the Major when he was going in, then I wished him luck, in fact I said, 'God be with you' to be precise." His voice tightened. "The breach will be any moment now."

The words had a galvanising effect, all eyes glued to the screens.

Seconds later 206 went black, causing John to utter an expletive as multiple cries of surprise and confusion rang out, all in Russian. The sound of the ram smashing the door was unmistakable. Ominously there were two strikes, not one— precious seconds lost. Multiple flashes of intense white light momentarily illuminated the room, each accompanied by an explosion, the sounds shattering in the confined space. This was followed by a number of grenade blasts, everyone praying the guards either side of the doors had been immobilised.

Bursts of automatic gunfire erupted, the muzzle flashes distinct in the darkened room, the only source of light being from the breached door. Cries from terrified and wounded men could be heard, along with splintering wood and what was thought to be cascading chandelier crystals.

Suddenly the lights went on, causing everyone in the van to sit more upright, were that possible. Smoke swirled throughout the room making vision difficult, but not to the point the widespread carnage wasn't shockingly evident. Guards lay dead, their bodies twisted in unnatural poses, blood spattered over them and across the walls. Two Cobet members were slumped on the table, killed in the crossfire, joining their comrade with the broken neck. Others were crouching beside their chairs or under the table, some crying out in pain, their wounds evident from blood-soaked suits.

The Major's men began hauling them back onto their

chairs, forcing their hands behind their back, applying cable ties as handcuffs. Dabylov was one of them, the fear on his face grotesque. Those who resisted were struck with the butt of a rifle to secure their compliance, the actions efficient and brutal.

As the smoke continued to clear, the vision in the room improved. Demyan and Igor were motionless in their chairs, miraculously unhurt, unnaturally calm, waiting their turn to be cuffed, in no way displaying any sign of apprehension or concern as to the events unfolding around them. The vision flooded Ballard with a sense of foreboding, triggering unease at what he was witnessing. "Vincenzo, this isn't good. Those two have something sinister up their sleeve, I'm certain of it." He recounted the scene in which Sergey was arrested during the Parliament House siege and managed to turn the tables less than thirty minutes later, Ballard finding himself a hostage aboard a chopper, handcuffed and hooded.

Vincenzo drew a reflective breath, analysing the situation. Making a decision, he contacted the Major, informing him he was coming in. He took his mobile and punched in a number, mouthing as he waited for a reply, "I'm ringing the Colonel." In the blink of an eye he delivered a short, sharp burst of Russian, the switch in languages effortless. Disconnecting, he ordered, "Let's take a look inside shall we? The Colonel's meeting us at security."

CHAPTER
36

Rising abruptly from his chair, the Colonel didn't bother to acknowledge Vincenzo or his three Australian colleagues, instead, with a curt nod he turned on his heel, assuming they would follow. The staff at security stood to attention, saluting as he strode past. Two flights of stairs followed, and after traversing a long corridor they came to the damaged doors leading into 206. Multiple streaks of blood on the tiled floor ended at 205, spelling out that the three dead guards had been dragged inside.

The scene greeting them when they entered 206 had everyone on edge. The images viewed on the monitors, while providing the mechanics of the raid, didn't prepare them for the brutal aftermath of the firefight as witnessed firsthand. Disbelieving what he was seeing, John's words were barely audible, "Jesus H. Christ, imagine being here when all this went off."

Bullet holes riddled the walls, interspersed with blood splatter, the guards lying where they had been shot, several with mutilated faces, the ammunition having torn flesh and bone. Above, the chandelier was in ruins, most of the crystal pieces now scattered across the table and on the floor. The huge tapestry on the far wall hung awry, the Russian coat of arms defaced by multiple bullet holes.

Despite the size of the room, it felt overrun as the Major's men herded prisoners into groups; those earmarked for Vincenzo formed a bedraggled bunch, many blood-stained, all in shock, including Dabylov. Vincenzo approached the group, asking questions in Russian. There was sullen silence, which enraged the agent. With a vicious backhand he struck Dabylov across the side of the head, dropping him to the floor.

The AC whispered out the corner of his mouth, "I'd suggest that staged smack in the mouth was for show, and it'll probably save the bastard's life." He focussed on Igor and Demyan who remained motionless at the head of the table, two of the Major's guards behind them, their weapons levelled.

The detectives continued their gaze around the room, coming to terms with high-stakes Russian military arrests where conventional rules didn't apply. Most confronting was the manner in which the Colonel moved throughout, viciously kicking prone figures with his boot to satisfy himself they weren't faking death. In a series of blunt instructions, he ordered the Captain's troops to herd the FSB allocation of Cobet members together. Within minutes they were removed from the room, almost certainly to be taken to the prison on the top floor and a very uncertain future.

Vincenzo made a phone call, and after a lengthy discussion with the Major, six of his men escorted the three Cobet members from the room, destined for the DGSE, MI6 and the Italian External Intelligence and Security Agency. Approaching the policemen, Vincenzo commented in a low voice so he couldn't be overheard, "I'm assuming you understood why

I did what I did?" They all nodded. "Dabylov demanded during his interrogation that I do just that to ensure no undue suspicion would be directed his way. I've also requested that the armoured vehicles park out the front and for those three to be locked inside one of them while we chat with our two ring leaders. I want to find out what's going on in their heads before I take them away. The second vehicle is for them."

As they were about to approach Demyan and Igor to interrogate them, it became apparent that the Colonel who had left the room earlier was now hell-bent on ensuring the necessary clean-up was completed as soon as possible. A series of trolleys were wheeled into the room by his soldiers, and the dead guards and deceased Cobet members were then dumped unceremoniously onto the stainless-steel trays; just as rapidly, they were removed from the conference room.

That left Vincenzo, the AC, Ballard and John in the room with Demyan and Igor, as well as five of the Major's soldiers, their officer still downstairs supervising the transfer of the three Cobet prisoners. Approaching the two Russians, Vincenzo grabbed a chair, and spinning it around, sat on the side of the table nearest Demyan, his forearms resting on top of the backrest. The policemen took a chair each and settled on the opposite side, the AC closest to Igor, the Russian displaying no surprise at the detectives' presence. Nobody spoke for almost a minute, with Vincenzo content to observe his prisoners, in no rush to begin his questioning.

For many criminals, as the detectives well knew, silences such as these often became unbearable, invoking offenders to confess without a question being asked. This was not and would never be the case with the two veteran Russians. Demyan turned his gaze on Vincenzo. It was neither hostile nor defeatist—rather it was a study of unreadable scrutiny. On the other hand, Igor produced the faintest of mocking smiles as he took in Ballard, his secondary perusal towards the AC and John nothing more than a disinterested observation.

Still nobody spoke.

Vincenzo finally broke the silence. "The most important question for me right now is whether Cobet can survive this … interruption." Again, no reaction from the Russians. "With you two in jail, I'm finding it difficult to comprehend how the group will ever—"

"We won't be going to jail." Igor's body didn't move a millimetre as he uttered the chilling words that struck dread in the policemen's hearts, now certain the two Russians had something ominous planned that would sway the odds in their favour. Not daring to look at Vincenzo for fear they would reveal how troubled they were, the policemen sat blank-faced, content to allow the agent to respond. Choosing not to, he sat staring at Igor, waiting for the Russian to elaborate. Over a minute elapsed before Demyan made the slightest of impatient body movements, which to the untrained eye would have gone unnoticed, but was taken by Ballard as a silent command.

Leaning back in his chair, unperturbed that his hands were bound behind him, Igor glanced upwards, his look reflective. "It never ceases to amaze me how the old ways are often forgotten, or believed to be ineffective despite hundreds, perhaps thousands of years of irrefutable proof that they work. Take torture for instance. Humans perfected that art a long time ago, the central principle being to inflict sufficient pain so the person has no option but to talk. There's no need for the modern techniques used today, although I do admit that good old-fashioned sodium pentothal is still very effective. No, that aside, give me a starving rat in a bottomless cage strapped to a man's naked stomach and I'll get you a confession any day."

It was clear that by monopolising the conversation, Igor was seizing psychological supremacy. Although fully aware of this, Vincenzo was unperturbed, content to afford the Russian full rein.

"Now take coercion for example, the one thing authorities throughout the world fear the most is heavy loss of civilian life and major devastation of infrastructure, this and the resultant eroding of public trust in the very authorities elected to protect them."

This time Ballard couldn't help but look at the AC and John, each convinced they knew what Igor was about to reveal, and they weren't wrong. Enjoying every moment, the Russian delivered the death blow as he maintained his unblinking gaze. "Cast your minds back to the Parliament House siege and the rig parked out the front filled with 40,000 litres of premixed ammonium nitrate and diesel fuel. We all know the destruction *that* would have caused had the load gone up. The whole concept was such a simple one to implement." He paused, now openly enjoying the concern growing on the policemen's faces, their endeavours to appear unfazed crumbling.

"Assistant Commissioner, Michael, John ... seeing you all here in Moscow is a pleasure, you really do get about. So, here's the deal ... I suggest that before *anyone* talks of going to jail, you make a phone call to your lovely superintendent. Ask her to look out the window into Spencer Street and tell you what she sees. She'll still be at work because it's only 5.30 in the afternoon back there, and ... well, let's just say a lot of activity is happening down in the street."

Feeling an immobilising numbness take over his body, Ballard sat silent, his thoughts racing. He stole a glance at the AC, aware of the emotions the senior officer must be experiencing, eyeballing the man who was responsible for his wife's kidnapping and subsequent injuries.

Igor switched focus, and with his expression turning to pure evil he addressed Vincenzo, driving fear into the CIA agent's heart. "And as for you sir, I've heard so much about you, and it's all very impressive. Now I strongly advise you make a call to your contacts at the CIA despite it being 2 a.m. over there. Get them to check out the west side of the administration building and describe what's in the executive car park. Once you've done that, put a call through to your Scotland Yard friends ..." He paused. "Silly me, I *should* say, *New* Scotland Yard. Oh dear, things change *so* rapidly these days, at times it's hard to keep up. Now, *New* Scotland Yard isn't so lucky because it's 8 a.m. over there and a lot of people are already in the building, with plenty more clocking on as we speak."

Igor's understated tone and manner was a well-proven psychological strategy which Vincenzo was conscious of but powerless to prevent. Demyan, having been silent throughout Igor's revelations, took charge, and while his delivery lacked Igor's flare and was heavily accented, it was equally shocking, nonetheless. "Should any one or all of those prime movers explode, not only will there be massive loss of life, but were it ever revealed you could have averted the disaster, well ..." He shrugged as best he could with his hands cuffed. "Imagine what would happen to your careers? So the *real* question has nothing to do with *us* going to jail. Rather, are we such a valuable prize that you would risk untold devastation and death to secure our arrest? This is a decision only you can make."

So there it was, the group's worst fears laid bare. Vincenzo gave a brief hand gesture and all four men rose and crossed to the far end of the room, glancing back at the Russians prior to exiting into the corridor.

The AC was tight-lipped, knowing their options were non-existent should Igor's threat be real. "Michael, make the call. Vincenzo, I'm assuming you'll be doing the same?"

A confirming nod followed.

With trepidation in his heart, John snarled, "Those two must have been tipped off about the raid … why else would they have gone to so much trouble?"

Vincenzo was perplexed, his ample self-assurance having taken a battering. "I agree they could well have got wind of what we were up to, but the thing that strikes me as odd is that they don't appear at all perturbed by the fact the Cobet hierarchy has been decimated." He added, "As for the tanker trucks John, with the resources this organisation has on tap, it would have been child's play to set that in motion." Taking out his mobile he moved away to make the calls that would undoubtably shatter their plans.

Dreading the result, Ballard phoned Delwyn. Five rings had him alarmed, but on the sixth his superintendent answered, her voice strained. "*Michael*, I'm *so* glad you rang. We have a major crisis unfolding here—"

"Delwyn, is there a tanker parked down in Spencer Street?"

"What? How did you know?"

"There's no time to explain, just tell me what's happening."

Delwyn didn't hesitate. "Over an hour ago the truck drove onto the tram tracks in Spencer Street, stopping opposite the headquarters building."

"Where's the driver?"

"There wasn't one."

"No driver?" John couldn't contain himself, his ear pressed alongside Ballard's mobile.

Delwyn responded. "It was a driverless truck John. This is Parliament House all over again. There are packs of C4 strapped on the outside of the two tanks. Traffic is banked up for kilometres."

"What about evacuating headquarters?" Ballard visualised the chaos such an incident would have created.

"That began the moment the unit arrived. Everyone was advised by the building's PA system to get out. Staff exited via the cross overs to the Crime building, then headed out the car park along Latrobe Street towards Docklands."

"The surrounding buildings?"

"You'd have been proud of your team. Taking a megaphone each, Susan dashed outside with Ken and Bobby to warn occupants in the nearby buildings to leave. It was incredibly brave of them. Thank God they're back inside now. The Remand Centre is hunkering down, praying its double-brick construction will withstand the blast. There's nothing more they can do ... the prisoners and guards *have* to stay where they are." Delwyn's voice was high-pitched, her stress levels redlining.

"Has a ransom demand been made?"

"No."

"Delwyn, your crisis is one of three. We believe a similar scenario is playing out at the CIA building in Virginia, and also at New Scotland Yard."

"Michael, don't tell me ... Igor's behind all this, isn't he?"

"Got it in one. We've captured him and Demyan, and they're threatening to blow the rigs if we don't release them."

Delwyn's voice dropped to a mere whisper. "Then you've no choice, you *must* let them go."

Ballard looked to the AC and John before answering. "As much as I hate to admit this, you're right. Delwyn … rest assured we'll do *everything* we can to keep you all safe. I have to go now, but I'll phone you back as soon as I know anything more. In the meantime, keep the chief updated. And Delwyn … make sure you and the team stay out of harm's way. Thankfully the Crime building's off to the side of where the rig's parked. Even so, stay towards the back of the building, away from the windows."

Disconnecting, Ballard saw Vincenzo complete his call, his expression foretelling equally bad news. "My CIA contact has confirmed there's enough explosives sitting in the car park to take out half the west wing of the main administration building. Evacuations have already begun." He marshalled his emotions. "I need to ring the Yard, but there's no doubt it'll be the same scenario. I'm assuming it's an action replay in Melbourne?"

Ballard nodded.

Less than a minute later Vincenzo confirmed the worst, that evacuations had also begun at New Scotland Yard. Pocketing his mobile, he claimed with as much enthusiasm as he could muster, "We began with multiple objectives, arrest key members of the Cobet hierarchy, well, we've achieved that more or less. Give the Russian President what he wanted by exposing those who were a threat to him and put them in jail—also in the bag. Arrest the two ringleaders …" He hesitated, his jaw muscles rippling. "We did that too, but now we've no choice but to let them go." His nostrils flared. "Does anyone have any alternate suggestions?" An almost tortured expression underscored the difficulty he was labouring under, having to admit defeat, his professionalism such that anything less than total victory was undeniable failure.

The AC placed a comforting hand on his shoulder. "You're right, we have no choice. You did everything possible to mitigate any unforeseen circumstances, but terrorism, and this has to be called out for what it is, unadulterated terrorism has unfortunately beaten us ... *this time*. And as much as it pains us to say, we can't let our pride get in the way of doing the only thing that makes any sense. You know better than me that we'll get these bastards ... it just won't be today."

Ballooning his cheeks, Vincenzo declared, "I'll call the Major and warn him, then I'll ring the Colonel."

After two brief discussions, one in Italian and one in Russian, Vincenzo faced the policemen, the rage in his eyes as fierce as ever. "The Colonel's on his way to discuss what we're doing."

"What's there to discuss?" John was shocked, fearful the Colonel would take matters into his own hands and unleash a wave of destruction.

Vincenzo acknowledged his concerns, stating, "He's Russian John. Doesn't that say it all? But there's something *we* can do, follow me."

Sprinting to Room 205, he burst in with everyone close behind. The entire floor was a jumble of clothing, weapons, bulletproof vests and an assortment of military gear, all in piles, the bodies of the three guards no longer there. On the walls the monitors were still relaying live footage of 206. A check confirmed Demyan and Igor at the head of the table, silent, ignoring the soldiers guarding them.

Vincenzo weaved through the piles of equipment and approached a slightly built man in civilian clothing wearing thick, horn-rimmed glasses that made his eyeballs appear to burst from their sockets. He was seated at a small desk on which lay a number of mobiles. The alarm the man displayed at the sudden intrusion was momentary, recognising Vincenzo as the agent got closer. Placing a hand on his shoulder, Vincenzo engaged the technician in a lengthy discussion in Italian. Pointing to two mobiles near at hand, the man nodded, indicating he had already worked on one of them.

After smiling down at him, and another pat, Vincenzo turned and headed back out into the corridor, again followed by the three policemen. He spun around. "I've instructed my guy to load spyware onto Demyan and Igor's phones."

"FlexiSpy?" Ballard was curious.

Vincenzo permitted himself a brief sigh of weariness. "No Michael, we're not parents tracking the movements of their children. The software the CIA use is three generations more advanced, with one key feature being it's virtually undetectable. We don't believe the Russians have stolen the code yet, and we *pray* the Chinese haven't."

Despite it being obvious, Vincenzo chose to detail what the software would allow them to do once the mobiles were handed back. Part way through the explanation the Colonel was spotted running towards them, his anger mottling his face a dullish purple. As he closed, Vincenzo held up a hand, indicating he wished to explain the circumstances, but the officer brushed past him, disregarding the group, instead heading into the room. Barking in Russian, Vincenzo ordered him to stop. The command was ignored, the Colonel determined to confront Demyan and Igor. The soldiers in the room braced themselves, desperate for direction, their weapons raised. Vincenzo ordered them to stand down.

Sprinting after the Colonel with justifiable fears he would unleash a disaster, Ballard and John contemplated tackling the raging officer. The AC followed, also in two minds as to what the Colonel's intentions were. It soon became apparent. Stepping behind Demyan and Igor, having pushed aside the closest soldier, in one smooth motion the colonel drew his pistol from his shoulder holster. Jacking a round into the chamber he rammed the barrel hard against Demyan's head, forcing it sideways towards his shoulder.

The three policemen stood stock still, noting for the first time that both handcuffed Russians were displaying open fear, aware the Colonel wasn't operating under the same rules of engagement as everyone else. Vincenzo roared orders in Russian, drawing his own weapon, levelling it at the Colonel, the tension in the room palpable.

The Colonel maintained his aim, then in what felt like slow motion he raised his gaze, his eyes as hard as ball-bearings, locking onto Vincenzo's. The two men faced off in a fierce mental battle, neither showing any sign of backing down. Deliberately reverting to English so the policemen could understand what he was saying, Vincenzo demanded, "Colonel, as I've explained, we have no option but to release these prisoners. To do otherwise will result in hundreds of lives being lost … I can't permit that. Believe me, I'm prepared to do whatever it takes to ensure these two men go free, and that includes shooting you dead."

To punctuate the point, Vincenzo ordered the soldiers to draw their weapons on the Colonel, which they did.

Ballard looked to the AC and John, fighting to comprehend the nightmarish situation unfolding before them, each aware that one false move would unleash unspeakable disasters in three separate cities.

At least fifteen seconds passed in which nobody moved, least of all Demyan and Igor who did their best to appear undaunted, failing miserably. Without notice the Colonel lowered his weapon, making to holster it. Instead, in a blur of movement he swung the pistol hard in an upward motion, striking Demyan on the side of the face, the barrel-sight tearing open the Russian's cheek.

The soldiers braced forward but Vincenzo commanded them to lower their weapons, their compliance immediate. Ignoring everyone, the Colonel then repeated his action, pistol whipping Igor to the floor.

"Excellent! Just what the shitheads deserved." John's hissed words escaped before he could stop them. Ballard and the AC cautioned him with a combined glare, yet secretly they cheered him on.

Holstering his pistol, the Colonel strode up to Vincenzo, his face centimetres from the agent's. In heavily accented English he snarled, "This is your problem ... clean it up." Marching from the room, he didn't look back.

CHAPTER
37

The disdain on John's face was total as he reluctantly joined Ballard in hauling the two Russians to their feet. Vincenzo drew his combat knife, cutting both sets of cable ties, deliberately refraining from offering either man the serviettes scattered across the table to stem the flow of blood from their wounds. Reaching out, he handed back their mobiles, one of the Major's men having fetched them from next door.

Uttering the words that he never dreamed would ever pass his lips, Vincenzo informed the Russians they were free to go, following up with, "We're holding up our end of the bargain, make sure you do the same." While the words were forceful, he was acutely aware there was no leverage available to him to impose the demand.

Neither Russian responded, confident they were in the box seat. Igor chose not to acknowledge the deep gash on his face, acting as though it didn't exist. Turning to face them, the intense look he levelled at Ballard and John had the coldness and intensity of a stalking lion, leaving them in no doubt they had become his prey. Unhurried, he joined Demyan, both men mustering what dignity they could as they began their slow walk to the door, their muscles tight from their incarceration. Vincenzo ordered three of his soldiers to escort them from the building.

Kicking one of the chairs so hard it skidded across the floor, John bellowed, *"Well that's a punch in the guts if ever there was one. And how do we know they'll keep their word—?"*

"We don't." The AC's words were meant to be blunt and had the desired effect.

"So, what's the plan to track them?" Ballard suspected the communications van was about to play a major part.

"As hard as this will be, we need to remain here for at least five minutes before heading downstairs and following those two. Without doubt they'll have henchmen staked out watching the building and reporting our movements. The last thing we need is for Demyan and Igor to suspect they're being followed. By delaying, there's a greater chance—not total mind you—but a greater chance they won't suspect their phones have been tampered with." He took in the three concerned faces. "As excruciating as this is, we *have* to trust the technology on this one. This is *not* a scenario where we follow on foot on the opposite side of the street, peering around corners like they do in the movies. When we do start tracking, I'll have one of my men drive the van while we're in the back, monitoring their movements. The second armoured vehicle will follow us should we get the opportunity to rearrest the bastards." The alarm on the detectives' faces caused him to add, "I promise that won't happen until *after* the trucks have been disarmed."

Entering commands in his mobile, his face broke into a much-needed smile. "Bingo, I have two distinct signals ... the software's working." He thrust the mobile out for all to see. "At least *something's* going our way."

Frustrated at not being able to leap into action, they slumped onto chairs, the mood dark, everyone in shock as they played over in their minds how things had gone so terribly wrong. Looking to Vincenzo, Ballard claimed, "I'll call Delwyn and explain that we *believe* the crisis is over. All they can do now is wait. When the time's right, the bomb squad will move in and disarm the rig."

Vincenzo agreed, speed dialling his CIA contact.

The AC leaned back in his chair as Ballard and Vincenzo made their calls. "My God John, check out this room. It's impossible to fathom what we've just witnessed."

With no meaningful words forthcoming, John replayed over in his mind the brutal actions that had taken place minutes prior, failing to make sense of it on any level.

Much quicker than expected, Ballard completed his call. "Delwyn says everything in Spencer Street is on hold. Traffic's blocked in all directions, and each of the nearby buildings have been searched and evacuated. She said the bomb squad is on standby for the order to go in and disarm the devices on the semi. She apologised she couldn't talk longer, saying she had another briefing scheduled with the Chief. Once that's over she'll ring me back."

Looking at his colleagues and guessing what they were thinking, Ballard spat out in disgust, "The real showstopper from now on is every time we get even remotely close to Igor or Demyan, they're going to wheel out the explosive tanker threat, and there's not a goddamn thing we can do about it!"

The AC studied his detective inspector, sympathising with his obvious disquiet. "Very true Michael, so all the more reason we do everything we can to catch these bastards, even if we have to offer a bounty for the Ndrangheta to take them out, effectively doing our dirty work for us."

Ballard and John observed their senior officer through narrowed eyes, attempting to determine whether or not he was serious.

Finishing his calls, Vincenzo rechecked the signals on his mobile, his optimism on the rebound. "Those two are still together, and it's clear by the distance they've travelled they're in a vehicle. So it's time to rock 'n 'roll my friends."

Desperate to be doing something constructive, the policemen leapt to their feet. On the one hand they admired the agent's cool head, accepting that should they have been seen charging out of the building as soon as Demyan and Igor had left it would have given the game away; on the other hand, they feared the delay could well cost them the opportunity to recapture the two Russians.

Minutes later, after seeing off the armoured vehicle with the three prisoners onboard, everyone scrambled into the back of the surveillance van, the driver already behind the wheel, peering over his shoulder as he waited for instructions.

Concentrating on entering commands on the keyboard, Vincenzo flashed a toothy grin as the GPS map appeared on the monitor: two white dots rhythmically blinking along a street with an unpronounceable name.

As they accelerated away from the kerb, Ballard's mobile prompted there was an incoming text. He prayed it was from Delwyn. Studying the screen, at first the words didn't register, but the instant they did he felt the blood roaring in his ears and his muscles weaken to the point he almost dropped the phone. John crowded alongside, demanding to be shown.

Sensing something was very wrong, Vincenzo ordered the driver to pull over, the armoured vehicle behind doing the same. John repeated aloud what he was reading on the screen for Vincenzo's benefit. "It says, '*I warned you that meddling in our affairs would lead to consequences. Igor*'." The colour drained from John's face as he watched Ballard frantically speed-dial Delwyn's number, switching the mobile to speaker.

To everyone's relief she answered on the second ring. Ballard's gut-wrenching anxiety subsided as his pulse rate slowed to something resembling normal. "Delwyn, has anything happened—?"

"No Michael. Why? What do you—?"

"Delwyn, we've just received a text from Igor warning us that he's about to blow the truck. You're *sure* everything is ok there?"

Delwyn caught her breath. "Yes … headquarters was cleared some time back, and we've done everything we can to evacuate the buildings near the blast zone. My God Michael, do you think he'll actually—"

"What about Ken, Bobby and Susan, are they with you?"

Instead of her reply, they heard a thunderous explosion through the mobile, along with a chilling cry of pain from Delwyn. The sound of shattering glass, combined with the rolling thunder of the detonation left no one in any doubt that Igor had enacted his ruthless threat.

Ballard was frantic, numb with shock, his despairing words echoing back at him. "*Delwyn … DELWYN … CAN YOU HEAR ME … FOR GOD'S SAKE … ARE YOU OK?*"

THE END

Ballard and John will return in
'Free Fall – When Duty Calls'

ACKNOWLEDGEMENTS

The alter egos of the four key support characters in 'Payback', 'The Heist', 'End Game', 'The Siege', 'Whatever It Takes' and 'Dead Man Walking' kick up another gear in 'Knife Edge'. Again, my thanks to Glenys Reid, Ken Sproat, Bobby Dzodzadinov and Susan Dodd for their continuing interest in my novels, and their spirited encouragement and involvement.

Leanne, my wife, applied her 'readability' test to the manuscript which was as insightful as ever. Her good humour, affection and street smarts are always appreciated, and it goes without saying that Natalie's character is based in no small measure on Leanne's delightful personality.

Peter Donelly, my former boss, features again in the action in 'Knife Edge'. The novels would not be the same without his influence as the stylish and capable detective superintendent. Thanks Pete, for continuing to be the complex, funny and deep-thinking individual whose namesake stands as a shining example for what we all would like our senior police to be. And sorry about getting shot in this episode!

It is with immense sadness that the passing of John Hutchison, the real-life gentleman who was the inspiration of the character of John Henderson (yes, also named John), has left me with an emotional ache that will last forever. He was a laconic larrikin who will live on in deed and spirit in my future novels.

Diane Howden, Leanne's school friend, has raised the bar yet again, and her 'take-no-prisoners', sharp and perceptive suggestions have, as always, added immeasurable value to the flow, pace and readability of the story. Her recommendations ensure this book is 'slick' and far more enjoyable as a read than it would otherwise have been. No novel of mine can be published without her astute input. Beware, Diane, book eight is underway!

Terry Read, a proven fan of the series, has immersed himself in the plots, and is now providing much needed grist for the mill for my forthcoming novels. His left-field thinking is appreciated, adding a no-nonsense, realistic dimension to the storylines.

It goes without saying that major thanks must go to Sid Harta publishing, ably led by Kerry Collison, along with Denise Taylor, my editor, whose astute changes 'sharpened' the text, and to Luke Harris, my typesetter and brilliant cover designer for the majority of my novels. For this novel he has exceeded his previous best!

Finally, as always, a big thank you to you, the reader, for choosing this novel and allowing yourself to be immersed in a world that thankfully most people never experience.

ABOUT THE AUTHOR

Harvey Cleggett worked for Victoria Police for forty-one years, affording him the operational experience to write realistic, gritty, fast-paced novels associated with the dark world of high-end crime. 'Knife Edge' is the seventh book of the crime/thriller series, 'When Duty Calls'.

ALSO BY THE AUTHOR

When Duty Calls (series)

PAYBACK: WHEN DUTY CALLS (Book 1)

Homicide Detective Inspector Michael Ballard is vigorously resisting retirement, not wishing to walk away from investigating and solving complex criminal cases. The brutal murder of a factory owner has him and his partner applying their 'old school' policing skills to hunt down the killer. But while Ballard is hunting the killer—is the killer hunting him? An absorbing murder mystery set in the often-violent world of modern-day law enforcement.

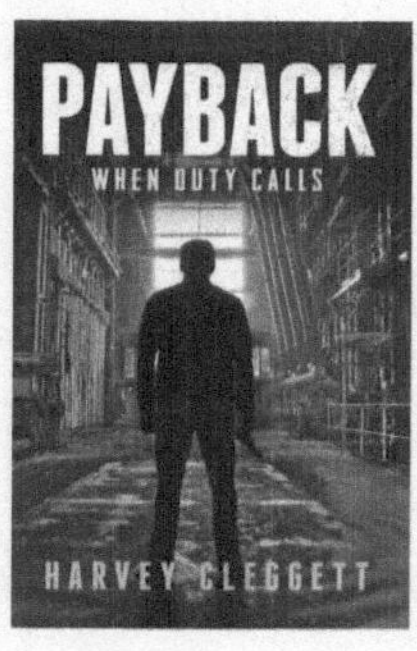

THE HEIST: WHEN DUTY CALLS (Book 2)

An audacious robbery that breaches the Note Printing Australia building with fatal consequences, sees homicide partners Michael Ballard and John Henderson pitted against ruthless professionals who

will stop at nothing to retain their ill-gotten $130 million in uncut bank notes. A pulsating country raid, followed by a heart-pounding boat chase in Port Phillip Bay has Ballard and John in the thick of the action. Throughout, Ballard fights to ensure his love for Natalie, his fiancée, doesn't place her in harm's way. 'The Heist' returns the characters from Harvey Cleggett's first novel 'Payback', catapulting the reader on a wild rollercoaster ride, culminating in a traumatic climax no one could foresee.

END GAME: WHEN DUTY CALLS
(Book 3)

Note Printing Australia has been breached, crashing a wrecking ball through the belief the building is impregnable. Despite the skill of the thieves, homicide detectives Michael Ballard and John Henderson have arrested a number of the gang while recovering a sizeable portion of the $130 million stolen, however, the ring 

leaders remain at large. The ongoing hunt takes the street-hardened cops into the dark world of bikie gangs and illegal guns, overseen by Russian mafia-style criminals linked to the Russian Embassy and senior members within the Kremlin. 'End Game' takes up where Harvey Cleggett's second novel 'The Heist' left off, turbo-charging the reader's adrenalin rush.

THE SIEGE: WHEN DUTY CALLS
(Book 4)

A group of terrorists are holding hostage the state's politicians inside Victoria's Parliament House. They are led by an elite Spetsnaz soldier demanding a billion-dollar ransom. A number of the captives have been executed to focus the attention of the Federal Government, which is adamant it won't pay, running the risk many more hostages will die. Detective Inspector Michael Ballard has proposed a daring rescue plan that requires precision timing from the police department's special Operations Group and the army's Special Forces, but there is just one catch . . . Ballard's bid to free everyone involves his capture and inclusion as one of the hostages.

WHATEVER IT TAKES: WHEN DUTY CALLS
(Book 5)

Terrorists are holding hostage the state's politicians inside Victoria's Parliament House. The siege is led by an elite Spetsnaz soldier who secures a billion-dollar ransom by murdering an ever-increasing number of hostages. Detective Inspector Michael Ballard proposes a daring rescue plan requiring precision timing by the police department's Special Operations group and the army's elite special forces. This saves lives but results in him being held captive by the Spetsnaz soldier. Escaping, Ballard discovers the ransom was part of a more sinister objective involving an elite criminal syndicate attempting to gain control of Australia's major shipping ports. The criminals have close connections to the Russian underworld, so thwarting the conspiracy requires all the expertise Ballard and his detective colleagues John and Peter can bring to bear.

DEAD MAN WALKING: WHEN DUTY CALLS (Book 6)

A Russian elite criminal syndicate known as The Board have infiltrated Australian ports, moving contraband at will. Detective Inspector Michael Ballard's relentless pursuit of the group's hierarchy, backed by colleagues John Henderson, and the Serious Crime Taskforce commander, Peter Donaldson,  has struck a hurdle. The Board's tentacles have penetrated the state's political system, the police force, and even big business. Alarmingly, direct threats have been made against Ballard and John and their families, warning them that should the homicide detectives' dogged investigations continue, their loved ones will suffer. If that isn't shocking enough, The Board has now set its sights on the first shipment of nuclear waste due to be entombed in the Victorian outback — a scenario that has implications for millions of lives. The three detectives' expertise and resolve are about to be tested to the full.